The Starlet and the Killer Gossip Column

Lisa Hall is the #1 bestselling author of six psychological thrillers, including *Between You and Me*, *The Perfect Couple* and *The Woman in the Woods*. Lisa lives in a small village in Kent, surrounded by her towering TBR pile, a rather large brood of children, dogs, chickens and ponies, and her long-suffering husband.

AF386302

Also by Lisa Hall

The Hotel Hollywood Mysteries

The Mysterious Double Death of Honey Black
The Case of the Singer and the Showgirl
The Strange Disappearance of Kitty Fox
The Starlet and the Killer Gossip Column

LISA HALL

THE STARLET AND THE KILLER GOSSIP COLUMN

canelo
HERA

First published in the United Kingdom in 2026 by

Hera Books, an imprint of
Canelo Digital Publishing Limited,
20 Vauxhall Bridge Road,
London SW1V 2SA
United Kingdom

A Penguin Random House Company
The authorised representative in the EEA is Dorling Kindersley Verlag GmbH.
Arnulfstr. 124, 80636 Munich, Germany

Copyright © Lisa Hall 2026

The moral right of Lisa Hall to be identified as the creator of this work has been asserted in accordance with the Copyright, Designs and Patents Act, 1988.
All rights reserved. No part of this publication may be reproduced or transmitted in any form or by any means, electronic or mechanical, including photocopy, recording, or any information storage and retrieval system, without permission in writing from the publisher.
No part of this book may be used or reproduced in any manner for the purpose of training artificial intelligence technologies or systems. In accordance with Article 4(3) of the DSM Directive 2019/790, Canelo expressly reserves this work from the text and data mining exception.

A CIP catalogue record for this book is available from the British Library.

ISBN 978 1 83598 169 6

This book is a work of fiction. Names, characters, businesses, organizations, places and events are either the product of the author's imagination or are used fictitiously. Any resemblance to actual persons, living or dead, events or locales is entirely coincidental.

Cover design by Leah Jacobs-Gordon

Cover images © Shutterstock.com

Printed and bound in Great Britain by Clays Ltd, Elcograf S.p.A.

Look for more great books at
www.herabooks.com | www.dk.com

1

For Timothy, because I know you like these books better than my other ones

Chapter One

The yellow rose hits the coffin with a faint thud, and a wail rents the air as the woman trips forward on heels slightly too big for her, almost stumbling headfirst into the open grave. Tilda gasps beside me, as a tall man reaches out and grabs the woman by the arm, catching her before she can end up in the hole. Her face obscured by black lace, the woman collapses into the man's waiting arms, sobs ripping from her chest.

'This is heartbreaking,' I mutter to Louis, who shifts beside me, sweating in a black suit under the midday sun. 'Is that Max's wife?'

Tilda presses a tissue to her nose and nods. 'That's Lizzie Hayden. God bless her.'

'Are you sure we should be here?' Unease prickles under my arms as I cast my gaze over the mourning crowd. I've never met the deceased, nor his wife or any of his family, and I feel a jolt of concern that any moment now someone will realise that and eject us from the graveside.

Tilda nods discreetly. 'Louella said I should cover the funeral for her piece in the paper tomorrow, and she never said I couldn't bring an assistant – or two – with me. If anyone asks, that's the only reason we're here.' Tilda's job as a reporter/assistant to renowned gossip columnist Louella Parsons can be the perfect cover sometimes.

Lizzie still weeps in the man's arms as the priest continues to speak about Max Hayden, darling of the Hollywood comedy movie scene, who was found drowned in the swimming pool at the Garden of Allah Hotel a week ago. I've never been to a Hollywood funeral before – the only funeral I've ever attended was my mother's after she lost her battle with breast cancer – and I never expected to be here, especially not in 1952. Despite the gravity of what is happening in front of me, there is still a tiny part of me that is overawed at finding myself – a displaced Brit from the twenty-first century – in Hollywood in the Fifties, with a job to die for as acclaimed film director Leonard Langford's assistant, and two of the best friends I could have ever wished for. I may be out of place and time, but I've never felt more at home.

Now, I peer out from beneath my black hat, surveying the scene ahead of me. Lizzie still weeps, and she's not the only one. Max was clearly very well loved by his peers. Bob Hope wraps an arm around Doris Day as she presses a handkerchief to her eyes, and Cary Grant is stoic as he stares straight ahead at the coffin. I feel it again, the sensation that none of this is real. How can I – Lily Jones, the girl who is a terrible driver, who misses boba tea, whose first job was working on the till in Tesco on a Saturday afternoon – be standing here, alongside some of the greatest stars Hollywood has ever seen? The cemetery, still a Hollywood landmark in my own time, is full of cinema's finest, all intent on paying their last respects to a man who I'd never heard of until Tilda waved a note in front of my face two weeks ago. A note that claimed Max Hayden was going to die in an accident – dated a week before Max's tragic demise. Could someone here be responsible for the note? Running my eyes over the crowd, I try to spot if anyone seems suspicious, but it's impossible.

It's not the first time Louis, Tilda and I have found ourselves embroiled in a mystery that it seems only we can crack. Whether it's rescuing Hollywood starlets from a horrible fate, getting swept up in mob activity, or solving mysterious disappearances, trouble has a way of finding us. With the whole of Hollywood believing Max's death is a tragic accident, I can't help but feel that it's found us again. After all, if it really was an accident, how did Tilda receive a note forewarning her, a week before Max died?

Leonard – my boss at the film studio – and his wife Jean stand together, Jean's eyes rimmed with pink. Of course they would have known Max, although I'm not sure if Jean's wan complexion is due to sorrow, or the fact that she's pregnant and suffering horrible morning sickness. Max's family cluster on the other side of the coffin, away from his wife Lizzie and the couple who stand beside her, each with an arm around her shoulders. That's odd. Could there be some animosity there? I would have expected Max's parents and Lizzie to be supporting each other.

'…Lil?'

Louis's voice in my ear pulls me from my thoughts. 'Huh? Sorry, I was miles away,' I whisper.

'You think someone here sent the note to Tilda about Max having an accident?' Louis murmurs back, his eyes raking over the crowd in much the same way mine have been.

'I don't know… Everyone seems devastated. Although…' I trail off. Ninety per cent of the people in attendance here are actors or affiliated with the movie business in one way or another. It would be easy for them to cover their tracks, wouldn't it? It wouldn't be difficult for someone who spends their days acting to pretend to be grief-stricken.

The pastor crosses himself, marking the end of his speech, and people begin to drift away from the cemetery. A worker leans discreetly against a tree, waiting for the mourners to disappear before he can get to work, burying Max six feet under forever. Lizzie grips her handkerchief in one hand, her face pale as she lets the couple beside her walk her towards a waiting black Lincoln Town Car. She slides into the backseat, the black veil of her hat obscuring her face, as the couple slip into the front seats and drive away without a backwards glance.

'Damn,' I hiss. 'I kind of wanted to try and speak to Lizzie, offer my condolences, you know? I know she doesn't know me from Adam, but I thought we could get a feel for her. See if she really is as devastated as she seems.'

'At her husband's funeral?' Louis gasps, shaking his head, clearly horrified. 'Lil, that's not really…'

'Lou, please.' Tilda rolls her eyes. 'You think Lily would be that crass? She just wants to… use her *powers* to see if she can figure this thing out.'

Oh, good Lord. I had forgotten that in order to explain how I know certain things about the time frame I find myself in, I had told Tilda and Louis that I was psychic, pretending that by touching photographs and newspaper articles I could 'see' what fate had in store for certain people. At the time it seemed a hell of a lot easier than trying to explain that I fell and bumped my head while working as a chambermaid at the Beverly Hills Hotel, then inexplicably woke up in 1949. Now I wonder if I made the right decision.

'Uh, yeah. That's it,' I say, following Louis as he makes his way out of the cemetery towards his pride and joy, a bright red Chrysler with white-walled tyres. 'But you're right, this isn't the time. Lizzie needs time alone to mourn.'

'Are you kidding?' Tilda stops in front of me, blocking my path as she sticks her hands on her hips. 'You read the note, right? It said Max was going to die in a tragic accident, and then one week later he drowns in a swimming pool. We need to speak to Lizzie while everything is still fresh. If there *was* foul play, then Lizzie might remember something that will help. Lou, you're gonna head right when you turn out of the cemetery.'

'We turn left to go back to your apartment, Tilda.'

Tilda grins and opens the rear passenger door. 'We're not going back to the apartment, Lou. We're going to Lizzie and Max Hayden's house. Obviously we're going to the wake.'

—

Max's house is on W Sunset Boulevard, set back from the road by a winding drive. As we approach, I realise I recognise it and press my hand to my mouth, stifling a gasp before Tilda notices. Eric, my twenty-first-century best friend, and I did a tour of the stars' homes one Saturday afternoon, fuelled by White Claw and Doritos, and had spent an inordinate amount of time hanging around outside this place in the hopes of bumping into its modern-day owner. I mean, who wouldn't want to meet Madonna? My mum was a huge fan, and Madonna was the soundtrack to my childhood.

'Do you think we should take the note to the police?' Louis says, as he pulls the car up to the kerb. 'I mean, that makes more sense than us questioning Lizzie, surely? Let the police look into things.'

'Come on, Lou,' Tilda snorts. 'Let's be real… You really think the police are going to investigate? They've already looked into things and immediately wrote it off as an accident. And besides…'

'What?' I turn in my seat to look at Tilda, surprised by the paleness of her cheeks. 'Til? What is it?'

'What if they think *I* had something to do with it? I didn't report the note, and now… now, Max is dead.' Her hands knot together in a very un-Tilda fashion. 'I'd rather take them the note when we have something concrete to show them that Max didn't die in an accident. Like a credible suspect.'

Louis opens his mouth and I shoot him a look. 'OK,' I say, quietly. 'I get it. But if we can't dig anything up, then we do need to talk to the police.'

I try not to gawp at the house as we step out of the car, Tilda smoothing her black dress down, and Louis holding out an arm for me to lean on as we make our way towards the arched front door. Huge oak double doors stand open, a butler dressed in formal uniform – even down to spotless white gloves – nodding as people enter. I take my place in line behind Irene Dunne, giving the butler a small smile as we enter.

'Where to?' Louis whispers as we enter a vast hallway. The floors are Spanish tile and the walls are painted a brilliant white, light streaming in through arched windows to the side. The whole place screams old money and understated elegance.

'Through there.' Bursting with confidence, as if she strides through the homes of Hollywood movie stars every day (and maybe she does – after all, she works for Louella Parsons, gossip queen of Hollywood), Tilda marches us through the hall to the back of the house. Stepping into the rear reception room, I pause to take it all in. The room is almost a ballroom, it's so big. A bar has been set up along one wall, and it looks permanent, a dazzling array of bottles on display. A bartender hands out saucers of champagne, which strikes me as a little odd. Isn't champagne a celebratory drink? We each take a glass anyway, Louis raising his in an odd little toast. As we make our way across the room, I notice that the plush carpet bears the dents of furniture that has been removed to make space for the dozens of people who fill the room, all peppering Lizzie Hayden with air kisses and condolences. The air is thick and warm, a fug of perfume and sadness, and when we reach the high arched windows on the other side of the room I let out a breath. The patio doors stand open, allowing the faintest hint of a breeze, and people spill out onto the lawn. Peering out, I can see a swimming pool, the water a crushingly bright blue. I turn away, my stomach flipping. I don't know how Lizzie can bear to stare out at the water, even though this wasn't the pool where Max drowned.

'Lizzie is right there.' Tilda lifts a finger discreetly in the direction of the bar. Lizzie stands, supported by the same man she wept on at the funeral, as a woman with dark blonde hair approaches and kisses her on the cheek. 'Do you think we should talk to her? Ask her if she knows anything about the note?'

'No,' I say urgently. 'This isn't the time or place. But we do need to speak with her at some point. Who are the two people with her? The guy was beside her at the gravesite too.'

Tilda runs her eyes over the couple. 'That's Jack Shaw. He's an actor. He starred in a few movies with Max way back in the beginning. I take it you're not a fan?'

I shake my head. Mum and I watched a lot of the classics, but she was never really into comedies. I've never heard of Jack Shaw before. 'Not really my thing,' I say. 'What about the woman?' She does look vaguely familiar.

'Ann Silver. She's pretty new on the scene – she's working on her second movie now. She's dated a few actors on her way up.' Tilda lowers her voice. 'There are rumours, if you know what I mean.'

'Uh, no?'

Tilda huffs. 'Rumours that she didn't make it into the movies on her talent, Lil. Jeez.'

Oh. 'You think she dated Max? Maybe there was bad blood.' Ann moves on to be replaced by a dainty woman with platinum curls. She reaches out and squeezes Lizzie's hand, and Jack places a hand at the small of her back.

Tilda shakes her head. 'No, they didn't date as far as I know, but they did work on a movie together. Her first movie, I believe. It was Max's last. She's working on the latest George Seaton movie now.'

Maybe that's where I know her from. George Seaton's latest is being filmed at the same studios where I work with Leonard, so maybe I've seen her around there. I wonder if I could ask her what she knows about Max. After all, if she worked on a movie with him there's a chance they might have been close, that Max might have opened up to her if there was something bothering him.

Tilda goes on, 'See that lady with Lizzie now? That's Mary Colman, Jack's wife.'

'They seem to be close to Lizzie. They've been taking care of her all day.'

'The four of them are close friends, I believe.' Tilda looks as though she wants to say more, but Lizzie is tapping a fork against a champagne saucer, urging the crowd to fall silent.

'Sorry, I'm sorry.' Lizzie's voice is lower than I imagined, with the faintest hint of a North Florida accent. 'I know this isn't usually the done thing, but I wanted to say a few words.'

A hush descends on the room, and Tilda and I exchange a glance, Louis shifting on the balls of his feet beside me. It appears we are not the only ones who seem caught off guard by Lizzie's intention to make a speech, as Jack Shaw presses his fingers against her arm and leans down to whisper in her ear.

'No, Jack,' Lizzie says, an urgent tone to her voice. 'I want to say something.' She surveys the room and swallows hard, her eyes glistening. 'Thank you all for coming to say goodbye to my dear Max. All of you know he was the life and soul of the party… sometimes a little too much.' There is a muted rumble of laughter, as though people aren't quite sure if Lizzie meant her words to be amusing. 'I don't know how we will go on without him…' she pauses and reaches behind her for a full glass of champagne, knocking it back in one go, '…but we simply must. This tragic accident—'

'Lizzie, that's enough now.' Jack reaches for her glass, but Lizzie yanks her arm away.

'No, Jack, I need to say goodbye to my husband.' Lizzie pushes him, not hard enough to make him fall but enough to make Jack's cheeks burn. 'As I was saying, this tragic accident might never have occurred if Max hadn't drunk so much that night—'

'I can't listen to this.' Jack glares at Lizzie, who stares defiantly back at him, before shoving his own glass onto the bar behind him and storming from the room. Mary watches him leave with tears in her eyes, one hand dithering at the sleeve of Lizzie's dress, before she too runs from the room after him. The only sound is the crash of the front door slamming closed, leaving Lizzie and the crowd of Max's mourners staring at one another in confusion. *What the heck was all that about?*

Chapter Two

'There's more to this than meets the eye,' Louis says as we arrive at Louis and Tilda's parents' house for dinner later that evening.

'Ha, no flies on you,' Tilda snorts as she steps from the car. She's changed out of her funeral garb into a cute green skirt that flares around her mid-calves and a white broderie blouse. I am also relieved to be out of my tight-fitting funeral dress, black and made of some awful shiny, man-made material that did not let my skin breathe at all, into a pair of baby blue capri pants and matching cardigan. 'I think the note I received tells us from the word go that there's more to this than meets the eye.'

'Maybe we should talk about this later,' I say, nodding in the direction of the front porch, where Tilda and Louis's mother, Debbie, stands with a big smile on her face. 'Hi, Mrs Jardine. Something smells incredible.'

'Lily, Mrs Jardine is my mother-in-law. You know to call me Debbie,' she scolds me lightly, hugging each of us in turn before ushering us straight to the dinner table where her famous meatloaf is waiting.

'So,' she says a short while later, once we've all eaten. 'How did the funeral go?'

'It was… great,' Tilda says, with a glance in my direction. 'Nice, you know. Huge turnout.'

'Well, he was a popular guy,' Andy, Louis and Tilda's father, says. 'Made a ton of great movies, and from what I've heard he was nothing short of a gentleman to everyone he met.'

'Clearly someone didn't feel that way,' Louis mutters under his breath as Tilda flicks out a foot under the table to kick him, catching me in the process.

'Ow,' I hiss, rubbing at my ankle. 'I guess we only know what we see in the press. Lizzie seemed devastated.'

'I remember when they got married,' Debbie says, with a dreamy look on her face as she begins to clear the table. 'It was a fairy-tale wedding. Huge event, they held their reception at Pickfair – you know, Douglas Fairbanks and Mary Pickford's place?'

'Wow.' A shiver runs down my spine. In my time the original Pickfair was demolished in the 1990s, and the idea that I could see it in its original glory right now makes my movie-loving heart contract.

'Apparently Douglas took Max under his wing when he first arrived in Hollywood,' Debbie goes on. 'And everyone was utterly thrilled when Max and Lizzie announced they would be married. Hollywood thought Max would be an eternal bachelor. He was always the life and soul of any party. Every newspaper photograph had him with a glass in one hand and a woman in the other. No one ever thought he would settle down.' She gives a fond smile. 'I was always a big fan of his. Anyway… it's terribly sad.'

'You see where I get my propensity for gossip?' Tilda says in an exaggerated whisper, and Louis lets out a burst of laughter.

'Hush,' Debbie says, setting the coffee pot on the table and taking her seat, a newspaper in her hand.

'It's collecting information, not gossiping, isn't it, Tilda? Although if you're not interested in gossip, I'm guessing you won't want to take a look at this.' She slides the newspaper across the table to Tilda, open at a page towards the back.

'What's this?' Tilda frowns as she scans the page, her finger running over the inky paper. 'Mom?'

'You don't know?' Andy laughs, clearly expecting Tilda to be aware of whatever it is as she pores over the page, biting on her lower lip.

'Til? What is it?' Louis leans in and I join him, trying to see what it is that has Tilda's brow crinkling in a way she hates.

'A gossip column,' she says faintly. 'I mean… it looks like a gossip column but it's not…'

I run my eyes over the newspaper. '*The Last Word*,' I read, the title glaring out from the top of the page. '*Shining the spotlight where the studios won't*. I mean, it's a catchy tagline… but it doesn't say who's written it.' There's not even a pseudonym attached to the column.

'So, this isn't you?' Debbie asks, her face mirroring Tilda's in a way that is uncanny. 'I thought maybe you got your own column and you were going to surprise us.'

Tilda shakes her head, pressing her lips firmly together. 'This isn't me. I have no idea what this is in the slightest.'

—

The evening falls flat after that, and it's barely an hour later when Louis pulls up outside mine and Tilda's apartment and we all tumble from the car.

'I need a drink,' Tilda mutters, pushing her way past us and upstairs to our front door.

'You think she's OK?' I ask Louis, as we watch her go. Tilda rarely gets mad about anything, but this seems to have thrown her for a loop.

Louis shrugs. 'Only one way to find out.' With a grin, he pushes me lightly in the small of the back towards the stairs. Sighing, I make my way up to the apartment.

Pushing open the door to the sitting room, I can see that Tilda is already perched on the couch, the newspaper open in front of her, a glass of whisky in her hand that I know she'll regret in the morning. 'Listen to this,' she says without even looking at us, as Louis and I slip into the sitting room. Louis pushes a bundle of clean washing off the armchair and slumps into it, and I move a stack of mystery novels off the coffee table so I can see the newspaper as I sit on the floor. We really need to spend a day tidying this apartment.

'Listen,' Tilda says again. '*Divorce is on the cards for this starlet – rumour has it she's more involved with the child in her life than the man… Perhaps someone should be checking on who she tucks into bed first at night?*'

'Woah.' Louis sits back, his shocked expression almost comical. 'What in the world…? Til, you sure you didn't know anything about this?'

'No,' she says hotly. 'And I don't know if Louella does either. This isn't our newspaper. This is some… some old rag that you see at the newsstands.' Tilda is right – the newspaper in her hand does hold the bold fonts and all caps that I would attach to something more suited to *The National Enquirer*. 'This isn't Louella's style, and besides…' She trails off. I know she sees herself as Louella's protegee, and the idea that Louella would work on blind items like this behind her back is hurtful.

'Hedda Hopper?' Louis names Louella's rival gossip queen. 'Do you think she has something to do with it? And who do we think it could be about? The whole thing feels a little dirty to me.' His mouth twists and he reaches for the whisky bottle. 'At least Louella *tells* us who the gossip is about.'

While I don't know who might be behind this new gossip column, I do know exactly who the blind item is referring to. It's Gloria Grahame. She was married – *is* currently married – to director Nicholas Ray, who I once saw striding about the gardens of Chateau Marmont, however he is about to divorce her and the rumour is – or will be – that he caught her in bed with his son, her stepson. She'll go on to marry her stepson in 1960. What a mess. Whoever is behind the column seems to have their facts correct so far.

'It's not Hedda – she's got her own column – but it could be someone who's worked under her,' Tilda muses, before she throws the newspaper to one side. 'Anyway, this is a ridiculous story. It could be about anyone, and it doesn't even really make sense. We have bigger things to think about.' She reaches into her purse and pulls out the note she received at her office two weeks ago, and a newspaper clipping. I pick up the clipping, running my eyes over the text.

MAX HAYDEN DIES IN HOTEL SWIMMING POOL

The headline shrieks out at me, accompanied by a photo of Max looking devilishly handsome, his blond hair swept to one side as he smiles a polished, professional smile, white teeth gleaming. It looks like a publicity still from one of his movies, and I feel a pang of something sharp in my chest. Max was barely forty, at the peak of his career. He shouldn't have ended up face down in a swimming pool.

'Could it have been an accident, Til?' I say, doubt tickling the back of my mind. 'It says here he was at the hotel for the wrap party for his latest movie. He was drinking… He could've tripped and fallen in. People say he didn't seem himself that night.'

Tilda snorts and tosses her red ponytail. 'Come on, Lily, don't be naïve. If Max just tripped and fell into the pool then how do you explain this?' She shakes the note in my face. It's typewritten, on cream paper – not expensive, but not cheap either. It reads:

> Here's something for your column – Max Hayden is about to meet his end in a tragic accident.

The bluntness of the note sends a shiver down my spine. There is no emotion, no dramatics attached to it, just simple facts. Max Hayden will die in a tragic accident.

'And you received this a week before it happened?' Louis says, as if checking to make sure he has all the facts straight. 'Why didn't you tell us before? Maybe we could have stopped it.'

'I kinda think we had our hands full with the Kitty Fox scenario, remember?' I say.

Tilda tuts, rolling her eyes. 'Do you know how many wacko letters we get sent to the newspaper office every week? Every crackpot in town seems to want us to write something or other about them, or the movie star who they think has done them wrong. Half of these letters don't even get read before they get put in the trash. This one only made it to me because it had my name on the envelope…' She trails off, running her fingernail over the words. 'Maybe I should have taken it more seriously, not just left it on my desk with the rest of them. Maybe I *should* have taken it to the police… and if I'd had any idea at all that whoever wrote this meant harm then of course I would have. But I thought it was just another hoax, another crazy, attention-seeking madman trying to get his words in the newspaper. And then a week later, Max dies in a swimming pool. *By accident.*' Tilda huffs and throws the note down on the coffee table. 'Like it or not, guys, something's fishy. And we're the only ones who know about it.'

I look up and catch Louis's eye, and he gives me a tiny nod. 'Well then,' I say brightly, 'I guess we just need to head over to Lizzie's house and find out exactly what was going on with Max Hayden.'

Chapter Three

'I thought we were going to Lizzie's house?' Tilda says the following morning, as I yell at Louis to come to a halt on W Sunset Boulevard outside the Garden of Allah.

'I want to check out the hotel first.' Without waiting for Louis to turn the engine off, I jump out of the car and make my way up the sidewalk to the entrance to the Garden of Allah Hotel. It's understated compared to the Beverly Hills Hotel, the wide driveway opening up to reveal a still impressive cream building, with Spanish tiles on the roof. Surrounded by a lush, green garden, palm trees gently obscuring the hotel from the road, a sign welcomes us to The Garden of Allah Villas. As I approach the hotel, Louis tugs at my arm.

'Wait, Lil. Should we really just walk in like this?'

'It's a hotel, Lou. Anyone can stay here.' Tilda strides past us, and I bite back a smile. Louis is always the one who is most cautious, the one who worries about us getting into trouble, while Tilda is the total opposite. Sometimes I wonder how they are even related.

Skirting around the edge of the hotel building, trying our hardest to seem as though we are meant to be there, the three of us make our way to the rear of the hotel, to the gardens and the pool that sits in the centre, surrounded by villas. I've heard stories about the hotel in my own time, now long since demolished and replaced by a strip mall, and I get that familiar tingle down my spine as we enter the gardens. That feeling of disconnection, of this whole experience being some sort of fever dream. How can I be standing here, in a hotel that was demolished over seventy years ago in the twenty-first century, a hotel that was a hub for celebrities of the time, a hotel that crawls with scandal and mischief?

'Lil,' Tilda hisses, with a jerk of her head. The pool, blue and clear, shimmers before us, bigger than I was expecting and oddly shaped. A lip runs around the edge of the pool, and it's easy to see how someone, even if they weren't drunk, could trip and fall in. 'This is where it happened.'

Movement at the edge of the garden catches my eye, and I tug Tilda and Louis away from the poolside to stand under a tree as a man who looks remarkably like Humphrey Bogart hurries towards one of the villas on the far side of the garden. Waiting until he is out of sight, I step back out and walk towards the pool, my Converse silent as I cross the tiles.

'You wouldn't even know,' I mutter to myself, sweeping my gaze over the pristine gardens. There is no evidence that there was ever even a party here, let alone a man dying.

'There are parties here all the time,' Tilda says. 'Pretty wild ones if you believe the rumours. It's easy to see how Max could have fallen in the pool. One trip over the edge of that lip there and you're in. He wouldn't be the first person.'

'And I guess if he'd had a few drinks...' I remember what Debbie said the previous evening, about Max always appearing with a drink in one hand and a woman in the other.

'Why didn't anyone help him when he fell?' Louis muses, peering down into the crystal-clear water below. 'I mean, if it was a party, there must have been people all around. Someone would have seen him fall. Surely someone would have just jumped in and dragged him out.'

Tilda shakes her head. 'He was found in the very early hours of the morning. It seems everyone else had left the party, and rumour has it that Max carried on drinking alone after the party was over... The story is he was out here on his own and "accidentally" fell in and drowned.'

'But that theory doesn't explain the note,' Louis says with a frown as he stares into the water. 'I mean... maybe someone knew about the party, knew that Max had a reputation for being a drinker and this is all just a coincidence—'

'No,' I say. I can't explain it – maybe it is simply the fact that I am still here in the 1950s when every morning I expect to wake up in my own bed, in 2021, Eric banging on the apartment door because I'm late for work – but my gut is telling me this is no coincidence. 'I don't think this was an accident, Lou. We definitely need to speak to Lizzie.'

—

Tilda squints in the bright sun as we head up the path to Lizzie and Max Hayden's house a short while later. I knew she'd regret that glass of whisky, and Louis nudges me with a grin as she slides her sunglasses off her head and onto her face. The house has a completely different air this morning to yesterday. There is no butler waiting at the door, no muted hum of conversation drifting from the hall, and the arched oak front doors stand firmly shut.

There isn't even the sound of birdsong in the immaculate garden, the lawn trimmed better than a millennial man's beard even though there is no sign of a gardener, and I remark on it to Louis.

'It's Saturday, Lil,' he replies. 'Maybe the gardener doesn't work on weekends.'

He's got a point, but even so the silence feels eerie, and I imagine Max's ghost stalking us up the garden path, even though I know it's ridiculous. He didn't even die here. Tilda presses her finger to the doorbell, wincing as the chime splits the air. We wait, the heat of the mid-morning sun warm on my back, but there is no answer. Tilda presses the doorbell again, this time holding her finger there for a few extra seconds.

'Maybe she's not home,' Louis says with a shrug. 'Maybe she's got things to sort out.'

'Oh please,' Tilda says with a roll of her eyes. 'Her husband – a huge Hollywood movie star, by the way – just died. I'm pretty sure Lizzie Hayden has people to sort these kinds of things out for her. Did you see how she was socking away the liquor yesterday? I'll bet she's just still sleeping.'

There is a tickle of something unsettling at the base of my spine as I picture the way Lizzie crumpled into Jack's arms after throwing her rose onto Max's coffin.

'Do you have the note?' I ask Tilda, and she nods and pats her purse.

'In here. But let's wait and see what Lizzie has to say before we mention it. After all, if Max had reverted to his old ways of whisky and women, there's every chance—' She breaks off as the door creaks open.

'Oh.' Mary Colman stands in the doorway, her face pale and her blonde ringlets drooping around her shoulders.

'Is Mrs Hayden home?' I ask.

'She…' Mary looks over her shoulder, back into the hallway as if not entirely sure.

'Hi, Miss Colman.' Tilda sticks out a hand. 'Do you remember me? Tilda Jardine. I work with Louella Parsons.'

'Oh. Oh, no.' Mary shakes her head. 'No, I'm sorry, Lizzie won't want to talk to you. We don't want people gossiping about Max, not after…'

'We're not here to gossip about Max,' I say gently. 'We're here to try and help, and we have a few questions we need to ask Lizzie. Do you think she'd see us?'

'No.' Mary's voice hardens. She steps out and half-closes the door behind her. 'You're vultures, the lot of you. It's disgusting, preying on a grieving widow.' She lifts her chin, peering down her nose at Tilda. 'And I know *exactly* who you are. I should have known you'd be sniffing around for a story.'

Tilda's eyes widen, and a flash of hurt crosses her face. Yes, she works for a gossip column, but Tilda always tries to be tactful and truthful. Mary Colman's words strike her like tiny bullets. 'Miss Colman…'

'What part of *no* don't you understand?'

I step forward, holding my hands up in a gesture of surrender. 'Miss Colman… Mary. I completely understand your reluctance to speak to us, but I swear we aren't here to cause you any harm.' I pause for a moment as Mary turns her gaze to me, her hostile expression giving way to something that looks like grief. 'My name is Lily Jones, and this is Tilda's brother, Louis. Please, could we speak to you for a just a minute? Tilda will wait outside if that makes you feel more comfortable.' There is a squeak of indignation behind me from Tilda.

'Lily Jones?' Mary's eyes narrow and she presses a finger to her lips, her brow crinkling. 'I know that name.' She smiles, transforming her from a pale, mousy little thing into a radiant young woman. 'You know Honey Black! I worked with Honey recently on a magazine piece about up-and-coming Hollywood stars... She mentioned you. She couldn't speak highly enough of you, to be honest. You're the girl who—'

'Mary?' A voice floats out from the back of the house. 'Who is it?'

Mary stands to one side, although she still gives Tilda a bit of side eye. 'I think maybe you all should come in.' Opening the door wide, she ushers us into the hallway and we follow her into a vast kitchen, where Jack Shaw stands at the counter, juicing oranges. He looks dishevelled, stubble scratching at his chin and his cheeks slightly crumpled, as if he hasn't slept well. He looks up, pausing as he frowns in our direction.

'Mary?'

'Jack, this is Lily Jones.' She gestures to me, and I find myself smoothing my wild dark curls down self-consciously. 'And her friends.' I'm not sure if Mary has forgotten their names, or if she doesn't want to alert Jack to the fact that Tilda works for a gossip column. 'They're here to see Lizzie.'

'Who's here to see me?' Lizzie sweeps into the kitchen, looking far more put together than I was expecting. She wears a long, navy-blue dress that falls to mid-calf, her hair is neatly curled and she wears the lightest application of make-up, just enough to make her skin glow. The scent of

Chanel No. 5 follows her as she passes by us and reaches for a glass of juice, just squeezed by Jack. There is no hint of the weeping, rumpled woman we saw at the funeral.

I introduce myself and Tilda and Louis again, then I explain that we are here to talk about what happened to Max.

'What happened to Max?' Lizzie's mouth purses as she frowns. 'Max fell in the pool, he was drunk. It was an accident.'

'Was there anyone who perhaps he didn't get along with? Someone who might have been at the party?'

Lizzie snorts. 'You clearly never met Max. There wasn't a person on this planet who that man couldn't charm.'

Jack makes a strangled noise that could be a cough and reaches for the inch of juice in his glass, tossing it back like a shot.

'What I mean to say,' Lizzie says as her hands knot together, 'is that Max was funny and kind, and although he could be a loose cannon at times he would never intentionally hurt anyone. Everyone loved Max.'

'Excuse me.' Jack pushes past us and heads for the hall as Mary throws a frantic look after him.

'So I don't really understand why you're here, or what you want to speak to me about.' Lizzie ignores Jack's exit, directing her question to Tilda. Of course, she must know who Tilda is.

Taking this opportunity while Lizzie is focused on Tilda, I whisper to Mary, 'I'm just going to pop to the bathroom.'

Without waiting for a response I head for the hallway, pushing open the first door I come to. I'm not sure exactly what it is that I'm looking for, but I'll take any opportunity I can to try and uncover more information on whatever Max had going on before he died. The door opens into a bedroom, Max and Lizzie's perhaps. The bed is unmade, a nightdress puddled on the floor as if Lizzie has only just stepped out of it. A pair of dainty slippers sit beside the opposite side of the bed, and there is the faintest hint of perfume in the air. A dressing table is littered with make-up tubes, open lipsticks and powder compacts, the mirror above it lit with stage lights. A black-and-white photo is tucked into the frame, and when I peer closely at it, I see it's a picture of Mary and Lizzie together, wearing matching dresses and beaming at the photographer. A door on the left leads to an en suite bathroom, the air inside still warm and slightly steamy, as though Lizzie has not long showered. Two toothbrushes sit in a mug, the mirror dotted with toothpaste. There is something that doesn't feel quite right about the room, but I put it down to the fact that two weeks ago Max would have been standing here brushing his teeth, and now he's dead.

Standing on the threshold of the bedroom I give a quick glance towards the kitchen, making sure the coast is clear before I cross the hall and push open the door to the sitting room. The sitting room is immaculate – a wide, generous space that could be a show home. Not a cushion is out of place, there's not a streak on the glass of the high arched windows, almost as though the room is never used. A photograph on the mantelpiece shows the four friends – Lizzie, Max, Jack and Mary – laughing at a funfair together, and I give it a cursory glance before moving to the next room.

The next room is another bedroom, and I step inside, quickly surveying the scene. The bed is made, but a jacket is thrown over the end of it and it feels as if I have interrupted something. The bedside table is clear but for a half-drunk glass of water and a photo of Max, his hand shading his eyes as he squints in the sun. Before I can turn to leave, the door to the en suite opens and Jack appears, his eyes widening when he sees me.

'I'm so sorry,' I gasp, 'I was just looking for the bathroom.' I can't help but peep into the bathroom behind him, taking in the towels on the floor.

'Down the hall. Second right.'

'Thank you.' My heart crashing in my chest, I stumble out of the bedroom and into the hall, only to find Lizzie ushering Tilda and Louis towards the front doors with Mary bringing up the rear.

'I'm sorry I couldn't be of more help,' Lizzie says, her eyes damp. 'Max let us all down, getting so drunk that he ended up...' She swallows as Mary wraps an arm around her shoulders.

'The thing is,' Tilda says firmly, 'we know Max's death wasn't an accident.'

'What?' Jack appears now, taking Lizzie's other side and staring at Tilda as though she's just dropped a bomb.

'There was a note,' I say, my heart still racing, 'hand delivered to Tilda at the newspaper a week before Max died. It said that he was going to be involved in a tragic accident.'

'I knew it,' Jack says, his voice ragged and broken as he turns to Lizzie. 'I told you! I told you this wasn't an accident. Max wouldn't have done this.'

'Jack,' Lizzie pleads. 'Max was an alcoholic. You know that.'

Jack turns to me, gripping my hands so tightly in his that I can feel the bones in my little finger crunch. 'I knew Max didn't fall into the pool by accident. If he was drunk that night, then someone tricked him into drinking alcohol. Max hasn't touched a drop of his own accord since 1949.'

Chapter Four

Jack's words are still ringing in my ears when I arrive at the studios on Monday morning. Tilda and I had spent Sunday cleaning our apartment and tossing around ideas over what really happened to Max that fateful night after the wrap party. Both of us came to the same conclusion – Jack's statement that Max hadn't touched a drop since 1949 doesn't mean anything. Max might have said he was sober, but the only person who really knows for sure is Max. If Tilda hadn't received the note, then I would have agreed with Lizzie that Max's death was a tragic accident. Except she *did* receive it, and I have no idea what to think or who to speak to. Surely Max would have tasted the alcohol if someone slipped it into his drink? I had half expected Jack or Lizzie to demand to see the note, or at least ask that we take it to the police, but neither of them had and that in itself makes me wonder if perhaps they know more about Max's death than either of them are letting on.

'Good morning, Miss Lily.'

Lost in my own thoughts, I look up, half surprised to see I have arrived at the back gate to the lot and Bobby, the security guard, is grinning at me. 'Hey, Bobby.'

'New movie starts shooting today, huh?'

'Sure does.' I smile at him and wish him a good day before heading onto the lot. I will never, ever get bored of working here, despite the way the last movie I worked on ended. A golf buggy whizzes past me, carrying a slight, dark blonde woman clutching a sunshade who I recognise as Ann Silver, and I make a mental note to try and track her down later on. After all, she worked with Max on his last movie, and she might have been at the wrap party. Extras bustle past me, herded by a woman with a clipboard, some of them feigning boredom as if they do this every day, but I watch the way their eyes drink in the backdrop greedily, the way their feet slow ever so slightly as they pass faces they've seen on screen a thousand times before. I know how they feel, because I still feel the same way every day, pinching myself that I get to work here.

The last movie I worked on with my boss, esteemed film director Leonard Langford, had the plug unceremoniously pulled on it when the main star mysteriously disappeared, but the studio wasted no time in getting started on the next big project. Today shooting starts on a mother-daughter movie with dark undertones, and butterflies swarm in my stomach. I'm not sure if it's excitement at being back on set, or nerves at feeling like the new girl as I meet the crew who will be working on the movie alongside me. There's also the fact that the studio has signed superstar Tipsy Jenner to play the mother – a movie star of epic proportions. There is a pang in my chest as I realise that the one person who would understand my excitement at working with Tipsy Jenner – my mother – isn't around to share it.

'Lily!' Bunny Truman, a runner who's worked her way up to become Leonard's second assistant, looks up with a grin, tucking her blonde curls behind her ear as I approach the small desk she uses in the corridor outside Leonard's office. 'Aren't you glad to be back on set today? It's so nice to get back to work properly.' She swipes a sheet of paper off her desk and tucks it into her drawer, and then straightens the pencils and ink ribbons beside her typewriter.

'Hi, Bunny. Don't tidy up on my account. This is your desk now.' Leonard has upgraded me to a desk in the corner of his office, although sitting right beside your boss instead of out of sight in the corridor doesn't always feel like an upgrade. 'Are there any messages?'

Bunny hands me a sheaf of papers and I groan aloud at the sight of Oskar Goldstein's name on the first message. A high-ranking studio exec, Oskar and I haven't always seen eye to eye, and if I can avoid him, I will. I tuck the message to the bottom of the pile, knowing Leonard would probably yell at me if he knew. Thanking Bunny, I push open the office door, pausing as I reach my desk.

'Bunny?' I call out.

'Yes?' Her face appears round the door frame, her cheeks slightly flushed.

'Has someone been in here over the weekend?' I can't swear to it, but it feels as though things on my desk – a framed photograph of me, Tilda, Louis, Honey Black and her husband Joe at their wedding, my favourite pen, a half-eaten packet of chips sealed shut with a hair tie – have been moved around a little.

'Uh, no?' Bunny's frown deepens before her face clears. 'Oh, I needed a pencil sharpener.' She grins and points at her eyes and the perfect dash of eyeliner. 'A girl has to look good in the movies, right?'

'Sure.' I nod, but I still feel unsettled and I'm not sure why. Maybe all this talk about Max and the note Tilda received has got to me more than I realised.

'You should get going, Lily,' Bunny says, seriously. 'Leonard wants you to go straight to make-up to introduce yourself to Tipsy. She'll be waiting for you – Leonard said you'd be there at seven thirty. You're already late.'

'Yikes, Bun! Why didn't you tell me that before?' Dropping the messages on Leonard's desk, I snatch up the huge bunch of studio keys I inherited from Jean and hotfoot it out of the office, scurrying across the lot without looking back, forgetting all about the unease that cloaked my shoulders.

–

'Hi!' I gasp, as I enter the make-up trailer, smoothing a hand briskly over my wild, dark curls. 'I'm Lily, Leonard's assistant.'

Tipsy Jenner looks back at me via the huge mirror in front of her, the spotlights giving her skin a shimmering glow as Veronica, the make-up artist, dusts her cheeks with powder. 'Lily, perhaps you can give us your thoughts on things?'

Tipsy looks exactly as she does on screen, despite her make-up only being half done, and I have to blink a couple of times. It's like this sometimes, living in LA. In my own time I would see a Real Housewife, or Anya Taylor-Joy, or Timothée Chalamet grocery shopping and have the urge to rush over and say hi, mistaking them for someone I knew from somewhere else. Now, it feels as though I am bumping into an old friend I haven't seen in years, aided by the fact that Tipsy is speaking as though we are in the middle of a conversation.

'My thoughts? On what exactly?'

'Pass me that.' Tipsy waves a hand towards the dressing table and the crumpled newspaper that sits on it. 'Come on, sit.' She opens the newspaper. 'Here it is. Page fifteen.'

Perching on the edge of the chair beside Tipsy's I lean over her shoulder, even though it feels absurdly intimate, and run my eyes over the page, my heart sinking as I see what she's referring to. 'The new gossip column?'

'Yes!' Tipsy turns to me, glee written all over her face as Veronica drops her powder compact, tutting under her breath as she stoops to pick it up. Tipsy's green eyes are shining, and she shakes her red hair away from her face. A single, lone grey hair sticks up from her hairline, and I wonder how long before the hairdresser arrives and yanks it out of her head. 'Isn't it the most delicious thing?'

'Well—'

'Listen to this…' Tipsy takes a deep breath and shakes the newspaper in front of her. '*Hollywood's latest starlet isn't quite what she seems… Might she be hiding a secret from her past? Studio publicity casts her as an all-American girl but rumour has it this chica has family roots that stretch far south of the border…*'

Veronica raises an eyebrow, a smile tugging at her lips as she wets a brush and runs it over a cake of black mascara. I swallow, trying hard to disguise my distaste.

'That seems a little…' *Racist* is the word I want to use, but Tipsy lets out a gust of laughter that carries the faintest hint of last night's gin and cigarette smoke.

'I *know*,' she says gleefully. 'It's absolutely delicious, isn't it? Far more snarky than Louella's coy little snippets. Everyone always knows exactly who Louella is talking about, since she doesn't do a very good job of hiding things.' Tipsy has a point there. 'This one though… I have no idea, and apparently neither does Veronica.'

'Well, we have our suspicions,' Veronica says, as Tipsy winks at her in the mirror. The two of them giggle like little girls, loving the scandalous nature of the column. 'So, what do you think, Lily?'

I pause, not sure how to respond. The twenty-first-century part of me – the part who was brought up to think that the colour of your skin doesn't matter a jot, it's who you are on the inside – wants to scream that from the rooftops, but the other part of me – the part who lives and works in Hollywood in the 1950s – urges caution.

'Well,' I say slowly, my internal battle raging. 'I guess I don't know who this could be about either. And I don't suppose it really matters, does it?'

'Doesn't matter?' Tipsy yelps, in a way I would find comical in different circumstances. 'Of course it matters. Someone is *lying* about who they really are. You can't do that in Hollywood, darling. You always get found out.'

'*Always*,' Veronica agrees, gesturing for Tipsy to close her eyes as the mascara wand hits her eyelashes. 'And something like this... Well, it's only natural that people will talk about it. It's *quite* the scandal.'

People lie about who they are in Hollywood all the time, but I don't think now is the best time to point it out. 'But it doesn't matter if someone is Hispanic. Or Black, or anything else for that matter,' I say, unable to keep my mouth shut. 'As long as whoever it is does their job properly they don't deserve to be treated any differently.'

'Ha!' Tipsy yelps again. 'Darling, you sound just like Clark. He threw a terrible fit at Victor over the segregation on the *Gone with the Wind* set.' *True.* That was another reason why I swooned when I saw him at Honey Black's birthday party in 1949. 'I don't mean that at all, of course. I just mean... the *deceit*. It makes the perfect recipe for a scandal soup.' Her eyes go back to the newspaper. 'Rita Moreno?' she mutters under her breath.

'No,' Veronica shakes her head. 'Everyone knows she's Puerto Rican.'

'Sorry I can't be of more help, Tipsy,' I say, as Tipsy finally drops the newspaper and lets Veronica carry on with her face.

'Pshaw.' Tipsy flaps a hand, and Veronica gestures for her to close her mouth. Veronica reaches for a jammy red lipstick and begins to dab it on Tipsy's lips, completing her transformation to glamorous movie star. 'It's all just a bit of fun,' Tipsy says, once her lips are a brilliant scarlet. 'Haven't you read the others? Hints about high-profile actors sleeping with people they shouldn't, divorce rumours… This entire industry thrives on gossip, Lily.'

Tilda wouldn't have a job if Tipsy wasn't right, I think, my mind whirring. I genuinely have no idea who the gossip column might be referring to, but I can't lie to myself. The whole thing leaves a nasty taste in my mouth and that uneasy feeling settles on my shoulders again.

'It's just a bit of fun,' Tipsy is saying again, 'and whoever is behind it all must be having the time of their life. But let's be honest, Lily, it's hardly going to kill anyone.'

Chapter Five

'Hellooo!' Bunny's face appears around the door frame of the make-up trailer, as she taps on the door simultaneously. 'Veronica, I have Mae for you.'

Bunny steps aside, wafting a hand to usher in a woman in her early twenties. She wears a blue-and-white-checkered dress, the waist cinched to tiny proportions, and matching pumps that I am immediately itching to know where she got them from. Her blonde hair curls softly to her shoulders, the right side styled so that it slightly obscures her face, giving her a shy, coy air. She steps hesitantly into the trailer, and I leap out of the chair beside Tipsy's and gesture for her to sit down.

'This is Mae Sinclair, our second lead. So thrilled to have you here, Mae.' Bunny claps her hands together excitedly. 'Lily, can I leave Mae with you? I have so much to do, but I love the first day of shooting!' And then she's gone, like a hurricane whirling in and leaving everybody reeling.

'Well,' I say with a grin. 'I guess you met Bunny.'

Mae gives me a cautious smile. 'She's very sweet.'

'That she is,' I concede. 'I'm Lily, I'll be taking care of you while we're shooting this movie. I work for Leonard, so if there's anything you want me to speak to him about, just let me know.'

Mae slides into the chair beside Tipsy, flashing her a quick smile. 'I think I can speak to Leonard about anything I'm concerned about, Lily, but thank you for the offer.'

Tipsy raises her eyes to meet mine in the dressing room mirror and I raise an eyebrow. Having worked with actresses before I thought I knew what to expect, but clearly not. I became good friends with both Honey Black and Kitty Fox, and I guess I was expecting Mae Sinclair to be the same – kind of needy, in need of a little hand-holding and a confidante – but clearly she's a different breed. I stifle a grin.

'You're all done, Ms Jenner.' Veronica steps back and Tipsy inspects herself in the mirror, turning her face this way and that and rubbing at her teeth with a fingertip.

'I guess that'll do,' she says, as she gets to her feet. Veronica turns her attention to her bag of colourful tricks, moving over to where Mae sits patiently. 'Gosh, I'm about dying for a cigarette. Do you have any, Lily?'

'I don't smoke, sorry.'

'Well, I guess I'll have to go and search some out.' Tipsy picks up her pocketbook and rummages through it, sighing when no cigarettes turn up. 'I'm sure one of the fellas out there will have one. I don't mind charming them a little if I have to.'

'Call time is in thirty minutes, Tipsy,' I say pointedly. The last thing I want is Tipsy disappearing in search of cigarettes. 'Wardrobe are waiting for you. Please can we not be late the first morning of shooting?'

'Darling,' Tipsy drawls, 'I am never late. Ask anyone, they'll tell you. Have a think, won't you, Lily?'

'About what?' It's been less than an hour in her company and I already feel as though Tipsy is giving me whiplash.

'About whom the gossip column might be about, of course!' And with a throaty laugh and a blast of Miss Dior perfume, Tipsy Jenner is gone.

–

'Well, that's not what I heard,' Mae says as the trailer door slams closed behind Tipsy. 'I heard she's late to set every day, but she's so high profile no one dares say a word.'

A tiny bubble of laughter escapes Veronica's lips as she sorts eyeshadow, searching for the right shade to make Mae appear five years younger on camera, and I bite my own lip before bursting into laughter. I, of course, have been prepped by Leonard, who told me Tipsy has no concept of time at all. Hence the reason why I told her we only had thirty minutes until call time, instead of the actual sixty minutes.

Mae shifts in her chair, loosening the belt around her waist and letting out a sigh, before twisting to look at me. 'Gosh,' she says, 'Lily, I am so pleased to meet you. I'm sorry if I came off as a little rude just now. I was just so nervous. This is my first movie and they cast me against Tipsy Jenner! My mother is having kittens at home.'

'My mother would also be having kittens,' I say with a grin, relief washing over me. I'm not sure how easy it would have been to work with Mae if she'd been unfriendly and stand-offish.

'Don't get me wrong,' Mae says, as Veronica gently turns her chair away from the mirror and begins to get to work on her make-up, running a pan stick foundation over her face before blending it. 'I know I deserve to be here. I know I'm talented enough, and I've done things I'm not proud of to get here, but I made it all on my own merit. I just hope that everyone else on set sees that too.'

'They will,' I reassure her, hoping that I'm right. 'Honestly, it's not that long ago that I was the new girl, and I remember exactly how it feels. Just work hard and be polite and you'll be fine.'

'So maybe I shouldn't get involved in all this gossip column stuff?' Mae asks, her skin porcelain perfect and her head perfectly still as Veronica turns her attention to Mae's brows, running a dark pencil over them.

'You heard about that?'

'Oh, Lily,' Veronica tuts as she slicks a little Vaseline over Mae's brows to keep them in line. 'Everybody has heard about it… It's the talk of the lot.'

There is a pause as Mae waits for Veronica to finish fussing with her brows, and she frowns as she catches sight of herself in the mirror, as if she isn't used to looking so flawless. 'I think Veronica is right – everybody in the whole of LA has heard about it. It's all anybody can talk about.'

'Well, I can tell you that Leonard will be less than impressed,' I say honestly. Leonard comes to work to make movies – he's not interested in the stars' private lives, or what happens off set, as long as nothing holds up his shooting schedule. And it's my job to make sure anything that might hold up shooting is squashed before it does. 'So maybe don't mention it in front of him.'

Mae gives a serious nod. 'Anything else I need to know?' There is a look in her eye now, something hungry that glitters with ambition.

'I don't think so.'

The door to the trailer flies open and a man I've never seen before pops his head in. He is maybe late twenties, his face framed by neat dark hair. His eyes flick past Veronica to Mae and then he turns his gaze to me.

'Good morning, ladies. Call time is in fifteen minutes.' He smiles, a thin, uncertain smile, and I grin back. His forehead is shiny with perspiration, and he glances towards Mae as if unable to believe he's in the same room as her.

'I know what time Mae is due on set, Mr…?'

He clicks the pen in his hand and I realise he's more nervous than Mae. 'Marshall. I've been sent to tell you to be on set at your appointed call time. Mr Goldstein doesn't want any hold-ups on this movie.' He swallows. 'He said, "Not after the last one."'

With a brisk nod at me and a weird kind of half-bow in Mae's direction, Mr Marshall strides out, and I find my mouth opening and closing, unable to articulate all the things I want to say. Just as the door is about to swing closed behind him, a hand reaches in and shoves it open again, and a gleeful Tipsy slides in.

'Darlings,' she says, a bottle in one hand, two shot glasses in the other, and the acrid scent of cigarette smoke on her clothes. 'You'll be glad to know I managed to find some smokes. I know you both must be nervous, first day on set and all that, so I thought I'd bring you a little something to calm the nerves.'

'Tipsy…' I look down at the bottle and shake my head. 'It's not even nine o'clock in the morning. I'm not drinking vodka so early, and neither is Mae. Nor are you for that matter.' Reaching out, I whip the bottle from her hands.

'That guy was right,' Mae says with a quick glance at her watch, smiling her thanks at the make-up artist as she slides out of the chair. 'We probably do need to get to set, if we don't want to be late.'

'I told you, I'm never late,' Tipsy says, scowling at me as I put the vodka out of reach.

'I think it's more that people wait for you, Tipsy,' I say with a grin, and give her a gentle shove in the back, guiding her out of the trailer and towards the back of the lot where the first scene will be shot.

As we cross the lot, I spot the dark-haired man hurrying along the other side of the road, his head down and a clipboard clutched to his chest. My heart sinks as I remember his words in the trailer. *Mr Goldstein doesn't want any hold-ups on this movie.* I was hoping Oskar Goldstein wouldn't be too involved, but I'm guessing he's going to be keeping a close eye on all of us given that the last movie we worked on got the plug pulled before shooting even finished.

'Hey, Tipsy?' I nudge her as the man reaches a stage door and presses his hand against it. 'Who is that guy? The one who was leaving the trailer as you got back?'

Tipsy squints across the street in his direction. 'Him? I think his name is Cliff... Martin? Markham?'

'Marshall?'

'That's it.' Tipsy runs her eyes over him and then shrugs as he pushes open the door and disappears out of sight. 'Darling, don't worry about him; he's just an assistant. He's nobody.'

Trying not to let Tipsy's words sting – after all, *I* am just an assistant – I watch as the door closes behind him and then Mae is tapping me on the arm and we hurry to the stage door, before Leonard realises we're late. Cliff might not be important to Tipsy, but I'm hoping I can get on his good side. Especially if he works with Oskar. I don't want anything to go wrong on this movie, for Leonard's sake as well as my own. This time, everything is going to be perfect.

Chapter Six

'Marks, please!' Leonard calls out, and I watch in awe as Tipsy switches from a chain-smoking, raspy-voiced gossip queen to an arrogant yet elegant woman, an air of haughtiness enveloping her as Mae takes her place on set opposite her. The slight sheen of nervousness that cloaked Mae as we entered the set has also drifted away, and I glance in Leonard's direction as Mae steps behind the bar, pouring Tipsy – her mother, in the movie – a strong drink.

The rumour on the set – flying already despite it being the first day of shooting – is that Leonard is the one who fought to get Mae for the part of Tipsy's daughter in this movie, the story of a girl who is beaten down by her overbearing mother until she meets the love of her life. Together, the two of them plot to get rid of Tipsy's character for good, the movie taking a dark and twisted turn in the final third. Word is that Leonard saw her audition and immediately told the casting agent that she was his Rita, fighting for her even when Oskar tried to tell him Rita should be played by an actress with a bigger name.

Now, Leonard's eyes gleam as Mae discreetly tips something into Tipsy's drink, using a drinks swizzler to stir the powder into the whisky. Her face is passive, and she keeps up a prattling stream of conversation as an oblivious Tipsy makes sly digs and snide remarks, fully immersed in her role as Mae's toxic mother. Moments later, Tipsy is gripping the edge of a chair, the whisky tumbler in one hand.

'I feel… a little odd,' she says, her eyes glazing over and her words slurring slightly. 'Rita… fetch me a chair.'

'Let's get you outside,' a nervous Mae says, playing Rita's fear and anxiety perfectly. 'You just need some fresh air.'

Mae takes Tipsy by the arm, flashing a glance towards the telephone, her character knowing that it will ring just moments after she has taken Tipsy outside into the garden, her future husband checking to make sure Rita's toxic mother is out of the picture. The camera follows as Mae leads the older woman out towards the pool, Tipsy tripping over her own feet.

'Oh gosh,' Tipsy's voice is muffled, her words sliding over one another in the most convincing display of intoxication I've seen on screen in a long time. 'These tiles are wet, I'm going to…'

'And *cut*!' Leonard calls out, clapping his hands together. 'Ladies, that was fantastic. Mae, excellent work.'

Mae gives Leonard a smile, but her cheeks are pale and she squeezes her hands together, her fingers knotting. Tipsy on the other hand gives herself a round of applause and throws an arm over Mae's shoulder.

'Fantastic, darling. Jolly good show. I almost believed you were about to throw me in for a moment.'

Mae smiles, but there is a sickly tinge about it, as if she has a bad taste in her mouth. I guess it is a difficult scene to film, the impending death of your mother at your own hands, and it was terribly convincing. Something about the scene has goosebumps rippling out all over my body, but I don't have time to think about it before Leonard is beside me, grinning wildly.

'See, Lily?' he says, clapping me on the back. 'Didn't I say Mae Sinclair was the perfect Rita?'

'You did,' I agree. 'Of course, none of us were ever in any doubt, except perhaps Oskar.' I grin as Leonard rolls his eyes. 'That scene was absolute perfection.' And it was, even down to the way it left an unsettling undercurrent of something dark and unnameable running through my body.

'Let's hope Oskar is ready to eat some humble pie,' Leonard mutters, as Oskar Goldstein glowers at Leonard from across the room, Cliff Marshall by his side. Cliff still clicks his pen and is looking at Oskar as though he's some kind of God. 'Excuse me, Lil. Can we catch up later? Jean said I'm to ask you to dinner next week, and to ask where you got those ginger cookies from? They're all she can eat without feeling sick.'

'I'll bring her some.' Jean, Leonard's wife and ex-assistant, is in the early stages of pregnancy. Her morning sickness shows no sign of abating, and clearly my ginger biscuits are the only thing she can stomach. I used to make them for my mother before she died, while she was undergoing chemotherapy, and I'm glad now I can make them for a happier reason.

Leonard strides after Oskar, leaving me to prepare for the next scene. It's very rare that scenes are shot in one take, so I'm taking this morning's work as an omen that everything on this film set is going to work out better than the last movie. Now, Tipsy is smoking a cigarette, waving her hand around and getting smoke in Mae's face as Veronica dabs at Mae's forehead with a powder puff.

'Lily, here are the pages for the next scene.' Bunny arrives at my side, clipboard in one hand, glass bottle of Coke in the other. 'And I brought you a drink. It's hot under these lights.'

'Thanks, Bun.' I take the clipboard and the bottle, the cold sweetness refreshing on my tongue. Checking my watch, I see we only have a few minutes before shooting resumes, and Leonard is still talking to Oskar, a fixed grin on his face. Veronica finishes dabbing at Mae's face and checks Tipsy over, before scooping up her bag and hurrying across the set to the exit. As she leaves, Cliff holds the door open for her and it looks as though he says something to her. Veronica blushes, pressing a hand to her mouth, before she glides out the door and I turn my attention back to Bunny.

'Wasn't it great, Lil? I have such a good feeling about Tipsy and Mae,' Bunny jabbers on.

'Great,' I echo, the image of Tipsy stumbling and slurring on the wet pool tiles etched into my mind. There is the faintest hint of something scratching away at my brain, something that I can't quite put my finger on. All I know is that it's something to do with Max. I need to see Tilda and Louis.

–

Cliff appears once Leonard has called cut for the last time today as I finish collecting call sheets and put up the 'HOT SET' signs, making sure none of the props or furniture are moved overnight.

'Lily, isn't it?' he asks, as he takes the other end of the rope I am using to section off the set without asking, looping it through the hook at the other end of the set.

'That's right. And you're Cliff Marshall.' Cliff flashes me a grin that transforms his entire face, as if surprised. 'How was your first day on set?'

'Great,' he says. 'At least… I think it went great? No one yelled at me, and I didn't bring Oskar the wrong coffee or anything.'

'Getting through any day unscathed by Oskar's wrath is a win in my eyes,' I say with a laugh. 'I would say his bark is worse than his bite, but that would be a lie.'

Cliff lets out a burst of laughter that rings across the empty set, and I find myself smiling too. 'Well, it's good to know I'm not the only one he barks at,' Cliff says, as we make our way out towards the lot. Holding the door open, Cliff ushers me through first. 'It was good to meet you, Lily. I think I'm going to enjoy working with you.'

'Me too,' I say, surprised to find I really mean it. 'Thanks for your help just then. I always get the creeps when I'm the last one on set. I always feel like someone might be lurking in the shadows… or I'm worried that a lighting rig might fall on my head and no one will find me until the morning.'

'Well, I don't mind sticking around. You know. Just in case.' Cliff grins, as Bunny steps out from the offices and starts making her way towards us. 'I should go. I have a date. See you tomorrow.'

Dusk has fallen by the time I say goodbye to Bobby on the security gate and step out towards the street with Bunny beside me. The afternoon's shooting went well, although slightly less smoothly than the morning, after Tipsy swore she saw a rat run across the set. No one else saw it, and I noticed that the vodka bottle had been removed from the make-up trailer, so who knows if there really was a rodent gatecrashing the filming. I'm just glad that Oskar wasn't on set to catch the delays. My feet ache and my back could do with a hot stone massage, so I am relieved when I see Louis leaning against his car in the parking lot.

'Hey. This is a nice surprise.' I lean in and kiss his cheek, breathing in his scent of limes and sunshine. Part of me wishes I could kiss him properly, but that's not what we are. Maybe if we'd both been born in the same decade – or if Louis knew where I really came from – things would have been so much different, but we weren't and they aren't. It doesn't mean either of us don't think about it though. 'I thought you were working.'

'Just got off.' Louis opens the car door for me and I slide inside, catching the scent of cigar smoke and beer on his uniform. Louis works as a bartender at the Polo Lounge at the Beverly Hills Hotel, where we met in 1949 after I first found myself out of place and time. 'I thought you might need a ride.' He glances over his shoulder. 'Err, am I… I mean, are we… Does Bunny need a ride too?'

I had forgotten about Bunny, and now she hovers beside the car with one hand lifted in an awkward wave. 'Sorry, Lou, I really need to talk to you guys alone.'

'Hey, Bunny.' Without missing a beat, Louis turns and gives her a brief hug. 'It's really great to see you, but Tilda is waiting for me and Lily to meet her for dinner. We need to head off.'

'Oh sure! I just wanted to say hi.' Bunny blushes in the dusky twilight and I stifle a grin. I don't know any girl who doesn't have some sort of crush on Louis. 'See you tomorrow, Lil.'

I wave at her as Louis slides into the passenger seat and we head out of the parking lot and onto Sunset Boulevard.

'So…' Louis takes his eyes off the road to look at me. 'What's going on?'

Settling back against the seat, I lean my head against the headrest and close my eyes. 'I need a stiff drink – preferably something spicy with tequila – and then I need to run some stuff by you two. It's about Max's death.'

'OK. A margarita hit the spot? I'm not sure about the spicy part though.'

'Leave that part to me.' I have a feeling the drink is not the only thing that will be spicy this evening.

Café Trocadero is still quiet when Louis pulls the door open and ushers me inside. It's one of my favourite spots in Los Angeles, and I can't help but run my eyes over the lobby as we wait for the girl to check our coats. It sets the tone perfectly for what awaits us inside – striped satin settees sit against a backdrop of the Parisian skyline, and it almost feels as though we are right there, in the centre of Paris. Following Louis through to the dining room, we make our way to the back of the room, past the polished, mirror-like dancefloor in the centre, to where Tilda is waving a hand in our direction, the picture window behind her offering a stunning view of the city.

'How did you guys know I'd need to see you?' I lean in and kiss Tilda on the cheek before sliding into the chair beside her.

'It's a tradition now, isn't it?' she says. 'First day of shooting equals drinks and a dissection of your new charge. You do have a new charge, right?'

I nod, grateful to Louis for snagging the waiter's attention. 'A margarita, please. And could you shake it with a fresh chilli?' I turn back to Tilda. 'I do have a new charge. Mae Sinclair. Have you heard of her?'

Tilda shakes her head. 'No, I don't think so. Is it true that Tipsy Jenner is also on the movie?'

'Yep. And she's just as wonderful as they make her out to be in the newspapers.' I lower my voice. 'Speaking of which, have you seen the latest gossip column blind item?'

'The one about someone coming from south of the border?' Louis asks, a frown etched onto his features. 'Yeah, and it stinks.'

The waiter brings our drinks – a kind of spicy margarita for me, beer for Louis and an old fashioned for Tilda – just as Ann Silver enters the café. She scans the room as if searching for someone, and I push back my chair.

'One sec, guys. I'll be right back.' Hurrying across the room I catch up with Ann just as she reaches her table. 'Hi! Ann, isn't it?'

Ann looks up at me, and as she squints, trying to place me, I notice her eyes are tinged with pink. 'Yes? Do I know you? Oh.' She picks up a napkin. 'I don't have a pen, I'm afraid.'

'Oh no.' I give a small huff of laughter to cover my embarrassment. 'I'm not after an autograph. I wanted to speak to you about Max.'

'Max?'

'Max Hayden. In light of his… accident. I'm so sorry for your loss. I know you worked together.'

Ann's brow creases further. 'We did, but I didn't really know him. Not well, not off set. Max was very professional.'

'So, you didn't notice if he was… I don't know, acting strangely, or drinking… or anything?' Ugh, I feel gross just saying it out loud.

Ann gives me a sidewards glance and looks over my shoulder as if hoping to be rescued. 'No, I'm sorry. Like I said, I really didn't know him terribly well. Although...'

'What?' My heart skips a beat, suddenly sure that Ann Silver is about to drop a nugget of information into my lap.

'Excuse me, I'm sorry. My dinner date is here.' Ann gets to her feet and waves over my shoulder, although she doesn't seem terribly excited to see them. 'It was nice to meet you.' Without another word, she moves past me towards the lobby and the doors to the cellar room downstairs, leaving me frustrated and sure that she might know more than she's letting on.

'Any luck?' Tilda asks as I return to our table and my slowly warming margarita.

'I think she wanted to tell me something, but she dashed off to meet her date. Did anyone see who walked in?'

Both Louis and Tilda shake their heads. 'Maybe we can catch up with her later,' Louis says. 'Anyway, Lil, what is it you wanted to tell us? You seemed pretty agitated when you got in the car.'

Taking a gulp of my drink, I let the tequila burn its way to my stomach before I speak. 'We filmed a scene with Tipsy and Mae today, where Mae put something in Tilda's drink. What if that's what happened to Max? What if someone spiked his drink to make him appear drunk?'

Tilda looks doubtful. 'I don't know, Lil. Louella has squashed a lot of stories about Max's behaviour before, stuff that even she thought was too scandalous to reveal. It seems more likely that he did drink that night.'

'But still, the note you received... Max didn't have an accident.' It's as if a lightbulb goes off over my head as I realise what it was at Lizzie and Max's home that struck me as odd. 'Drink up, guys. We need to get back over to Lizzie's house.'

Chapter Seven

The doorbell chimes again as I press my finger hard against it, and Tilda gently pulls my hand away.

'Lily, she'll answer. Pressing the bell repeatedly isn't going to help any.' Just as Tilda speaks, the door flies open and Mary Colman stands there, like before, her face pale and lined with worry.

'Lily Jones!' she exclaims, the worry fading into a smile as she claps her hands together in a way that's more animated than I've ever seen her. 'Are you…?'

'I wondered if I could speak with Lizzie. Is she home?'

Mary glances over her shoulder, her demeanour growing slightly chilly. 'She is, but she's resting.'

'That's all right,' Tilda says with a smile, pressing her foot over the threshold so that Mary has to take a small step back. 'Maybe we could speak with you instead. It won't take a moment, I promise.'

Mary pauses, her eyes narrowing as her gaze goes to Tilda's foot, before she nods reluctantly and stands to one side to let us enter the vast, airy hall. Tilda makes her way towards the kitchen at the back of the house and Mary scurries along behind, pushing her way past me.

'I'm not going to disturb Lizzie for you,' she says, her jaw set. 'Whatever you want to ask, you'll just have to make do with me. Lizzie will have to telephone you about anything I don't know.'

'That would be great,' I say with a reassuring smile, as Tilda's eyes flit about the kitchen. It's not as tidy as it was on our last visit, a marble bowl on the table oozing with overripe fruit, an array of dirty glasses on the worktop beside it. 'I wanted to speak about Max. I've got a couple of questions. I'm sorry, I know it's painful. You're all close, aren't you? You, Lizzie, Max and Jack?'

Mary nods, her eyes filling with tears. 'It's a terrible business, all of it. I'm not sure quite what we're going to do, if I'm honest.'

Mary reaches for the coffee pot, and I see Tilda slope out of the kitchen from the corner of my eye. Louis comes to stand beside me, effectively shielding Tilda from Mary's eyeline as she pours coffee that smells acrid and burnt. 'What is it you want to know?' she says, wrinkling her nose as she lifts her cup to her lips.

'Do you really think Max had been drinking that night? The night of the accident? Jack swears Max hadn't had a drink in over three years. It seems odd that Max would suddenly decide to break his sober streak.'

'Well...' Mary says, sipping at her coffee. It's an old stalling tactic and I stay silent, waiting for her to fill the gap. Also an old tactic, but an effective one. 'I guess he just... couldn't help it. The temptation was too much. It was a party after all.'

'Was there anything bothering him? Anyone who might have had it in for Max?' I lean in, my eyes fixed on Mary's face. 'Is there any chance that someone could have—'

'Could have what?' A stern voice comes from behind me and I turn to see Lizzie Hayden, her face make-up free, her long brown hair twisted up into ringlets, a silk dressing gown cinched tight around her waist despite the fact it's still early evening.

'Lizzie! Lily wanted to speak—' Mary fumbles with the coffee cup, dark, bitter liquid seeping across the worktop. Ever the gentleman, Louis reaches for a cloth and begins to clean it up.

'Could have what?' Lizzie repeats, her eyes narrowing as she takes me in. 'I thought I'd told you everything you wanted to know on your last visit, Miss Jones.' She lifts her chin, but I think I catch a flash of fear in her eyes before it's gone, leaving me wondering if I might have imagined it.

'I was going to ask whether you think there might have been a chance that someone may have spiked Max's drink that night.' The idea came to me fully formed, after watching Tipsy stumble around on set with her spiked whisky, slipping on the wet tiles. 'If Max was sober, perhaps someone slipped something into his drink, making it seem as though he was intoxicated.'

Lizzie pauses for a second, her mouth opening and closing. 'Why on earth would someone want to do that? Max was… Everyone adored Max. The only people who attended the party were people from the studio, people who worked on the film. Max brought hundreds of thousands of dollars in for the studio. Why on earth would anyone want to…' She swallows, her fingers knotting together until her knuckles turn white.

'Did you attend the party?' I ask. Louis looks up sharply, the coffee-stained rag still in his hand.

Lizzie flicks her eyes towards Mary. 'Yes. Of course I did. I was his wife.'

'We were all there,' Mary offers up in a voice barely above a whisper. 'Lizzie and I left early. Lizzie was up for an audition early the next morning and she wanted me to run lines with her.' It sounds plausible, but there is something about the way Mary won't meet Lizzie's eyes that makes my spine prickle.

'The idea that Max…' Lizzie shakes her head. 'That note you received was clearly a cruel prank, nothing more. A terrible coincidence. Now, if you'll excuse me, I have an early start in the morning. Mary,' her voice softens and I feel a wave of sympathy for Lizzie, even though I'm pretty sure she's lying about something, 'please see Miss Jones and her friend out.'

It's only when Lizzie refers to my 'friend' that I realise there is no sign of Tilda. Keeping my mouth shut, I watch as Lizzie stalks off towards the bedroom and then turns to Mary.

'I'm sorry,' she says. 'It's been a very testing time. Let me see you out.' Louis exits the kitchen first, and as I follow him, Mary hurries to walk alongside me, her cold, pale hand resting on my forearm.

'Miss Jones,' she says in a low voice, ensuring Louis doesn't overhear us. 'Can I trust you?'

'Of course.' I lower my voice to match hers, my heart pounding a frantic double beat in my chest. 'You can tell me anything. Your secret – whatever it is – is safe with me.' *Drugs? Prostitutes? Gambling? Just what did get Max Hayden killed and what does Mary know about it?*

'The thing is, you seem… different to everyone else.' Mary stops in the hall, tilting her head to one side. 'I'm not sure what it is but it's as if…' She trails off, shaking her head. 'Ignore me.'

'No,' I press. 'What is it?'

'It's almost as if you're from another time.' She frowns. 'There's just an air about you, as if you've seen and done more than the average person. Gosh, I'm just being silly. My grandmother was a psychic, and she always said I had the gift, but honestly— Oh!' Mary breaks off and presses a hand to her mouth, just as goosebumps ripple out all over my body. 'I didn't know you were in there!'

Tilda has popped up from behind a sofa in the sitting room, a grin on her face. 'Sorry, got lost looking for the bathroom.' She comes out, running a hand over her skirt as if she's been touching something dusty, but my gaze drifts past her to the mantelpiece and the gap where a photo used to stand.

'Mary? Liz? I'm back.' The front door slams closed and Jack bursts in, his hair rumpled and a faint fug of whisky on the air around him. 'What's going on?' He looks from Mary to Louis and then past me to the sitting room. 'What is this?'

Pushing past Tilda, Jack crouches next to the sofa and tugs on the corner of a box that has been inexpertly hidden behind it. 'Mary? What is this?'

Mary's eyes are wide and she holds out her hands in a placatory gesture as she moves towards Jack, kneeling beside him. 'Jack, darling, don't be—'

Jack has already ripped the packing tape from the box and is rummaging inside. 'These are Max's things,' he says, his voice gruff. 'All his stuff, his awards, letters… photographs. You've boxed up all of his things.' The photo that once stood on the mantelpiece has been tucked inside the box, a college scarf laid on top. 'Who did this? Was it Lizzie? The man has only been gone a couple of weeks and you're already trying to erase him!'

'Darling,' Mary tries again, one hand rubbing his shoulder. Jack shrugs her off, running his hand through his hair before tugging the photo free. I catch sight of a grinning Max, standing beside a pool in swimming trunks that date the photo to the 1930s.

'You had no right,' Jack rasps. 'Max is barely in the ground.' He gets to his feet, storming out of the sitting room into the hall. 'Lizzie? Lizzie!'

Mary's eyes fill with tears as she glances into the box and then towards us. 'You have to go,' she says urgently as Jack's roars come from the bedroom, the sound of a door bouncing on its hinges making her wince. 'Please, leave now. Jack's a little upset, but he'll calm down. It'll be fine.' She shoves us along the hallway, and before any of us know it, the front door slams closed behind us and we find ourselves on the front path.

'Well,' Tilda breathes after a moment. 'That was…'

'Horrible,' Louis says, one arm around my shoulder as we make our way down the winding front path towards the street.

'You never really told us why you needed us to go back to that house, Lil,' Tilda says. 'Although I'm glad we did, despite what just happened.'

'It was the photograph,' I say. 'The one of Max in swimming trunks, that was on the mantelpiece before it got boxed up. It looked as though it was taken at some sort of tournament, and then I started thinking about the photos that were on display in the house. There was one of Mary and Lizzie together, and one of all four of them on the fireplace, but there were none of Max and Lizzie together.' I pause, letting the other two digest what I've said.

'Mom said Max and Lizzie's wedding was a high-profile affair,' Louis says, 'so you'd think they'd have their pick of neat photographs to display.'

'Not a single wedding photograph anywhere in the house,' I agree, 'and they've only been married, what, three or four years?'

We reach the car, Louis leaning down to open the door for me. 'So, do we think there was trouble in paradise?' he asks.

'Lizzie admits she was at the party that night, and there was something about the way Mary looked when she said they left early to run lines that made me think her explanation didn't quite have the ring of truth about it,' I say, my mind whirring overtime.

'Maybe that's why Lizzie is so adamant Max's death is an accident,' Tilda says. 'Because she knows it wasn't.'

Chapter Eight

Maybe that's why Lizzie is so adamant that Max's death was an accident. Tilda's words repeat on a loop in my head all night long as I toss and turn in my tiny single bed. When the first rays of dawn begin to lighten the room, I give up and sigh, shoving back the blankets and heading to the bathroom.

As I yank Tilda's pantyhose off the shower rail – clean and dry, thank goodness – and step under the stream of hot water, I wonder if Lizzie Hayden could be a killer. Could she really bump Max off at a wrap party in full view of everyone? It's the most plausible explanation – I've watched enough true crime documentaries on Netflix in my own time to know that it's always the husband. Or the wife. Or someone close to the victim at the very least.

'Morning, Miss Lily.' Bobby beams at me from his position on the gate as I arrive at work, my head still full of Max and Lizzie. 'You might want to hotfoot it inside this morning.'

'Oh?'

Bobby shakes his head. There's not much he hasn't seen from his position as a security guard on the lot, so I step up my pace and hurry towards the trailers. Even from thirty feet away I can hear Leonard's voice booming out of Tipsy's trailer.

'…unacceptable, Tipsy. What were you thinking?'

Tapping lightly on the trailer door, I push it open to find Tipsy sitting with a pout on her face. Leonard looms over her, his hair sticking up in spikes where he's run his hands through it.

'It's *method acting*, Leonard,' Tipsy says with a scowl. 'Surely you've heard of it.'

'Good morning, Leonard.' I tiptoe my way inside, the scent of alcohol and cigarette smoke hitting my nostrils. 'I don't mean to interrupt but is everything all right?' I glance at our director, who presses his lips tightly together as if afraid of the words that will tumble out. 'I could hear you almost at the parking lot… and I'm pretty sure that means everyone else can too.'

Leonard sighs, throwing a hand in Tipsy's direction. 'Smell her, Lily. Alcohol. It's six thirty in the morning, she hasn't even been to make-up yet, and our star is drunk.' He glares at me, hard enough to make my insides quail. 'I don't have time to deal with this.' With a shake of his head, he storms out of the trailer, banging the door closed behind him.

I step across the carpet and perch on the chair beside Tipsy. Leonard's right, she stinks of alcohol. Fresh alcohol. 'Tipsy… what the fuck?'

Tipsy looks at me, shock written all over her face. 'Excuse me, Lily? What kind of lang—' She stumbles and takes a breath before trying again. 'What kind of language is that to use? Don't you know who I am?'

Stifling a groan, I move to the coffee pot, pouring her a cup of strong, black coffee. 'Yes,' I say, 'I do know who you are. You're Tipsy Jenner and you are a legend on the screen. You don't need booze to get you through. Now, what's really going on?'

Tipsy takes the coffee mug and makes a face as she takes a sip. 'It's method acting, Lily. You know, where an actor stays in character even when they're not shooting. My character is filming a scene today where she's drunk and plotting a way to get rid of her daughter's awful boyfriend before he can trap her into marriage. I was just trying to get into character.'

'Tipsy, you've been in the business for over twenty years. You don't need to use method acting.'

Tipsy sniffs and a fat tear plops onto the robe she wears. 'I'm old, Lily. I'm nearly forty. There won't be many more roles for me – I'll be cast as the mother for a couple of movies, and then the grandmother, and then that'll be it for me. All over.' She raises her eyes to mine. 'Did you see Mae on set yesterday?'

'Yes. And she was wonderful.'

'Exactly,' Tipsy hisses, slopping coffee over her sleeve. 'She was a knockout. Absolutely top drawer. She made me look… old, and past it. I thought maybe I should try the method thing, that that would make Leonard praise me the way he praises Mae. If it's good enough for Marlon…'

'Oh, Tipsy. I mean it. You don't need method acting. Leonard praised both of you yesterday, and you absolutely smashed that scene by the pool.' Just thinking about it makes a shiver run down my spine. 'He's giving Mae extra encouragement because this is her first movie, but you don't need that. Mae does – I bet she'd be thrilled if you mentored her a little bit too. You're brilliant – if you weren't, you wouldn't have sacks of fan mail delivered to the studio every day.' I gesture to the mail bag in the corner of the trailer, bulging with envelopes.

'Excuse me, ladies.' The trailer door flies open and Cliff appears, his nose wrinkling slightly as he glances between us, blinking rapidly. He swipes at the corner of his left eye with one finger. 'Is everything OK in here?'

Tipsy sighs and leans towards the well-lit mirror, running a finger under her eyes to scoop up her smudged mascara, and I step towards the door and lower my voice. 'Not the best start to the morning,' I say, nodding in Tipsy's direction.

'Can I smell… hooch?' Cliff delicately sniffs the air and turns a worried gaze on me.

I nod. 'Afraid so. Tipsy thought she'd try her hand at method acting. I've given her some strong coffee, but she's a sloppy drunk, it seems. God knows how I'm going to sober her up enough to get to set on time. Oskar's going to have my guts for garters.' The very thought of Oskar seeing Tipsy in this state makes my heart sink to my boots. Or Converse trainers, as the case may be.

Cliff pauses for a moment, his eyes running over Tipsy as a smile tugs at the corners of his mouth. 'Give me just a minute. Don't go anywhere.'

A few moments later, in which Tipsy has sniffled into a clean hanky and refused any more coffee, Cliff reappears with a small glass in his hand.

'Cliff, what the hell?' I round on him, fury sparking in my veins. 'You're supposed to be helping – that's a shot glass! The last thing she needs is any more booze.'

Cliff holds out the shot glass to Tipsy, who takes it with a brief side eye in my direction before she necks it in one and winces, letting out a yelp. 'Lily, it's OK,' Cliff says, clapping a coughing Tipsy on the back. 'It's a shot of pickle juice. Guaranteed to sober up even the most pie-eyed.'

Tipsy coughs again before swigging at her coffee, as Cliff rests a hand gently on her shoulder. 'Ms Jenner, you're wanted in make-up.'

'I just need five minutes, please, darling?' Tipsy gives him a watery smile, and Cliff nods enthusiastically.

'Yes, ma'am. No problem.'

'Gosh, that stuff burns.' Tipsy pulls a face in the mirror as Cliff squeezes past me, giving me a shy grin as he steps out into the fresh morning air.

Waiting until the trailer door closes behind him, I hand Tipsy a tissue and pull her into a hug, relieved to find she now smells like coffee and pickles, and Cliff's shot seems to have done the trick. 'Honestly,' I say, 'you're the best actress I've ever seen, and you have years ahead of you yet. Look at Gloria Swanson – she wasn't playing a mother in *Sunset Boulevard*, and she was fifty. You're still in your thirties.' Thinking about it, perhaps Gloria wasn't the best example – Norma Desmond was a washed-up has-been in that movie.

Tipsy gives me a wobbly smile and takes the foil-wrapped stick of Wrigley's gum I hold out to her. 'Thanks, Lil. You're first class, all the way.'

'So, no more method acting?'

'No more method acting.' Tipsy hurries away to the make-up trailer, and I gather up the script pages she's left on the dresser before heading out of the trailer, exhaustion already tugging at my bones and it's not even seven o'clock. It's going to be a long day.

'Hey, wait a second!' I pull Tipsy's trailer door closed and call out to Cliff, hurrying down the steps after him until I catch him up. 'Thank you for stepping in this morning. You've just saved my bacon, I reckon.'

'Ah, it was nothing.' A blush rises to his cheeks, and he looks down at the sun-baked asphalt.

'How did you know pickle juice would sober her up? I've never heard of it before.' I fall into step beside him. He blinks again, as though he has dust in his eye.

'My, err… my mother,' he says quietly. 'She, um… she likes a drink. So you pick these things up, you know?'

His blush deepens, and I feel as if I've wedged my foot firmly in my mouth. 'I'm sorry,' I say, 'I didn't realise. I just want to say thank you again. You're my hero this morning, Cliff.'

He nods curtly and starts walking again, and I follow, grateful for once to have someone on this lot who isn't making my life harder.

—

'And… cut! Excellent work – Tipsy, you were great.' Leonard claps his hands and we break for lunch, finally. Tipsy catches my eye and gives me a wink before she links her arm through Mae's and they wander off to find the pathetic chicken salad that the canteen serves up to the female stars.

I should eat something myself, but before I can finish collecting the continuity notes I've made during this morning's shooting, Bunny appears, breathless and wringing her hands together.

'Oh, Lil. I'm glad I caught you. I heard about Tipsy… She wasn't really drinking on set, was she?'

'Bunny!' I hiss. 'Where did you hear that? No, she wasn't drinking on set. Jeez. And don't go around repeating gossip like that.'

'Sorry. Veronica said…' Bunny flushes and I feel guilty for snapping at her, but honestly, if she wants to get ahead in this game she should know better. 'Listen, there's someone here to see you.' She bounces on her toes. 'He's in the office, waiting.'

I resist the urge to sigh. My stomach is growling, and I have to type up the dialogue changes before we start shooting after lunch. 'Is it urgent?'

'*Very*,' Bunny says, her eyes wide.

Five minutes later I step into the tiny corridor Bunny uses as an office, my own eyes widening when I see who is sitting there.

'Jack,' I say, holding out a hand. Jack Shaw gets to his feet and pumps my hand in a tight handshake.

'Miss Jones, I'm sorry to barge in here, but I needed to see you away from the house. Away from Lizzie.'

Oh. This is intriguing. 'Bunny,' I say, turning to the doorway where Bunny stands, wringing her hands. 'Do you think you could fetch Mr Shaw and me some coffee?'

Bunny nods frantically. 'Of course. And Mr Shaw I just *loved* you in *Pilot 457*.' With a simpering grin, Bunny scampers off and I lead Jack into the office I share with Leonard for some privacy.

'I'm assuming this is about Max,' I say, watching Jack carefully as he picks lint from his jacket, fumbles in his pocket for cigarettes and straightens the pens on my desk. Anything to avoid meeting my eyes. 'But before you tell me anything, can I ask you something?'

'Of course.' Jack finally meets my eyes, and I am not surprised to see the weariness in them. Losing Max, his best friend and confidant, has hit him hard.

'Lizzie… Does she take sleeping pills?'

'Sleeping pills? What, you mean like yellowjackets?' Jack's accent makes the slang term come out as *yeller*. 'I don't think so, why?'

I shake my head. 'Just a hunch, but it seems I might be wrong.' There is a tap at the door, and Cliff peers around the door frame.

'I'm sorry to interrupt.' He steps inside, a coffee cup in each hand. 'I said I'd bring these in for Bunny. Lily, she said she'll type up your continuity notes while you're in your meeting.'

'Swell coffee, kid,' Jack says after taking a sip, ignoring the way Cliff lights up like a beacon.

'My pleasure, sir.'

'Thanks, Cliff.' I wait a few moments, until the door is firmly closed behind him, and then I turn back to Jack. 'So, how can I help you, Jack?'

Jack sighs, silent for a moment as if ordering his thoughts before he speaks. 'Max didn't drink that night, I know he didn't. He worked so hard to get sober, and there's no way he would have thrown it all away for one stupid wrap party.'

'Do you think he could have been spiked?'

Jack's eyes widen. 'Is that why you asked if Lizzie was on the yellowjackets?' He shakes his head. 'I don't know if he was spiked. I was with him almost until it happened, but I didn't see anything out of the ordinary. I went to the bathroom and then to the cloakroom to fetch my jacket but I got waylaid by someone. I don't even remember who it was now, someone from the studio. We were practically the last ones at the party. By the time I got back to Max, it was too late... He was in the water.'

'Oh God, Jack. I'm so sorry.' I hadn't realised that Jack was the one to find Max. No wonder he's been so distraught. 'Have you gone to the police about this? I mean, if you're sure that Max wouldn't have relapsed, and with the note—'

Jack shakes his head vehemently. 'No, I haven't. Who would believe me? Max, whether we like it or not, had a reputation as a party boy. Or – if I'm being brutally honest – as a drunk. My point is, it wouldn't have mattered if Max had been spiked, or drunk. Max could swim.'

'Yes, but that doesn't mean—'

'No,' Jack cuts me off. 'Max could *swim*. I mean, even if he was drunk, Max wouldn't have drowned. He swam in college, he was going to the Olympics until he ruptured a ligament, and then he gave it up. If he couldn't go to the Olympics then he wasn't going to swim at all, not competitively. Everything was all or nothing with Max.'

'I had no idea.' *But I'd had an inkling, hadn't I?* I'd seen the photo of Max in swimming trunks on the mantelpiece before it was boxed up, and I'd thought about wedding photos, not done what I should have and taken a closer look. 'The photo of him by a pool. It was at a tournament?'

Jack nods, his eyes reddening. 'That was the last tournament he swam in before his injury. The last photo of him at the top of that particular game. After he recovered, he joined the drama society and the rest is history.'

'Why didn't Lizzie tell the police that Max was a strong swimmer?' Something still doesn't add up.

'She didn't know.' Jack looks away, shifting in his chair. 'Max would get up early and go down to the ocean to swim every day. She was asleep.'

'But she was his *wife*.'

Jack shoves the chair back, stumbling slightly in his haste to get up. 'I should go, Lily. I really can't tell you any more than that. I'm sorry, maybe I shouldn't have come at all.'

'Wait, Jack.' Shoving my own chair back, I snatch at his sleeve, snagging the thick tweed between my fingers before he can leave. 'You really believe that Max was murdered?' Jack looks me dead in the eye. 'I don't believe it was an accident, Lily. I can't possibly see how it could have been.'

Chapter Nine

I slump back in my seat, lingering in the office for a few minutes after Jack leaves, my mind racing as I try and compose myself before I return to the set. The weight of our conversation hangs heavy in the air, Jack's words a burden on my shoulders as I realise I have to find out what really happened that night. My conscience won't let me leave it, and I know Tilda and Louis will feel the same way when I tell them what Jack revealed today. *Max was a strong swimmer and could have gone to the Olympics.* My blood runs cold at the thought of someone holding him down under the water, the desperate panic he must have felt.

Voices outside pull me from all thoughts of Max, and glancing at the clock, I shake my head. I need to get back on set before Leonard realises I'm late. Opening the door to the corridor, I see Cliff perched on the edge of Bunny's desk, his lips almost touching her hair as he murmurs something in her ear. Bunny's cheeks are pink, and when she spots me she gasps.

'Oh, Lily! I thought you'd already left. Here.' She hands me a sheaf of neatly typed notes. Cliff slides off the desk and lifts a hand in goodbye as he slopes off around the corner.

'Thanks, Bunny, that's a huge help.' I look down the corridor after Cliff. 'So, Cliff, eh? What's that all about? Do you have a crush on him?'

Bunny shakes her head vehemently. 'No, Lily! Absolutely not. Cliff is the last person…' She shakes her head again. 'He's just a colleague, Lil, you know that. And seeing as he's Oskar's assistant I feel like…'

'Don't say he's your superior, Bunny,' I scold. 'He's an assistant, just like you are, just like I am. In the pecking order of the movie business, we're all on the same level. He's quite cute though. And he got me out of a jam this morning. You could do worse.' With a quick grin in Bunny's direction, I hurry down the corridor towards the set, pulling up short as I round the corner to see Cliff hovering, his hands tucked into his pockets.

'Oh! I didn't see you there.' I move to scooch past him, but he moves in the same direction, unintentionally blocking my way. We both pause, and I utter a brief, awkward laugh before Cliff finally steps to one side and lets me pass.

'Sorry, my fault,' he mumbles, one hand rubbing at the back of his neck as his gaze flicks past me, back towards the corridor where Bunny sits.

My heart double-beats in my chest, something feeling off about the odd interaction. Turning back to look over my shoulder, I see he is heading back around the corner and I think about the way he was leaning over Bunny, the way there was something intimate and private in the air between them. *Oh no*. Does he have feelings for Bunny? Did he overhear the way she so emphatically denied feeling that way about him? Yikes, I hope I haven't caused any awkwardness between them. Uncertainty gnaws at me and I wish I'd never said anything at all to Bunny now.

I don't have time to think about it any further as I reach the sound stage. Thankfully the red light above the door that indicates filming is in progress is not yet lit. Pushing open the door, the scent of cigarette smoke and sawdust fills my nostrils and I inhale deeply. It's like the scent of a library, the kind of smell you could never be bored with.

'Lily!' Tipsy waves a hand at me, as she and Mae huddle together over a small table, just to the left of the set. The three-walled set of Tipsy's house is immaculate on the inside – the sofa covered with a thick lace doily, the low coffee table, the bar where Mae spiked her mother's drink the day before – but the edge of the set is raw and rustic, the wooden frame structure liable to leave deep splinters in your fingers, and trails of lighting cables and sandbags holding things steady make the walk across the set treacherous. I whistle at a member of the prop crew as he almost tumbles over a sandbag, the rolled rug in his arms blocking his view.

'Lily, over here!' Tipsy calls again, her tone impatient. 'You're going to want to see this.' She looks up at me with glee in her eyes as I approach her and Mae. 'Listen to this, it's a new Last Word column: *Studio execs are whispering about a certain matinee star, who seems to be stumbling through his lines with glassy eyes and a lazy grin. Following rumours that the tough guy's cigarettes contained more than just tobacco – a story that made headlines roar – all eyes are on this fella… If the rumours are true there's a chance he'll lose more than his contract.*' Tipsy slams the newspaper shut and Mae presses a hand to her mouth. 'Isn't this the *most* delicious scandal you've ever heard?'

If the anonymous gossip columnist is referring to marijuana, then no. As a twenty-first-century girl living in LA in a time when weed is legal, this is not the most scandalous rumour I've ever heard. As the assistant to a prominent director in the 1950s though… this is a pretty big deal.

'The tough guy has to mean Robert Mitchum, right?' Mae pipes up.

'Right,' I muse, taking the paper from Tipsy and running my eyes over the blind item again. Robert Mitchum was busted with a small amount of marijuana back in 1948 and ended up doing a couple of months' jail time, but since then what the item says is right. Mitchum's arrest was a huge scandal at the time and ever since then the studio does look closely at any actor who shows up with red eyes, or that grassy scent clinging to their clothes.

'Do you think it could be Vic?' Tipsy names the actor playing Mae's toxic boyfriend in the movie.

'Could what be me?' Speak of the devil and he shall appear. Vic Romano strolls onto set, nodding at Veronica, the make-up artist, to come and powder his shiny fore-head.

'Nothing,' I say quickly, before Tipsy can open her big mouth and put her foot in it.

'Silly gossip,' Mae says shyly, tucking her hair behind her ear. She lays a hand on Vic's arm, tactfully guiding him away from Tipsy and her newspaper. 'Vic, we should run our lines quickly before Leonard gets back. You can get powdered while we do it.'

Tipsy watches Mae lead Vic away to the other side of the set, waiting until they are a safe distance away before she speaks. 'Did you smell that? I swear his jacket smelled like…' she lowers her voice, '…*funny cigarettes*.'

'How do you even know what they smell like if it's illegal?' I say with a raised eyebrow as Tipsy smirks. 'And I don't think I smelled it, but…' But Vic did have that sleepy look about him, the sure sign of a quick smoke. Don't get me wrong, plenty of people in Hollywood smoke grass and pop pills, but they've learned to be subtle about it. On the surface, anyway.

'It could be that guy on Ann Silver's movie,' Tipsy muses, 'or what about Steven Hess?' She names another actor, well known for his late nights and regular girl-friends. 'He definitely parties.'

'We should take a wager.' Vic is back, freshly powdered and smelling only of the waxy, oily scent of the greasepaint Veronica uses, and clearly keen to join in the gossip despite Mae's best efforts. 'Because Tipsy, darling, it surely isn't me.'

'Oh.' Tipsy has the good grace to blush.

'I like your thoughts on Steven Hess though,' Vic goes on, giving her a devilish grin. With his slicked-back dark hair and straight white teeth, he is swoon-worthy, pure matinee idol material, and Tipsy is definitely under his spell despite the twenty-year age gap. 'Put me twenty dollars on Steve, and I'll buy you a martini when I win.'

'That's illegal.' Cliff has appeared beside us like an apparition, making me jump. 'Gambling, I mean. Betting. All of it, it's illegal. If the studio heads hear about gambling on set then that's it, you'll all be fired.' He blinks in that funny way he has, and I wonder if it's dust or a tic.

'Vic was joking,' I say. 'Weren't you, Vic?'

Vic shrugs and Tipsy lets out a filthy cackle, raunchy enough to make the tips of Cliff's ears turn red.

'Ignore them,' I whisper to Cliff. 'They're like a herd of wild cats. It's almost impossible to keep them under control.' We share a brief grin, and then the exterior door flies open.

'What the hell is going on? Lily?' Leonard storms in, his face like thunder, Oskar Goldstein marching along behind him.

Oskar throws a glare in Cliff's direction, snapping his fingers at him. 'You, there. Messages? For God's sake, don't keep me waiting. You lot think time costs nothing and money grows on trees.'

Cliff scurries over to Oskar, handing him a bunch of messages before anxiously standing to one side and pushing his glasses up his nose, his eyes going to Bunny who stands by the door.

'Marks, everyone!' Leonard booms, his brows knitting together. 'I told all of you what time recall was. Lily, dialogue notes, please.' His brows knit even more tightly together if that's at all possible, and I can almost see the stress pulsing off him in waves. I dread to think what tiny thing Oskar has been chewing him out over this lunch break. 'Vic, what is that hair? I've told you a million times, you are a *rake*. Hair needs to be over the forehead, not swept back like that.' Leonard clicks his fingers to summon a hairdresser. 'Lily, you should have picked that up already.'

I apologise and hand Leonard the notes, watching in awe as he organises everyone to their places, checks on the set to make sure everything is ready, then points at a light that needs adjusting before moving to his director's chair.

'Lily.' Tipsy places a hand gently on my arm before she moves to her mark. 'Did I see Jack Shaw coming out of your office earlier?'

'Err, yes. Yes, you did. You really need to go and hit your mark, Tipsy. Leonard is waiting.'

'What did Jack want? Was it about dear Max?' Her fingers dig into my forearm now, her red nails scratching through my thin blouse.

'Yes, it was. Tipsy, your fingers…' I tug away, the fabric of my blouse snagging slightly. 'We did speak about Max, as a matter of fact.'

Tipsy nods solemnly, her grasp finally loosening. 'I thought so. Listen, Lily, are you busy after we finish shooting for the day?'

'I'm meeting some friends for a drink at the Polo Lounge.' Louis is working the evening shift, so I have already arranged to meet Tilda there for a quick drink after work.

'Excellent, I love the Polo Lounge. The McCarthy salad is to die for.' Tipsy looks as though she wants to say more, but Leonard is glowering in our direction, tapping at his watch and pointing at Mae who stands poised and ready, flawless under the heat of the lights. 'I'll meet you there after we finish shooting.' And then she scurries into position, blowing Leonard an over-the-top kiss and patting her red hair into place.

Clutching my battered steno pad, I jot down the complaints listed by Leonard throughout the day to be entered into today's log – that wardrobe were late with bringing Tipsy's dress and that Mae's curls keep wilting under the lights – my pen pausing as I wonder whether to log the gossip over the Last Word column. Realistically, I should. It would count as unprofessional conduct, but everyone on set is involved, from Veronica and her make-up brushes, right the way up to Tipsy. All of us have read the blind items and all of us have speculated at some point who they may be about. But this log is used in case the studio calls – if Oskar calls, more importantly – and wants to know about delays and problems on set. I don't want anyone to get into trouble; I like Tipsy, and Mae is a sweetheart. Even Vic is friendly enough. I move on, jotting down a note about the sandbags left in the wrong place. Besides, if I make a note about the gossip, Tipsy might not want to talk to me – and I definitely want to talk to her this evening over a gimlet or two. I get the feeling that she knows more about Max Hayden than she's letting on.

Chapter Ten

Stepping into the lobby of the Beverly Hills Hotel is like coming home. Every time I walk along the path behind the hedges that ensure the guests' privacy, every time I step onto the red carpet that leads through the double doors into a lobby filled with flowers and smiling hotel staff, I feel as if I am back where I belong. Not that surprising considering in my own time I worked here as a chambermaid, and this is where I found myself that first awkward, confusing, topsy-turvy morning when I woke up for the first time in 1949.

Now, despite the long day – shooting overran, thanks to Vic being unable to get his lines right – I almost skip through the lobby towards the thick oak double doors of the Polo Lounge. Pushing them open, the first thing I see is Burt Lancaster sipping on a cup of tea as Fred Zinneman gestures wildly to him, a Bourbon highball on the table next to him. The movie buff in me is desperate to hear what they're talking about – is Zinneman, who is about to direct *From Here to Eternity*, trying to woo Burt into playing Sergeant Milton Ward? Because if so, I am itching to tell them both that Burt will agree to play him, and the movie will win best picture at the Oscars in 1954. The second thing I see is Louis polishing a glass behind the gleaming oak bar and Tilda sitting on a stool with a gimlet in her hand.

'About time,' she says with a grin, as I plop down on the empty stool beside her. 'I'm two gimlets in and Lou won't let me have any more.'

'They're not your friend, Til,' Louis says with a smile. 'Lily, what can I get you?'

'Something non-alcoholic,' I say. 'It's been a long day. Vic Romano couldn't get his lines right, so shooting overran. I thought Leonard was going to have a coronary.'

'Was he high?' Tilda reaches over and snags an olive from the bowl on the bar and pops it into her mouth. 'Vic, I mean.'

'You've seen the newspaper today,' I say with a sigh. Was Vic's inability to say the word 'possession' correctly down to marijuana? Or simply a failure to run his lines before bed the previous evening? I don't know, but I'm sure Tipsy will have something to say about it when she arrives.

'Of course I have.' Tilda shrugs. 'And so has everyone else in LA.'

Louis pushes a Shirley Temple towards me. 'To be fair, Lil, that's true. It's all anyone has talked about in here today. You wouldn't believe the names I've heard being suggested as to who it could be.'

Of course the latest Last Word column is a hot topic of conversation; it's exactly what it's designed to be. I could just do with the speculation being about someone other than the actor working on my movie. I have my work cut out trying to keep Tipsy in line, and trying to figure out what really happened to Max, without this as well.

Tilda groans as Louis pushes a Shirley Temple towards her too, but the groan dies on her lips as the doors to the Polo Lounge swing open and Tipsy Jenner makes her way towards us, a huge pink hat covering half her face.

I'm not sure if it's meant to grant her anonymity, but it's just succeeded in drawing everyone's attention to her. Knowing Tipsy for the brief time I have, perhaps that was the aim after all.

'I forgot to tell you,' I murmur. 'Today is about to get even longer. Tipsy is joining us. I had a surprise visitor at the studio today, and I think Tipsy might know more about things than she's letting on.' I quickly bring Tilda and Louis up to speed with Jack's visit today as Tipsy veers off in the direction of Fred Zinneman.

'He was an *Olympic swimmer*?' Tilda's mouth hangs open, her whispered gasp louder than she anticipated.

'Shhhh,' I hiss. 'Not quite – but strong enough that Jack is convinced he would never have drowned, drunk or not. Hey, Tipsy!'

Tipsy pecks me on the cheek, leaving the scent of Chanel No. 5 and greasepaint on the air. She hasn't washed away her make-up from shooting earlier, and she looks just the other side of garish without the cameras on her. 'Lily, darling. Are these your friends?'

'This is my friend, Tilda,' I say, 'and that's her brother, Louis, over there.' I point to where Louis is shaking a martini for a man in a fedora.

Tipsy removes her hat, her eyes narrowing as she rakes them over Tilda's slight frame, over her bright red hair and the matching lilac skirt and cardigan she wears. 'You're that girl, aren't you? The gossip columnist.'

Tilda lifts her chin slightly. 'I am a journalist, yes. And I do work with Louella Parsons, but I wouldn't call myself a gossip columnist, per se.'

I gesture to Louis to bring Tipsy a drink. Hopefully something strong and vodka-based will make her more amenable. 'Tipsy, Tilda is a really good friend of mine. You can trust her, I promise.'

'Are you sure?'

'Believe me,' Tilda leans in and lowers her voice conspiratorially, 'I know things about people in this town that would make your hair curl and I've never breathed a word to anyone, not even Lily.'

I don't know whether to be put out by this or impressed with Tilda's restraint.

Tipsy's eyes are wide. 'Gosh, I can only imagine.' A fleeting expression crosses her face and I know she's just dying to ask Tilda for some juicy gossip. 'I mean, you think you can trust someone and then boom, they blow things up in your face. I've been burned before, by people I thought I could trust.'

'Do you mean Larry Bernhardt?' Tilda asks gently, ignoring the sharp look Tipsy gives her. 'I'm so sorry he treated you that way. You deserved better.'

'Lily, let me tell you something,' Tipsy says, clearly reading my confusion. 'Most men are cads. Not all of them, but most of them. I learned the hard way after I gave my heart to Larry Bernhardt and he quite publicly trampled all over it. After he left me in the most appalling way – for my cousin, did you know that? And it was all over the papers – I swore off men forever, which is a real shame because all I ever really wanted was a family and a daughter of my own. It's one way to make headlines, I suppose, being jilted at the altar like that. Anyway...' She shakes her head and takes a huge sip of the martini Louis has placed in front of her. 'Enough about all that nasty business. It was very dear of you to invite me along to your evening drinks.'

I don't remember things happening that way, but I shrug it off. 'Tipsy, about Max. You know Jack came to see me today? He said some things that… well, gave me some concern over Max's accident. You knew Max, didn't you?'

Tipsy takes another huge gulp of her drink and Louis catches my eye, discreetly picking up the cocktail shaker to fix her another one. 'Everybody knew him, darling. Max was a force of nature. I worked with him on a movie years ago, but we saw each other at parties, awards ceremonies, that kind of thing. He was always incredibly kind to me. He sent me flowers after Larry… left.' She looks down at her drink, toying with the olive on her cocktail stick.

'What about Lizzie? Are you friends with her?' There is still something about Lizzie that I can't put my finger on, something that makes me feel that she's not being entirely honest about things.

'Lizzie?' Tipsy frowns. 'No one is really friendly with Lizzie, apart from Mary Colman.'

'She seems like a nice lady though,' Louis pipes up. 'Not as lovely and charming as yourself, obviously, but it's odd that she doesn't have many friends.'

Tipsy preens a little at Louis's flattery. She may say she's sworn off men but I'm not entirely sure I believe her. And I'm not jealous. Not in the slightest. 'Lizzie is perfectly nice,' she says. 'But it's more that she keeps herself to herself. She works hard and isn't really one for parties. Max was always the party animal.'

'Max didn't die by accident, Tipsy. I'm pretty sure there was some foul play.'

Tipsy's eyes widen and she leans in close. 'What do you mean?'

Glancing at me, Tilda rummages in her bag before smoothing out a sheet of paper, worn thin in the crease through the middle of it. 'I received this note a week before Max died.'

Tipsy runs her eyes over the page, biting down on her lower lip as she takes in the words written there. 'Lily, you need to stop poking—'

'Tipsy!' Before Tipsy can finish her sentence, Mae hurries through the door, her jacket and the ends of her hair wet with rain. Close behind her is Cliff, who is bone dry. 'I'm so sorry I'm late.'

A flicker of confusion runs across Tipsy's face before she nudges me, gently hinting at me to give up my stool to Mae. 'No problem, darling. We barely got started, and Lily was leaving soon anyway. Let me get you a drink.'

Cliff hovers awkwardly on the fringes as Mae requests a Tom Collins – my own personal favourite too – and shakes out her hair. 'I was walking back from the studio and got caught in the rain,' Mae explains. 'Cliff very kindly pulled up in his car and offered me a ride, and then he insisted on walking me in.' She turns to Cliff. 'Thanks so much, you've been a gentleman. I'll see you on set tomorrow.'

There is an awkward moment while Cliff processes the fact that he has been dismissed, and then he gives a small bow in Mae's direction, a fixed smile on his face. 'Of course, Miss Sinclair. Have a lovely evening.'

We watch Cliff weave his way between the booths towards the doors and Mae lets out a sigh of relief. 'I'm sorry to crash your party, but Cliff wanted to drive me all the way home! As we were passing I suddenly "remembered" I had a meeting here. Thank goodness you were here, Tipsy. He seems like a nice fella, but I'm not sure I feel comfortable with him knowing where I live. I barely know him.'

'He's a lovely guy,' I say. 'He seems a little shy, and I think Oskar is probably going to bully him, but he really helped me out this morning.'

'And he's hardly dangerous, Mae,' Tipsy scoffs. 'He's only got eyes for Veronica.'

'Veronica?' I raise an eyebrow, as I remember the way he sat close enough to smell Bunny's hair earlier.

Tipsy nods enthusiastically, the whiff of gossip on the air livening her up. 'Veronica tells me she's been out with him a few times. Rumour has it things are getting serious. But that's all it is – rumours.' Tipsy turns to me. 'I guess you should be getting home too, Lily.' Louis has removed his apron and come around from behind the bar, his shift over for the evening. 'This young man is waiting to give you a ride. It was lovely to meet you, Tilda. Be sure to keep me updated on any juicy titbits you may hear in your line of work.' She slides off her stool, linking her arm through mine as if to walk me to the door and make sure I really am leaving.

'I was going to have another drink,' I say, my tone muted as Tipsy leads me gently towards the double doors. Tilda and Louis have already gone ahead to get the car.

'Best not to,' Tipsy says with a smile. 'You have an early start in the morning. Mae will be fine with me, don't worry.'

'You won't be late for your call time tomorrow?' I ask sternly, still feeling as though Tipsy is giving me the bum's rush.

'I swear. But listen, Lily.' She leans in close, so close I can see the make-up clogging her pores and smell the olive brine on her breath. 'Let it go, with Max. He's gone.

There's nothing that you can do to bring him back, so please, for all our sakes, just stop digging, OK?'

Chapter Eleven

'That was a little odd, huh?' Tilda says from the backseat as I slide into the front seat beside Louis. 'What was Tipsy saying to you as you were leaving?'

'She was warning me off,' I say slowly, my mind whirring. That was definitely what it was, no question about it. *But why?*

'Warning you off?' Louis gives me a sharp look as he pulls onto Sunset Boulevard. 'About Max?'

'Yeah, no doubt about it. She told me to stop digging, that there's nothing I can do to bring Max back.'

'All the more reason for us to keep on digging,' Louis says, and my heart contracts. That's part of the reason why I can't help but love him. I know he doesn't want to keep searching for answers about what really happened to Max, I know he thinks one of these days we're going to find ourselves in boiling water so hot it's impossible to jump out, but still he goes along with things, just to make me happy.

Tipsy's words play on my mind all the way back to mine and Tilda's apartment, so much so that I'm not even disappointed when Louis cries off coming in for a nightcap, saying he wants to squeeze in an hour's rehearsal time with his band before he goes to bed. Clearly it plays on Tilda's mind too, and when we are in the bathroom getting ready for bed, both of us covered in cold cream and smelling of toothpaste, she presses a picture into my hand.

'What's this?' I look down at the photo, at Max's smiling face, his hair ruffled by a breeze. He looks relaxed and happy, the ocean and a sandy shoreline in the background. The photographer casts a long shadow to the side of the photo. 'Tilda, where did you get this?'

Tilda has the good grace to blush as she tips baking powder onto her toothbrush. 'I may have stolen it from that box of Max's things when we were at Lizzie's house.'

'Tilda!' I know she's prepared to do anything to get to the truth but this feels… grubby, almost. 'This belongs to Lizzie. You can't steal a photo of her dead husband, no matter how much we need to figure out what happened to him.'

'I'm sorry! I didn't plan to. It was just there and I saw you walk along the hallway and I thought…' She looks up at me, a gleam in her eye despite the regret she's professing. 'I thought you could use the photo. You know, for your *gift*. I thought you might be able to feel something, or see something if you had the photo, a clue that might help us get to the bottom of it.'

Oh, man. It's my own fault that Tilda nicked the photo – she still genuinely believes my story that I can see things psychically when I touch a photograph or article. I let out a long sigh.

'OK,' I say, wearily. 'I'll see what I can do.'

—

Of course, I can't do anything. I don't have a psychic gift. Everything I've known ahead of time here in 1950s Hollywood has been things I read online or watched documentaries about on streaming platforms in the twenty-first century. I lie awake for hours, the photograph clutched tightly in my fist as I rack my brain trying to remember any tiny detail I can about Max Hayden, but there's nothing. I don't think I ever even watched a movie that starred him.

'Anything?' Tilda asks eagerly the next morning, as we sweep out of the apartment together and head to the bus stop on the corner of the street.

I shake my head. 'Nothing, sorry. And now we have to get this picture back to Lizzie without her noticing.'

'I'll figure something out. That's a real shame though. I was hoping we might get some sort of breakthrough. Some sort of clue to point us in the right direction.' Tilda sighs as we board the bus, and it's only as I perch on the seat beside her that I realise she's going in the wrong direction. 'Til, you're on the wrong bus.'

'No, I'm not,' she says with a grin. 'I'm coming to work with you today. I'm at the studios, interviewing that new guy on the Ann Silver movie. Louella wants a piece about "young Hollywood". She tried to tell me Vic Romano counted, but I told her he's got more grey hairs than Spencer Tracy.'

I burst out laughing at this despite the fact that it's not true at all. Vic has a head of thick, black hair and he's barely ten years older than us. We agree to meet after shooting is over. I hurry onto the lot, waving at Bobby and rushing past the backlot streets, weaving between runners on bicycles carrying reels of film and memo pads towards Leonard's office.

By the time I am done catching up with messages, typing up notes from the previous day and trying not to dwell on Max's untimely demise, it's time to hustle Tipsy and Mae to the sound stage. Unusually, Tipsy's trailer is empty, only the scent of Miss Dior and cigarettes filling the space when I pop my head in. Mae's trailer is also empty.

'Bunny?' I catch her as she hurries past, today's script pages clutched in one hand. 'Have you seen Mae and Tipsy?'

'They're on set, silly,' Bunny says with a little shake of her head, 'and you'd better hurry – they're just about ready to start.'

Shit. I hadn't realised time had got away from me so much. I hurry across the lot, pausing as I reach the sound stage. The red light isn't lit, but a notice hangs on the door.

CLOSED SET – DO NOT ENTER

Ignoring it, I push the doors open and step inside, inhaling that familiar sawdusty smell. Tipsy sits in a director's chair, Veronica primping and fussing at her face.

'…root beer float, and then he even sprung for a slice of cherry pie,' Veronica is saying as she dabs at Tipsy's cheeks. 'Of course, *she* doesn't know about that but they're saying…'

Realising I've wandered into a rumour mill on overdrive, I move towards the stage floor where Leonard spots me immediately and waves me over.

'Lily, you're here.' He talks quickly, a cigarette burning at the corner of his mouth. I wonder if Jean knows. He promised her he'd stop when they found out about the baby. 'I need absolute quiet on set today, so no one is to be in here who isn't essential to the scene. Vic and Mae are shooting a love scene and Mae is a little nervous; it's her first one. Keep the set locked down and silent – I want to get this in the can on the double.'

'Righto.' I look around the set, at the staged room – complete with bed – and the bright lights that burn over the section where the action will take place, at the chalk crosses that mark where Mae and Vic will stand. Vic waits in the wings, a cigarette in one hand as he pores over his script pages, that errant strand of hair flopping over his forehead. Tipsy is still in the make-up chair, her lips moving silently as she recites her own lines and prepares for the moment when she will burst in on her daughter and her boyfriend. 'Where is Mae?'

Leonard looks at me, his brow crinkled. 'How the hell would I know, Lily? That's your job.' I watch his retreating back stalk away and I am about to go and hunt Bunny down to find Mae, when the doors creak open and she appears. She looks tired, her eyes slightly puffy, and she gives me a wan smile as she tugs the ever-so-slightly too big cardigan wardrobe have given her up onto her shoulders.

'Mae,' I hiss. 'You're late! You're lucky Leonard is too preoccupied to notice. Here, sit down.' I push her gently into the chair just vacated by Tipsy. 'Are you OK?'

Mae swallows and nods as Veronica begins to work her magic with her brushes. 'Yes, just… nervous, that's all. I've never done a scene like this before.'

'It's just a little kiss,' Tipsy says with a belch of laughter, as she hovers nearby. 'Just pretend you're kissing a date. I mean, I've had to kiss Clark and everyone knows the rumours about him and garlic. Lord knows Vic isn't diffi-cult on the eye.' She flaps a hand, swishing cigarette smoke and dust motes through the air. 'You'll be fine. You must have kissed worse frogs than him.'

Mae blinks, her mouth gaping open. 'I haven't… I don't…'

'Mae, Tipsy is just being silly, trying to relax you, that's all. You'll be fine,' I say in a soothing tone. 'It'll be over before you know it.'

Mae nods reluctantly, and once Veronica moves away she gets to her feet and takes her mark. Vic moves in, and a hush falls over the set. I can barely breathe as Vic tells Mae that he loves her, he'll do anything for her. And once her mother is out of the picture they can be together forever, the world will be theirs. He leans in, one hand brushing her hair away from her face, the other curling around her waist, and then the air splits with a resounding crack. Vic pulls away, one hand cradling his face as Mae rears back, her eyes wide and her face pale.

'Mae? What in the name…? This isn't in the script.' Leonard throws down his clipboard and steps forward.

'You'll pay for that,' Vic hisses, his cheek a burning bright red as he presses his fingers to his skin. 'You don't slap me and get away with it scot-free.'

'You touched me!' Mae says, her voice cracking as she shrinks away from him.

'Of course I touched you,' Vic sneers, his lips twisting, an ugly shadow passing over his face. 'It's a love scene, and we can't shoot a love scene without touching. I know this is your first rodeo, darling—'

'You didn't have to touch her like that.' Tipsy's voice is like ice, dripping with disdain. 'I saw you, Vic. Your hand was not where it was supposed to be. You're lucky I didn't slap you too.'

Yikes. 'Tipsy, I think maybe you and I should let Leonard deal with this.' Pushing her gently towards Bunny, who stands on the edge of the set biting her lip, I turn back to Leonard, who is already taking control of the situation in the calm, measured manner I've grown so used to from him.

'Mae, you need to get used to being touched on set, especially for a love scene. It's the way I do things – I want our picture to look authentic, to seem as though you really are about to throw everything away for this man, so you need to relax and look as though you're enjoying it.' Leonard's eyes are on Mae as Vic smirks and I'm not sure whether I want to punch him or our director first, but then Leonard continues. 'And you, Vic. You're a disgrace. You ever use one of my scenes to behave inappropriately and I'll make damn sure you never work in this town again.'

Tipsy gives a smattering of applause and Leonard glares in her direction until she lowers her hands, a smug grin on her face. Vic takes his place on his mark with a sullen glance in my direction, where I stand next to Mae.

'Ready?'

'I'm not sure.' Her skin looks waxy beneath her make-up. 'It's been a long time since I even kissed on a date with a boy I liked, let alone...' She looks from beneath her lashes at Vic.

'You've got this,' I say. 'Think of the pay check. Think of the Oscar nomination.' I lean in. 'Think of the hand-print that must still be throbbing under all that pan stick.'

Mae grins and takes her mark, and this time the scene is shot in one. Despite Mae's upset she pulls her role off with pure professionalism, almost as though the slap gave her an added confidence boost. Relieved, the cast and crew scatter the moment Leonard calls cut, and it's a blessing to step out of the sound stage into the bright sunshine, where I immediately bump into Cliff.

'Hey.' I smile at him, as he juggles an armful of dry cleaning. 'You need some help with that?'

Cliff shakes his head. 'All good, thanks, Lily. I thought I'd give up collecting dry cleaning once I was promoted to Oskar's assistant, but you know how it is. What Oskar wants, Oskar gets.' He smiles, but it's weary. 'I dropped an ashtray on his foot earlier,' he confesses. 'I think picking up six months of dry cleaning is the punishment, but at least he called me "boy" instead of "you, there".'

I pat him on the arm. 'I think Leonard believes sending me to collect his dry cleaning is a treat. Thanks for dropping Mae to the hotel last night, and I'm sorry if Tipsy came off rude. You should have stayed for a drink.'

Cliff shakes his head, but the weariness is gone when he smiles again. 'I couldn't… I was taking Veronica for dinner.'

Before I can reply, Tipsy appears beside me. 'Lily? What's going on?'

I pause, taking in the scene around us. Something feels… off. There isn't the usual bustle of golf carts whizzing by, or hordes of extras being shepherded from one stage to the next, but there is a crowd of people by the studio gates, a buzz of chatter like a cloud over their heads.

'I don't know.' I think I can make out Tilda's red pony-tail on the edge of the crowd and I make my way over, calling her name. She swings around, her face chalky, and struggles her way through the extras to meet me.

'Til? What the hell is going on?'

'Heck,' she corrects me automatically. 'It's awful news, Lil.'

'What is it? I thought you were interviewing that new guy on Ann's movie today? We've had a closed set, so I have no idea what's going on.' Thoughts run through my head at warp speed. *An accident. A fire. Oskar got run over.* Maybe that last one was wishful thinking.

'It's Ann Silver,' Tilda says. 'She's dead.'

Chapter Twelve

'Dead?' Shock makes my teeth feel numb, and judging by the expression on Tipsy's face, she's as stunned as I am. 'Are you sure?'

'It's true, Ann Silver is dead!' A runner dashes past us, barely slowing as he confirms the news and we all stare after him, Tipsy pressing a hand to her mouth. How can Ann Silver be dead? I just saw her the other night at Café Trocadero. Cliff's eyes are as wide as saucers as I turn to Tilda.

'What happened?'

Tilda takes a deep breath, her voice choked. 'She didn't turn up on set this morning. At first people just thought she'd overslept, or had a heavy night, you know? When she missed her call time the production secretary called her house, but there was no answer.'

'Did they find her at home?' A vision of Ann slumped in bed and covered in blood flashes through my mind, even though Tilda hasn't said what happened to her.

Tilda shakes her head, her eyes filling with tears. 'She wasn't there. The atmosphere on set was more… frustrated than concerned at first, you know? Ann didn't seem like a bad girl, but you never know what some of these people get up to behind closed doors. There was a lot of whispering going on. Obviously no one wanted me to overhear anything, seeing as I work with Louella. I guess everyone just assumed she thought she was bigger than the studio.' She pauses, her eyes meeting mine. 'And then the police showed up.'

'Oh!' Tipsy clutches the chunky necklace at her throat. 'Poor dear Ann.'

'You, boy!' Appearing seemingly out of nowhere, Oskar clicks his fingers in Cliff's direction. 'Why are you just standing there, like some sort of empty-headed nitwit? Get rid of those reporters!' He marches past with two police officers in tow, and I watch as he leads them into the building that houses his office, wishing I could be a fly on the wall. A red-cheeked Cliff swallows, shifting the dry cleaning in his arms before he gives me a nod and hurries towards the security gate.

'Ann's body was found at the bottom of the Hollywood sign by a city worker who headed up there to do some maintenance on the sign this morning,' Tilda goes on. 'He didn't even realise it was a body at first, let alone a movie star. He thought someone had dumped a pile of garbage.'

'Oh!' Tipsy says again, blinking hard as if she might faint. 'Oh, good Lord.'

'Was she…?' I don't want to voice the thought out loud, not in front of Tipsy who clearly isn't dealing with the news very well.

'The police are saying she jumped.' Tilda's voice is solemn, and she quickly crosses herself. 'Rumours are already flying about how Ann was depressed, about the way she had been withdrawn from the rest of the cast and crew lately. Word on the set is that she didn't want to socialise with anyone after shooting finished for the day, she just scurried home. People thought she was stand-offish but now they're saying it's because she was depressed.'

'No. No, this is all wrong.' Tipsy shakes her head. 'That's not Ann at all.' She looks over at the crowds still swarming the gates, gossip buzzing on the air. 'Let's not talk here. Let's go to my trailer.'

–

Tipsy's trailer is far more untidy than I remember it, clothes and shoes spilling all over the floor, the scent of perfume heavy in the air. The vanity, lit by big, bright bulbs, is spattered with powder, and two pairs of silk stockings are draped over the armchair. Magazines are piled on the table, alongside crumpled script pages, coffee rings on many of them, and fan mail in half torn envelopes. A bottle of bourbon has leaked a sticky brown mess onto the table, and half-empty Coke bottles, the rims stained with pink lipstick, are dotted all over the trailer.

'Here, sit.' Tipsy snatches up the stockings and shoves an evening gown off the end of the daybed to make room for us to sit down. 'Drink, anyone?'

'Not for me.' Tilda casts her gaze about the trailer, her nose wrinkling slightly, which is rich seeing as she is the untidiest person I know.

'Tell us about Ann,' I say, as Tipsy pours herself a hefty shot of bourbon, topping it up with the dregs of some warm Coke from the glass bottle on the table.

'She wasn't depressed, I can tell you that much,' Tipsy says after taking a gulp of her drink. Some of the colour has come back into her face now, but her hands still shake slightly. 'I've known Ann ever since she first arrived in Hollywood. A little slip of a thing she was. She was an extra on a movie I worked on and you could tell she was going to be a star.' Tipsy pauses, her eyes far away as she remembers. 'She caught the eye of the studio, and I'll never forget when they said they wanted to screen test her – she was overwhelmed, she was so excited. Ann was living her dream in Hollywood, Lily. She wasn't depressed in the slightest.'

I'm not convinced. I've seen it all before, how the bright young star gets dragged down by the seediness of Hollywood, by the pill popping, the scandals, the long working hours that mean you're exhausted from sunup to sundown. Life in Hollywood is never as glamorous as it looks on the screen.

Tipsy catches sight of my doubt and shakes her head firmly. 'I'm telling you, Ann would never do that. She was always the life and soul of the party, always so… so *grateful* to be working in the movies.'

'Was there anyone she didn't get along with?' I try for tact, but it's difficult. I need to ask the question. 'Anyone who… might not have wanted her around? Anyone she argued with?'

Tipsy shakes her head again, her hair flying. 'Absolutely not. Ann was a sweetheart, she was a joy to work with, and she always knew when to keep her mouth shut. All these people saying she was depressed because she didn't want to socialise… Wanting to go home to a hot bath after a long day doesn't mean you're depressed. Sometimes after spending hours on set, the last thing I want to do is spend my evenings with those same people, but it doesn't mean anything sinister. I don't know what she was doing up there at the Hollywood sign, but she must have slipped and fallen. Another tragic accident.'

Tilda and I exchange a glance, and my heart flips in my chest. *Another tragic accident? Or something far more sinister?*

Tilda shouts Louis's name over the crash of drums and guitars, the music cutting out with a horrible screech of feedback as he and his two bandmates realise we are standing in the doorway of the garage, interrupting their practice.

'Oh hey.' Louis turns with a grin and my heart flips over. He's slightly sweaty from playing guitar, and his hair is adorably mussed. 'What are you guys doing here?'

'Cutting your practice short.' Tilda turns a megawatt smile on the two other band members, friends of Louis's from high school. 'Beat it, fellas. Lou can come out to play again tomorrow.'

The two friends slope off and Louis leans his guitar in the corner, wiping his face with the hem of his shirt, turning his back so as not to give me a flash of his tanned stomach. Not that I would have minded seeing that, but… it is 1952. 'Thanks, Til,' he says with a groan. 'It's taken us two weeks to all find a time to play together and now—'

'And now I'm about to tell you that we have another dead body on our hands.' Tilda plants her hands on her hips, daring Louis to argue.

'Well, son of a gun.' Louis raises his eyebrows. 'What in the heck happened? Who?'

I give him a brief rundown of what happened at the studio today, and the rumours surrounding Ann's death.

'And what do we think?' Louis says eventually, his brow creased. 'We don't actually believe Ann killed herself, do we? Not when Tipsy is so sure she wasn't depressed.'

'And Tipsy is sure,' Tilda says. 'She said Ann was always the life and soul of the party.'

'There's no way to tell for sure,' I say. 'Maybe she was feeling low. People who feel that way can often hide it, and it's not as if it's easy to talk about that kind of thing. Or maybe there was something else going on with her. Something worrying her.' I think of Ann at Café Trocadero, the way she seemed as though she would rather be anywhere else than there. 'You know what I think we should do?'

'What?'

'Go and take a look at where it happened for ourselves.' I half expect Louis to argue with me, but instead he simply nods.

Thirty minutes later we find ourselves at the foot of the hill that holds the Hollywood sign, the air still warm despite the sun lowering in the sky. I have never been more grateful for my Converse sneakers – the only remnant from my twenty-first-century life – as I survey the twisting dirt path ahead of me.

'Up we go, I guess.' Tilda looks as uncertain as I do. *What the hell was Ann doing coming up here at night?*

We start to make our way along the winding path, feet sliding on the loose gravel and our sleeves and ankles snagging on the overgrown brush. The path is steep, and in places a thin wire fence has been erected in a pitiful attempt to keep trespassers at bay. Clearly it hasn't worked. Dust rises and the sky above is a rainbow of peach, lilac and red as we reach the letters.

'I wouldn't fancy doing that hike in the dark,' Tilda says, panting slightly. 'Ann left the studio at around seven thirty last night, and she told a crew member she was going to Musso's to pick up some food, and then back to her apartment. There was a box from the restaurant on the counter, so she definitely didn't get out here until late.'

The letters loom over us, almost unnervingly huge, the exposed steel supports behind them giving easy climbing access to anyone daring enough. I can see the attraction – the city sprawls out beneath us, lights beginning to glow as dusk falls – but even so, I wouldn't want to climb it in full darkness, if that's what Ann did.

'There are footprints here.' Louis crouches beside the support of the H, tapping a finger in the dirt at a neat shoe print, smaller than mine, and perhaps a perfect fit for Ann.

'There are footprints everywhere,' Tilda says, gesturing to the ground. She has a point. Uniformed officers, detectives and reporters have all been up here today, trampling what could be a crime scene. Now, the footprints are the only sign that Ann was ever here at all. 'I'm not sure that footprints are going to help.'

'Even when they're right beside the ones that could be Ann's?' Louis points again, to a shoe print in the dirt. It aligns perfectly next to Ann's, as if she took a step up to climb onto the support structure, and then the person behind her did the same.

'So maybe she wasn't here alone?' I glance up at the H, my stomach turning at the sheer size of it. 'We have to go up there.'

'Lil! It's getting dark!' Tilda is the bravest person I know, apart from when it comes to heights. 'And it's really, really high.'

I already have one foot on the steel, and Louis comes up behind me to give me a boost. I begin to climb, my heart in my mouth and my palms sweaty, until I manage to clamber onto the small ledge at the top of the H. It's narrow – wide enough to stand on, but only just – and the breeze that whips up from the valley below makes it all feel even more precarious. I can understand why, in my own time, there isn't any access. My breath sticks in my throat as I look out over the city, a vision against the fading light.

'It's beautiful,' Louis breathes beside me a few seconds later.

'And deadly,' I reply. It's a long way down from here, and I wonder if Ann stood with her feet on the edge, plucking up the courage to fall, or whether it was a split-second thing, a hand in the small of her back sending her tumbling over the edge before she realised what was happening. Louis still stands with his eyes on the ground below, swallowing hard and stepping back a little as if dizzy. As he does, something catches my eye. A glint of something shiny tucked against the structure of the sign. Something dropped by accident, unnoticed.

'Lil?' Louis turns as I gingerly bend to pick it up, aware that one slip of my foot means I'll end up the same way as Ann Silver. 'What is that?'

I turn the object over in my hands, inspecting it the best I can in the dying light. 'It's a lighter,' I say. 'A fancy one. It looks like there's something engraved on it.'

Louis takes it and holds it up, angling it so the last rays of sun hit the body of the metal. 'It says *Silver Circle 1949* on it. What does that mean?'

'Hey! You two! It's really getting dark, so you need to come back down before you kill yourselves!' Tilda calls up from the ground. 'If you die, I don't have time to plan your funerals. I have things to investigate.'

With a roll of his eyes, Louis tucks the lighter into his pocket and we begin to climb back down. It's easier going down than it was climbing up, and it's only a matter of minutes before we are both on firm ground and showing Tilda our discovery.

'Do you think it might be Ann's?' Louis asks, as Tilda turns the lighter over in her hands.

'I don't think she smokes,' she muses. 'At least, I've never seen her with a cigarette. Tipsy could probably confirm that. Although we don't even know if this could be Ann's at all – someone could have dropped it up there weeks ago.'

I shake my head. 'I don't think so, Til. You've seen how dusty it is down here? It's ten times dustier up there. That lighter didn't have any dust on it when I picked it up. If I had to guess I'd say it had only been there a few hours, a day at most. I don't think Ann was alone up there, and I don't think she jumped or fell. I don't think this was an accident at all.'

Chapter Thirteen

Early the next morning Tilda and I slide into a booth opposite Louis at Nickodell's, a popular place on Melrose, not too far from the studios. Two steaming mugs of coffee await us. Even though tea is more my jam, like all good British girls, this morning definitely calls for maximum caffeine. It's early enough that despite the fact Nickodell's is a prime haunt for studio staff, it's relatively empty and we can talk in peace. Come lunchtime though, this place will be swarming with folks in the business, grabbing a bite, doing business and downing one or two – or more – drinks.

'You get much sleep last night?' Louis asks, his hands around a cheese egg muffin.

I shake my head. 'Nope.' The smell of the fryer and the sizzle of bacon in the pan makes my stomach turn. 'Barely slept a wink. I just kept thinking about Ann. About how frightened she must have been if what happened really wasn't suicide.' My hand slides into my purse and I wrap my fingers around the silver lighter. 'Do you think we should go to the police? I mean, Tipsy said Ann "knew when to keep her mouth shut". What does that mean? And what if Ann *didn't* know when to keep her mouth shut about something?'

'Like what?'

'I don't know... What if she saw something she shouldn't? What if that was the case with Max too? Don't you think it's odd that there have been two high-profile deaths in as many weeks?' I'm spitballing, throwing out suggestions as they hit my brain, but there's no denying something feels off about it all.

'There's no point calling the police,' Tilda says, dropping this morning's newspaper onto the table with a thud. The headline screams out at us:

SUICIDE AT THE HOLLYWOOD SIGN
Ann Silver dead at 24

'There's a two-page article inside,' Tilda says, her brow crinkling. 'The Chief of Police has already chalked Ann's death up to suicide. Her funeral will be held next week, but not here. Her parents are taking her home – they never wanted her to come to Hollywood in the first place, so you can hardly blame them. There's a couple of sad quotes from crew working on the movie, and Oskar has dropped a line or two in there about how she'll be missed, but the real issue is that an unnamed source told the reporter that Ann had seemed down recently. If she really didn't commit suicide then it's down to us to prove it.'

I flick the flint on the lighter, the flame burning a bright orange as my heart sinks. Everything feels huge – Max's death, Ann's dive from the top of the Hollywood sign, keeping Leonard's movie on track after the way the last picture was derailed. It's not the first time I've felt this way, I remind myself, and every time we figure things out in the end.

'Lil?' Louis's voice is gentle, and he reaches out and tugs the lighter from my hand.

'Sorry, I just feel a bit overwhelmed. I don't even know where to start. I can't believe that Ann's death is just accepted as a suicide with no investigation. It's all just taken at face value.' In my time, this would never have happened. TikTok sleuths and Instagram detectives would have taken to the internet, intent on proving things weren't as they seemed. A Netflix documentary would have been made, or Louis Theroux would have gone on a deep dive on camera, but poor old Ann won't get any of them. She'll just get me, Tilda and Louis. My eye catches the engraving on the lighter. *Silver Circle 1949*. Maybe Tilda, Louis and I will be enough.

'We need to figure out who this lighter belongs to. If it *was* Ann's somebody at the studio might recognise it,' I say. 'And if it's not hers then whoever's it is was there at the same time as Ann, or very recently. Even if they're not involved they might have seen something.'

'Let's get to the studio.' Tilda flips the newspaper over, hiding Ann's face, and slides out of the booth. 'If we get there early enough we can visit Ann's set before you're late for your own movie, Lil.'

Glancing at the clock on the wall, I see Tilda is right. If we hustle, we can poke around on Ann's picture before anyone notices I'm late. Kissing Louis on the cheek, I promise to update him afterwards.

A few minutes later, Tilda and I approach the security gate to the lot.

'Holy shit. I was hoping we'd be able to sneak in with only Bobby noticing us.' A crowd has formed in front of the gates, a swarm of reporters, photographers and rubberneckers waving clipboards and calling out to the security guards for information. Small bundles of flowers are already being left at the gates, and Bobby looks harassed as he steps around the edge of the crowd to scoop them up.

'Language, Lil,' Tilda says, bending to help Bobby. 'Here, Bobby. You'll be here all day at this rate, and it looks as though you have more important things on your hands to deal with.'

Bobby turns to look at the crowd, worry drawing his mouth into a droopy, thin line as he adjusts his hat. 'I don't know what they're hoping to achieve,' he says, wearily. 'Some of them have been here half the night… Oskar's already fed the papers a line, and everyone else has been instructed not to talk about that poor, sweet girl.'

'How well did you know her?' I take some of the flowers from Bobby, freeing up his hands for more. The petals are damp with the morning air, and the smell that rises already carries the tiniest hint of decay about it. My stomach rolls and I swallow, nausea leaving a sour taste in my mouth.

'Oh, you know.' Bobby flaps a hand. 'As well as I know anyone who turns up here day after day. She was a nice girl. She gave me a pair of leather gloves at Christmas, after I told her about the arthritis.'

'She does sound lovely,' I say, a lump forming in my throat. 'Listen, Bobby, do you mind if we sneak in around the back? I don't really want to face those baying reporters, especially with Tilda with me… and Leonard will string me up if I'm late.'

'Sure thing, Miss Lily!' Bobby finally smiles as he opens the gate for Tilda and me to sneak in unnoticed, and we hurry towards the sound stage on the other side of the lot where Ann's movie is filming.

It's eerily quiet over here. Where usually there would be a bustling set – the sound of hammers carrying through the early morning air as the carpenters get to work, rolling racks of clothes being wheeled to wardrobe, and call sheets being handed out all amid the scent of coffee and cigarettes on the air – the place is practically empty. Thick silence envelops us as we move through the lot, the doors to the sound stage closed and locked. A man in a suit hurries past, a clipboard in his hand, his neat side part and shiny shoes giving him away as a studio lawyer. He marches past without a second look in our direction, and I tug on Tilda's arm.

'There's no one here, Til. We should probably get out of here before someone does show up and starts asking questions.' Tilda is the last person people will want to see on the lot today, given her role as Louella Parsons's protegee.

'Wait a minute.' Tilda holds up a hand to silence me. 'Listen.' There is the muffled sound of a sob, then a sniff, from around the corner.

'Someone *is* here.' Rounding the corner, I see Ann's trailer. A bouquet of flowers has been left outside and the door is shut, the thin curtains at the trailer windows pulled closed. A young girl sits on the steps to the trailer, her head in her hands and her shoulders hitching. Picking up speed, Tilda and I hurry across to her, dust coating my Converse.

'Hey,' I say gently as we reach the girl. She lifts her hands from her face to look at us and I have to bite back a gasp. She looks eerily like Ann. 'Are you OK? The set is closed today.' The girl nods, but her wan pallor and the way her breath hitches tell me otherwise. 'Do you have someone you want me to call?'

The girl shakes her head as Tilda crouches beside her and takes her hands in hers. 'Did you know Ann well?'

The girl nods, sniffing again. 'I'm her stand-in. You know, for the lighting and blocking and things? I've worked with her on every movie she's done.' She tugs her hand free and holds it out for me to shake. 'I'm Kate.'

'Lily. I work here at the studios. And this is Tilda. She's… a writer.' I pause. 'Did no one tell you the set was closed today?'

Kate shakes her head. 'I was sick yesterday. A horrible stomach bug. I saw Ann the day she…' Her voice cracks. 'I didn't know. I didn't know she'd died until I got here and saw the flowers and all the people outside. My wireless is broken and I hadn't seen the newspapers…' A sob erupts and a fresh wave of tears start to fall.

Tilda and I share a glance as we wait for Kate to get herself under control, and it's only a few minutes before she is pressing a hanky to her nose and apologising. 'You don't need to apologise,' I say, with a gentle smile. 'But I do need to ask you a couple of questions, if you feel up to it.'

'We're trying to find out what happened to Ann,' Tilda says. 'We're not sure things are as clear-cut as the media – and the studio – is saying. We've heard rumours that Ann was depressed, but others are saying she wasn't at all. As her stand-in you probably know her better than anyone else on set. How was she, really?'

Kate pauses, her foot scuffing along the edge of the step where it meets the ground. 'She was always so happy to be at work, you know? Acting was her life – I never wanted to be anything more than her stand-in, but Ann wanted the world to know who she was. She wanted to win an Oscar, and she wanted to set up her own acting school one day for kids who were less fortunate. For the kids who come from a different background, not the ones whose parents are already in the movies. She was a good person.'

'Everyone liked her?'

'Sure!' Kate nods enthusiastically. 'Everyone liked Ann – she always had a kind word for everyone, right down to the janitor. She never forgot where she came from, never forgot how fortunate she was.'

'How was she, that last day?' I ask, my tone soft. I know this is hard for Kate to talk about, but she is surely the best person to judge Ann's state of mind that day.

Kate sighs. 'She was… not her usual self. She hadn't been for a couple of weeks.'

'How so?' Maybe she was depressed after all. Maybe Ann just didn't want to be here anymore… Maybe I'm making Kate relive Ann's last few days for no reason.

'She was quiet. She didn't want to eat lunch with anyone, not even me. A lot of stars don't want the stand-in in their trailer, but Ann was never like that. She used to laugh, saying if I looked enough like her to be her stand-in then I deserved to use the trailer too. But the last couple of weeks she holed up in here every time we took a break, like she was avoiding someone. I thought maybe she was just exhausted – the movie is a Western and there's a lot of violence on set – and I thought maybe she was just feeling a little put through the wringer, you know? But then that last day…' She trails off, knotting her hanky through her fingers.

'What?' I press. 'What happened that last day?'

Kate meets my eyes, hers rimmed with pink and her nose shiny. 'It was like a switch was flipped, and not in a good way. It felt as though Ann had been pushed to her limit. She was *furious* about something, but when I asked if she was all right she just said everything was fine. I knew

it, though. I knew *her*. After shooting finished for the day
I asked if she wanted to get a drink. I thought maybe she
would talk about things away from the set.'

'But she said no.' We already know that Ann went to
Musso's to pick up food and then back to her apartment.
Could whatever had been playing on Ann's mind have
been enough to make her want to jump from the Hollywood sign?

'She said no,' Kate confirms, her voice barely above a
whisper. 'She told me she was going to grab some food
and then she had an appointment. Ann was never planning
to stay home after she picked up dinner. She was meeting
someone after work.'

Chapter Fourteen

'I knew it,' Tilda hisses as we leave a tearful Kate on the steps of Ann's trailer and hurry towards the set for Leonard's movie. 'Ann might have been worried about something, had something on her mind, but I don't think she was depressed.'

'She definitely wasn't herself though – Kate said she was furious about something. And who did she meet? If we can figure that out then we're halfway to finding out what really happened on the top of that sign.' Showing Kate the lighter hadn't given us any joy. She thought she might have seen it before but couldn't tell us where or who owned it. Now, Tilda peels off to head back to the newspaper office.

'Til? Before you go… not a word about any of this, yeah?' I know I don't have to say it, and it's compounded by Tilda rolling her eyes.

'*Obviously*,' she huffs. 'But I have to give Louella something this morning… I'm thinking Vic's wandering hands might make for an exciting snippet in the column today.' With a wink – and before I can protest – she is gone.

Although things are still rolling on Leonard's movie, shooting carrying on as usual, there is a sombre air on set. The crew doesn't whistle, there is no sharp banter being tossed around between the lighting crew and the props men, and everyone seems to be tucked safely away in their trailers. Perhaps that's why I notice him. A man in a sharp suit, tall, with black and silver hair and a moustache Tom Selleck would be proud of, sliding out of the warehouse that houses the wardrobe department and skirting around a golf cart parked outside. Usually I wouldn't pay him any attention, but after sitting with Kate and hearing about Ann's state of mind, perhaps I'm on red alert. Watching him as he makes his way towards the exit, I rack my brain to see if I recognise him, but I'm sure I've never seen him before.

A studio lawyer, maybe? Or an exec's assistant? I don't pay much attention to the studio executive assistants, not when I have Leonard – and sometimes Oskar himself – bellowing in my ear. *Could he be a reporter?* My heart sinks at the thought. The last thing the studio needs is an inside scoop from a rogue journalist. I am about to turn and head towards Bobby's security gate to ask him if I can take a look at the log for this morning, when movement at the wardrobe door draws my attention. Mae appears, not yet dressed in her costume, her hair and make-up still untouched. With a furtive glance, she steps out onto the path that runs between the wardrobe warehouse and the trailers, the packed gravel crunching slightly beneath her slippered feet. She peeps over her shoulder, as if checking she is unobserved, and then hurries towards the commissary, presumably to grab a bite before hair and make-up.

Intrigued by the subterfuge, I follow after her, wondering why she was in wardrobe but still not dressed in her costume. Should I ask her outright? Was it a secret love tryst, an affair Mae wants to keep secret? But when I push open the door to the commissary, a burst of chatter assaults my eardrums.

'Lily! Oh, there you are, at last!' Tipsy calls, grabbing my attention with an extravagant wave of her arms. 'You simply *must* see this!' The newspaper is spread out before her, and as I cast my eyes around the canteen I see multiple copies of the paper spread across the tables, Ann's face smiling up from a couple of the front pages. Everyone is poring over the inky pages, some shocked, some delighted, but all bubbling with questions.

'Tipsy, you haven't even been to make-up. And your hair…' Her red hair is curled up in rollers, and she raises a cigarette to unpainted lips. Leonard is going to kill me if I can't shepherd her into her trailer in the next five minutes.

'What is it, Tipsy?' Mae slides into the seat beside Tipsy, an apple in her hand. 'Another Last Word?'

Tipsy nods delightedly and I half expect her to give a squeal of delight. 'And it's a doozy!'

'Ladies, I understand that the gossip is exciting, but we really need to get you—' I break off as the commissary door opens and Cliff steps inside. He pauses, his face impassive as he clutches his pen and surveys the scene. As his eyes settle on Mae a smile lifts the corner of his mouth, and he takes a couple of steps towards us. I watch as Mae meets his eyes for the briefest of seconds before ignoring him and turning back to Tipsy. Cliff falters to a stop before pivoting in the other direction, as if he never meant to come our way at all, and I feel a lurch of sympathy for him. Getting to my feet, I announce that I'm going to grab some coffee and hurry across the room to where Cliff is helping himself to an overripe banana from the fruit bowl.

'Morning,' I say, as Cliff turns to smile at me. 'How are you?' I haven't forgotten the way his eyes widened as Tilda spilled the news about Ann yesterday. 'There's a weird atmosphere here today, don't you think? It's going to be impossible to stop people gossiping about poor Ann.'

Cliff glances over my shoulder, towards the table where Mae and Tipsy are sitting. 'Did Mae say anything to you about Ann?'

'Mae?' I frown. 'No. She's not said anything at all to me. I'm not sure she even knows Ann. Why?'

Cliff fiddles with the end of his banana, peeling the skin to reveal a bruised, darkened fruit. 'It's nothing. Only...' He peers over my shoulder again and sighs. 'Lily, you know I'm not one to gossip, but rumour has it that Mae and Ann didn't really see eye to eye.'

'Mae and Ann?' I turn to glance in Mae's direction, watching as she laughs at something Tipsy says.

'It's just a rumour.' Cliff shakes his head. 'Apparently there was some rivalry there but I don't know...'

'What, do you think...?'

Cliff throws the banana into the bin without taking a bite. 'Forget I said anything, Lil. It's just idle gossip. You know what it's like around here... I've heard a hundred different things about Ann already this morning. Look, you'd better take the girls their coffee. Catch up with you later?'

'Sure.' Feeling a little bemused, I grab two black coffees and take them back to the table, where Tipsy is still holding the newspaper aloft.

'Quickly, Tipsy. What does it say?' Mae grins up at me as she takes her coffee. 'Lily is about to chew us out for being late, but I don't want to be the only person on set who doesn't know the juice!'

'It says...' Tipsy clears her throat and shakes out the newspaper, ever the actress. '*A darling blonde bombshell who lights up our screens with her chirpy charm seems to have a little extra spark off screen. She's moving in suspicious circles – and whispers are that she's got a soft spot for causes that may make the Feds raise an eyebrow. Be careful, dear, affection in the wrong places can cost more than just box office appeal...'* Tipsy looks up at me with glee. 'This is even better than the rumour about the funny cigarettes!'

A darling blonde bombshell... causes that may make the Feds raise an eyebrow. Knowing what I know about Hollywood in the 1950s, the rumour can only be referring to Judy Holliday and her supposed involvement in the red scare. In the 1940s and 50s Hollywood was rife with rumours that people within the movie industry were involved in communism, and I know a bunch of people were black-listed because of it. Judy Holliday was not one of them.

'This is a load of old rubbish, Tipsy.' I snatch the news-paper, ignoring her protests. 'You can't spread rumours about things that aren't true. You need to get to your trailer now, before Leonard comes and gives us all what for.'

With a grumble Tipsy gets to her feet, Mae following suit, but by the time I get them both prepped and on set, they've missed their call time and Leonard is quite rightly fuming.

'Lily?'

'Yes, sir.' Although I've known Leonard for a long time, and I know he's a lovely guy deep down, he still has the ability to make my legs wobble when he's angry.

'What are we running here?'

'A... uh, a movie set, sir.'

'Exactly! Not a damn daycare! Why is everyone late to set? Tipsy, I expect it of her – you did give her a call time thirty minutes before I actually need her, didn't you? But

Mae? And *you*? Lily, I need to be able to rely on you.' His eyes bore into me, and I find I have no excuses.

'There was a new blind item,' I say, my mouth dry. 'It's pretty bad, and everyone—'

'I *don't care*,' Leonard says through gritted teeth as he shoves the day's script notes into my hand. 'Get them here on time. Please.' He turns a ferocious glare on Tipsy, who beams back at him. 'Marks, people. For God's sakes, on your marks.'

—

We don't break for lunch, Leonard punishing all of us it seems for being late. By the time we finish shooting in the late evening, Mae looks about ready to keel over, and I enlist Bunny to grab her a bottle of Coke and a piece of fruit. I've learned through previous experience that there is no point trying to get these women to eat a Baby Ruth or a Twinkie between takes – the actresses won't want it and the studio won't allow it.

My relief at Leonard wrapping for the day is short-lived when he gestures for me to follow him. He turns a finger on Mae, Vic and Tipsy too, and it's with some trepidation that we follow him across the lot. I was right to worry as we approach Oskar's office, Cliff standing outside with a nervous Bunny beside him.

'Bunny, what's all this about?' I whisper as she steps into line behind me. 'Cliff? Do you know?'

Cliff shakes his head, clasping his hands behind his back. 'I've no idea. Sorry, Lily.'

'I don't know either,' Bunny whispers, her fingers shaking as she pushes her hair behind her ear, 'but I think it's probably to do with what's been happening on the lot.

You know. *The gossip.*' She widens her eyes at me, and I stumble slightly as we enter the office.

Oskar Goldstein, studio exec and general arsehole, sits behind his desk, glowering over his clasped hands at us as we take seats on the chairs lined up in front of him. I feel like a child, up before the headmaster.

'I'll make this brief.' For a man who seems perpetually pissed off, I didn't realise it was possible for him to sound even more aggrieved than usual. 'We've got a serious problem, and *you,*' he points to each of us in turn, 'are part of it. The delays on set today cost us daylight, crew overtime and money we can't afford to throw around. Some of you should be more aware of that than others.' At this, I squirm in my chair. I know the studio lost a lot of money after the last picture folded before it was finished shooting.

'I'm sorry...' Vic leans in, his voice as smooth as caramel. 'Are you saying that we shouldn't bond as a crew? We shouldn't spend time together in our break periods? Because I'm pretty sure the union—'

Oh yikes. Oskar's face turns an alarming shade of purple. 'That's damn well not what I'm saying and you know that, Romano.' I see Cliff's eyes widen at Oskar's tone and he jots a little note on his pad. 'I want professionalism on my set at all times. Gossip, rumours, idle chit-chat... all of it stops now.' He pulls out a cigar and furiously snips the end off. 'I should fire you all.'

Leonard raises an eyebrow at this.

'I can't make a film if my actors and crew aren't on set on time, if you're treating this place like a damn beauty parlour, sitting around, running your mouths. I don't want to hear another word about this gossip column, you hear?

Anyone caught engaging in these rumours will be off the lot. For good.'

'Oh, come now,' Tipsy drawls, a suggestive smile playing about her lips as she looks at Oskar, who scowls as he lights his cigar. 'A little chatter doesn't hurt anyone. If anything it boosts morale.'

'*Morale* doesn't pay the bills,' Leonard snaps. 'You want to gossip? Do it on your own time, not on mine.'

I press my foot lightly on Tipsy's, urging her to be quiet. 'No more gossip on set,' I say, as Mae keeps her eyes on her lap and Vic smirks. 'I'll make sure I nip it in the bud before anyone can even open the newspaper in the morning.'

'Good.' Leonard gives a weary nod and gets to his feet. All of us scramble to our own feet, relieved that the meeting – bollocking, if we're being honest – is over. 'All of you out of my sight. You have an early start tomorrow.'

Tipsy opens her mouth to speak and I give her a tiny shove in the small of her back, pressing her towards Cliff, who now holds the door open for us all to leave.

'Thank you, dear.' Tipsy smiles at him, and Cliff beams back in return before Oskar's voice pulls us up short.

'I mean it,' he says ominously. 'The next disruption on this set will have real consequences, especially if it's down to this ridiculous column. I'm talking fines, suspension – even the termination of your contract. We're here to make movies, not headlines.'

—

'Fuuuuck,' I hiss to Bunny as Tipsy and Mae walk off arm in arm, Vic Romano swaggering along behind them. 'Oskar is fuming. Which means Leonard is going to be on my ass about this now.' All I want is for one movie to go off without a hitch.

'Lily,' Bunny presses her lips into a firm line, 'I've told you before, you've got to stop with the sailor talk. People will think you're *common*.'

I stifle a laugh. As a girl who grew up on the outskirts of Peckham, East London, I would be surprised if anyone thought I was anything other than that. The laughter dies on my lips as I catch sight of the moustachioed man I saw this morning, walking away from the door that leads to Leonard's office, and the corridor where Bunny's desk sits.

'Bun? You know that guy?' I nod discreetly in his direction, and Bunny turns to look.

'No,' she says faintly, something unreadable flashing across her face so quickly that I can't be sure it was there at all. 'Never seen him before in my life.' She keeps her eyes on the street ahead as we make our way towards the security gates. As we reach them, Bunny turns to peer back over her shoulder but the man is long gone.

'You sure you don't know him? He looked like he was coming out of the corridor to Leonard's office.'

Bunny shakes her head, her short blonde curls flying. 'I swear, Lily. I've never seen him before.'

I pause to let Bunny through the gate first, peering back over my own shoulder. Because if Bunny, who seems to be the eyes and ears of our entire operation, who always seems to know everything before anyone else, says she's never seen him before – and I'm not one hundred per cent sure I believe her – then what is he doing coming out of that corridor?

Chapter Fifteen

'Lily, we have to go.' Tilda is pacing the apartment floor when I let myself in, while Louis stands in the doorway to the tiny kitchenette, jangling his car keys in one hand.

'Go? Go where? Til, I just got home.' All I want to do after the dressing down from Oskar and Leonard is take my make-up off, strip off my bra and change into my nightclothes so I can spend the evening pondering on whether the mysterious man on the lot is Mae's secret lover or someone more sinister.

'Lizzie called me at the paper.' Tilda snatches up her purse and makes a shooing gesture towards the door.

'Lizzie? Lizzie Hayden? What does she want?'

'She wants to talk to us.'

Suddenly the fatigue that hit me on the way home melts away and a buzz of anticipation ripples through my veins. I catch Louis's eye and he grins.

'Yeah, we thought that might liven you up. Rough day?'

'Long day. But none of that matters if Lizzie is finally going to open up to us about Max.' Hurrying down the stairs and out the front door, I hop into the passenger seat and Louis has us en route to Lizzie's house in a matter of minutes.

'Step on it, Lou. Can't this thing go any faster?' Tilda hangs over the headrest, pressing her fingers into his shoulder, and I wish – not for the first time – that seatbelts were law in 1952. 'I want to get there before Lizzie changes her mind. I still can't believe she called.'

'Did she give you any idea about what she wants to tell us?' I twist around in my seat to look at Tilda, even though it'll make me car sick.

'Nope.' Tilda shakes her head, her red ponytail flying. 'But she said it's going to be *off the record*. Pull in here, Lou.'

Louis parks, and we make our way up the winding path that leads to the house. There is the scent of jasmine on the air, and as the house comes into view every light is on, the whole place lit up like a Christmas tree. It's such a stark contrast to the other visits we've paid to the house that goosebumps rise on my arms as Tilda presses her finger to the doorbell.

Lizzie herself opens the door and ushers us inside. Her eyes are pink and she seems to have lost weight in the brief time since we last saw her, the belt on her skirt cinched in to the last hole. She leads us into the kitchen, where Jack and Mary sit on opposite sides of the marble island. Jack has a drink in front of him, something dark and peaty, and there is the faintest whiff of old booze about him.

'Thank you so much for coming over.' Mary slips off the stool and gives us a wobbly smile. 'Can I fetch you a drink?'

I'm already shaking my head when Lizzie replies, 'Mary, please. Can we just get this over with?'

Chastened, Mary sits back down at the island, her eyes on the marble in front of her. The atmosphere is thick, the tension so palpable you could cut it with a knife.

'Lizzie, for goodness' sakes,' Jack says, wearily. 'Don't take things out on Mary. We all agreed that we should talk to Lily and her friends. We have to trust someone.'

'Do you think…' Mary swallows, her gaze darting from us to Lizzie to Jack. 'Do you think maybe we should make them sign something? A contract, of sorts. To say they can't repeat anything.' The words seem to take everything out of her and she falls silent, her chest hitching as if she's been running.

Tilda and I exchange a glance as Louis runs his eyes over the trio in front of us, as if searching for a clue as to what Lizzie is about to reveal.

'You can trust us,' Louis says. 'Whatever it is, Lizzie, you can tell us. We want to know the truth about what happened to Max… We want to help you.'

Lizzie turns her gaze to Jack, who nods abruptly. 'All right. The truth. But whatever is said here tonight stays in this room.' She swallows and Mary reaches out and squeezes her hand. 'According to the rest of the world, to the media, to all of Hollywood, Max and I were love's young dream. I was the one who finally managed to tame the playboy of the movie business, the loveable rogue who no one believed would ever settle down.' A small laugh escapes and Lizzie blinks. 'We met on a movie five years ago – Mary was on the same movie, and Jack and Max had been friends for years. We instantly clicked – all of us, not just Max and me. By the time we finished shooting the movie, I was in love.' Her fingers reach out and her hand creeps into Mary's, squeezing tightly together.

'It was never you and Max,' I say, realisation dawning. 'It was you and Mary.'

'*What?*' Louis gasps, as Tilda presses her hand to her mouth. 'Lily, what on earth are you talking about? That's ridiculous, of course Lizzie and Mary aren't...' he swallows, '...*in love*. That's not... I mean, it's not...'

'It's not a big deal,' I say, as Mary's eyes fill with tears. I mean, it is a big deal right now – in 1952 homosexuality was criminalised in California – but for me, as a twenty-first-century girl, this is nothing. 'It's shocking, yes, and of course you don't want this to get out, I completely understand.' Lizzie and Mary will lose their jobs, the scandal will rock Hollywood to its core, and there's a very real chance of jail time for them both. 'That's why you didn't want to contact the police... You were worried that if they dug around too much you two would be exposed.'

'It's true,' Lizzie says, lifting her chin defiantly as Louis looks unconvinced. 'Mary and I fell in love on set. I knew right away there would only ever be Mary for me, but I didn't know how we could be together.'

'And then Max told Lizzie about he and I.' Jack speaks now, tossing back the last of his drink. Louis blinks, as if stunned. 'Max and I had already been together for two years by then. We met in San Francisco, at a party thrown by Orson Welles and Rita Hayworth. We were working together on getting Max sober – finally, he was happy, and we couldn't afford for him to be drunk. Couldn't afford to risk him slipping up and giving the game away about us. When Max realised the truth about Lizzie and Mary, he knew there was only one way we could all openly be together.'

'Becoming best friends,' Tilda says slowly, with a nod of her head. A ghost of a smile plays about her lips, and it seems as though she is doing her best to appear over the shock of Lizzie's revelation. 'It's a genius idea. The four of you, all living together under one roof... the one safe space where you could all be yourselves.'

'That explains why there were no wedding pictures of you and Max together,' I say to Lizzie. And it explains why there were two sets of ladies' slippers in the bedroom, why the second bedroom felt so masculine. Why Lizzie didn't know that her husband had been a swimmer in college. Everything was there, right in front of us. We just didn't see it.

'Max gave up a lot to be with Jack… and so that I could be with Mary,' Lizzie says, her voice trembling.

'Wait,' I say. 'Is that why Max's parents didn't support you at his funeral? Did he cut them off to protect you all?'

Jack nods, his eyes rimmed red. 'We let them think that Lizzie didn't like Max's family, and Max "took her side" against them. He was devastated, but he knew that to have his family in and out of our lives would risk everything for all of us. It's not so bad for the rest of us, our families are scattered across the country, but Max's weren't.'

'I don't understand,' Louis says now, his brow crumpled. 'Why are you telling us this? Aren't you worried we'll spill the beans? Tilda works on a gossip column after all.'

'Well, of course we've thought about that. Why do you think it's taken us so long to decide to speak with you?' Lizzie says.

Tilda pipes up now, her face earnest as she presses her hand to her chest. 'I swear, you can trust me. I won't say a word to anybody. Not everything I hear gets published in the column. Some things need to be kept quiet.' She pauses. 'I know Hollywood loves to gossip, but I'm not out to ruin anyone's life.'

Lizzie and Jack share an uneasy glance, and there is a pause before Jack speaks.

'I found something,' he says, 'in Max's things. Wait here.' He heads out of the kitchen, returning a few moments later with a bundle of papers in his hands.

'What's this?' Intrigued, I take the envelope that Jack holds out to me, running my eyes over the thick black ink on the letter inside. 'Oh my God, this is…'

'A blackmail letter,' Jack confirms with a sharp nod. He throws the bundle of papers onto the counter. 'All of these, dating back to the beginning of the year. I found them in the box of Max's things that Lizzie had bundled up to sell at auction.'

'I had to,' Lizzie protests, her voice thickening. 'There's no money left, Jack. We have to auction Max's belongings to make the mortgage payment on this place. If we lose this house too…'

'Someone was blackmailing Max,' I say, my eyes scanning over the vicious dark strokes of the pen.

> *You know the kind of secret you're keeping is*
> *enough to destroy more than one life… What price*
> *is your silence, Max? You missed the deadline.*
> *This is your final chance to protect yourself and*
> *the ones you love. If the envelope isn't left at the*
> *third payphone on Hollywood & Vine by ten p.m.*
> *Friday, there'll be a different kind of deadline.*
> *A Friend*

'They were threatening to tell the truth about your relationship with him, Jack. Who knew? Who knew about the two of you?'

Jack shrugs. 'We tried to be discreet – hell, Max even went to the trouble of marrying Lizzie and cutting off his family to protect all four of us – but of course there was the odd rumour every now and again. I think someone Max had a fling with once tried to sell a story, but Max had a fixer on it and it died before it got anywhere.'

I've heard about Hollywood fixers – guys (and women in my time) whose job it is to make things go away in Hollywood. 'Do you have a name?'

Jack shakes his head. 'It was years ago. I can't believe Max never told me this was happening. We could have figured this out together. We would have found a way.' He sounds so defeated, so broken, that my own heart breaks for him.

'Did Max pay the blackmailer?' Tilda asks, and I could kick myself for not thinking to ask the question myself.

Lizzie lifts her shoulders in a shrug as Mary pats her on the back. 'There was no money left. Max made plenty of cash withdrawals, but he'd always done that. Who knows where the money went? All I can think is that Max couldn't bear the pressure anymore. He couldn't bear the thought that someone would expose us all…' A sob rips the air, and Mary covers her mouth with both hands as if trying to stem a tidal wave of tears. 'The idea that he would rather die than let Jack be dragged through a scandal…'

Louis claps a hand on Jack's shoulder. 'It sounds as though Max was an excellent man.'

'He was,' Jack chokes out. 'But please, now you know the truth, you have to stop digging. I thought maybe there was something more sinister going on with Max's death but now I've found these letters… I have to accept that Max simply couldn't take it anymore. He couldn't bear the shame, or the idea that all of our lives would be ruined.'

'We should leave you,' Tilda says, her tone solemn. 'I'm so very sorry for your loss.'

Lizzie kisses Mary on the side of the head and then comes to see us to the door, leaving Jack sat at the counter, his head in his hands. 'Thank you,' she says as we step out onto the porch. 'For being so understanding. I appreciate that what you've heard tonight is beyond scandalous, but it really is love, that's all. You won't...' She looks Tilda dead in the eye. 'You really won't write about us, will you? Swear to me?'

'I swear,' Tilda says.

'Will you promise me one thing?' Lizzie asks, lowering her voice. 'If anyone asks you, please tell them that Max's death was just a tragic accident. I can't bear for Jack to have to deal with the shame of Max being named a suicide.'

'Of course.'

'And if you find out who wrote those letters...' Her face changes, her jaw set and fury burning right behind her eyes. 'Send them my way. I have things I want to say. I might not have been Max's wife in every sense, but I still loved him.'

I nod, and it's only once the door is firmly shut behind us that Tilda speaks.

'Well,' she says. 'Talk about a plot twist. I never would have guessed that about Max Hayden.' She pauses. 'I can't imagine living like that, hiding your true self away. I guess I never really thought about how it might affect someone... But even so, I still don't believe this was an accident, and I certainly don't think Max committed suicide.'

Chapter Sixteen

'Tilda, we were just told that the man was being black-mailed over something that would destroy his entire life if it came out,' Louis says crossly, as we make our way back towards the car. 'Of course he took that way out – he had no other option.'

'No. Someone sent a note to me, and I think they were hoping that I would investigate and then expose Max, but I ignored them,' Tilda says. 'What if someone decided Max had to go?'

'Like who?' I ask, as we get into the car and Louis starts the engine with a throaty rev. 'Everyone liked Max, Tipsy said it herself, and let's be honest, there's not much that woman doesn't know.'

Tilda leans forward, peering over the seats. 'The Last Word column in the newspaper… There was one a few months ago that I think might be relevant. Hold up.' She rummages in her purse and brings out an envelope stuffed with clippings. 'I can't believe I didn't put it all together before, but of course we had no idea about Max and Jack.'

'You've kept them all?' Louis glances in the rearview mirror at Tilda shuffling through, her fingers stained with old ink.

'Of course I have,' she snaps. 'I knew they'd come in handy. I just wasn't sure if it would be work or… something like this. Aha. Look, Lil.' She hands me a scruffy piece of newspaper and I hold it close to my face, squinting as I try and read by the glow of the streetlights whizzing by.

> This wild leading man may have been tamed by a Hollywood princess, but he's keeping a scandalous secret off screen. While fans and moviegoers gush over their storybook romance, whispers on the inside suggest our dreamboat is more devoted to the handsome 'pals' visiting his dressing room than his blushing bride.

'See?' Tilda peers over my shoulder, pointing at the ink. 'Hollywood princess – Lizzie played an Egyptian princess in 1947. It was a tiny movie that didn't do so well, but someone knew about it. Handsome "pals" visiting his dressing room – Jack visited Max on every set he worked on. The blind item has to be about Max.'

'And this came out after the blackmail letters started arriving.' My mind starts ticking over, running through everything that we've discovered tonight, trying to make sense of the timeline. 'What night did Max die?'

'The twenty-third of May,' Tilda says.

I glance over the sheet of newspaper. 'This was published the week before he died.'

The car brakes suddenly, jolting us forward, and I put out a hand to the dashboard to steady myself. 'Sorry,' Louis says. 'My foot slipped... The week before Max died? That's the same week Tilda received the note on her desk.'

'Holy shit,' I breathe. 'You're right, Til, this is all connected. It's too coincidental not to be.'

'What if…' Tilda strokes her chin, presumably thinking but it makes her look more like a cartoon villain. 'What if the blackmailer was writing Max letters, and when the money ran out the blackmailer somehow got the blind item published. It would have been an attempt to push Max into finding the money. When the rumours didn't swirl hard enough to put pressure on Max, they sent me the note in the hopes that I would investigate and expose Max for them.'

'I still think Max did this to himself,' Louis says solemnly. 'I agree that the blackmailer could have arranged somehow for this blind item to be published, but surely that would have been the final straw for Max? Knowing that people might figure out his secret and there's no money left to pay the blackmailer. He wouldn't have been able to bear the shame.' There is the faintest curl to his lip, and I realise that Louis isn't as accepting of Max and Jack as I hoped he might be. I remind myself that he's the product of a time when homosexuality was considered a criminal act, but I still have to fight the urge to lecture him.

'I think we need to—' I'm cut off as Louis slams on the brakes, causing Tilda to almost headbutt me over the back of the seat.

'Jiminy Cricket, Lou! You almost had us through the windscreen.' Tilda presses a hand to her forehead, as I try to calm my racing heart.

'There was…' Louis clutches the steering wheel, his face white. 'A person.'

Reaching for the door handle, I tumble out onto the road, the thick darkness only broken by the headlights further up the road. Movement comes from ahead and then the figure of a woman appears, one arm raised above her head in a wave.

'Is that…?' Tilda squints and then she's hurrying towards the woman, her hair flying and her feet slipping on the gravel road. 'Mae Sinclair? Is that you?'

Oh shit. What the hell is my newest charge doing on the deserted back roads, late at night, flagging down cars? Mae stumbles towards Tilda, and behind her I see the back of a car, skewed towards the ditch beside the road, deep gouges in the gravel made by the tyres.

'Mae? Are you all right?' I rush towards her, taking in her wild eyes and shaking hands. 'What happened?'

Mae shakes her head, unable to speak for a moment. Like the gentleman he is, Louis takes off his jacket and wraps it gently around her shoulders. 'Is that your car?' he asks gently. Mae nods, her teeth chattering. Her mascara has pooled in dark circles under her eyes, and her lipstick is long gone. Two spots of rouge stand out on her cheeks, as if they've been pinched sharply. 'I was just… Someone ran me off the road. I was driving back from…' She tails off. 'There were headlights in my rearview and they were getting closer and closer… I waved for them to go around but they sat on my tail and then slammed into the back of me, pushing me off the road.' She shudders, clutching Louis's jacket tightly around her.

'Did you see who it was?' I peer down the road, as if I will somehow be able to see who did this, but it is dark and silent.

'I didn't see. I didn't even see what car it was really, just their headlights in my rearview.'

Louis has stepped over to Mae's vehicle and is peering at the fender closely, scratching his chin. 'Definitely some damage done here,' he says with a low whistle. 'They pushed you right into that ditch. We can call a tow truck, but it's the middle of the night. Who knows how long you might be out here.'

Mae opens her mouth to speak, fear rippling over her features.

'We won't leave you here,' I say. 'We can give you a ride home and then we can wait while you call the tow truck. Or I can get Bunny to call and get it recovered in the morning. But really, Mae? We just need to get you into the warm and off the side of this road.'

Mae nods and Tilda and I help her to the car. She slides onto the backseat beside Tilda, and then I approach Louis, who is still inspecting the car.

'I'm no mechanic,' he says, 'but they definitely did a number on her. See here?' He points to the crumpled metal on the side of the car. 'They must have rammed her pretty hard to force her into the ditch like that.' He straightens up and looks me dead in the eye. A lock of dark hair has fallen over his forehead and my stomach flips. Maybe one day I'll be able to look at him without wishing everything was different. Maybe one day I'll be able to look at him without seeing a home, a ring, two little babies with his eyes and my hair.

'Lil?'

'Sorry.' I smile at him, shaking away thoughts of everything that might have been if I'd been born in the right decade.

'I said, do you have any idea who might have done this?'

I shake my head. 'No, none at all. As far as I can see on set, everyone likes Mae.'

'Yeah,' Louis says softly. 'Everyone liked Max too.'

The roar of tyres on the road behind us rips through the air, and then the twin beam of headlights rockets around the corner. The car – I can't see what make it is or who is behind the wheel – is going too fast, dust and tiny stones flying as it roars towards us.

'Lily, run!' Louis grabs my hand and we sprint to our own car, throwing ourselves into our seats. He guns the engine as the car roars past us.

'Oh my Lord!' Tilda shrieks as I sit back against my seat, my heart in my throat, my pulse clattering under my skin. 'I thought he was going to hit you!'

'Just a… a crazy kid on a backroad, Til, no need for dramatics,' Louis says, but his breath comes in little pants and he's gripping the steering wheel so tightly his knuckles are white.

'They swerved,' Mae says, her voice so small I can barely hear her.

'What?'

'They swerved towards you, they were trying to hit you,' she says, her eyes filling her face. 'They almost did hit you! It was the same car that ran me off the road, I'm sure of it.'

I press a hand to my chest, fear making it hard to draw in enough oxygen. 'You're sure?'

'Pretty sure. The headlights were the same shape. I couldn't tell you what make the car was, but they looked different to the usual shape.'

Louis's eyes are on the rearview mirror. 'Kinda like they were set into the fenders a little?'

'Yes,' Mae gasps. 'Exactly like that!'

My heart sinks as I look in the side mirror. Headlights are in the distance, gaining on us quickly, and I bite my lip. 'Lou?'

He gives a terse nod. 'I know. They must have pulled in to let us pass so they could get behind us again.' He presses his foot further to the floor and I see Mae's hand creep into Tilda's. Behind us, the headlights grow brighter, the full beam shining straight in through the rear window. The road ahead of us is winding with a steep gradient, carved into the hills with a sharp drop off on one side, without even the protection of brush and bushes, let alone a solid railing. It's a back road used by locals who want to head home away from the bright lights and occasional stop–start traffic on the boulevard, a supposed shortcut although the steep gravel track means it's impossible to drive fast safely. Despite that, we pick up speed, but the car behind is still gaining on us, the lights making it impossible to see who is behind the wheel.

It's on a straight stretch that the first bump comes. A tap against the rear bumper that causes Mae to shriek and Louis to curse under his breath. He presses the accelerator to the floor, the car starting to whine a little. The sheer drop on one side of the road whips past, and I swallow down the bile that rises in my throat at the thought of the tyres skidding on gravel, Louis's car crumpling like a cardboard box as we sail over the edge and hit the ground below. The car drops back a little and I catch my breath, my nerve endings singing.

'They're coming back,' Tilda whispers, fear lacing every word. She twists to look out of the back window, her hand still gripping Mae's tightly. 'Lou, they're coming back. They're going to run us off the road!'

'No, they're not,' Louis mutters through gritted teeth. He grips the steering wheel, his eyes never leaving the road as the speedometer inches further and further to the right. 'Hang on, ladies, as tight as you can.'

I grip the passenger door, my chest constricting as I see the bend looming ahead. Louis reaches out and flicks off his headlights, and I know for sure then that we're going to die. The road is twisty and we can't see a thing. Louis wrenches the wheel to the right, throwing us around the bend in the road, my head hitting the passenger window with a thump. The engine roars, and after a few seconds Louis eases off the gas.

'Everyone OK?' he asks, the faintest tremor to his voice.

'Uh, yeah,' Tilda's voice comes from the backseat. 'Way to go, Lou! We lost them!' She high-fives a wan-looking Mae. I look in the side mirror, still not sure we really have lost them, until I see the spiral of steam coming from the ditch on the other side of the road behind us.

'Don't worry, Lou,' Tilda says with a breathless laugh. 'I won't tell Mom you drove with your lights off.'

Chapter Seventeen

'Do you think she'll be all right?' I ask, once Mae is safely home, albeit with still slightly shaking hands and not a lick of colour in her cheeks, and the three of us are safely holed up in mine and Tilda's apartment.

'Who, Mae?' Louis looks up from where he sits on the floor, idly strumming his guitar. 'Sure. She's a plucky gal. Those lunatics might have run her off the road, but she sure was brave, flagging down our car. We could have been the ones to do it for all she knew.'

Tilda appears in the doorway from the bathroom, her red hair in rollers and her face slathered in cold cream. 'I'm just glad we all got home in one piece,' she says, a faint tremor to her voice. It's rare to see Tilda shaken – she's been through the mill more than once since I arrived in the past – and seeing her like this now makes my own nerve endings sing.

'I was thinking,' I say slowly, reaching for the mug of hot chocolate on the coffee table. Louis wanted to lace it with brandy, but I want to keep a clear head.

'Should we be worried?' Tilda makes a lame attempt at a joke that falls flat, as Louis lays down his guitar and scooches closer to me.

'I was thinking,' I say again, 'that we know Max was being blackmailed, right? And whoever was blackmailing him… there's a possibility that they somehow got this gossip published about him in the Last Word column.'

'I would say it's a strong possibility,' Tilda says, reaching for her own mug with cold-cream smeared fingers, the waft of brandy filling the air. 'That blind item seems to fit Max's situation perfectly.'

'So, people are saying that Max did this to himself, or it's a tragic accident, but it seems more likely that whoever this blackmailer is could have had a part in it…' I toss the idea around in my mind again, the thought that has been pressing against my brain since Tilda first brought the blind item clipping out of her purse. 'What if… Max isn't the only one?'

'Huh?' Louis frowns, his brow creasing in that adorable way it does when he's confused.

'What if Max isn't the only one?' I repeat, something sharp and bubbly zinging through my veins, chasing away the last vestiges of exhaustion. 'These blind items… There might have been more than one blackmail victim. Tilda, get your purse.'

Tilda hops up and grabs her bag, upending it over the coffee table. The envelope with the clippings spills out and she tugs them free, arranging them over the table so all are visible. My eyes land on the one that I am almost one hundred per cent sure is about Judy Holliday, and I skip over it, knowing that she's going to be just fine.

'What about this one?' Louis plucks one from the spread. 'Who do we think this one could be about?'

Running my eyes over the ink, I pass it to Tilda. It's something about *a rising blonde bombshell* posing for photos that aren't exactly family friendly. I remember a rumour about Marilyn Monroe posing for nude calendar photos and shake my head. Marilyn is safe, at least for now anyway.

'The one about the cigarettes… that meant drugs, right?' Louis scowls at the page in his hand. 'Who could that be about?'

Tilda scoffs. 'Half of Hollywood, Lou. Everyone is taking something, whether they admit to it or not.' She pauses, her brow furrowed as she stares at the clipping in her hand. 'Lil… if your theory is right, and the blackmailer really is behind what happened to Max, then might it make more sense to look at other people who have had accidents recently?'

Tilda's words hit me like a bolt of lightning. Of course, Max could be the first person to have refused to pay the blackmailer – that's if my theory is even correct. There's still a chance that Max just couldn't take the shame and the pressure of living a lie anymore, or it really could have been a tragic accident, but if it wasn't…

'Ann,' I breathe, that familiar tingle running through my body from my hair to the tips of my toes. 'What if Ann was being blackmailed too?' I think about the lighter we found at the top of the Hollywood sign, the way it wasn't covered in dust like everything else. 'What if the person who dropped the lighter was the person who was blackmailing her?'

—

Cliff is stepping out of a studio car as I arrive at work the next morning. I raise a hand in a brief wave, and he smiles.

'Hey, Cliff,' I say, my fingers going to the lighter in my skirt pocket. I haven't been able to stop thinking about Ann since we started putting together puzzle pieces last night. 'Just the guy I wanted to speak to.'

'Oh yeah?' Cliff smiles again, looking absurdly pleased. 'What can I do for you, Lily?'

'You've worked here a while, right? On other sets before Oskar promoted you to his assistant?' When Cliff nods, I pull out the lighter and hand it to him, watching as he turns it over in his hands. 'You don't happen to recognise this, do you?'

'Where did you get this?' Cliff peers at the inscription, his brow furrowing as he blinks.

I hesitate, not sure I want to reveal the fact that Louis, Tilda and I are digging into Ann's death. 'I… found it. I wanted to return it to its rightful owner, that's all.' I take the lighter back as Cliff shakes his head, and tuck it deep into my pocket again. 'Hey, are you all right?' Cliff looks pale, dark rings circling his eyes. He looks exhausted.

'Late night,' he says, his shoulders slumping. 'My mother called. She was… *under the weather*. She does that sometimes. The phone rings and then she's on at me about where I've been, who I've spoken to and what I've been eating. The calls can go on for a while and I usually come away feeling… a little worn down.'

Poor Cliff. 'I'm sorry. The last thing you need is me pouncing on you the moment you step out of the car.'

'You're not the problem, Lily. I should head inside, before Oskar arrives. Sorry I couldn't help with the lighter.' Cliff gives me a brisk smile and starts for the gates. I follow in his footsteps, giving a smile to Bobby as I sign in. Then I head for Bunny's desk.

'Morning, Bunny.' I smile at her as I tug off my cardigan and adjust the scarf I've tied at a jaunty angle around my neck. I will never, ever get bored of 1950s fashion, although at the same time I'm not sure what I'll do when my trusty Converse trainers give up the ghost.

Bunny looks up with a gasp, jumping slightly as she drops the sheet of paper she's holding to the floor. 'Oh, Lily! I didn't hear you come in.'

'Leonard's got you busy this morning.' I lean down to pick up the paper she dropped, but Bunny beats me to it, snatching the page up and crumpling it into a ball. 'Is there anything I can help you with before I get started?' I cross my fingers behind my back, hoping she'll say no. I have my own things I need to do before I head to make-up to fetch Tipsy and Mae.

'Always busy, Lily,' Bunny says curtly. 'You of all people should know that.'

'Right. Of course.' It's unusual for Bunny to be snappy. She's usually a perpetual ball of sugary sunshine, to the point that Tilda says she makes her teeth rot. 'Are you…?'

'I'm fine.' Bunny blinks, turning her attention back to her typewriter. 'I'll type up Leonard's messages and then you can bring them to him on set. The dialogue changes are ready to go too.'

'Thanks, Bun.' I give her an appreciative smile and wonder whether Lou, Tilda and I should invite her for a drink. Something doesn't feel quite right, and while Bunny can be annoying sometimes she is a very sweet girl and I hate the thought of her being upset.

'I'm sorry, Lil,' she says, sighing. 'Oskar keeps asking me to help out with things for this party he's throwing for Tipsy, and I feel a little overwhelmed… I mean, Cliff is supposed to be his assistant, but only for movie-related stuff it seems. Anything else — like entertainment and throwing parties — is women's work.' She rolls her eyes.

I had forgotten about the party for Tipsy, celebrating her twenty years in the business. I'm not entirely sure whether the party was Oskar's idea or whether Tipsy —

knowing her the way I do – demanded the party herself. Either way, it's set to be extravagant, loud and vibrant, just like Tipsy herself.

'Let me know if I can help with anything,' I say, before reaching for the telephone. 'I just need to make a quick call to the recovery company. Mae's car got rammed off the road last night.'

Bunny gasps, her cheeks draining of colour. 'Is she all right? Is she in the hospital?'

'She's fine but shaken up. I just need to get her car recovered to a local garage to get it fixed.'

Bunny flaps a hand in my direction. 'No, Lil, you have enough to do. At the very least I need you to get these pages to Leonard before call time. Let me telephone them. I can get Mae's car recovered.'

Blowing a kiss in Bunny's direction, I snatch up the pages she hands me and hurry out onto the lot. I'll be cutting it fine, but I just have time to slip into Ann's trailer before call time. Time to uncover if Ann Silver was hiding secrets from the world after all.

Chapter Eighteen

There is no weeping stand-in sitting on the steps of Ann's trailer this time, but the set is once again quiet. I was half expecting shooting to have resumed, but either they are filming on location today or everything is halted until they find Ann's replacement. Something about the idea of the movie going ahead – even though I know the studio needs things to make financial sense so that we're not all out of a job – makes me feel knotted up inside, as if we haven't given people enough time to grieve Ann before moving on.

Part of me is expecting her trailer to be cleared out but her name is still stencilled onto the door, and when I press down on the door handle it springs open and I am relieved to see the trailer is still full of Ann's things. The trailer is long and narrow, smaller than Tipsy's, the centrepiece the vanity table with a make-up mirror surrounded by bulbs. Powder compacts, lipsticks, a cake of mascara and a big bottle of perfume stand neatly on the vanity, a blonde wig draped over the edge of the mirror. The waste basket is full of tissues neatly daubed with the imprint of lipstick marks, and there is something about them that makes my heart twist in my chest. The idea that that small mark is the only real proof that Ann was a living, breathing person perhaps.

Moving on, I rifle through the costumes hung neatly on a rack on one side of the trailer. Blouses, skirts, a huge heavy fur coat. Although a part of me wrinkles inside at the idea of touching a dead animal, another part of me longs to run my fingers through the soft fur for a second time. There is another wig, a silver tray with a pitcher of water on it, the edges of the pitcher marked with a water stain where the level has dropped. The entire trailer has a sad, desperate air about it, the heeled sandals hastily discarded by the daybed giving the whole place a *Mary Celeste* vibe.

'Come on, Ann,' I mutter under my breath, aware of time marching on. I don't have long before Tipsy and Mae's call time, and I haven't even set eyes on them yet. 'If you've got a secret, let me find it.'

Standing back with my hands on my hips, I survey the trailer, trying to figure out where I would hide something if I were a famous movie star. The drawers in the vanity come up empty of anything scandalous, instead full of lipstick tubes, tissues and a couple of fan letters arranged neatly in piles. A stark contrast to Tipsy's chaotic trailer. Equally the pockets of her robe, hanging on the back of the trailer door, are empty too. There is a stack of books beside the daybed, and I step towards them. Was Ann a reader? According to this pile she was, although in my experience I've found that most actors on movies tend to spend any free time they have in their trailer going over their lines, but maybe Ann read to relax. Opening the first book, I flick through the pages but nothing falls out and there are no notes in the margins. The second book is the same, as is the third, but the bottom book in the pile feels different when I pick it up. Lighter. As though there aren't enough pages inside to match the spine. Glancing towards the door, I lick my lips, my mouth suddenly dry as I flip open the cover. I blink. It isn't a book at all, but a small jewellery box disguised as a book.

Why on earth would Ann hide her jewellery in a box designed to look like a book? Suspicion rumbles through my veins as I pick over the few items in the box. A small pair of stud earrings, gold but not real judging by the way they are tarnished. A tiny silver ring, the kind little girls get as a christening gift. A medal on a chain, a saint I don't recognise staring piously out at me. Underneath the jewellery is a pair of small, white gloves, the fingertips yellowing with age. But it's the final item in the box that gives me pause, and I reach in and lift it out.

It's a silver tiara, delicate but not ornate. The stones that catch the light as I turn it over in my hands glitter, but they are cheap paste gems, not real diamonds, which may explain why it isn't locked in a safe somewhere. The combs on either side that hold the tiara in the hair are slightly bent and there's something about it that doesn't seem quite right. My eyes go to the gloves, to the ivory white of the satiny fabric. *Could this be a wedding tiara? Could Ann have been secretly* married?

Before I can think much about it, the door to the trailer flies open and Tipsy is silhouetted against the door frame.

'Lily!' she gasps, clearly just as shocked to see me and I am to see her. 'What are you doing here?'

Getting to my feet, I slide the tiara into my skirt pocket and gently chide her. 'I could ask you the same question. You're supposed to be in make-up with Veronica. You're going to miss your call time.'

'Ha,' Tipsy huffs. 'I should be in make-up but that dunderhead Vic Romano showed up late, and seeing as his call time is before mine, Veronica gave him the chair. Car trouble, apparently, that was his excuse.'

'Car trouble? What kind of car trouble?' My chest tightens, my breath sticking in my throat. 'Did he have an accident?'

'Oh golly, I don't know.' Tipsy brushes past me towards Ann's wardrobe. 'He just said he had car trouble, although he could have just called for a studio car like the rest of us. That's what Oskar's boy did this morning, I heard him bragging about it to Bunny. I don't know why Vic insists on driving in every day like some… common—' She catches sight of my face. 'He could get a ride, that's all I'm saying.'

'That still doesn't explain why you're here in Ann's trailer.'

Tipsy has her head inside the small closet beside the costume rack. 'I was looking for these.' She backs out, holding a pair of black lace gloves above her head. 'Ann wore these for a scene and they are just to die for.' Tipsy doesn't seem to realise what she's said as I feel my mouth drop open. 'She said I could wear them for my party tonight, as long as I returned them before her call time the next morning… Obviously, I don't need to worry about that so much now. Poor, dear Ann.' She sniffs dramatically and fumbles for a handkerchief from her sleeve, the gloves still gripped tightly in her other hand.

'Well, I guess it doesn't…' I trail off as Tipsy turns to face me. 'What happened to your face?' There is a small cut right above Tipsy's eyebrow, an ugly pink slash that slices across her skin. Almost as if she's hit her head. I press my fingers to the lump and small cut on the side of my skull where my head hit the passenger window last night.

'Oh, this?' Tipsy points a finger to her eyebrow. 'Isn't it hideous? I hope Veronica can disguise it. I don't want an ugly old gash immortalised in my pictures forever.'

'But how did it happen?'

'Lily, really? Does it matter?' Tipsy makes a show of smoothing the gloves out and folding them together. 'It's nothing, just a tiny mark.'

It's not just a tiny mark. It's almost half an inch long and it must have bled a lot – it probably still hurts now. Before I can probe any further the trailer door flies open again, and Cliff appears.

'Why are you in here?' He looks at us both in confusion. 'You're both meant to be on set. Leonard is looking for you and Oskar... Well, let's just say Oskar is less than impressed that we're having to search for you before shooting can start.'

'Darling, please. Let's not be dramatic. We're not even late.' Tipsy drifts past him without a second glance, almost as if she is relieved to have an excuse to leave and escape from under my searchlight.

'Tipsy needs to get to make-up,' I say to Cliff. 'Her call time isn't for another hour.'

'Sorry, Lily.' He nods at me. 'I'm just following orders.'

I glance around the trailer one more time, making sure I'm not missing anything, my eyes snagging on the small space under the daybed. 'How did you think to look for us here?'

Cliff looks puzzled, his brow crinkling as he rubs at one eye with his ring finger and sniffs. I wonder if he has allergies, and if Piriton has been invented yet. 'Someone saw you walk this way, that's all. They said maybe you'd be here. Like I said, just following orders.' He gives me a beseeching look. 'I'm sorry, Lily, but do you mind if we hustle? Oskar is… Well, he's on the warpath.'

'OK.' I flash him a smile, also keen to leave Ann's trailer now. 'Sorry. I don't want you getting into trouble too.' Waiting for Cliff to exit, I turn and pull the trailer door closed behind me, catching sight of the navy-blue trunk stashed under the daybed as I do. I'd spotted it as I did my final glance over the trailer, but there was no way I was going to draw attention to it in front of Cliff and Tipsy. As I follow Cliff towards our own set my hand creeps into my pocket, brushing against the tiara. Instinct is telling me that the tiara was hidden for a reason… the question is, why?

Chapter Nineteen

Oskar hovers on set all day, meaning everyone is walking on eggshells and the little vein that pops out of Leonard's head when he's stressed is visible even after several cups of coffee and an afternoon's shooting that goes swimmingly. The only person who doesn't seem bothered by Oskar's presence is Tipsy, who beams her way through make-up touch-ups and retakes, clearly looking forward to her party.

Once the set is clear, I scoop up the production log for the day and head over to Oskar's office to drop it off before I can finally leave for the night, to go and get ready for Tipsy's party. My head is full of what I'm going to wear, and whether Tilda will help me with my make-up when raised voices slow my feet as I reach Oskar's office door.

'…useless?' Oskar's voice filters out through the closed door, full of venom and rage. 'What am I even paying you for?'

'Mr Goldstein—'

'It was a *simple* task, one that should have been easily completed by a *simpleton*.' There is a snort of disgust. 'Get out. I can't even look at you.'

Before I can scramble away from the door, it flies open and a red-faced Cliff appears, the door swinging shut behind him as he walks past with a brief, shame-filled glance in my direction. Looking down at the production log in my hands, I shove it under my arm and hurry after Cliff.

'Cliff? Cliff, wait a second.'

Cliff stops under a blinking streetlight between two sound stages, his shoulders heaving.

'Gosh, are you OK? I'm sorry, I couldn't help but overhear.' I hold up the logs. 'I didn't mean to eavesdrop. I was bringing these to Oskar.'

Cliff pushes his glasses up his nose, his cheeks still a burnt pink. 'He's so... so...'

'Yeah. I know. What happened for him to speak to you like that?'

'I misplaced a memo. An important one. I put it in with the general files instead of locking it away and Oskar flipped on me. He said anyone could have got hold of the information on there, and he was right.'

I place a hand on his arm and squeeze reassuringly. 'You're not useless – anyone could have misplaced a memo. Hell, I've done it before, more than once! Oskar is just... a handful, that's all. He flies off the handle. You're not the only one he yells at, even though that doesn't make it right.'

Cliff sighs. 'Maybe I'm letting him get to me too much, but he touched a nerve. I didn't mean to misfile it, but... What if he fires me? What will I tell my family? My *mother*?'

'Your mother?' I frown. 'Why would she be angry?' Cliff is a grown man, not a child.

'You don't know my mother,' Cliff says gloomily.

'Listen, Oskar isn't going to fire you over a memo. That would be ridiculous. And you know what he's like. All fire and brimstone. Don't take it to heart too much.'

Cliff nods, but his mouth is downturned and he blinks, as though holding back tears. 'He just said all the things my mother says about me. Maybe I shouldn't have taken this job. Maybe it's all too much.' He pauses. 'It's not like I'm being well paid. My mother reminds me of that too. She's always keen to let me know on her evening calls that not only am I useless, I'm also not worth half the amount my father is.'

My heart breaks a little at the crack in his voice as he gives me a small smile that doesn't reach his eyes. 'You're not useless, Cliff,' I say. 'In fact, you've been nothing but helpful to me. And you do have one thing that Oskar doesn't.'

'What's that?'

I grin. 'I actually like you.'

—

An hour later, Louis toots the car horn outside the apartment, and I scurry downstairs to meet him, ready to head to the hotel to celebrate Tipsy with him as my plus one. He's finally got the message that I don't need him to come up to the apartment to collect me every time, but I still smile as he opens the car door for me.

'You look lovely,' he says, taking in my outfit. I've borrowed a dress from Bunny, a strapless number by Christian Dior that she bought on her father's credit account, apparently. The bodice is fitted, in a deliciously rich shade of cream with a bow tied under the bosom, before the skirt switches to a velvety black, sweeping down to my feet. I feel like a million dollars.

'Thank you. You don't look so bad yourself.' Louis is wearing a traditional tux, his hair slicked back with a pomade that smells of sandalwood and bergamot.

'No Tilda?' He glances over my shoulder before closing my door and coming round to the driver's side.

'She left already with Ty. She said she'll meet us there.' Tilda's sort-of boyfriend is a police dispatcher, and I wonder if she's pumping him for information about Max and Ann as we speak.

Conversation is light on the ride to the Hollywood Roosevelt, where the party is being held tonight. I'm not sure if it's just me, but since Louis and I agreed to be just friends, things feel a little awkward sometimes when we're alone. As if there are things the two of us want to say but know we never can. Sometimes I wonder what would happen if I just told him the truth – that I was born in 1995, that I came here through some weird missed stitch in time. I sigh. Even if I did tell him the truth, it still wouldn't mean we could be together. Instead, I just give him little sidewards glances as he drives, the glow of the streetlamps illuminating his profile.

Pulling up outside the Hollywood Roosevelt, Louis tosses the car keys to the valet, and I step out onto the sidewalk, checking to make sure I still have Ann's tiara tucked into my clutch. A red carpet has been rolled out from the slightly tired façade of the hotel, and I spot some of Hollywood's finest milling about, as flashbulbs pop and reporters call out to grab the attention of the guests. The Hollywood Roosevelt isn't the kind of place I was expecting Tipsy to choose for her twentieth anniversary party – there are grander places in Hollywood for sure, the Beverly Hills Hotel being one – but I can see why she chose it. The twelve-storey building stands out against the boulevard's skyline, tall and elegant, and despite the slightly tired air about it, it still shimmers with glamour. The cream-coloured stucco on the outside of the building is less fresh than I imagined, but the red-tiled roof set off by the wrought-iron balconies and arched windows below more than makes up for it.

'Ready?' Louis holds out an arm and I slip mine through. Vic Romano struts down the red carpet ahead of us, a blonde I don't recognise on his arm. It's only as we approach the ballroom from the lobby that I spot the huge cameras.

'Louis, wait.' My feet slow and my stomach rolls. I didn't realise the event was being televised, and now fear spikes in my veins. What will happen if I'm caught on film forty years before I've even been born?

'Lil, what is it?' Louis follows my gaze. 'The cameras? Surely you're not shy?' He gives a huff of laughter, as if he already knows the answer to that.

'No, it's just...' There is a commotion behind us, and I turn to see Elizabeth Taylor on the carpet behind us with her new husband Michael Wilding. Behind them, Marilyn Monroe is graciously smiling and waving, although the reporters seem more excited by the fact that Joe DiMaggio is on her arm. I realise that this might be the first time Marilyn and Joe have been officially seen out together, and I manage to stifle my starstruck feelings at being in the same room as Marilyn for just long enough to slip into the ballroom behind her and Joe, fairly confident that the TV cameras will have been focusing on them, not me and Louis.

The ballroom is warm and inviting, despite the carpet reminding me of the Overlook Hotel in *The Shining*. The walls are a cream plaster, accented by dark wooden beams, and there is a polished hardwood square in the centre of the room that serves as a dancefloor. A band has set up on the raised stage at the other end of the room, already singing about the loveliest night of the year. The lighting is soft and forgiving, so many of Tipsy's guests being older stars of Hollywood, and the thick scent of a dozen different perfumes hangs in the air. Mae stands with Vic Romano and his girl, laughing at something Vic has said – something scandalous, no doubt. I remember what Tipsy said about him having car trouble and my stomach lurches. *Could he have been the one to try and run Mae off the road?* Watching them laughing together now it seems ridiculous to think that Vic could have had any part in Mae's accident. Cliff and Veronica enter, Veronica clinging tightly to Cliff's arm. Cliff looks much more his usual self and I'm glad, not wanting Oskar's tirade to dampen his evening. He looks down at Veronica, who gazes adoringly back at him, adding fuel to Tipsy's theory that they are very much a couple. They weave their way through the throng of guests toward Vic and Mae, and Vic leans down to whisper something in Veronica's ear that makes her blush. Cliff puts his hand on Mae's elbow and I watch as she smiles tightly at him, before extricating herself and heading towards a waiter holding a tray of champagne saucers, snatching up one for herself and one for James Stewart, who takes it with a look of surprise. The entire room is a who's who of Hollywood – from James Dean to Clark Gable, from Grace Kelly to Humphrey Bogart. There's no sign of Tipsy yet, but there is one face I am thrilled to see.

'Tilda!' I wave at her across the room and she runs lightly across the carpet without spilling a single drop of her dirty martini, Ty trailing behind her.

'What a turnout,' Tilda says after she's kissed us hello. 'I'm glad Tipsy invited me personally, instead of having to work… Although I'm not saying I won't be listening to any conversations this evening.' She winks at me and I roll my eyes.

'Listen, Ty, would you mind grabbing me a drink?' I turn to Tilda's on/off boyfriend. 'I'd love a Tom Collins if you can get someone to fix me one.'

Tilda watches Ty hurry away before she turns back to me. 'OK, what do you want to tell us? You weren't exactly subtle there.'

'You know me too well.' Reaching into my purse, I pull out the small silver tiara. Lou and Tilda lean in over it. 'I found this in Ann's trailer, hidden inside a jewellery box disguised as a book. I got the feeling it might be important... I mean, when I say hidden, I mean *hidden*. The pages were hollowed out completely. I thought it was an actual book until I opened the cover.'

'Oh.' Tilda presses a hand to her mouth as she runs her eyes over the tiara.

'Golly,' Louis breathes. 'This is... Well, very unexpected. I thought she was from Kansas or Ohio, somewhere like that? Somewhere that grows corn.'

'What's so unexpected?' I look from one sibling to the other, my frustration mounting. 'What's so special about this tiara? I found a pair of gloves too, ivory and satin. Very bridal. I was thinking that perhaps she'd been married and that was her secret—'

Tilda widens her eyes at Louis. 'Ann wasn't married,' Louis hisses, as he peers over my shoulder, checking we are not overheard. 'And she wasn't from Ohio. She was *Mexican.*'

Now they've really lost me.

'This tiara...' Tilda turns it over in her hands, the silver crown seeming smaller than I remember it. 'Along with the gloves you found... Was there anything else?'

I pause, thinking. 'Uh… Some earrings, little gold studs. And a chain with a kind of medal on it. It had some kind of saint engraved on it.'

Tilda raises an eyebrow. 'This would be from Ann's quinceañera, Lily. Not her— Oh, hi, Bunny.'

Whipping the tiara out of sight, I smile at Bunny as she approaches. She looks radiant in a pale pink gown, her hair plaited into a crown.

'What are y'all doing?' Her eyes go to my side, where the tiara is pressed into the depths of my voluminous skirt.

'Just waiting on drinks,' I say. 'Who are you here with?'

Bunny shakes her head. 'Nobody. I did have a date but he let me down at the last minute, and there's no way I'm missing this party – not after all the hard work I put in. It's not like Oskar would let me miss it anyway.' She sighs. 'And technically I am working this evening, so no matter that I don't have a date.'

'At least let me get you a drink,' Louis says, smoothly putting his arm around her and steering her away, leaving Tilda and I to the tiara.

Once Bunny is safely out of earshot, I flash the crown again. That's what was bugging me about it – the quality of the crown. It's cheap and flimsy, like something you'd buy at Claire's Accessories. Not the kind of quality a bride would expect on her wedding day. 'Mexican? But like Louis said, wasn't Ann Silver from Oklahoma or some such… Oh.' It dawns on me then, the horrible reality. 'The studio lied about her background, about her whole identity. They pitched her as an all-American girl, when really she wasn't even American at all.' That explains the horrible dye job on her hair, the blonde wigs left in her trailer. She must have worn them once her roots started growing out.

'Ann Silver was supposed to be the perfect American doll,' Tilda says, just as shocked as Louis judging by the expression on her face. 'From her very first movie the studio had her down as the perfect girl next door – the girl the rest of us should aspire to be. Pretty, polite and patriotic. But looking at this… She was *Mexican*. This tiara would have been from the celebrations when she turned fifteen. She would have worn it with the gloves, the medal and a huge, extravagant dress.'

'It explains why there was no huge fancy funeral. When the studio said her parents had taken her home to bury her, we all assumed Oklahoma, but they took her back to Mexico.' Saliva spurts into my mouth, hot and sour. I feel nauseous at the fact that Ann had to hide who she really was to fit in. *Did she have any choice at all in the matter? Or was she truly prepared to die to cover up who she really was?*

Tilda is speaking, but I can't take in what she's saying as I catch sight of a familiar face, his moustache wiggling as he talks. 'Til, you know that guy?'

'Him?' She cranes her neck to get a better view of the guy I've seen sneaking around Bunny's office, the guy who reminds me of Tom Selleck. 'I think his name is Freddy. I've seen him around but I'm not entirely sure who he is or what he does.'

'Can you find out?'

'Sure. You think he might be related to all this?'

I shake my head. 'I don't know, but I've seen him sloping around on set a couple of times now, but only since all this stuff started with the Last Word column. I'd just feel a little better if I knew who he was and what he's doing at the studio.'

Tilda nods in agreement. 'No problem. I'll dig up whatever I can.' There is a commotion then and Tipsy makes a grand entrance on Oskar's arm, smiling and waving, air kissing her way into the room. She looks radiant, and the gash on her head is barely noticeable.

The rest of the evening goes off without a hitch, the dancefloor filled with glamorous couples as the big band play old favourites all night. I dance with James Dean, although he doesn't seem to remember that we've met before, and Grace Kelly spills her gin on my skirt, but my heart only truly skips a beat when Louis asks me to dance with him. He whirls me around the dancefloor to an old Nat King Cole song, my heart thumping hard in my chest as I breathe him in, his arm gripping my waist. We spin past Tilda and Ty, Tilda scolding Ty for having his hands too low on her back, and then past Bunny in her pink dress.

'Wait, Lou.' I accidentally stand on his foot as I try to manoeuvre him back to where Bunny is huddled in a corner with Cliff. Her cheeks are pinker than the fabric of her dress, and as I catch sight of her again, she looks as if she might cry. 'Bunny and Cliff are over there.'

Louis spins me so he is facing them. 'You think she's OK?' His breath is warm against my ear.

'I guess we just dance our way over and find out.' Twirling our way towards the darkened corner, we sink into the chairs against the wall, closest to Bunny and Cliff.

'…that's not what I…' Bunny's voice is barely audible. I lean down to fiddle with the strap on my shoe, leaning in her direction discreetly. '…you said.'

Cliff puffs on a cigarette, the smoke swirling around his head in a grey-blue cloud that tickles the back of my throat. 'Bunny, you know…' He turns his head, his eyes widening as he catches sight of Louis and me perched on the chairs, clearly trying to listen.

Bunny grips the sleeve of his suit jacket. 'Yes, I know, of course I know, but—'

'We'll talk about this later,' Cliff says in an urgent whisper, tugging his sleeve free as he pushes past Bunny and hurries out of the ballroom, weaving his way between dancing couples. Veronica turns to watch, making her excuses to Donna Reed before following Cliff from the room.

Louis reaches for Bunny, wrapping an arm around her shoulder as she blinks, tears glistening on the ends of her lashes. 'You OK, sweetheart?'

Bunny nods, and it's only when she speaks that I realise she's not upset, she's furious. 'If only all men were like you, Louis,' she says, pressing her lips together. 'I'm quite all right, thank you. But I am in need of a drink!'

With that, she marches away. Before I can ask Louis what he thinks all that was about, Tilda descends on us, her eyes bright with excitement or dirty martinis. I'm not sure which.

'The blind item,' Tilda hisses in a loud whisper as she reaches us. 'It came to me when the band started playing that old Gene Autry song.' She hums a few tuneless bars of a song I don't recognise. 'Remember? The blind item that mentioned a star whose roots might have been more *south of the border*? That could have referred to Ann, if someone found out where she was really from.'

'Holy shit.'

'Language, Lil.' Tilda slugs back the dregs of her dirty martini, handing her empty glass to a passing waiter. 'You think Ann could have been blackmailed too?'

'There's one way we could find out.' I need to get back into Ann's trailer and see what's inside that trunk.

Chapter Twenty

Part of me wants to sneak away to Ann's trailer now, while everyone is too busy having fun at the party to notice my absence. But then Leonard is tapping me on the shoulder and asking where Bunny is, and I find myself stepping into her shoes for the rest of the evening, making sure the band has refreshments when they take a break and ensuring Tipsy is having the best time.

'*Wonderful,*' she slurs, wrapping an arm around my neck when I ask her, almost suffocating me with her heavy perfume. 'Just wonderful, darling. And look at all my friends.' She sweeps an arm across the room, stumbling slightly. Thank God the cameras are gone for the evening now. 'I don't need silly little gossip items in the newspaper to make me popular. I'm already a star. The things I could tell you about these people!'

'What do you mean?'

Tipsy hiccups. 'Darling, you don't know *the half* of what goes on in this town. Look at him.' She gestures drunkenly towards Oskar. 'He's not as perfect as he makes out, let me tell you.'

I want her to tell me more, but she spots Ingrid Bergman across the room and swoops on her, calling out to her about 'those dear little babies'. Remembering that Ingrid has just had twins thanks to her scandalous relationship with Roberto Rossellini, I leave her to it, hunting down Louis and Tilda who I find huddled together in the lobby.

'So this is where you two have got to.' People are beginning to drift away from the party now, and I become aware how much my feet are aching.

'Just bringing Lou up to speed with things,' Tilda says. 'He agrees that it's possible Ann could have been black-mailed.'

'It makes sense,' Louis says. 'Kate told us that while she thought Ann wasn't depressed, she had been a bit quieter over the previous few weeks. I know she might have been able to hide it, but Kate knew her so well that I think she would have picked up on the fact that something was wrong. And then there's the tiara. Hollywood might have tried to take it from her, but her true identity clearly meant a lot to Ann. Do you think she would have done that to her parents?'

I shake my head. 'And the lighter – I think someone was up there on the Hollywood sign with Ann. If we can find out who the lighter belongs to, we'll be a step closer to finding that out.' I look around at the stream of guests leaving, most of them tipsy and laughing. 'Where's Bunny? Is she all right? I think there might be something going on between her and Cliff.'

Louis nods. 'She's furious with Cliff, but she wouldn't go into detail. Just called him a snake and then marched into the ladies' room.'

'I checked on her,' Tilda reassures me. 'She's all right, but she was all undone. I told her to leave and said we would fix it if Oskar asked where she was.'

Thankfully Oskar has been too in his cups to even notice Bunny's absence. 'Tomorrow night,' I say to the others, as we head out of the lobby towards the valet.

'After shooting has finished. Meet me in the back lot and we'll go to Ann's trailer and see if we can find anything that points to her being blackmailed.'

–

Tipsy is not the only decidedly green face I see on my way to pick up messages from my office in the morning. Even Leonard seems subdued, pressing his fingers to his temples before slurping a large black coffee. The party was such a roaring success that no one stopped to think about the morning after and the fact that we will still be shooting – Oskar is hellbent on getting this movie made on time, and he doesn't care who's hungover. My first stop is my office, or more specifically, Bunny's desk. She is behind her desk when I arrive, but the only thing in front of her is her typewriter.

'Bunny? Are you all right?' I hover in her eyeline as she drags her gaze up to meet mine. She gives a faint smile.

'Fine. Tired, you know, after the party.' She leans down and opens a drawer, starting to rummage through it as if too busy to talk.

'You are OK though? I know you were upset last night. Tilda told me she sent you home.'

Bunny doesn't stop rummaging. 'I could have stayed, I was fine.' She doesn't look up, but I can see her cheeks flushing a dark pink.

'Was it Cliff? Did he do something to upset you? The two of you seemed—'

'Sorry, Lil, did you want something? I'm terribly busy this morning.'

I pause, eventually deciding not to press the issue. Bunny will talk when she's ready. 'No, all good. Just...

checking in.' Bypassing her desk, I spend an hour sorting through the messages that have come through, leaving most of them on Leonard's desk, and confirming today's shooting schedule, cross-checking who is called when and what wardrobe requirements they have, and typing up the minutes of Leonard and Oskar's last meeting. The entire time, my mind wanders back to Ann and what really might have happened to her.

'I'm going to drop these minutes off to Oskar's office and then get Tipsy and co to set on time,' I say to Bunny, my eyes on the pages in my hand as I walk back into the corridor. 'Oh.'

Cliff is backing out of the room, Bunny staring at him with wide eyes, her cheeks no longer flushed. Now, she looks pale and pallid, and she grips the water glass in her hand until her knuckles are white.

'Cliff was just leaving,' Bunny says, with a slight lift of her chin before she cuts her eyes to me. 'Please could you take these to Oskar too, Lily.' She puts down the glass and hands me a sheaf of papers.

'Sure.' I hover for a moment, wondering if Bunny will tell me what's wrong, but she turns back to her desk and rolls a fresh page into her typewriter. Clearly there is something going on between Bunny and Cliff. If he's led her on while he's involved with Veronica, I'll be furious with him. Hurrying down the corridor, I spot Cliff's lanky frame pushing open the outer doors to the lot. While Bunny clearly doesn't want to talk about it, if this guy is screwing around with her heart then I won't stand for it.

'Cliff?' Catching up to him, I match his stride, even as he lengthens it.

'Yes? Oh, Lily. Hi.' He smiles at me, as if he didn't just leave Bunny shaken in her office.

'You and Veronica… You're dating, aren't you?' I give him a grin. 'At least, that's the rumour flying around on set.'

Cliff pauses and finally looks me in the eye. 'Yes. What of it? Oskar knows about it, and he doesn't mind.'

I lean in close, so close I can see the fresh stubble sprouting on the underside of his jaw. 'I don't know what the deal is with you and Bunny, but she's my friend.'

Cliff shakes his head. 'Oh no, Lily, you've got the wrong idea.'

'Have I?' I tilt my head, studying him closely, but his face is impassive, just a hint of pink shading his cheeks. 'If I have, then I'm sorry.'

'Bunny and I… We're just friends. Barely even friends. I mean, I hardly know her.' Cliff swallows, blinking rapidly.

'Well, all right. Whatever it is, just be gentle with her, please. I've seen you going in and out of her office. Don't make promises you won't be able to keep. She's very dear to me, you understand?'

Before Cliff can respond Veronica appears, carrying the small leather case that she keeps her make-up in. 'Oh, there you are.' She beams at Cliff, reaching up to plant a small kiss on his cheek. 'Lovely party last night, wasn't it, Lily?'

I nod, keeping my eyes on Cliff as his hand goes around Veronica's waist. 'Certainly was. You look much fresher than the rest of us do today.'

Veronica flashes her dimples at me, as Cliff takes her case and then clasps her other hand tightly. Veronica blushes. 'Isn't he a gentleman? Thank you, Cliff.'

'A real gentleman,' I say. And to be fair, Cliff is – as long as he's not stringing Bunny along. 'I'll leave you two lovebirds to it.' And I sweep on ahead, all the way to Oskar's office.

–

'Hello?' After knocking twice and receiving no response, I gently push open the door to Oskar's overdone office, expecting to find it empty. Instead, Oskar is behind the huge mahogany desk, his face beetroot red as he fumbles to close his desk drawer.

'Can't you knock, Miss Jones?'

'I did. Twice. I'm sorry, I assumed you weren't here.' My feet sink into the plush carpet as I make my way to his desk.

'*Assume* makes an ass of you and me, Miss Jones.' Oskar mops at his sweaty forehead and runs a finger around the edge of his collar. *Ew.* Pit stains show at the edge of his shirt and right now I am *assuming* I've caught Oskar looking at something he shouldn't have been.

'Are you OK, Mr Goldstein? You seem very flushed and it is awfully hot in here.' I move to the window on the pretence of opening it, trying to peer behind his desk to figure out what he was actually up to.

'Fine,' he blusters, tucking his hanky away and reaching for a cigar. He snips the end off and lights it, blowing a plume of thick grey smoke in my face. 'What is it you want, Miss Jones?'

I hand him the pages Bunny gave me and the minutes of the last meeting. He pulls open the drawer to fetch his glasses and I catch a glimpse of a small red book, open and filled with his scratchy handwriting. It's impossible to read upside down, but it looks like notes in some sort of code, figures and letters intertwined. One of the names looks familiar, but the writing is barely legible, and I tilt my head to try and decode it. Catching my gaze drifting downwards, Oskar slams the drawer with a huff.

'Will that be all?'

'Just wanted to let you know that we're starting with scene twenty-seven inside the house this morning and then moving to stage nine to shoot the exterior scenes after lunch.' Giving Oskar a respectful nod, I turn and make my way out of his stifling office, thinking about the little red book and how keen Oskar was to hide it. Could Oskar be turning his hand to writing screenplays? Or a memoir, perhaps? Coding his writing so no one steals it. The idea makes me want to laugh, but it soon dies as I think of something more sinister. Was that Max's name I saw in the notebook? Surely Oskar Goldstein couldn't be the one behind the Last Word column? Another thought strikes me, even more sinister than the last. It couldn't be *Oskar* blackmailing Hollywood stars, could it?

Chapter Twenty-One

Filming is a shambles, and it's not just the fact that everyone – crew included – is nursing stonking hangovers. My mind is distracted, thinking over the way Oskar shoved the little red book into his drawer as I entered his office. Could he really be the one writing the blind items? In part it would make sense – who better to have all the industry knowledge? But that's where the idea falls flat. Oskar may have all the information, but as a studio exec, he's the one most likely to want to keep the scandals under wraps. I can't see him blackmailing anyone either. Surely he wouldn't risk his job for a few extra dollars?

Tipsy is late, her hand shaking as she tries to light a cigarette (although I think that is down to a hangover rather than Leonard's ferocious roar when she eventually turned up on set), and when the time comes for Mae and Vic to shoot together the two of them can barely look at each other.

'What the hell is going on?' I mutter to Tipsy as we wait in the wings, Tipsy's script on my lap as I try and help her brush up on her lines.

'Again!' Leonard shouts, the cigarette at the corner of his mouth wiggling furiously. 'Places, you two – and for Pete's sake let's see some damn chemistry this time.'

Mae hits her mark, and this time when Vic places his hand on her shoulder I see her entire body stiffen. She shifts, turning her face to his, a fleeting expression crossing her features before Leonard calls cut again.

'Take a break,' he says. 'Go get a cigarette, a drink, splash water on your face. I don't give a damn what you do as long as you get back here in ten minutes and be ready to damn well *act*.' He sweeps past us, slamming the door to the set behind him. Vic steps aside, a smirk on his face as Veronica homes in on him and starts patting at his face with powder.

The moment Vic steps away from her, Mae relaxes, her features softening. I turn to see if Tipsy has noticed, but she's snapping her fingers in the direction of Cliff.

'Boy!' she calls, clearly having forgotten his name. 'Yes, you, boy. Bring me the newspaper.'

Cliff snatches up the paper and brings it over, a smile etched onto his face. Watching the way Veronica's eyes flick towards him, and still feeling aggrieved at the way he seems to be upsetting Bunny, I head over to Mae, collecting a cold bottle of Pepsi and a banana on my way.

'Here.' I hand them both to her. 'You look like you could use the sugar.'

'That bad?' A feeble puff of laughter escapes Mae's lips as she takes the bottle, her eyes gazing over my shoulder as she does.

'What's with the two of you this morning?' I know Vic is behind me, know exactly where Mae's eyes are landing.

'What? Nothing. Did he say something to you?' Mae's eyes are wide as she sips from the bottle of Pepsi.

'No, but you two are weird with each other today. Usually you set the screen alight, the tension between the two of you is crackling, but today...' Today something is off. I know it and Mae knows it too.

'It's just a hangover, Lily. That's all. We all drank too much at the party last night.' She holds the bottle aloft. 'I'll be fine once I've had this. A sugar high is all I need.' Her eyes go to Vic again, and I feel a spark of something tug at my belly.

'Is it Vic? Did he do something?' Vic's car trouble springs to mind, and my heart lurches. Was it Vic trying to run Mae off the road? Did something happen after the party, something that convinced Mae that Vic was responsible? Before Mae can answer, Tipsy is calling my name, yoo-hooing at me from the edge of the set.

'Sorry, Mae. We'll talk later?' Excusing myself, I head over to where Tipsy sits at a rickety table, one of the props for the living room scene. 'What is it, Tipsy?'

Tipsy shakes the newspaper at me, her eyes wild and a grin to match. 'You *have* to see this,' she hisses, the air of gossip thick around her. 'Look.' She hands me the paper and watches in delight as I scan the front page.

'Well,' I say eventually, my heart sinking. 'I guess we know why these two are stumbling this morning.' The photograph on the front page is of Vic leaving the party last night, Mae tucked under his arm in a way that can only be described as cosy.

'I guess it wouldn't be a big deal,' Tipsy says with an affected air of nonchalance, 'if the girl Vic arrived at the party with last night wasn't supposed to be his fiancée.' My own eyes must widen as Tipsy nods, her face alight with the joy of sharing news that isn't common knowledge. 'He proposed to her last month, although nothing has been formally announced. Of course Hedda Hopper knew all about it – most of us did, in an open-secret kind of way – but now the world is about to see Vic Romano as a cheater, not the hero he longs to be.' Tipsy sits back and folds her arms in satisfaction.

'Tipsy, come on,' I chide her. 'This could be completely innocent. What did Oskar say about rumours and gossip on set? You'll get us all fired at this rate.' Oskar has tried to impose a media ban on the studio but it's almost impossible to enforce, as the newspaper in Tipsy's hands proves.

'The evidence is right there in front of you.'

'A photograph is not evidence,' I say, realising how ridiculous it sounds as the words leave my mouth. Tipsy must realise that just because a photograph exists, it doesn't mean the context is right – she's been in the newspapers enough times herself. 'Vic could have just given her a ride home. Or got Mae out past the photographers if they were giving her a hard time.'

Tipsy shrugs. 'Maybe. Or maybe they were just heading home to *practise their lines.*' Tipsy drops me a lascivious wink and reaches for the paper, but I hold it above my head.

'Tipsy Jenner, you need to stop,' I say, shaking my head. 'I'm going to hide this newspaper in your trailer before you get us all fired, and *you* are going to sit here quietly and hope that Mae and Vic nail this scene, before Leonard loses his head.'

Tipsy's trailer is just as much of a tip as it was the last time I was in here, and I groan internally. Leonard is such a stickler for perfection that I think if he walked in here and saw the state of the place, he might have a heart attack. Scooping a bunch of tangled stockings from the floor and placing them on the end of the daybed, I move to the small desk to stuff the newspaper into a drawer. It would be just my luck that Oskar will decide to drop by on Tipsy later, and if he sees she's broken the media ban, she'll have no problem with dropping me in it and telling him I brought the paper to her trailer.

'Jeez, Tipsy.' As I open the drawer, it erupts with hair clips, costume jewellery and pages of scrawled hand-writing. At first I think they're fan letters, but when I run my eyes over the pages I realise it's something else entirely. Written in violet ink, in sprawling, feminine writing that I recognise as Tipsy's, words leap out from the page at me. *Scandalous. Vicious. He asked me to marry him even though he was already engaged. She left more than her dignity in Reno.* What is this? A novel? Her memoir? A tell-all exposé of her life in Hollywood? Names leap off the page, and a sour taste fills my mouth. Tipsy loves gossip, that's no secret and of all the people on set she seems to be the one who revels in it the most, but some of what's written here has a spiteful edge to it. She describes one unnamed actress as 'attention-seeking and fame-hungry', which doesn't seem so bad until she refers to her as sleeping her way to the top. *Could this be referring to Ann?* I remember what Tilda said about there being rumours that Ann had slept her way to the top and I press my hand to my mouth. I had thought Tipsy only had good things to say about Ann. It feels bitchy and underhand, and I drop the pages back into the drawer as if they have burned me. I always thought Tipsy's love of gossip was just harmless fun, but what if it's not? What if she's been using her knowledge to blackmail the stars of Hollywood?

–

Mae and Vic seem more relaxed as we shoot through the afternoon, although there is still something in the air between them that doesn't seem quite right. Tipsy makes several cutting comments under her breath about the two of them, and where before I might have nudged her and told her to hush, now I leave that to Bunny and busy myself with jotting down continuity notes until finally Leonard calls cut.

'Darling, let's get drinks,' Tipsy says, stopping me as I'm about to leave the set. 'I'll just hop along to my trailer and change and then you and I can head over to Browns for a cocktail.' She leans in close. 'We can talk about Mae and Vic and what the *real* story is there.'

'There is no story, Tipsy,' I say, on my guard and very aware of Vic jovially calling out his goodbyes to the rest of the crew. 'Just idle gossip. I can't come for drinks anyway, I'm afraid. I already have plans.'

'Oh.' Tipsy's face falls. 'Well, no bother. I'm very busy anyway, plenty to do. Lots of people to see.' She flashes me a brief smile and turns on her heel, hurrying away towards her trailer and leaving me feeling oddly guilty, although I'm not sure why.

It's easy to be invisible when you are a woman who *isn't* an actress on a film set, and even easier when you're the director's assistant and can move around the place freely. It's not long before everyone else has left, and I make my way across the lot to Ann Silver's trailer. As I reach it, Louis and Tilda pop out from behind, an old camera slung around Louis's neck.

'Do I need to ask about the camera?' I say, no greeting needed.

Tilda grins. 'Just a prop in case Bobby wasn't on the gate. If it was the new guy we were going to tell him that I was here to conduct an interview and Louis was my photographer, so we had to make it look authentic.' Tilda beams with pride. 'It was my idea. And it's Dad's camera.'

'And did you need it?'

'Uh, no.' Louis gives me a sheepish grin. 'Bobby just let us straight through when we said we were meeting you.'

Somehow the two of them always seem to lighten my mood, even when it's been a rough day. After informing them about the notebook in Oskar's office and the pages in Tipsy's trailer, Tilda pulls out her notebook and starts scribbling. 'This could be important, Lil,' she says before I can ask what she's doing. 'You really think Tipsy could be behind the blackmail?'

I shrug. 'I don't know. I never would have said she was vindictive like that but… some of what she'd written was pretty harsh. If it's a memoir she's writing I'm not sure anyone would ever have the nerve to publish it.' Footsteps echo across the lot behind us, and I turn back to Ann's trailer. 'We'd better get in and out of here before anyone finds us.'

Ann's name stencil has been removed from the door, and when I press down on the handle it doesn't budge. 'It's locked.'

'Not for long.' Tilda pushes me out of the way and pulls a bobby pin from her hair. Bending it to the right angle, she shoves it into the lock and wiggles until the handle turns under her hand. 'I've been practising,' she says with a wink, standing to one side to let me and Louis inside.

Stepping into the trailer, my heart sinks. While the daybed and vanity dresser remain, anything personal that belonged to Ann is gone, including the trunk under the bed.

'It's cleared out,' I say, disappointment bitter on my tongue. 'The trunk is gone. There's no way we can find out what Ann was hiding now.'

'Really?' Tilda raises an eyebrow. 'Come on, Lily. It's not like you to give up so easily. Ann's stuff was here just the other day – the studio knew where Ann really came from, and it's not likely that it all got boxed up and shipped to Mexico on the same day. It'll be on the lot somewhere.'

'You think?' Louis sounds doubtful, but there's no time to expand on it before the beam of a flashlight sweeps across the door, illuminating the inside of the trailer.

'Shit,' I hiss, ignoring Tilda's tut under her breath. 'Someone's out there.' The three of us freeze as the beam sweeps across the room again, and the sound of my breathing fills my ears. My heart crashes against my ribs and I can see my own fear reflected back on Tilda's face. Louis slides towards the small window, pressing his face to the glass.

'What if it's the blackmailer?' Tilda's lips barely move as she hisses the words, her face drained of colour. 'What if they've come to do the same thing we have – find any evidence Ann might have left behind?'

I want to tell her that that's ridiculous, that surely whoever it is wouldn't be that stupid, but then the handle on the trailer door begins to turn. It's too late. We're caught.

Chapter Twenty-Two

There is a roaring in my ears as the door creaks open, and then Tilda lets out a yelp.

'Bobby!' His name is a sigh of relief on my lips, as I squint at the bright beam shining in my face. 'You scared the crap out of me.'

Bobby looks taken aback, before his mouth twists in a smile. 'I could say the same about you, Miss Lily. What in the heck are y'all doing in this old trailer? Shouldn't you be at home?' He lowers the flashlight so it's no longer blinding me, scanning it over Louis and Tilda as if double checking who they are. 'And how in God's name did you get in here?' He turns the flashlight back on me.

'The door was unlocked,' Louis says hurriedly. Behind him, Tilda slides the bent bobby pin under the daybed, out of sight.

'Even so… What are y'all doing in here? This is Miss Silver's old trailer.'

'We just had to…' I tail off, not exactly sure what excuse to give Bobby for why we are in Ann Silver's old trailer after hours.

'I asked Lily and Louis to help me.' Tilda steps forward, brushing her hands over her skirt and smoothing her hair down before she turns a bright smile on Bobby. 'I have to write a piece for the newspaper about Ann – nothing salacious! Almost like a… a eulogy, if you like. Something sweet about her life and the impact she made. They'll probably show it at the Academy Awards next year.' Tilda's face takes on a dreamy expression, and I press my foot firmly over the top of hers to bring her back to the present. 'So, I was hoping to find some… inspiration in here.' She beams at him, a picture of innocence.

'Well, Ann's things aren't here anymore,' Bobby says with a shrug. 'If you'd told me what you were up to when you came through the gate I coulda told you that, but I thought you were just here to meet Miss Lily.'

'Yeah, Til,' Louis says, with a roll of his eyes. 'Maybe we should have just told Bobby what we were here for.'

Tilda opens her mouth but before she can speak I jump in. 'So, where can we find her things, Bobby? They didn't get shipped back to…' I pause. 'Oklahoma, did they?'

Bobby shakes his head. 'Aww nah, not yet. At least I don't think so. They'll be in the storage shed at the back of the lot, out past the stables and all.' He frowns. 'Although I'm not sure you should be heading back there.'

'Oskar knows about it,' I say without thinking. 'I mean… he said we should probably look at her things to make sure the piece Tilda writes represents Ann accurately.'

'And the studio,' Louis says solemnly. 'Oskar wants to make sure the studio is painted in a favourable light too.' He leans in and lowers his voice. 'You know how Oskar can be.'

I'm not sure how us looking through Ann's things will have anything to do with the studio looking good, but it works. Bobby nods, stroking his chin. 'It's kinda dark out. Don't you think you'd be better off coming by in the morning, Miss Tilda? I can let you in at first light.'

Tilda is already shaking her head. 'Oh, Bobby, you know the world of journalism is a cutthroat one. I have to file my copy by five a.m. or someone else will beat me to it. We'll be just peachy, I promise. We'll be super careful. And we won't mention your name. If anyone asks, we never saw you, or you us.' With a wink she sashays past him, the tips of his ears turning pink. Louis claps him on the back, and the pair of us follow Tilda before Bobby can ask any more questions. It's not until we're out of sight that my pulse finally returns to normal.

—

The storage sheds are large warehouses at the very far end of the studio lot. Mostly full of old junk, props and costumes that are past their prime. While some people might see it as a graveyard of movies past, the contents of these sheds are worth their weight in gold to Hollywood collectors.

'Locked.' Tilda stands back and surveys the padlock with her hands on her hips. Bobby was right – it is dark out here, the yellow glow of the lights from the studio not quite reaching this far.

'I might have a key.' I pull out the huge bunch I inherited from Jean when I took over her job as Leonard's assistant. The keys to the various storage sheds and sound stages are big and unwieldy, and most of the time I begrudge having them clipped to the belt of my skirt all day, but tonight they might finally come in handy. 'I've never really needed to use these before, but Jean was insistent I have them. You never know when you might need to get into somewhere to fetch something.' And Jean was right. Fumbling through to find any key that could fit the padlock, it's the fifth one that finally turns with a click, the padlock dropping to the ground. Louis tugs the heavy outer door open, and we step inside to a treasure trove of lost items, dust motes swirling on the shards of moonlight that slice through the slatted walls.

'Wow,' Louis breathes. 'This is crazy… Look at this!' He points to a backdrop of a beach, intricately painted, the edges frayed and curling. 'And this!' A replica of a Civil War musket leans against the wall, and Tilda slaps his hand away before he can touch it. 'It's a prop, Til!'

'You hope,' she says, sarcasm lacing her words. 'This place gives me the creeps. Let's find Ann's stuff and get out.'

Theoretically you'd think Ann's things would be at the front of the store, given how recently they were moved, but it takes us a good half hour to find the trunk, tucked away beneath a layer of moth-eaten costumes.

'Almost as if someone was hiding it,' Tilda muses, as she pulls out another bobby pin, strands of red hair floating around her face. She fumbles with the lock, hissing under her breath about our lack of a torch, and I can't help but give an audible gasp when the lock finally springs free.

The faint scent of lilies wafts up from the trunk, presumably from the scarf and gloves laid on top. Gently I pick them up and place them to one side on top of a balding fur coat, careful not to get sawdust on them. Beneath those items are two children's books, the spines broken and the pages worn in both. Clearly old favourites of Ann's from her childhood. A bottle of perfume in a different scent from the one that wafted out of the trunk – her mother's maybe? – and a small porcelain doll dressed in a fancy gown.

'These must have been from her quinceañera,' Tilda says in a hushed whisper. 'Girls carry the doll as a symbol of their transition to womanhood. Ann would have worn a dress to match the doll's.'

While Tilda is running her hands over the white lace of the doll's gown, I peer into the depths of the trunk, moving aside a sweater to get to the very bottom. My breath catches as I pull out a pile of envelopes.

'Guys,' I say, slipping a sheet of paper from the first envelope. 'Look at this.' Twisting the page so that a shaft of moonlight hits it, I run my eyes over the words, my mouth suddenly dry. The letter reads:

> *Dear Miss Silver, or perhaps I should refer to you as 'plata'. After all, isn't that how you say 'silver' in Spanish?*
>
> *You've never been to Oklahoma in your life, and I have the proof of where you are really from. Bring $500 in an unmarked envelope and leave it under the seat in the far right booth at the back of Musso and Frank. Tuesday at eight p.m. You don't want to know what will happen if you don't.*
>
> *A Friend*

'Tuesday? Which Tuesday? Do we think she went?' Tilda doesn't take her eyes from the letter, from the typewritten words stamped deep into the page.

'There's another one.' Louis has been filtering through the envelopes, discarding letters from home in his search for any further blackmail letters. 'Here. Golly, it's bad.'

> *Miss Silver,*
>
> *Perhaps you misunderstood my previous correspondence. The price is now $1,000. The same*

'She never paid the first instalment,' I breathe, a wave of admiration washing over me at Ann's bravery. 'And clearly whoever was blackmailing her wasn't happy about it.'

'Lil.' Tilda's voice trembles as she hands me the last letter. It's short, just a few words, but it's enough to make my blood run cold.

Hollywood sign. Friday at eleven p.m.

'Bloody hell.' My stomach lurches, the proof in my hands that Ann wasn't alone up there and there is a very real chance she didn't jump. 'She never paid the blackmailer. She can't have done. I think they wrote to her threatening her, and when she didn't pay up they called in the blind item.'

'In the hopes it would force her to pay up or…?' Louis frowns, shoving his hands into his pockets as he begins to pace, trying to connect all the dots. 'Tilda, the letters Lizzie and Jack gave you, the ones Max received. Do you have them?'

Tilda nods, rummaging in her ridiculously oversized purse. She pulls out the two letters Max Hayden received. 'They have to be from the same person, right? Surely there can't be two blackmailers in Hollywood at the same time?'

Anything is possible, but I take the envelope with Max's name on it anyway and hold it up to the watery light. Both envelopes are handwritten, in blocky, black pen, with no discernible flourishes. It could have been written by a man or a woman. The writing itself gives away no clues.

'The envelope is handwritten,' I mutter to myself, 'but the letters themselves are typewritten. So whoever it is has access to a typewriter.' Not that that narrows things down. We're in Hollywood, for Pete's sake, where every other person is a wannabe screenwriter. 'No stamp. No post-mark. Whoever delivered these knew where both Ann and Max lived and they hand delivered the letters.' Not for the first time I feel a burst of frustration. If this was in my own time there would be CCTV, or an IP address if it was sent digitally. I'd be able to watch as the culprit marched up the driveway to Max and Lizzie's house, or slipped into the booth at Musso's. As it is, we have none of that.

'M!' Tilda shouts, yanking the letter out of my hand.

'What?' Louis stops his pacing. 'Til, are you just randomly yelling stuff or—'

'Look at the letter!' Tilda waves it in my face and I snatch it up, peering closely at the words. 'Look at the letter M on both letters. It's wonky, see? The M sits slightly higher on the page than the rest of the letters.'

Tilda's right. This is the proof we needed to show that both Ann and Max were being blackmailed by the same person. The only question is… who?

Chapter Twenty-Three

Slipping out of the storage shed into the darkness, Tilda fiddles with the padlock as I slide the blackmail letters into my purse, swiping my fingers over my skirt. I feel grubby at the thought of them festering in my bag, the vicious threats to expose Ann making me feel tainted and dirty. The idea that she went to meet her blackmailer is even more terrifying and heartbreaking than the idea that she might have jumped from the Hollywood sign.

We are halfway across the lot when I see the side door that leads to my office open, and a tall figure looks both ways before stepping out into the street.

'Wait.' I tug on Louis's arm, holding him back as the man marches towards the side exit, away from Bobby and the security gate. He knows his way around, that's for sure. Only a few people know to use that gate after hours. 'That's the guy, Tilda. Freddy someone.'

'Huh.' Tilda watches him go, frown lines etched into her forehead. 'I started digging on him but people are oddly reluctant to talk. There's word that he used to be a police officer but I'm still trying to get my source to verify him.'

'You got a name for him yet?'

'Working on it.'

Whoever he is, police officer or not, there is no reason for Freddy to be on set long after shooting has finished.

I am pondering the idea of checking my office to see if anything is missing when the door opens again and Mae appears.

'Is that—?' Louis asks.

I nod. 'Yeah. I thought she left as soon as shooting finished. I wonder if she was meeting with our guy there.' I turn to see if Freddy is still there, but the lot behind me is empty. 'In fact, I'm going to find out. Guys, I'll meet you back at the apartment.'

Louis and Tilda head off to the parking lot at the back of the studio, and I hurry after Mae, calling out to her as she steps through the gates and onto the pavement.

'Mae! Wait!' Finally she slows, turning to look at me with a frown.

'Lily? What is it?'

'Did you not call a studio car to take you home?' I am panting slightly from hurrying to catch her up and my hair is starting to frizz, the scent of rain on the air. 'I can wait with you if there's one coming.'

'There isn't one coming,' Mae says, as she starts walking down the boulevard again. 'I can walk, it's fine. I don't live far.'

I fall into step beside her, wondering how I can broach the topic of Freddy whatever-his-name-is without sounding crazy. 'I live this way too.' Not true, Tilda and I live in the opposite direction, but maybe Mae will open up to me on the walk. 'So, how are you feeling now?'

Mae mumbles about feeling better, and we talk about the afternoon's shooting, but when I mention Vic's name she clams up, and I don't feel able to mention Freddy. A crack of lightning splits the air, and there is a rumble of thunder in the near distance, then moments later the heavens open.

'Shit!' I yelp, holding my purse over my head. It rains so rarely in LA that I've fallen out of the habit of carrying an umbrella with me, and now as rain slides down inside my collar I regret my life choices.

'My apartment is just up here!' Mae has to raise her voice over the rain hitting the pavement. 'Come on, you can come in and wait for the weather to pass.' Mae turns onto Harper Avenue and leads me up the path to a small Art Deco-style apartment building. 'Sorry,' she says, 'I'm on the third floor, and there's no elevator – but there is a bathtub, so you know. You take what you can get.'

The apartment is small but cosy, and Mae has made it feel lived in by throws arranged artfully over the sagging couch and church candles on the small mantelpiece.

'Let me get you a cup of tea,' she says, throwing her bag onto the sofa. 'And the bathroom is just there, if you want to dry off a little.'

'Thanks.' Mae heads off to the tiny kitchen and I make my way towards the bathroom, pausing as I reach Mae's open bedroom door. There is the sound of running water then the click of the stove, and before I know it my feet are taking me past Mae's neatly made bed to the dressing table. Her room is small, cosy and neat, the dresser holding a navy velvet jewellery box and a pink ceramic piggy bank, a handful of dollar bills sticking out of the top. I catch a glimpse of myself in the small vanity mirror, my curls dripping down my neck and a run of black mascara under my eyes. It's not my reflection that has my attention though, it's the small book on the dresser, bound together with a rubber band. Slips of paper are tucked inside, and I swear it's only because I catch sight of Ann's name that I slip the bands off and open the book.

'What the…' Pressing my hand to my mouth, I scan over the page, over the neat, blocky handwriting. It's a list of the blind items that have been published so far, Ann's name scrawled next to the one about someone being from 'south of the border'. Some of the others have 'true' scribbled next to them, and the one that referred to Max has something unintelligible scribbled next to it.

'Lily? You want sugar in your tea?' Mae calls from the kitchen.

'Uh, no… thank you.' Fumbling with the list, I try to shove it back inside the notebook, when another, thicker paper falls out. The list falls from my hand as I pick up the page. 'STATE OF CALIFORNIA – DEPARTMENT OF MOTOR VEHICLES' shouts from the top of the sheet, the California state seal embossed on it. It's a driver's licence, with a pale-faced, sombre-looking Mae in the photograph. Only the name on it isn't Mae Sinclair. It's Mabel McAllister.

The ground seems to shift beneath my feet as I try to piece together what I've found. Mae isn't Mae. Mae is Mabel. And what about the list of blind items? I swallow, suddenly feeling nauseous, and then there is a creak from outside the room.

'Lily?' Mae appears, a steaming mug of tea in her hand. 'What are you doing?'

Chapter Twenty-Four

'Mae!' I turn, my back shielding the notebook and driver's licence. 'I was just… looking for a hair tie. Sorry. Cheeky of me, I know, but you know with hair like this…' I gesture to my wild mop of curls and laugh. 'Rain is not my friend. But anyway, not to worry, because it turns out I had one after all. See?' I hold up my arm to show the hair tie around my wrist and walk towards her, pushing her back out into the small hallway. 'That tea looks good. Do you mind if we sit down for a bit?'

Mae's eyes narrow, and there is a brief moment where I am sure she's about to yell at me and throw me out, and then her face softens. 'Sure.' She hands me the cup of tea. 'Let me fetch you a towel too.'

Moments later I am ensconced on Mae's squashy and slightly uncomfortable sofa, my hair wrapped in a towel as I sip tea.

'So, Lily,' Mae says, her eyes never leaving my face. 'How long have you been friends with… Tilda, is it? The reporter?'

'A couple of years,' I say. 'We met when I was working with Honey Black on the set of *Goodtime Gal*. I actually met her brother first; he's a bartender at the Beverly Hills Hotel. I was staying there at the time.'

Mae arches an eyebrow. 'How lovely. So, Tilda… She works with Louella Parsons, right? The gossip columnist.'

If there's one thing I know Tilda hates being referred to as it's as a 'gossip columnist'. 'She works with Louella, yes. She worked really hard to get her position. We're very proud of her.'

'Does she share things with you?' Mae's eyes twinkle as she looks at me over the steaming cup of tea in her hands. 'Come on, Lily, I bet you hear things well ahead of everyone else.'

My stomach lurches. Is Mae trying to find out what I know? I think of the list in her bedroom, the scrawled notes beside the blind items, and wonder again exactly what her involvement might be. I shake my head. 'I know nothing. Sorry. It's lucky I ran into you at the lot tonight. I wouldn't have wanted you to walk home alone in the dark.'

Mae flaps a hand. 'Don't be a daft thing, Lily,' she says. 'There were plenty of folks about if I ran into trouble.'

'Well, you are in Hollywood now, Mae, and people know your face.' I lean forward and avoid her gaze, putting my cup on the table. 'Speaking of which, I've noticed a new face around the lot this past week or so. A tall fella, with a thick moustache. You know the guy I mean?' I look up now, fixing my eyes on Mae's face.

She stares at me guilelessly, her eyes wide and innocent, but I notice the slight whitening of her knuckles around the handle of her cup. 'No, I'm ever so sorry, Lily. I have no idea who you're talking about.'

I pause for a moment, letting Mae's lie dissolve on her tongue. 'My mistake,' I say with a smile. 'I thought perhaps… Anyway, thanks for the tea. I should probably be getting home.'

Mae gets to her feet, an air of relief surrounding her as she walks me to the door and I hand her back the towel.

'I'll see you tomorrow,' she says, almost hustling me out into the corridor. As she gives me a gentle shove in the back, I almost trip over a small box in the hallway, left right outside her door.

'Oops.' I stoop down and pick it up, noticing Mae's name in thick black pen on the top. 'You've got a parcel.'

Mae takes it with a frown, before sliding her finger under the tape and ripping it off. Her face pales as she pulls out a bottle of whisky, the bird on the label giving it away as John Wayne's favourite tipple.

'Wild Turkey?' I say with a laugh. 'I never pegged you as a whisky gal, Mae. We could have done with that half an hour ago when we were soaking wet and freezing.'

'I'm not a whisky gal, Lil,' she says quietly. She shoves it back into the box, her mouth twisting with distaste. 'Can you put that in the trash on your way out? There are trash cans for the apartments by the gardens.'

'Sure, but…' I take the box, peering inside to see if there's a note. 'Don't you want to know who it's from?'

Mae shakes her head. 'It'll be some creep, Lily. A man who thinks he knows me. It happens all the time once you're in the pictures, just ask Tipsy.' She tries to sound tough, but there is a tremor to her voice.

'Are you sure you're OK? If it is someone creepy then they know where you live…' I glance over my shoulder and down the stairwell, as if I might catch sight of whoever left the parcel. 'I can wait, if there's someone you want to call to come over so you're not alone tonight.'

'It's nothing, Lily. Honestly. You should go, I'm tired after getting caught in the rain and I have a long day tomorrow.' And she closes the apartment door in my face.

'Lily!' Heart pounding, I gasp my way into consciousness, squinting at the early morning sunshine forcing its way through the thin curtains at my bedroom window. 'Lily! Wake up!'

Pushing myself into a sitting position, I see Tilda in the bedroom doorway, still in her nightgown with a fat roller in the front of her hair. She'd gone out to meet Ty after our little trip to the storage shed last night and I was asleep by the time she got home. She looks far perkier than I do this morning though. 'What time is it?'

'Six o'clock.' She bounces into the room and scrambles onto the end of my bed. 'I figured your alarm would be going off soon anyway.'

'Why are you in my bedroom at the crack of dawn? And without even bringing me a cup of tea.'

'No time for tea, and anyway this is America. We drink coffee and it's about time you did too.'

I can't help but notice the newspaper Tilda has tucked under her arm. 'What is that? Don't tell me…'

Tilda nods, opening the paper and jabbing a finger at one of the middle pages. 'Right there. Another blind item. And, Lil, this one is a doozy.'

Dread pools in the pit of my stomach, a heavy weight that brings a sour taste to my mouth as I start to read.

> Which high-flying studio powerhouse has flown a little too close to the sun? Word has it, he's been courting Lady Luck a little too often, only she doesn't seem to be on his side. A certain syndicate seems to be taking his calls faster than anyone at the studio ever has. Still, he puts on a great show for the red carpet.

'What on earth?' I frown, my brain still not fully awake as I try to make sense of the vague snippet of gossip. 'Syndicate? What does that mean?'

Tilda arches an eyebrow in that way she has. 'If you ask me, I would say *gambling*.' She lowers her voice, even though it's just the two of us in the apartment. 'Lady Luck? Doesn't seem to be *on his side*. Doesn't that sound to you like someone has been playing with something they shouldn't?'

'Gambling? What, like, cards or something? How is that so scandalous?'

Tilda sighs. 'Lil, I know since we've been to Vegas and all, you think gambling isn't a big deal.' I never said that, but even so, I'm not sure someone having a flutter on the horses warrants a blind item in a gossip column. 'It's illegal, Lily. You can go to *jail* for gambling in this state.'

Of course. I feel like an idiot, my cheeks heating as I shift further up the pillows. 'Sorry, Tilda, I didn't realise.' That makes more sense. No one gambling would want it to be common knowledge, especially if... 'Oh blimey, Til. A studio powerhouse. Who do you think it could be?'

Tilda shrugs. 'Honestly? Any one of them. Louis Mayer?'

'He stepped down last year,' I point out. 'This reads as if the person involved is still working. What about Jack Warner?'

'I think he does like a trip to Vegas,' Tilda muses, 'but then if I know that then a ton of other people know it too, so it's hardly something to gossip about.'

'What if Lady Luck is a woman?' There's every chance it could be, and Lord knows people jump in and out of bed with each other in Hollywood all the time. Things are decidedly less wholesome than the studios would have you believe. 'Someone is screwing around where they shouldn't.'

'Ew, Lily.' Tilda wrinkles her nose. 'Don't say "screwing around", it sounds so… common.'

Before I can respond the alarm clock on the bedside table erupts into a shrill ring and I slam my hand down on top of it. There's something so satisfying about the way the noise cuts as my hand hits the bell. It hits different to just pressing a button on my phone.

'I have to get to set,' I say, pushing back the covers, a knot of nervous energy pulsing through me. 'Let's catch up later. Maybe ask around at the paper? See if anyone has any idea who it could be about.' I know before I even step foot on the set that this latest item is going to be causing havoc… and I'll be the one expected to diffuse the situation.

–

The canteen trailer is buzzing with gossip when I arrive, but at least Tipsy and Mae have already been to hair and make-up, so that's one cat already wrangled. Veronica and Cliff sit together at a table, coffee in front of them both. 'I know who *I* think it could be,' Veronica is saying, a teasing smile on her lips as Cliff shakes his head. 'What? Come on, Cliff, you know what I told you the other night! No one is free from speculation.' Veronica throws back her head and laughs, as Cliff catches sight of me.

'Here, take my seat.' He drops a kiss on Veronica's head and shoves his chair back, but I shake my head as I hear my name over the rumble of gossip.

'Lily!' Tipsy waves me over and pulls out the chair beside her, a browning apple core on the table in front of her. The cut on her head looks less severe this morning, a smear of slightly too dark foundation covering it. 'Darling, you must have seen it already. A studio powerhouse! How delicious!'

'Good morning to you too, Tipsy,' I say with a faint smile. 'Morning, Mae.'

Mae gives me a sharp smile, before turning back to the cup of hot water and lemon in front of her. She seems much more herself this morning, no sign of the shaken Mae I saw yesterday evening.

'Thanks again for last night,' I say. 'The tea and the towel and everything.'

'What's this?' Tipsy glances between me and Mae, her eyes sharp. 'Lily, I thought you had plans last night.'

'Oh, I did. But I ran into Mae and we got caught in the rain and she very kindly helped me to dry off.'

'No big deal,' Mae says with a shrug, before she points to the paper as if eager to change the subject before I can mention the parcel left on her doorstep. 'So what do we all think about this? What's the story?'

Tipsy leans forward, resting her chin on her steepled fingers. 'Well, it has to be someone important – they referred to him as a powerhouse, didn't they?'

Mae mimics her pose and I sit back, that familiar nasty taste in my mouth. Both of these women could be behind the blind items – both of them love to gossip, and I've found evidence showing that either one of them could be involved. The issue with this is that I like both of them, and the idea that either one of them could be blackmailing their peers and potentially killing them off makes my heart skip a beat.

There is a commotion by the door, and I hush Tipsy and Mae as a red-faced Oskar marches in, Bunny scurrying along behind him.

'Right,' Oskar barks, sweat stippling his temples. There are already stains in the armpits of his suit jacket and the day has barely begun. 'Before anyone says a word, I am aware of another blind item in the newspaper today and I am nipping this in the bud, *right now*. Anyone overheard discussing this will be fired with immediate effect, do you understand? I've warned you all countless times, and yet here you are, sitting around in the canteen, gossiping and speculating, when you should be running your lines.'

Mae flushes a deep red, the heat stretching up from the neckline of her blouse to creep across her cheeks, but Tipsy lets out a bark of laughter.

'Honestly, Oskar, anyone would think this blind item is about you, the way you're carrying on. My call time isn't for another forty minutes, and I'll thank you for your concern but I already know my lines and I am entitled to get breakfast.'

Oh, for God's sake. 'Tipsy, please,' I whisper, pressing my foot over the top of hers. 'You can't speak to him that way.'

'You can't speak to me that way,' Oskar echoes, his voice dangerously low. He steps forward and leans over the table, his fists banging down on the Formica, dangerously close to Tipsy's hands. 'You might be Tipsy Jenner, but you might want to remember who put you where you are.'

The canteen has fallen deathly silent, and Mae swallows audibly as Tipsy and Oskar stare at each other. I am already frantically trying to figure out how I am going to manage this situation, in a way that will minimalise it and also somehow stop Leonard from finding out, when Oskar presses his face close to Tipsy's. She stands her ground, refusing to pull back even though his cigar-laced breath must be hitting her right in the face.

'I know exactly who put me here,' she says coldly, 'and that's not the only thing I know about this town. You'd be surprised by the things I've heard lately.'

Oskar flounders for a moment, his eyes narrowing. 'If you know who put you here, then you know exactly who can make this all tumble down for you.' Straightening up, Oskar's face twists with rage and fury, an already not especially handsome face becoming uglier by the second.

'Mr Goldstein, sir.' Cliff steps forward and taps Oskar lightly on the shoulder. 'Maybe this isn't the right place or the right time for this conversation. How about you let me handle this and we get Miss Jenner to come to your office later on, after shooting?'

Oskar turns his anger on Cliff, as Bunny steps back to avoid getting caught in the crossfire, her face pale. 'You? Who do you think you are to tell me what to do?' He runs his eyes over Cliff, a sneer etched onto his face. 'You're nothing but an *assistant*, boy. I only took you on as a favour to your parents. You're lucky to have a job at all. And if you want to stay working for me you'll mind your damn business.'

With that Oskar storms from the room, leaving only the faint, damp smell of cigars and the remnants of his rage behind.

'Cliff—' Bunny steps forward, but Cliff shoots her a venomous look as Veronica wraps an arm around his waist. He shakes her off and moves to the counter, pouring himself a cup of black coffee, bitter and burnt.

'Cliff?' Touching his arm, I say his name quietly but he doesn't look up from the coffee pot. 'That was uncalled for. There was no need for Oskar to go off at you like that.'

'Just leave it, Lily. It doesn't matter.' Cliff turns to me now, his mouth twisting. 'Oskar, my mother, just about everybody in this studio…' His tone is defeated, and I position myself so he has to look at me. 'It's always the same.'

'You should speak to Oskar, tell him not to talk to you that way.'

Cliff snorts. 'So he can fire me and prove my mother right? I don't think so.' He stares at me. 'One of these days people are going to sit up and take notice of what I actually do, and then maybe I'll get some recognition.'

'Oh dear,' Tipsy says as she comes to join me, watching Cliff sweep out of the canteen with the last shreds of his dignity. 'Someone really got stung.'

'Tipsy, please.' I close my eyes. 'Please just head to set. I'll bring you fresh coffee.' Tipsy sashays away, calling out to Bunny and holding out a hand to Mae as if this entire exchange didn't just happen. Me, though… All I can think about is the way Tipsy hissed in Oskar's face that she knew things about this town. Remembering that night in the Polo Lounge when she warned me off looking into Max's death, my blood runs cold, unable to shake off the feeling that her words are more than just an idle threat.

Chapter Twenty-Five

I can barely hear my own knock on Leonard's office door over the thud of my pulse in my ears as I bravely attempt to speak to him before he arrives on set. I'm hoping that I have got to him before Oskar, and when his stern, 'Come in,' rattles through the door I take a deep breath before entering the office.

'Lily? Why on earth are you knocking?' Leonard gestures to my desk, just a few feet away from his. 'This is your office too.'

'I wasn't sure…' I swallow, my tongue sticking to the roof of my mouth. 'I thought Oskar might have come to see you.'

'Oh?' Leonard sits back, lacing his hands behind his head. Unusually for him there is the faintest five o'clock shadow grazing his chin, and his eyes are ringed by dark circles.

'There was a bit of an incident in the canteen,' I say, sinking into the chair opposite Leonard. Quickly I recount the events that transpired, even down to Tipsy and Oskar's final exchange. Leonard closes his eyes, scrubbing a hand over them. 'I'm sorry,' I say quietly, my throat thickening as tears sting my eyes. 'I really tried to defuse the situation before Oskar even arrived but it's these blind items… They're sending everyone half-mad with trying to figure out who they relate to.'

Leonard sighs. 'I know. And I know you're trying your best to keep everyone in line. Jean used to tell me it was like herding cats.' He gives a huff of tired laughter.

I pause for a moment, swiping my hands over my skirt. I've never had a dad. My mum raised me by herself, until she passed away from breast cancer not long before I came to Los Angeles. My dad was long gone before I was born, and I never missed him – how can you miss what you've never had? – but if I was ever going to look at someone as a father figure it would be Leonard. Now, I have the overwhelming urge to tell him everything.

'What if it's not just idle gossip, this Last Word column? What if it's something more?' Knotting my fingers together, I look up at Leonard but he's smiling and shaking his head. 'What if it's serious and the police need to be involved? I'm feeling a bit... overwhelmed by it all.'

'Lily, don't get yourself worked up. It's gossip, that's all. Someone with far too much time on their hands – I hardly think the LAPD will be interested. Gossip is what makes Hollywood go round after all. Listen, I know I've been tough on you, telling you it's your job to squash the rumours, but you've seen how Tipsy is. You give her an inch and she'll take a mile.' He reaches out and squeezes my hand briefly. 'Don't tell Jean but you're the best assistant I ever had, and I know you can accomplish whatever you put your mind to.'

His words buoy me up. *I can. I moved to LA and got into the movies when everyone said it was a pipedream.* OK, things might have been a little unconventional, but I made it and I'm not going to let whoever is blackmailing the stars of Hollywood get away with it.

'Thanks, Leonard. How is Jean anyway?'

Leonard sighs again. 'Bored. Frustrated. A little low, I think. Say, you wouldn't come over and see her, would you, Lily? I think it would really lift her spirits. I'm here so late every evening going over the rushes that I'm sure she wouldn't say no to a little company.'

'Sure. Leave it with me.' I leave Leonard's office, his faith in me making me feel a little more confident that we can get to the bottom of what's going on with the black-mailer and the blind items. It helps that Jean has worked with Tipsy many times before, and after what Tipsy said earlier about knowing what's going on in Hollywood, I feel like perhaps we should focus on her a little. Bunny's desk is empty, so I perch on her chair and place a call to Tilda at the newspaper office. It takes a few minutes for them to track her down.

'Lil?' She is breathless as she comes to the phone, and I picture her with her pencil behind her ear in that way Louis tells her is uncouth. 'What is it?'

'A baby shower for Jean. Tonight. At the Langford's house.'

'A what now? What in the heck is a *baby shower*?'

Yikes. I'd forgotten that such a thing doesn't really exist yet. 'A party for Jean to celebrate her pregnancy and to cheer her up. Leonard says she's feeling a little low. I was thinking we could pick up some snacks, some balloons and maybe a cute outfit for the baby and swing by and see her tonight.' I pause. 'Shooting starts in a few minutes, but if you could call Louis and let him know I'm sure he'll pick up a cake for us.' Louis's apartment doesn't have a phone yet and it's too early to call him at the Polo Lounge.

'Lily…' Tilda's voice is serious. 'I know we love Jean and all, but don't you think we should be working on who this blind item might be about? Whoever it is clearly hasn't paid the blackmailer, which puts them in danger.'

'Yes, and that's exactly what we're going to do tonight. With Jean. Tipsy made some comment this morning about how she knows all kinds of things about what goes on in Hollywood, and Jean has worked on movies with Tipsy for years. We can speak to Jean about Tipsy and see if she thinks she could be behind the blind items, and cheer Jean up at the same time. We can kill two birds with one stone.'

'OK.' Tilda's voice grows fainter as she briefly covers the receiver for a moment, calling out to someone that she's on her way, but I don't miss the last thing she says before she hangs up. 'Let's hope the two birds are the only things killed this evening.'

The pool shimmers under the lights, and Tipsy grinds out her cigarette as Leonard calls for everyone to take their marks. We're shooting the scene that Tipsy has been the most excited by for the entire movie – the scene where she dies.

'OK!' Leonard calls. 'Vic, you're going to walk Tipsy back into the water, the two of you tussle, and then you hold her down. Tipsy, struggle for a moment, and then go still. Got it? I want this in one take if we can. It's cold in here and I don't want anyone getting sick.' Leonard drops a wink in my direction. 'Lord knows what we'll do if Tipsy can't talk.'

Tipsy raises an eyebrow and then a hush falls over the set. I never realised the pool scene would be filmed on the lot in a sound stage pool. I had assumed we would move out to another location, and I am fascinated as I watch the scene unfold.

Vic and Tipsy argue, Tipsy's voice loud and belligerent, slightly slurred from the alcohol she is supposed to have imbibed. She berates Vic, telling him she'll never let him marry her daughter, as Vic moves towards her, gripping her by the upper arms and pushing her back towards the water, telling her she won't be around to stop him. I can't help my hands flying to my mouth as Vic presses down on Tipsy's head, her hair floating out around her. Her arms flail and her face briefly rises above the surface of the water, her mouth open in a gasping O before Vic shoves her back under. He holds her there for seconds that feel like minutes, until she finally stops moving.

'And cut!' Leonard strides forward, clapping loudly. Vic grins, shoving his wet hands through his hair, but Tipsy still floats face down in the water, her skirt ballooning around her legs. 'Excellent work, folks. Vic, you were chilling. You nailed it.'

'Tipsy? She's not moving. Tipsy!' Mae steps forward from the shadows, her face bone white. 'Someone do something!' she shrieks, her eyes wild as she searches the crew for someone to help her. 'Get her out of the water!'

'Mae? Everything is OK. Look.' I point to the pool, where Tipsy has rolled onto her back and is lazily bobbing around in the water. A runner stands at the edge of the pool, holding a huge white fluffy towel, waiting for Tipsy to emerge.

'I can't breathe.' Mae gasps, her chest hitching, her hands clawing at the high-collared blouse her character wears. 'Lily, help me.'

'Deep breaths, slowly,' I coach, realising that Mae is about to have a full-blown panic attack. 'Mae, come on, listen to me.' But Mae isn't listening. The colour drops out of her face, her eyes roll back in her head and she slumps to the floor, unconscious.

'I feel like an idiot,' Mae says a couple of hours later, sitting up in the nurses' station. 'I don't know what came over me.'

'Well,' I say, perched on the end of the bed, 'Tipsy didn't help by bobbing around face down in the water after Leonard yelled cut.' I smile, but Mae's face remains sombre.

'Is everyone mad at me?' Mae's voice is small and she swallows, blinking hard.

I laugh. 'No, silly. Leonard was worried about you. But Mae…' I reach out a hand and squeeze hers lightly. 'What happened? What panicked you? It was as though something triggered you.'

Mae yanks her hand away. 'Nothing *triggered* me. What an odd expression. Why would you say that? I just didn't eat this morning, and it was hot under the lights, that's all. I… Tipsy was under the water and I just… felt over-whelmed. Nothing more than that.'

The nurse enters, a clipboard clutched to her chest. 'Miss Sinclair, I'm just going to check your blood pressure one more time and then you're good to go.'

'I'll leave you to it, if you're sure you're OK.' I get to my feet, a nagging sensation in my stomach that Mae isn't being entirely truthful with me. 'Make sure you rest this evening. Leonard will want you on top form tomorrow.'

Mae nods and the nurse begins to bustle around her, so I step outside only to bump into Cliff.

'Oh.' His face lights up with a smile as he realises it's me he's walked into. 'How is Mae? Oskar asked me to check on her.'

'Fine, but she's getting checked over now. She's not to be disturbed.' Cliff nods but seems oddly reluctant to leave. 'You can walk me to the lot though, if you want to be a gentleman.'

As we walk through the service alley that runs behind the nurses' station towards the parking lot, I catch a glimpse of someone headed to the station from the other direction. Thinking it might be Leonard checking on Mae, I pause for a moment and wonder whether I should let him know that I'm planning on dropping in on Jean tonight. But when the figure pulls open the door, the yellow light from inside the building illuminating his features, it's not Leonard. It's the guy I keep seeing creeping around on set. Freddy someone. The guy Mae claims not to know.

–

'Are you guys… going to a party?' Cliff frowns as we arrive in the parking lot where Tilda and Louis lean against the car, waiting for me.

'Uh, kind of?' I am amused to see the backseat is filled with balloons. 'Louis, what the heck is all this? Tilda is going to have to sit in the trunk.'

'You said get balloons!' Louis cries, as Cliff lets out a burst of laughter and Tilda rolls her eyes. 'I got balloons! And a cake. Although I didn't know what flavour Jean would like so I got two and some ice cream, which is probably melted.'

'You did good.' I pat him on the back and turn to Cliff, who hovers awkwardly. 'Thanks for walking me out.'

'My pleasure.' Cliff's eyes go to the balloon-filled car again. 'Do you… Do you want me to give you a ride? I'm not sure how y'all are going to fit in there together. If you give me the address of the party I can drive you, and give you a hand bringing all the stuff in…'

Tilda shakes her head. 'Thanks, but we'll manage. It's not really a party, more of a… shower.'

'Thanks again, Cliff,' I say. 'See you tomorrow?'

Cliff rubs at the corner of one eye and smiles briskly. 'Sure. See you tomorrow.'

I turn back to Tilda and Louis as Cliff makes his way out of the parking lot. 'I've just come from the nurses' station. Mae passed out today – we were shooting a scene by the swimming pool and she just… I don't know if it was her nerves or what, but she said she couldn't breathe and then, bam, she was on the floor.'

'Oh, poor Mae.' Tilda frowns. 'Is she OK now?'

I nod. 'But the weird thing is as I was leaving, that guy, Freddy something, was headed into the medical bay. He must have been going to visit Mae as she's the only patient there, but when I asked her about him before she said she didn't know him. Something isn't right there.'

'Maybe you should ask her about it.' Louis nods over my shoulder and I turn to see Mae and Tipsy making their way towards us, Tipsy's arm around Mae's shoulders. Mae still looks pale and fragile and I'm glad she's not leaving alone.

I shake my head at Louis and paste on a smile as the two actresses approach us. 'How are you feeling now, Mae?'

She shrugs. 'A little tired. I'm fine though. Don't worry, Lily, I'll be on set on time tomorrow and ready to go.'

I'm more concerned about the moustache guy creeping around her on the set, but before I can mention it, Tilda's purse slips out of her hands and explodes over the pavement.

'Oh shoot, I'm sorry.' Tilda starts scrabbling around on the floor as I stop a lipstick from rolling away with my foot. Mae also bends to help, but Tipsy is too busy batting her eyelashes at Louis to notice.

'Here.' Mae scoops up a wedge of notes, pausing as she's about to hand them back to Tilda. 'Wait. What is this?' She runs her eyes over the page, her smile becoming stilted and stiff.

'It's nothing.' Tilda reaches out to swipe the page from Mae's hand, but Mae holds it above her head out of reach.

'It doesn't look like nothing. It looks like gossip.' Mae cuts her eye to Tilda. 'Like something that would appear in a newspaper column.'

Tipsy turns her attention to us now, her head whipping round. She's lit a cigarette while talking to Louis and the smoke curls around her head like a halo. 'Like a blind item? Well, well.' She arches an eyebrow.

'Don't be ridiculous.' Louis's eyes darken and he steps around the bonnet of the car to stand beside Tilda, who gives a weak laugh.

'Please, Mae. You don't honestly think—'

'I don't know what to think. But imagine if I could tell Oskar Goldstein who was causing all this trouble on set.' There is a vague air of satisfaction to Mae's tone, one that almost seems tinged with relief.

'Come on, Mae. I'm a reporter – these are just notes for Louella for her column, and there's nothing blind about that.' Tilda's voice holds an air of desperation, and I know she's anxious about being kicked out of the studio for good. It's not like Oskar was ever happy to have her around, and it's only on Leonard's good word that she gets as much access as she does.

'I guess we'll see, won't we?' Mae shoves the notebook in Tilda's direction. 'Tipsy, are you ready? I'd like to get home now.' Without another word Mae stalks off towards the security gates, as Tipsy opens her mouth as though she wants to say something. She doesn't though, for once, instead just giving me a brief nod and following after Mae. As they head out of earshot, Tilda lets out a long sigh.

'They don't really think that I could be behind that Last Word column, surely?' She bites her lip, worry etched onto her features.

The whole exchange has left a nasty taste in my mouth. 'I guess there's only one way to prove them wrong,' I say. 'We need to figure out who it really is. And you, Tilda, need to find out everything you can about this Freddy character. He might be the key to clearing your name.'

Chapter Twenty-Six

Tilda is especially subdued on the way over to Jean and Leonard's house. After we pull up and get out of the car, I take her arm.

'Listen, I know you don't have anything to do with the blind items, but everyone is hooked on the mystery. And who's to say Mae wasn't double bluffing, turning the spotlight on you? I found that list in her bedroom, remember? She's definitely more interested in things than anyone else, besides Tipsy.'

Tilda nods. 'I guess I was always going to come under suspicion eventually. After all, it is my job.'

'Lily?' The front door creeps open and Jean stands there, one hand resting on her little bump. 'What on earth are you all doing here?'

'Surprise!' Louis wraps one arm around Jean in a hug, balloons clutched tightly in the other hand. I reach into the car and bring out the cake, icing smudging my fingers.

'It's a baby shower!' I say with a grin, trying to let the worries of the evening over Mae, the blind items and the mysterious Tom Selleck lookalike slide off my shoulders for an hour or two. 'Don't ask me what it is, just let us in and enjoy yourself.'

Jean stands to one side, a smile splitting her face. The first time I met Jean I never would have imagined that we'd become friends, but she's grown on me, probably because I don't have to work under her watchful eye and strict rules anymore. She hides a heart of gold under her tough exterior, and I know anyone else wouldn't have had the patience she's had to train me up before she left the studio.

'This is lovely,' she says, a short while later when we are all settled in her and Leonard's spacious sitting room. Although it's a large room, with deep arched windows looking out on to a turquoise swimming pool in the backyard, it somehow manages to feel cosy and intimate. A floor-to-ceiling bookshelf holds leather-bound screen-plays, and a tasteful black-and-white photograph of Leonard and Jean in their wedding finery looks out at us from the mantelpiece. The large coffee table, sat between two squashy cream sofas, is covered with the cake, the gifts we brought, and a bottle of champagne Jean rustled up from somewhere – although I am relieved to see she barely touches hers. 'And such an unexpected surprise.'

'Leonard said you were feeling a little low,' Louis says, one foot planted firmly in his mouth.

'And we've missed you,' I say, hastily. 'Working on set isn't the same without you around.'

Jean primps at her hair, tucking it neatly into place. 'Well, Leonard did always say I was the best assistant he ever had.'

Stifling my smile in my champagne glass, we talk a little about Jean and how she's feeling (tired and hoping for a girl, naturally), before the conversation turns to the movie.

'All this nonsense with the gossip in the newspapers,' Jean tuts. 'I hope you're managing to keep a lid on things, Lily.'

'Trying,' I say, unable to keep the smile on my face. 'It's harder than it seems though. Tipsy Jenner – you've worked with her before, haven't you?'

Jean sighs and places her glass on the coffee table, bubbles still fizzing up the inside of the saucer. 'Yes. She's a dear woman, but golly, she loves to tattle. The things that woman knows… I honestly don't know where she gets her information.'

'So this isn't a new thing? Her love of gossip?'

Jean lets out a laugh. 'Oh gosh, no. I mean, the whole industry is full of gossips – there's nothing Hollywood loves to do more than direct the spotlight – but Tipsy has always been right in the thick of it. She'll get herself in trouble one day.'

'Trouble?'

'If there's one person you'll need to watch on set for stirring things up, it's Tipsy. Be discreet though. She doesn't take kindly to being pulled up on things.'

I think of the way Tipsy reacted to Oskar earlier, the venom that leached into her voice when he scolded her in front of the entire crew. The cut that appeared on her head the morning after Mae was run off the road. Before I can ask Jean any more questions, the shrill ring of the telephone pierces the air.

'Excuse me.' Jean hefts herself up from the sofa, pressing her hand into the small of her back even though she's not even six months pregnant yet.

'Blimey,' I say once she's out of earshot. 'It's easier said than done, keeping that lot in line on set.'

'What do you think about what she said about Tipsy?' Louis leans in and lowers his voice. 'Do you think Jean was trying to tell us Tipsy was behind the blind items?'

Tilda shakes her head. 'It could be anyone, let's be honest. Mae had the list of items in her things, Tipsy said herself she knows things *and* she had stuff written down... and let's not forget me. I'm a suspect now too.'

Reaching out, I squeeze her hand. 'Til, no one would ever think you could blackmail anyone – because let's be honest, that's the real issue here. Whoever is leaking the blind items to that Last Word column is blackmailing those involved, and potentially hurting them. You would never.'

Jean appears in the doorway, her face drained of colour, one hand pressed to the base of her throat. 'I'm so sorry, Lily. I think...'

'Jean? What is it? Is everything OK?' Leaping up, I grab her arm and guide her to the sofa, while Louis pours her a short brandy from the sleek bar in the corner of the room. 'Is it Leonard?'

Jean shakes her head, her hands trembling as she takes the brandy from Louis. 'It's the most awful thing,' she says, quietly. 'That was Leonard on the telephone. He's not coming home...' She looks up at me, her eyes wide. 'It's Oskar. There's been a terrible accident and he's hurt. He's been rushed to hospital. They don't know if he's going to make it.'

—

For the second time in a matter of weeks Louis drives like a professional stunt driver, getting us to the Cedars of Lebanon Hospital in East Hollywood faster than I ever thought possible, leaving Tilda behind to sit with Jean until Leonard gets home. He throws the car into a parking space and the two of us hurry up the front steps and into the lobby. The hospital is impressive, more like a building from a movie set than an actual hospital, and the soles of my Converse squeak on the polished floor as we head to the reception desk.

'I'm looking for Oskar Goldstein,' I say, my breath catching in my throat as the nurse on duty stares at me over the rim of her glasses. 'He was brought in this evening, by ambulance.'

'I'm sure he was. Are you family?'

'Well, no, but—'

'Lily!' My name is a shriek on the air and then Tipsy Jenner is hurtling towards me, her arms outstretched. 'Oh, thank goodness you're here. No one seems to know what has happened. The doctors aren't telling us anything...' She trails off, her hair mussed and her lipstick smudged into the lines around her mouth. 'You are here for Oskar, aren't you?'

I nod. 'Yes, of course we are. How is he?'

'Asleep. Or unconscious. I'm not sure which, to be honest.' Tipsy pushes her hair back with a shaking hand. 'They think he slipped on the tiles out by the pool. He took a blow to the head, and the doctor was telling Leonard that he has some broken ribs. They're keeping an eye on him because of internal bleeding. Oh, Lily, isn't it dreadful?'

'The worst,' I agree, as I try to process Tipsy's ramblings. 'Can you take us to his room?'

'Oh, they won't let you in.' Tipsy shakes her head gravely and pops a cigarette out of the silver holder in her hand.

'I'd like to speak to Leonard.' I eye the cigarette cautiously, wondering if she's actually going to light it inside a hospital. There are some things about the past that I don't think I'll ever get used to. 'Is he with Oskar?'

Tipsy nods, placing her cigarette to her lips. She fumbles in her pocket and pulls out a lighter, the silver case glinting under the harsh corridor lights overhead. Louis's eyes widen as Tipsy lights her cigarette and my stomach flips as I see what he's looking at. 'I'll take you up there. Come on, follow me.'

Tipsy leads us to the elevator. Before she can slide the lighter into her purse, Louis holds out a hand and Tipsy drops it into his palm.

'Tipsy, is that real silver? It's a beautiful lighter. Where did you get it from?' As he turns it over in his hands I can clearly see it's the same as the one found at the top of the Hollywood sign the night Ann jumped, and my stomach somersaults.

'The studio handed them out a couple of years ago. See?' Tipsy points at the tiny engraving. *Silver Circle, 1949.* 'It was to commemorate something. I forget now. There were a few of us who received them, stars and higher-ups at the studio. A nice little gift, I suppose. But,' she leans in and whispers, even though it's just the three of us in the elevator, 'don't tell anyone, this is my second one. I lost the first one and had to beg, borrow and steal to get another.'

Louis catches my eye and I feel something sharp and spiky run through my veins, the sensation that we might just be moving closer to some answers, as the elevator comes to a halt, jolting my stomach.

Tipsy steps out first, none the wiser to the gestures and glances being exchanged between Louis and me behind her back, and leads us to a closed door at the end of the silent corridor. A police officer sits outside, back straight and eyes dead ahead. When he sees Tipsy, he gets to his feet.

'Miss Jenner.' He tips his hat. 'And you are?'

'Friends of Mr Goldstein,' Tipsy says haughtily. 'Could you ask Mr Langford to step out, please?' The police officer nods and I marvel at the power Tipsy has, just from being on screen. Moments later, Leonard appears, his face pale and dotted with stubble. Tipsy takes his place, slipping inside the room to sit beside a sleeping Oskar.

'Lily. What are you doing here?' Leonard scrubs a hand over his face. The poor man looks exhausted.

'We were with Jean when she got the call. Don't worry, Tilda stayed with her. What on earth happened?'

Leonard shakes his head. 'No idea. I got a call to say he was hurt, that he'd been found at home covered in blood. He was awake briefly when I arrived, but when I asked him about what happened he couldn't tell me. He doesn't remember a thing.'

'And Tipsy didn't know what happened?'

'Tipsy?' Leonard scratches his head, worry lines burrowing across his forehead. 'No, why would she?'

Matching worry lines creep across my own forehead as I ponder. 'I just assumed she was with Oskar, or at least she was the one who called you. We raced over here as soon as you called Jean, and Tipsy was already downstairs.'

'The cops called me.' Leonard glances towards the closed door of the hospital room. 'I don't think Tipsy was with him, although I haven't really had a chance to speak with her about it. Listen, I should get back in there with Oskar, just in case he does wake up. I appreciate you folks coming to see if he's all right but there's really no point in you staying. I'll make sure to let him know that you visited.'

I know a dismissal when I hear one, and Louis stands to one side and lets Leonard re-enter the hospital room.

'Tipsy was already here when Leonard arrived?' Louis hisses to me, low enough so that the police officer can't overhear. 'Don't you think that's odd?'

'And the *lighter*,' I hiss back. Everything feels decidedly wrong, and my heart sinks. I like Tipsy. She's a brilliant actress, witty and funny, a joy to spend time with. I just hope she's not also a blackmailer with a taste for murder.

The door to the hospital room opens and I clam up, expecting Tipsy, but it's not her.

'Cliff? I didn't know you were here. Leonard never mentioned it.' My eyes drift down to the coat slung over his arm, recognising it as belonging to Tipsy.

'I'm the one who found him.' Cliff's eyes look slightly pink, and I feel a pang of sympathy for him. 'Called the ambulance, everything. It was very… shocking.' He blinks and I wonder if maybe he should see a doctor too, if he's in shock.

'Do you need a ride?' Louis asks. 'We're heading out now, so we can give you a ride back home, if you'd like. The last thing you'll want to do is get a cab after the night you've had.'

'Uh, no thanks.' Cliff holds out an arm, and it takes me a moment to realise he's holding Tipsy's coat out to me. 'I'm going to stay a little longer, just until Oskar is fully awake and talking and I know he's all right. I just need to pop down to the car and fetch his overnight bag. But Tipsy asked if you'd mind taking her coat to the all-night dry cleaner on Melrose on your way home?'

'Tonight? I mean… Sure.' I take the coat, my nose wrinkling slightly at the smudge of crimson on the sleeve. 'Are you headed to the car now? Come on, we'll walk out to the parking lot with you.'

Cliff is silent on the way to the parking lot, his face pale, and while part of me wants to reassure him that Oskar will be OK, I don't want to lie to him. I hold Tipsy's coat, careful not to let the damp smudge of crimson touch my clothes. Does she realise there is a stain on the sleeve? Is that why she's so eager to get it cleaned tonight? I barely even notice Cliff veering off towards his car when Louis gives a gasp, which turns into a cough as he tries to disguise it.

'Hey, are you OK?' Cliff springs into life, hurrying back towards us and clapping Louis on the back as he coughs and splutters. It takes a moment before Louis gets his breath back and he nods.

'Thanks. I must have… swallowed a fly or something.' Louis widens his eyes at me, giving a slight incline of his head to where Cliff has returned to a car a couple of spaces down from where he parked. At first I don't understand what Louis is so het up about, and then I notice the headlights of Cliff's car and the way they are set into the fenders, just like the car that tried to run us off the road. Shooting a glance at Louis, who is finally losing the pink sheen to his cheeks, I move towards Cliff.

'Do you need a hand with Oskar's things?' I ask, as Cliff delves into the backseat, pulling out a brand new Brics weekend bag, hastily packed judging by the way it bulges. 'I can—'

'No, no.' Cliff shakes his head, blinking. 'I'll be fine. I want to get this up to Oskar straight away. I'm not sure he'll even be awake to need any of these things but…'

'You want to be useful.' I nod.

'Sweet ride, Cliff,' Louis says, running one hand over the bonnet of the car. 'This yours?' He carefully avoids looking at me, keeping his gaze on the car as I watch Cliff's reaction. *Surely it wasn't Cliff who tried to run us off the road? The thought of it makes me feel sick.*

But Cliff is shaking his head as he hoists the overnight bag onto one shoulder. 'I wish, Louis. It's a pool car from the studio.'

'Pool car?'

'Yes, Lil,' Cliff says impatiently, his eyes going to the entrance to the hospital as if eager to get back inside. 'A pool car. The studio owns them but anyone can use them – didn't you know that?'

'Lil doesn't drive,' Louis says darkly. 'It's not that she can't… I mean, she can, but really, really badly.'

I glare at him and turn my attention back to Cliff. 'We should let you get inside. Be sure to let us know how Oskar is, won't you?'

Cliff gives a stiff nod and disappears back inside the hospital. I wonder how long Oskar will let him stay once he wakes up – Oskar doesn't seem to have much patience for poor Cliff, but Cliff is quietly persistent in his role as Oskar's assistant.

'The headlights,' Louis says, once Cliff is out of earshot. 'Just like the ones on the car that night.'

'You know what this means?' I ask, my pulse pounding in my ears. 'Anyone at the studio could have used this car. If this *was* the car that tried to run us off the road, then that means someone at the studio is involved.' I run my gaze over Tipsy's coat sleeve again, my eyes snagging on the stain.

'Does that look like—'

'Blood,' Louis says before I can finish speaking. 'You think it's Oskar's?'

That seems to be the only explanation, which begs the question again of how Tipsy knew about Oskar so fast. Cliff said he's the one who found him, not Tipsy. Then there's the 'memoir' I found in Tipsy's trailer, and the lighter that's an identical match for the one found at the Hollywood sign – the one Tipsy said she lost. As an employee under contract with the studio, Tipsy could have used the pool car at any time. Sliding my hand into Tipsy's coat pocket hoping to find the lighter tucked away so I can inspect it again, my fingers brush against a small square of card.

'Oh.' I look at Louis, who is waiting impatiently for me beside the car. 'Lou. I think we might have just found out Freddy's name.' I hand him the business card I've pulled from Tipsy's coat, the name 'Freddy Carver' and a telephone number etched in white onto the navy-blue card. 'Now we can find out who he really is.' *And what his business card is doing in Tipsy Jenner's coat pocket.*

Chapter Twenty-Seven

The lot is silent the next morning as Tilda and I sneak in through the back gate before the sun is even up, Freddy Carver's business card burning a hole in my pocket.

'You're sure no one will be around?' Since Mae's accusation against Tilda last night over the blind items, Tilda has definitely lost her spark a little. Usually she wouldn't give a damn about being caught breaking into Oskar Goldstein's office but this morning she's jittery, checking over her shoulder as we hurry through the lot, our footsteps echoing between the buildings.

'Oskar certainly won't be,' I say dryly, 'and shooting is suspended for today at least. I'm not sure if Bunny or any of the other assistants will still come in though, so we need to be quick.' As we approach Oskar's office I tug my keys from my belt, flipping through them until I find one that looks as though it might fit.

'And you're sure you have the key to his office?' Tilda's brow crumples as I insert the first key and then the second with no luck.

'Honestly? No.' I grin at her as I try the third key. 'Jean just told me this bunch opens almost every door on the lot – it's taken her years to collect them all. So I'm hoping one of them fits, but there's no guarantee.' And I quickly realise that Jean was right – these keys open *almost* every door on the lot. Just not the one to Oskar Goldstein's office.

'Maybe this is the Lord's way of telling you this isn't a good idea,' Tilda says. 'Why don't we just head over to Oskar's house? Surely the housekeeper will be up by now.'

I do want to head over to Oskar's house, to the scene of the crime, but I want to get my hands on that little red book first. Wandering around the side of the building, my heart skips a beat. All is not lost.

Tilda follows me around the edge of the building, shaking her head when she sees the tiny window, open just a crack to let out Oskar's cigar smoke. 'No. Nuh-uh. No way.'

'Til, I'll never fit through there. You're *tiny*. And it'll only take you a second. Come on, have you really lost your spritz?'

'My *what*?' She turns to face me, planting her hands on her hips the way I knew she would. 'Lily Jones, are you calling me yellow?'

Bullseye. 'No, of course not but… Louis is usually the cautious one. He's usually the one who tries to knock some sense into the pair of us. You know, if you don't want to—'

'Give me a bunk up.' Tilda glares at me as she waits for me to make my hands into a cradle she can step into. Moments later, she's got the window as far open as it'll go and she's wedged at the waist, shimmying her way inside.

'Once you're in, flick the lock on the door but don't turn the lights on,' I hiss. Footsteps ring out from around the corner and without thinking I reach up and shove Tilda through the opening, wincing as she tumbles to the ground with a muttered *oof*. The footsteps come closer and my heart is in my mouth as I press myself against the corner of Oskar's office, the bricks hard against my shoulder blades.

'Lily?'

Shit. Adjusting my stance so I look as though I am just resting against the wall, not hiding *at all*, I paste a smile on my face. 'Bunny. You're here early.'

'I got a garbled message from Leonard to say shooting was suspended, but I have a lot of paperwork to go through so I figured I should come in anyway.' Her eyes narrow. 'What are you doing here if we aren't shooting? And why aren't we shooting? Is Mae OK after yesterday?'

'Yesterday?' I have to think for a moment, before I remember Mae's fainting fit. So much has happened since then that I'd almost forgotten about it. 'Oh, yeah, Mae is fine. It's Oskar.'

'Oskar?' Bunny's eyes flick towards his office, shifting on the balls of her feet. 'What about him?'

'He was found at home last night covered in blood. They're saying he slipped on the wet pool tiles.' I give Bunny the bare facts as I know them, and by the time I am finished she is almost translucent she's so pale.

'I knew something like this would happen.' She speaks so quietly under her breath that I can barely make the words out. 'Thank you for telling me, Lily. I'll arrange a fruit basket to the hospital from all of us.' Before I can ask what she meant by saying she knew this would happen, she's hurrying along the alley towards her own office, her head down, and then Oskar's door flies open and Tilda stands there, rubbing at her shoulder.

'Let's do this,' she says.

—

Oskar's desk is a riot of marked-up screenplays with a thick red 'CONFIDENTIAL' stamp punched across the front pages, studio memos and, oddly, Twinkie wrappers. A half-smoked cigar lays in the crystal-cut ashtray, ash littering the mahogany desk, and I wrinkle my nose as we approach. A framed photograph of Oskar shaking hands with Frank Sinatra has pride of place beside the blotter and a shiver runs down my spine, memories of our time in Vegas rising to the front of my mind.

'Oskar isn't into housekeeping,' Tilda muses as she flips through the memos on his desk, brushing a finger through the cake crumbs beside them.

'Too busy and important for all that,' I say, as I pull open the desk drawers and begin rummaging. 'And to think Oskar yelled at Cliff for misplacing an important memo, when he's left them scattered all over the desk for anyone to see.' I feel a pang of sympathy for Cliff, who looked so distraught last night but can't seem to do anything right by Oskar.

At first, I think I've forced Tilda through a tiny window on a breaking and entering spree for nothing, the drawers containing only pens (posh fountain pens, not your cheap tacky biros), a folded handkerchief (clean, thank God) and an unopened box of expensive cigars. I am about to move on to the filing cabinet in the corner of the room, when my fingers brush against something hard and round in the top of the drawer. Curious, I press my fingers against it, and then with an audible click a tiny drawer in the centre of the desk pings open.

'Is that…?'

'A secret compartment, yeah.' The secret drawer appears empty at first glance, but the green felt in the bottom doesn't seem to sit properly. Sliding my fingernail under the edge, I lift the corner of the felt and pull it up, a surge of satisfaction running through me when I spot the cover of Oskar's little red book. 'Aha. Funny place to keep a notebook.' The fact that Oskar has hidden this so well speaks volumes.

After a quick check outside to make sure we're not about to be discovered, Tilda opens the red leather cover and scans the first page. 'It looks like some sort of list.' She frowns, running her finger down the scrawled list.

Peering over her shoulder, I take a peek. I was expecting some sort of diary, or a shitty version of the screenplays Oskar reads every day, but this is something totally different. There are lists of names, some first names only, some only initials, some weird references that could allude to someone but you would never know who. Some have asterisks beside their names, some have tiny hearts, but all of them have dollar amounts beside them.

'This is no diary, Lil,' Tilda says. 'This is a log. An accounts book.' She flips the page, poring over the scratchy list made by Oskar's pen before she gasps, dropping the book onto the desk. 'Holy moly.'

'Tilda? What is it?' Snatching up the book I read over the page she was on, but I can't make head nor tail of what has her gasping like that.

'See here?' She jabs a finger at a name in tiny font in the bottom corner of the page. 'Freddy Eyelash. That's our guy, Lil. I knew I should have recognised his name when you showed me his business card.'

'Freddy Eyelash is Freddy Carver?' It still doesn't make sense to me. 'But who is he? Why is he always hanging around on set? And why does Oskar have his name scrawled in this book?'

Tilda looks up at me, her eyes wide. 'Freddy Eyelash is a big deal, Lil. Possibly mob-connected. He's a fixer.'

Before I can respond, the door to Oskar's office swings open and Cliff appears, looking rumpled and exhausted.

'What are you doing here?' Confusion crosses his face as he looks from Tilda to me and back again, and I thank God Tilda had the foresight to slip Oskar's red book into her purse as the door creaked ajar.

'Just checking on things. Dropping off memos. In fact, I should probably get going. I need to catch up with Bunny.'

'She's in?' Cliff perks up a little at this.

'She's busy,' I say firmly. Clearly Cliff is still harbouring a little bit of a thing for her, even though he's supposed to be dating Veronica. 'Shooting might be off but we still have other things to do.' I run my eyes over him, over his crumpled shirt collar and his pale cheeks. 'How are you feeling today? Last night must have been an awful shock for you.'

Cliff nods, his Adam's apple working as he swallows. 'It was. Terrible. It was the last thing I expected when I went to the house.'

'What about Tipsy?'

'Tipsy?'

'Wasn't she at the house when you arrived?' I'm still trying to figure out how Tipsy got blood on her coat sleeve.

'Uh, no?' Cliff's brow crinkles. 'I don't think so. To be honest, Lily, it's all a bit of a blur.' Cliff runs his eyes over Oskar's desk one more time, his gaze skittering over the piles of scripts and admin before returning to my face. 'Let me walk you out. Oskar will be furious if the office isn't locked up properly.'

Standing to one side, Cliff props the door open as Tilda and I leave, my heart crashing against my ribcage at how close we came to being caught stealing from Oskar's office. It's only as Tilda and I step out through the security gates, waving to Bobby and with Cliff out of sight, that it dawns on me. Cliff never said why he was in Oskar's office this morning.

–

'It sounds obvious, but a fixer fixes things,' Tilda explains, as we make our way over to Oskar's lavish mansion on the other side of Hollywood. It's a bus ride away, but Louis is working and let's be honest, he's never going to let me drive Christine, his car. 'You know, something happens and he's the one to swoop in and brush it all under the rug. Half the things that happen in Hollywood we never hear about because of people like Freddy Eyelash.'

'Why on earth do they call him Freddy Eyelash, of all things?' Part of me isn't sure I want to know.

Tilda grimaces, her mouth twisting. 'Legend has it that in his previous career as a police officer he wasn't averse to using whatever tactics he could to get information out of people… including removing their eyelashes. I guess that's what made the mob think he might be such a handy addition for them.' She pauses. 'I mean, that's if he even *is* in with the mob. That's all speculation too.'

The stink of diesel that permeates the bus is making me nauseous, and I am relieved when the bus rumbles to a stop just off Stone Canyon Road. 'So he would know all the gossip?' A frisson of something icy runs down my spine. 'He'd know exactly what was going on… and how to make people pay up if they didn't want it to get out.'

Tilda nods, clutching her purse to her side as we step off the bus and into the blessed fresh air. 'He's well known, at least his name is. I don't think many people know what he looks like, not until they use his services anyway. I could kick myself for not realising.'

'Well, Mae and Tipsy both know who he is,' I say, as we approach the winding, gated drive that leads to Oskar's house. 'Tipsy had his card and I've seen Mae with him more than once.'

'You think they might be working together?' The idea has crossed my mind, but still I can't reconcile Tipsy – generous, hilarious Tipsy with her loud laugh and constant haze of cigarette smoke – or even Mae, with her quiet demeanour and subtle humour, as murderous blackmailers. Pressing my finger to the buzzer at the gate, I explain to the housekeeper that we're from the studio and have come to pick up a few things for Oskar. The gates slowly open. At the front door, a stout older woman with thick, black hair pulled into a pristine bun stands with a sombre expression on her face.

'Mr Oskar isn't coming home yet?' she asks as we step inside the wide, sweeping hallway. 'How is he?'

'He's stable,' I say, although I have no idea if that's really the case. Taking in the vast staircase ahead of us, and the many, many side tables littered with porcelain trinkets – not what I would have expected of Oskar at all – I can see the housekeeper has her work cut out for her. 'We just need to pick up some things for him, pyjamas and such, if you don't mind showing us to his room.' I cross my fingers behind my back, hoping she hasn't realised that Cliff has already collected an overnight bag for Oskar.

We follow her up the stairs, her voice floating back over her shoulder towards us. 'I could have packed him some things,' she says. 'I've worked for Mr Oskar for a long time. He's been very kind to me and my family. It was such a terrible shock to hear what happened to him.'

Tilda moves into the bedroom the housekeeper gestures to, but I stay on the landing beside her, aware that she seems keen to keep talking. 'You weren't here when it happened, Mrs...?'

'Rosie. Rosie Delgado,' she says. 'No, thank goodness. I had left for the evening. Mr Oskar asked me to prepare some snacks for him and his friends – chips, sandwiches, that kind of thing. I made sure there were cigars and whisky, and then I left for the night. I only saw on the news that he had been hurt.'

'His friends? Oskar had friends over the night of the attack?' My stomach lurches, my mouth suddenly dry. If Oskar had people over, someone might have seen what happened.

'It was Tuesday. Mr Oskar always has his friends over on a Tuesday. He lets me leave early, as long as I have prepared the snacks.' She frowns. 'Such a horrible accident to happen to him.'

'Did you recognise the friends that he had over?' Was it Cliff? Or Tipsy? I still don't know how Tipsy found out so quickly.

She shakes her head. 'No, I left before they arrived. The news... It said he fell outside by the pool and hit his head. He was lucky to be found at all. He could have died!' I open my mouth but I don't know what to say, for some reason still not entirely sure this was an accident.

'Lily? I could use a hand.' Tilda's voice floats out of the bedroom, a sharp edge to it.

I turn to the housekeeper, who is dabbing at her eyes with a pristine white hanky. 'I'm sorry about Oskar but I'm sure he'll be home soon, and he'll be very grateful to you for holding the fort. I'll let you know when we're done here.'

As soon as Rosie descends the staircase, I head into Oskar's bedroom, where Tilda stands beside the bed, the red book clutched tightly in her hand. Papers are strewn across the bedspread – a garishly trendy shade of aqua that matches the padded headboard – and a picture frame containing an oil painting leans against the bedroom wall, revealing a small alcove hidden behind it. I frown as I take in the scene, running my eyes over the horrible oil portrait of Oskar. 'You found something.'

Tilda nods. 'Oh yeah, I found something. In the alcove, there. The picture was hanging over it – I only checked because it looked askew. Look.' She gestures to the papers and I reach out and snatch one up, my hands suddenly cold as I skim the words.

> *So, the little red book is where you run your ledger,*
> *is it? My dear Mr Goldstein, what would people*
> *think if they knew the nasty truth about you? You*
> *think of yourself as a polished studio exec, when*
> *the reality is you're nothing but a lowlife addict,*
> *addicted to the thrill, and there are others who could*
> *perform your job far better than you ever could.*
> *If you don't want the ugly truth revealed to the*
> *world, you'll bring $10,000 and the red ledger to*
> *the bench behind the chapel at ten p.m. on Friday.*
> *Come alone. If you don't, you'll have rolled your*
> *last dice.*
> *A Friend*

'Holy shit,' I breathe, my chest tight. 'It's a blackmail letter. Signed the same way, complete with wonky M. It's from the same person who blackmailed Max and Ann.'

Tilda holds out the ledger and then tucks her hand into the alcove and pulls out a red poker chip. 'This isn't a souvenir from Vegas, Lil. And this book isn't any kind of diary. The letter is right. It's a ledger of people who owe Oskar money, and who he owes to. He's been running illegal poker games.'

I think of Rosie telling me how Oskar would have friends over every Tuesday night, the way he fumbled the red book out of sight when I went to his office that day, and then another thought hits me. 'The blind item… You said it was gambling. Tilda, you were right.'

The blind item was about Oskar, and this was no accident. Oskar never slipped on any wet tiles. He was attacked and left for dead – but by who?

Chapter Twenty-Eight

'There's no way this could have been an accident,' I say to Louis later on that evening as we head to the hospital to visit Oskar. He's awake now, and although he's feeling a little sore I'm hoping he might be able to tell us something about that night. 'The latest Last Word piece was about Oskar for sure, and there were blackmail letters hidden behind a picture in his bedroom. Whoever got to Max and Ann got to Oskar too.' I am not surprised by this. Knowing how stubborn and block-headed Oskar can be, there was never any doubt that he would refuse to pay up for a blackmailer.

'Maybe now he's awake he'll remember something. Even the tiniest thing could help.' Louis holds the elevator door for me and we ascend to the private floor where Oskar is being cared for, away from the general public.

'Hello, Oskar.' Peering around the door frame, I stifle the wince that hunches my shoulders as I take in Oskar's bruised and battered face and the thick bandage wrapped around his head. 'How are you feeling?'

He pushes himself up the pillows, screwing up his face as pain makes itself known. 'You should see the other guy. Didn't happen to bring me a cigar, did you?'

I am about to shake my head when Louis slips his hand inside the pocket of his jacket and pulls out a fat Cuban, snipping the end off and handing it to Oskar. 'Here you go, Mr Goldstein.'

Oskar droops a black eyelid in a poor imitation of a wink and runs the cigar under his nose, inhaling deeply. 'Ahhh. That's the ticket.'

'Maybe just keep it at sniffing the cigar, for now,' I say, perching on the edge of the hospital bed. A huge bouquet of flowers sits on the locker beside the bed, along with get well cards and a fruit basket that, if I know Oskar, he won't ever touch. 'How are you really?'

'Sore. Tired. But I'll be back at my desk before you know it, Lily, so the schedule better not be out of whack. Is everyone filming today? And what about messages, did you bring them?'

'Oskar,' I say gently. 'The schedule is fine. Everything at the studio is fine, and no, I didn't bring your messages. You nearly died. You need to focus on recovery, not your messages. I wanted to ask you about the... accident.'

Oskar shifts in the bed, gesturing for Louis to pass him a glass of water. 'Where's the other one? The little girl you run around with – the redhead.'

'She's working.' Tilda has gone to the newspaper office to start digging up as much as she can on Freddy Eyelash, now we know his name.

Oskar tries to cock an eyebrow. 'Typing up her little gossip column, no doubt.'

'About that. The blind items... You know Tilda isn't the one behind them, right?'

'So you say. I don't know who's behind them, but I do know they need to stop.' Oskar coughs, pressing a hand to his broken ribs. 'The devil makes work for idle hands and there's none more idle than those who gossip.'

Louis catches my eye and I shake my head discreetly. Now isn't the time for him to come riding to defend Tilda's honour. 'Oskar, can we talk about the blind items? More specifically the one about you.'

'Me?' He tries to look indignant but it falls flat on his bruised face.

'I've seen the letters,' I say. 'The blackmail letters? I think whoever sent them to you was the one to write the Last Word piece in the newspaper about someone being too close to Lady Luck. And I think that piece was about you.' He looks so despondent I want to take his hand, but I am aware that he is still a studio exec, still my boss's boss, and still very much my senior. 'You were hosting poker parties, weren't you?'

'I don't know what you're talking about. Blackmail… illegal gambling…' He swallows hard. 'It all sounds like a plot from a movie, Lily. I'm respected at the studio. I don't know why on earth you'd think—'

'Oskar, if you're not going to be honest with me then I'll have no option but to ask around, talk to other people who might have been at your poker parties, although I'd rather just speak with you now and keep it all under wraps. We found a chip and the blackmail letters in your room. So, please. Let's not play games now.'

Oskar closes his eyes, the purple–black stain of a bruise spreading across his eye socket and along his cheek. 'It was only once or twice and only with trusted friends. We just played a couple of hands and had a few drinks, that's all. We weren't harming anyone.' His hand shoots out and grips my wrist tightly. 'You won't tell anyone, will you, Lily? About the blackmail letters? In fact, you should probably go to my house and burn them.' He pauses, wincing as he breathes in. 'I got the first letter and laughed it off as one of the others playing a game. And then I got a second letter, and then a third. I was furious by then. I wasn't going to pay anyone for something that was…'

'Illegal,' I say, quietly. 'Sorry, Oskar, but it is. You were taking a risk.'

'I know,' he snaps. 'But you don't understand, Lily. It's the thrill of it – there's nothing like it. It doesn't mean I should hand over my money to some… lowlife, because they see fit to blackmail me.'

Louis pulls the chair from beneath the window and sits beside the bed. 'Mr Goldstein… Oskar. That night, the night of the accident. Do you remember anything at all?'

Oskar pauses, hissing as his eyebrows draw together. 'Honestly? No. I remember feeling incensed during the day, after I'd seen the Last Word piece, but I convinced myself nobody knew it was me. The next thing I remember was waking up in here with the mother of all headaches.'

'Your poker party… Rosie said you held them on Tuesdays, so surely you held one that night? Is there anyone who would be willing to talk to us about what happened?'

Oskar plucks at the bedspread, avoiding my eyes. 'You don't need to speak to anyone, Lily. I'd really rather you didn't.'

'But—'

Oskar sighs, rubbing a hand over his forehead. 'You don't need to speak to anyone about that night, Lily, because I cancelled the poker party. The blind item did put the wind up me so I thought it was best to cancel, avoid trouble for any of the others. I was home alone that night. I must have fallen… I don't remember. That's what Tipsy told me.'

Louis and I exchange a brief glance, Tipsy's name on Oskar's lips making my stomach somersault. 'Oskar, I don't think you did fall, and I don't think this was an accident at all. I can't go into all the details, but you aren't the first person to have received a letter from the blackmailer. But you are the first person to have survived.'

—

I don't sleep well after breaking the news to Oskar that he isn't the only one on the blackmailer's hit list. He was furious when I refused to elaborate. When I suggested that perhaps it was time to go to the police, he became even more incensed, telling me that there was no possible way any of this was connected, and he'd simply drunk too much and fallen. I suspect that he is more concerned with the police finding out he was running a gambling racket than catching whoever it was who tried to off him. Now, as I arrive on set the following morning, my stomach is in knots as I realise I have no idea who I can trust.

'Meeting, in the commissary,' Bunny whispers to me as she hurries past, a clipboard clutched to her chest. 'Hurry, Lil, you'll be late.'

Taking her cue, I scurry through the lot towards the canteen trailer, the knot in my stomach growing ever bigger. As I slip in the door behind Bunny the chatter ceases and I spot Tipsy and Mae sitting together, an empty chair beside Mae, and then Vic Romano on the next chair, his long legs sprawling across the floor.

'We thought you weren't going to make it,' Tipsy whisper-shouts across Mae in my direction. 'Even

Romano made it on time.' She drops him a wink, as Mae flashes me a quick smile.

'You look tired, Lily,' she says, tilting her head to one side as she looks me over. 'Were you out late last night?'

'No. Just a touch of insomnia.' I try not to read too much into Mae's words – surely she doesn't know that I was at the hospital last night visiting Oskar? I think about the driving licence I found in another name in her room. Mae wouldn't be the first person in Hollywood to change her name, but to find it in with the list of blind items makes me feel oddly uneasy and I make a mental note to speak to Tilda about it again.

'Have you heard the latest?' Tipsy nudges Mae glee-fully, nodding to her to get my attention. 'There's another Last Word column!'

'There is?' My heart sinks and for a moment I feel faint and dizzy. Another blind item means another death. 'What was it this time?'

Tipsy pauses for a moment, stretching out the dramatic tension. '*Which hotshot director, known for his love of fast cars and even faster women, has been seen stepping out on his latest wife? Spotted having dinner in Malibu, he definitely wasn't discussing camera angles… It's not the first time this love rat has cheated, and it seems it won't be the last.*' Tipsy claps her hands together, her eyes gleaming. 'This really is delicious gossip, don't you think? One of the best so far. I wonder who it could be about. I know who my money is on – Billy Wilder is *quite* the ladies' man.'

I don't speak, my fists clenched by my sides as my eyes go to the keys on the table in front of Leonard as he prepares to speak. The flat silver key on a distinctive oval keychain to his brand new 1952 Porsche 356 coupé. His pride and joy, and a present to himself before the baby comes. With its meticulous silver exterior, split screen windscreen and plump red leather seats, it's the sports car of more than one person's dreams on set.

'Everyone!' Leonard claps his hands together. The dark circles still ring his eyes, and a tiny splash of coffee mars his shirt. He doesn't look like the usual well-kept Leonard that I am used to and I feel another sickening lurch in my gut. 'As most of you know, Oskar suffered a fall the other night and sustained quite a nasty head injury.' A murmur goes through the trailer, and there is a clang as someone drops a coffee cup. 'He's going to be out of action for a few weeks, but obviously the show must go on. So, in his absence we will be working with someone who is the perfect fit to step into his shoes temporarily and keep things ticking along.'

Leaning against the wall opposite me, I see Cliff give a small smile to Veronica, who stands beside him. Bunny hovers beside Leonard, and I see her glance in Cliff's direction too, her fingers tightening on her clipboard. Mae shifts in her seat beside me, and I realise we are all waiting with bated breath to see who will take Oskar's place.

'Thank you, Henry, for stepping in at such short notice to help us get this picture over the line on schedule. Everyone, welcome Henry Ginsberg.' A short, grey-haired man in a sharp suit steps forward and begins talking, but my eyes are still on Cliff. He almost visibly slumps and I realise a part of him must have been hoping that he would be trusted to help out in Oskar's absence, seeing as he is his right-hand man.

Henry makes a short speech and then Leonard is reminding everyone of call times and Bunny is handing out fresh script pages. Cliff stands alone by the coffee pot, having sent Veronica to Mae's trailer to start on her make-up.

'I wasn't expecting that.' I nod in Leonard and Henry's direction as Cliff pours me a cup of the bitter, acrid coffee. 'I'm guessing you weren't either. I'm sorry, Cliff.'

Cliff gives me a sharp look, before passing me the cream. 'I'm just an assistant, Lily. Even if I do bear the Marshall name.'

'Marshall? Wait… Marshall as in Tully Marshall? The silent movie star?'

Cliff nods. 'He was my grandfather. Movies are in the family, so I was never going to do anything else. Although I've never hit the dizzying heights of stardom that he did. Something my mother never fails to remind me about.'

'I had no idea.'

'No one ever does.' Cliff gives me a droopy smile, dropping two sugar cubes into his own cup and stirring slowly. 'Aside from the movies my grandfather lived a fairly quiet life. He was living out in Palm Springs at the end – we still have the house. Secluded, private, it's a perfect getaway.'

Raising my eyes to where Leonard is laughing with Henry Ginsberg, his face still etched with dark shadows, it's as though a lightbulb goes off over my head. The blind item could refer to any director, but Leonard is the only one I know with a brand-new sports car. The reference to his 'latest wife' and that it's not the first time he's cheated, given the way he and Jean came about, makes fear strike icy shards into my heart. I can't run the risk of Leonard dying. Not if there's anything I can do to stop it.

'Cliff? Your grandfather's place. Is there any chance you'd consider renting it out to me, just for the weekend?'

If the blind item is about Leonard then I might have just found a way to get him out of the picture.

Chapter Twenty-Nine

'Honestly, this is too much. You are too good to us.' Jean presses a hand to my cheek as Louis swings her little travel bag into the trunk of Leonard's sports car. 'I don't quite know what you think we've done to deserve a weekend away,' she says, leaning in close, 'but I am very, very grateful to you, Lily. I've barely seen Leonard since this movie started shooting.'

Pasting on a wobbly smile, I run my eyes over her outfit. Jean is as chic as ever in a flower-print day dress, white gloves, a vibrant red headscarf and sunglasses. You can barely see the small bump of her stomach. 'You both deserve a break,' I say. 'And look at you! You look like Audrey Hepburn.'

Jean looks surprised, whipping her sunglasses off. 'Oh, these are hers,' she says. 'She left them at our house when she came for drinks a few weeks ago.' She presses a hand to her mouth, hiding her grin. It's nice to see Jean a bit giddy for once. 'If she asks, you didn't see them – I'll return them when I'm home.'

'Here are the keys.' Cliff hands over a small bunch of keys to Leonard. 'There isn't an alarm or anything… and you should help yourselves to anything while you're there. I did ask the housekeeper to get a few essentials in. Wine, caviar, you know.'

I raise an eyebrow as Leonard claps Cliff on the back, almost knocking him over. 'You're a gem, errr...'

'*Cliff,*' I hiss quietly.

'Cliff. Anything that makes my wife happy makes me happy.' Leonard's voice is gruff as he moves to check the trunk, cutting Cliff off before he can respond. 'Jean? Are you ready? We need to head out if you want to make it before sunset.'

Jean kisses Tilda and Louis on the cheek as I approach Leonard, Cliff standing awkwardly to one side. 'You could smile a little bit,' I tease him. 'You're getting a weekend break with your beautiful wife.' Part of me feels as though I should be reminding Leonard of this, especially if the blind item does refer to him. Jean will be destroyed if Leonard has cheated on her, and I would feel the same way. These two are the closest I've had to parents for a long time.

'I'm missing the private screening of *The Bad and The Beautiful* tonight,' Leonard grumbles as he leans in to kiss me on the cheek. 'And what about the rushes over the weekend? Now really isn't a good time, Lily. I have too much to do—'

'You have a couple of months before you have a new baby,' I say firmly. 'And a wife who's complaining that she never sees you. Plus, you work too hard. Henry Ginsberg can sit through the rushes this weekend, and I'm sure Cliff will help out too. And as for the private screening, we're going in your name. Besides, you and Vincente have been friends for years. He'll always give you another, even more private showing if you ask him.' *I need you out of town in case you're the next one on the blackmailer's hit list.*

'Anything — any little thing at all and you'll call me?' Leonard hovers by the driver's side door as I resist the urge to shove him into the car.

'I swear.' It's only once Leonard and Jean are heading out onto the boulevard, Jean twisting in her seat to turn back and wave at us, that I finally let out a long breath. 'You checked the car over, right?' I ask Louis.

'Yep. Told Leonard I was taking her to fill her up before he left. It's a hell of a car, Lil.' Louis's voice takes on a dreamy tone and Tilda tuts, kicking him lightly in the shin.

'But did you check the tyres? And the brake line?' she says, as the silver Porsche turns a corner and disappears from view.

'Why do you need to check the car over?' Cliff looks puzzled. 'It's brand new. There can't be anything wrong with it.'

Tilda's eyes widen and I jump in before she says something I'd rather she didn't reveal. 'It's me… sorry. When I lived in London I drove an old banger all the time, and it was forever breaking down and getting me in a jam. I have to check these things, even when it's not my car. And besides, it's Leonard… If the car does break down on a trip I've organised, I don't want you or I to get in trouble for it. Louis, you're sure everything is OK?' I don't know exactly how the director in the blind item is going to end up in an accident, but if it is Leonard, it won't be down to the car – not if I can help it.

Louis nods. 'All good. Although I still can't believe he agreed to go. I was half expecting him to bow out at the last minute.'

Me too. When Leonard's initial reaction was to decline, saying he already had plans, my heart had sunk, wondering if he was meeting up with someone he shouldn't. But when the plans turned out to be the private showing of

Vincente Minnelli's new movie, I knew I could swing things. Speaking of which…

'Guys, we have to hustle. The screening starts in an hour and I want to be there early.' I'm going to examine every face who enters – just in case our blackmailer decides to put in an appearance.

–

As I get Tilda to zip me into a dress more suited to an evening at a legendary film director's house than running errands on a studio lot, my hands are shaking. I am going to *Vincente Minnelli's* house. The only downside is that he and Judy Garland have already separated, so there's no chance of her giving us a song this evening.

The nerves are still there as we approach the house, through huge double gates and immaculate gardens, although they are more down to the thought that the blackmailer might be in attendance than meeting Vincente. Painted white, the house looks more imposing by the contrast of the black window frames and black double door that stands open as a maid admits the guests. I see Gene Kelly and Cyd Charisse entering the hallway, and then Vincente's producer Arthur Freed appears, a glass of scotch in one hand. I feel out of place, and not just because I've slipped here from the twenty-first century. This feels *huge* and not for the first time I want to pinch myself to see if I'll wake up.

'Lily? I didn't know you were invited this evening.' Mae Sinclair appears, stunning in a navy-blue, off-the-shoulder dress that sparkles under the huge chandelier in the hall.

'Representing Leonard,' I say. 'You look wonderful.' And she does, although a little overwhelmed at the clientele she's surrounded by.

'Really? Leonard isn't coming?' Mae's brow creases. 'Where is he?'

I open my mouth to tell her when I remember the list of blind items I found in her things, names etched in her neat handwriting. I don't think I saw Leonard's name but I can't be too careful. 'Away with his wife,' I say vaguely.

'Oh.' Mae almost seems put out by the news. 'Well, that's a shame. I haven't really spent much time with him away from the set.'

'And why would you?' Tipsy gusts in on the conversation on a wave of gin and cigarette smoke. 'Isn't this darling? Although rumour has it Vincente doesn't have a soul to share it with. Apparently Judy took everything, even the baby.'

It seems odd to hear Liza referred to as a baby when I've only ever known her as a loud, brash, funny cabaret star. Mae wanders away to fetch another drink and Tilda nudges me.

'She seemed keen to know where Leonard was,' she whispers out of the side of her mouth. 'You think she might have something to do with it?'

I shrug, accepting a cocktail from Louis. 'I don't know. She's hiding something though. Why else would she be hanging around with Freddy Eyelash and then telling us she doesn't know him? Did you find out anything about the name on the driving licence?'

'Not yet.' Tilda lowers her voice as Mae moves past us towards the oak doors at the end of the hallway. People are beginning to take their seats for the showing in Vincente's private cinema room. 'It's difficult when we don't know where she's really from – there are no other records for a Mabel McAllister other than the driver's licence. I hate to say it, Lil, but I think we're going to have to get into Mae's things again.'

As we follow the other guests into the cinema room, with its heavy velvet drapes in a rich shade of crimson and seats that are probably more comfortable than in any other cinema in America, a wave of exhaustion washes over me. I have too many suspects and not enough clues pointing me in one solid direction. Mae and Tipsy enter together, Mae whispering into Tipsy's ear as they settle at the end of the row, and then the lights dim and a swell of music filters through the cinema. I wish I could say I enjoy the movie, but having seen it several times with my mother before she died, it's easy enough to tune out as I keep my attention on the guests instead.

The big stars sit in the front row and are rapt the entire time, Kirk Douglas stealing glances at Lana Turner beside him every time she appears on screen. In the rows at the back are the lesser-known faces, including some of the crew who worked on the film. Mae and Tipsy sit in the second row, right in my eyeline. Tipsy smokes her way through the movie and seems more interested in trying to attract Kirk's attention than watch the screen. Mae, however, doesn't seem interested in the film or the screening attendees. She fidgets in her seat, checking her watch every now and again as if waiting for someone to arrive, but the heavy doors remain closed.

By the time the movie is over, I have a headache and I wish I had a mobile phone so I could call Jean and make sure they've arrived OK at Cliff's grandfather's house.

'That was incredible,' Tilda breathes, as we stand to all file out, squinting as the overhead lights come on. 'You think Louella would let me write a film review for the paper? It's a scoop, huh? No one else has seen it.'

'You're not even really meant to be here,' I say, my words trailing off as we hit the hallway to find Vincente in conversation with a housekeeper, his face stricken as tears course down her cheeks. There is a buzz of conversation filling the hall but it isn't the chatter of people who've had an enjoyable evening. It's a dread-laden babble of shock.

'What is it? What's happened?' Mae appears, looking fragile, her hair slipping out of the chignon she's tucked it into.

'I don't know.' I scan the crowd, searching for someone I can ask, my eyes eventually landing on Tipsy whose mouth is drawn into a tight circle, her eyes hollow. 'Tipsy?'

She blinks, frowning as if she doesn't recognise me for a moment. 'Lily? Oh, Lily, isn't it dreadful, dreadful news?'

My stomach lurches and I get that weird, off-kilter feeling you get when your blood sugar drops. 'What is? Tipsy, I don't know what's happened.'

'Oh.' Her eyes widen, and for once I get the feeling that Tipsy isn't happy about being the one to share the news. 'The housekeeper... she heard it on the wireless while we were all in the picture room watching the film.'

'Heard *what* on the wireless?' Tilda butts in, her tone filled with enough frustration for all of us. 'What happened, Tipsy?'

'An accident.' Tipsy hiccups, tears spilling over and causing black rivers of mascara to run down her cheeks. 'A horrible, terrible car accident.'

'What?' Mae goes deathly white, her fingernails digging into Louis's arm so hard that he winces.

Tipsy presses a hanky to her eyes, dabbing ineffectually at the tears that keep pouring. 'No one survived, that's what they're saying.'

'Who was in the accident?' Louis is calm and steady as he holds onto Mae with one hand and rests his other hand on Tipsy's shoulder, bringing her attention to him. 'Tipsy, take a deep breath.'

Tipsy obliges. 'No one is quite sure who was involved yet, but they're saying it's a big-name director. Someone we've all worked with before. It happened out in San Bernadino Valley, but they haven't reported the full details yet.'

'Oh.' Mae stumbles, sinking into a chair against the wall, all colour completely drained from her face now as she covers her eyes with her hands.

'San Bernadino Valley?' I cast a panicked look in Tilda and Louis's direction, my knees feeling as though they are about to give way. That's the road that Leonard and Jean would have taken to get to Cliff's grandfather's house.

Chapter Thirty

'I need to use the phone.' Fear makes the words stick in my throat, my tongue feeling too big for my mouth as I make a beeline for the teary housekeeper.

'Through there.' The housekeeper points a shaky finger towards the kitchen. Louis, Tilda and I hurry inside, the buzz of chatter from the hallway muting as Louis closes the door.

'It can't be them, surely not.' Tilda is pacing, her brow furrowed, her hands knotting together. 'First of all, surely Leonard wouldn't cheat.'

I say nothing, remembering how Jean and Leonard had stolen kisses behind his first wife's back until eventually they were forced to go public. After fumbling in my purse, I finally locate the slip of paper with Cliff's scrawled writing on it, the number of the house in Palm Springs in bold black ink. The phone is a heavy-set cream number, mounted on the wall of the kitchen, the cord spiralling down the wall. Picking up the handset, I listen for the dial tone and then begin the laborious task of dialling out, my anxiety growing with every second the rotary dial takes to spin back into place. Finally, the burr of the ringtone sounds in my ear. It rings. And rings. Louis and Tilda both watch with wide eyes, my own fear reflected back at me as the phone goes unanswered.

'Hello?' A breathless voice finally picks up and I close my eyes, the sting of tears hot behind my eyelids.

'Jean? Is that you?' Static hisses down the line for a second, and my heart feels as if it's going to burst right out of my chest.

'Lily? Yes, it's me. What's wrong? Did something happen?'

A cold wave of relief washes over me and I sag against the kitchen wall, the phone cord wrapping around my fingers. 'Thank God. Is Leonard there too?'

'Leonard? No. He just stepped out to get some firewood. Lily, there's a beautiful fireplace here and I know it's not really cold enough yet but—'

'Has he gone out in the car? Or is he still on the property?' My heart rate spikes, the receiver slipping in my damp palm.

Jean gives an impatient sigh on the other end of the line. 'Yes, Lily, Leonard is here on the property with me. He's out in the backyard at the woodstore, fetching logs, I just told you that.'

The tears I've been trying to hold back slide down my cheeks now, and Louis hands me a hanky before wrapping his arm round my shoulder. I say goodbye to Jean, apologising for disturbing her, and let Louis wrap me in a hug as I sob.

'I'm sorry,' I say moments later, my eyes pink and raw, my nose probably a shiny red beacon. 'I was just so relieved it wasn't them in the car accident.'

'This whole thing is too much,' Tilda says. 'We need to go to the police, let them deal with it.'

'Deal with what though?' I say, moving to the kitchen sink to run my wrists under the cold tap, finally feeling more under control. 'We don't really have any proof – the letters are evidence, but they don't prove that Max didn't break his sober streak and fall into the pool, or that Ann didn't jump off the sign. If anything they point to those events being even more believable. And Oskar has already refused to involve the police. No, this is on us to prove. And it's on us to catch whoever it is.'

The kitchen door swings open and Vincente Minnelli stands there, a frown drawing his brows into a deep valley. 'What are you doing in here? Everyone is leaving.'

'I'm sorry, Mr Minnelli.' I blink, unable to believe that I am standing in Minnelli's kitchen, speaking to him face to face. 'I'm Lily Jones, Leonard Langford's assistant. I attended on his behalf this evening, after he had to leave for Palm Springs. After the news broke about the accident, I had to check that he wasn't involved.'

Vincente's face softens and he nods. 'It was Julian March.' He names a prominent director, who I know Tipsy has worked with before. 'There was someone else in the vehicle but she hasn't been identified yet. A sad day for Hollywood.'

A sad day indeed. And also a terrifying one. Just how far is the blackmailer prepared to go to get what they want?

—

Ten days later Hollywood gathers at the Hollywood Memorial Park Cemetery – known in my time as the Hollywood Forever Cemetery – for the second time in as many months for yet another prominent funeral. The town is reeling from the death of Julian March, known for his hard-hitting movies that dig at Hollywood's seedy underbelly. Touted as a tragic accident – Julian was apparently seen in a bar shortly before he went off the road –

rumours have swirled anyway about Julian owing money and the mob possibly being involved. And then there's the woman who was found in the car with him. Her name has been revealed only as Sophie, and she was some twenty-odd years younger than Julian, fuelling additional rumours that he was having an affair.

'You think the blackmailer is here?' Tilda whispers, her face half hidden by a huge black hat that I'm pretty sure she's borrowed from her mother. I can't say much though, having had to borrow my black dress from the wardrobe department.

I scan the crowds. It's hard to say – anyone who is anyone in Hollywood is here. 'Who knows?' A flicker of fear burns low in my belly. Things seem to be escalating, and we're still no closer to who might be responsible.

A pastor drones on about the good Julian March did throughout his life as his wife Phoebe dabs at her eyes. Their young daughter, a tiny thing who can't be more than five years old, peers around the gravesite curiously, as if not entirely sure what's going on. Vic Romano stands beside the widow, one hand on her elbow, and I wonder what the connection is there, as clearly they are close. Tipsy gives an audible sob when the casket is lowered, and is comforted by Elizabeth Taylor, who gives her hand a tight squeeze. At the back of the crowd, Bunny stands with her head bowed, Veronica and Cliff a little further along. Cliff wraps an arm around Veronica's shoulders, and she leans against him, tears running down her cheeks. Everyone is downcast and subdued, Julian's death casting a pall over the whole town.

An hour later we are stepping inside Julian March's vast Hollywood mansion, alongside everyone else in the movie business it seems. The hall is filled with people, faces that

I've grown up watching on the big screen, and I've never felt so out of place in my life.

'Is this really the time, Lil?' Louis asks as I make a beeline for the staircase. 'I mean, it's a wake for Pete's sake. Surely we could come back another time and do this?'

I shake my head, one foot already on the bottom stair. 'Lou, come on. I've never met Julian March in my life, and neither have you. His wife has no idea who we are, so what makes you think she's ever going to let us into her house again? I know it's the wake, and I fucking hate the fact that we are using this opportunity to go through Julian's stuff, but I am ninety per cent sure this wasn't an accident, and we're going to prove it.'

'Prove what?' Bunny appears at the foot of the stairs, a martini in one hand and a celery stick in the other. Her eyes are red and her lipstick has worn off, and I realise she's already a little drunk.

'That Julian might have been murdered,' Tilda says.

Bunny's eyes nearly bug out of her head. 'What? Are you kidding me, Lil?' She shakes her head but the celery stick trembles in her hand. 'You have got to stop with all of this nonsense. I've heard the things you've been saying about Max and Ann and it's... absurd. It's speculation, that's what it is. Please, Lily, just leave things alone.'

'Bunny, I heard Cliff is looking for you,' Tilda interrupts Bunny's pious tirade. 'And I'm pretty sure that Tipsy is looking for cigarettes. Can you find her some? You know what she's like when the craving takes her and we don't want her causing a scene here, do we?'

Bunny opens her mouth to argue but thinks better of it as Tipsy's voice floats out from the sitting room. Narrowing her eyes at me one more time in a way I think is supposed to be mildly threatening, Bunny turns on her heel and flounces away, leaving me free to head upstairs to Julian's inner sanctum.

—

Julian's bedroom is more of a man cave than a boudoir. Decorated in varying shades of taupe and grey, with a lot of heavy wood furniture, there doesn't seem to be much evidence of Mrs March occupying the space at all – a fact that is confirmed by the closet only containing suits, and a room further down the hall painted in vivid colours and smelling of L'Heure Bleue.

'So they sleep separately. Huh.' Tilda nods as she rifles through the suits hanging neatly in the closet.

'That doesn't mean much,' I say, as I yank open a dresser drawer to find neatly rolled ties. 'I mean, lots of people sleep in separate bedrooms, don't they?' I'm pretty sure in the Fifties they do, not so much in my time. 'That doesn't mean he was having an affair.'

Louis scoffs as he peers out of the bedroom on to the landing to check the coast is still clear. 'He did die with another woman in his car, Lil. One whose full identity hasn't been revealed. I'd say there's a pretty high chance.'

'Even if he was, he didn't deserve to *die* over it,' I say hotly, as the ties yield nothing and I move on to the next drawer of neatly rolled socks. 'Louis, sometimes you can really—'

'Guys.' Tilda's voice is sharp and the irritation I'm feeling drains away as she steps out of the closet, an envelope in her hand. 'Julian got a letter too. Same threat – *meet me here with $15,000 this time or else I'll spill your secrets* – same sign off, same wonky M. Julian *was* being blackmailed.'

'So this means it wasn't an accident. And the blind item really was about Julian.' Louis steps inside the bedroom, the door latching shut behind him. 'And whoever is blackmailing Hollywood stars is responsible for two deaths at once now. Everything is escalating.'

I am already deep inside the closet, searching for more letters or anything that can give us a clue as to who might be responsible. All we need is one tiny hiccup on the blackmailer's part – a posted letter instead of hand delivered, a smudge of a postmark. Anything that can point us in the right direction. Spotting that the carpet in the corner of the closet has lifted slightly, I run my fingernails underneath, gently tugging it up to reveal a loose floorboard. Narrowly avoiding a huge splinter, I manage to pull the floorboard up, revealing a dark, cobwebby space underneath, a musty scent rising from the gaping hole. Tilda's nose wrinkles as I shove my hand inside, my heart skipping a beat as my fingers land on paper. It's another envelope, this time with a postmark.

'There's another one. With a San Fran postmark.' The envelope is typed this time, and I know even before I've unfolded the page inside this isn't a blackmail letter.

Dear Julian, the letter begins, a faint waft of something floral rising from the pages. *You knew my mother, back in 1930. You met on the set of your first movie...*

Holy shit.

'Julian wasn't having an affair with Sophie,' I say, my mouth dry. 'Look – she says she wants to meet him for dinner in Malibu... just like it said in the blind item. But Sophie wasn't his mistress. She was his daughter.'

Chapter Thirty-One

Before we have the chance to process things any further, the door handle moves on the bedroom door and Tilda gasps.

'In here.' Sliding back inside the closet, I make room for Tilda and Louis and pull the closet door closed, just as a foot appears on the plush carpet of Julian's bedroom. Muted sounds of conversation and the clink of glasses float up from the bottom floor as the person enters.

The figure crosses the carpet, pausing at the chest of drawers where I had my hands deep inside Julian's socks only minutes ago. Did I close the drawers properly? I can't remember, the excitement of Tilda finding a blackmail letter eclipsing anything else. Pressing my face to the crack in the louvered doors, adrenaline pumps through my veins as the figure opens a drawer, runs a finger over the contents and then closes it again. When he turns to the bed, I catch a glimpse of his face and I am drenched in an icy waterfall of fear.

'Freddy Eyelash,' Tilda whispers in my ear, her mouth barely moving as she too presses her face to the louvered doors. 'What the heck, Lil?'

'Shhh.' All of a sudden Louis's aftershave is tickling the back of my throat and a strand of Tilda's hair is brushing the end of my nose, and I don't know whether I am going to cough or sneeze. Gripping my nose between forefinger and thumb, I squeeze, holding my breath, my eyes watering as Freddy Eyelash moves to the bedside cabinet, his eyes raking over the less than perfect bedspread. There is a clear dent where Tilda perched on the edge of the bed when she was searching through the cabinet and now Freddy pauses, his eyes narrowing as he straightens up. He lifts his chin, almost as if he's smelling the air, and I want to curse Louis for drenching himself in the aftershave that I usually love so much. He moves to the window, bending down to peer under the bed, and while my urge to sneeze has gone, I have no breath in my body. Tilda clearly feels the same as her hand snakes into mine and I give it a squeeze, pressing my finger against my lips.

Freddy is a fixer, Tilda said, and while I don't really know much about what a fixer does, I'm pretty sure he's paid to do whatever it takes to make things go away. Freddy looks sharp and gentlemanly in his black suit, his hair neatly parted to one side, but his hands are big and I'm pretty sure that's the bulge of a gun at his waistband. Yeah, I think Freddy Eyelash has done whatever it takes to make things disappear… and now it looks as though we might be on his list.

He steps around the bed towards the closet and beside me Tilda closes her eyes, her breath hitching in her throat. Louis shuffles back and I frown at him, questioning him with my eyes. He reaches down and picks up the only weapon available – a shiny brown loafer. I try to swallow, but my throat is bone dry as the floorboards creak outside the closet. Freddy reaches out a thick hand, so close I can see the black hairs on his knuckles, and grips the door handle. *This is it. The moment Freddy Eyelash discovers us and probably kills us.* Like I said, I don't really know what a fixer does, but I reckon murder is probably on the menu. But before the door can be wrenched open, a voice filters in, high and sweet.

'Freddy? What are you doing in here?'

Freddy drops his hand and I finally breathe out as he turns to the doorway, stepping away from the closet. 'Just checking. Someone saw people coming upstairs, and Mrs March said this floor was out of bounds. What are you doing up here?'

There is a pause. 'Looking for another bathroom. I guess we should both get back downstairs before we find ourselves in trouble.'

Freddy crosses the room, and a second later there is the click of the bedroom door closing. I drop Tilda's hand, swiping my sweaty palm over my skirt.

'Oh Lord, I've never needed to pee so badly,' Tilda says, stepping out of the closet. 'We need to get out of here before he decides to come back.'

The air outside of the closet feels fresh despite the faint tang of cigar smoke from downstairs, and I take a deep breath before I turn to Louis and Tilda, something troubling on my mind. 'Did you hear who it was, who came looking for Freddy?'

Louis shakes his head. 'I don't think I really took it in. All I could think was, please Lord, let us get out of here without being discovered.'

'She said she didn't know him,' I say, 'but I knew she was lying. It was Mae. Mae was the one who just came to find Freddy.'

It's Vic who holds court at the commissary trailer the following morning when I arrive at the studio. The smell of frying bacon wafts on the air, but even that isn't enough to give me an appetite, and the handwritten sign announcing today's special as tuna salad makes me feel even more nauseous. The idea that the blackmailer had got things so wrong about Julian March kept Tilda and me up until the small hours, discussing how he could have got things so twisted. My instinct is that perhaps whoever is blackmailing the stars and then releasing blind items isn't as close to the action as they like to think they are. Did they spot Julian and Sophie having dinner in Malibu – the dinner where Sophie introduced herself as the daughter Julian never knew he had following a brief affair over twenty years earlier – and jump to conclusions? The whole thing leaves a nasty taste in my mouth, as I slide my hand into my purse and check that the blackmail letter Julian received is still there.

'So, who do we think this one is about?' Vic asks, his voice booming out across the lot as two crewmen lean on the counter, their sleeves rolled up to show tanned forearms.

Lounging in a chair with her customary cigarette between her fingers, Tipsy yawns. 'Read it again, Vic. I need to digest it.'

Vic, ever the actor, clears his throat dramatically. '*One of Hollywood's newest darlings may have even more skeletons in her closet than the props department. She's caught the public's attention with her sweeter than apple pie demeanour, but a little bird from back East says she vanished right around the time a local "accident" made headlines. Things were swept under the rug faster than you can say "fixer" but keep your eyes peeled, my dears. Things have a nasty habit of resurfacing in the third act in this town.*'

Tipsy grinds out her cigarette and claps her hands together. 'Golly. That sounds even worse the second time around.' She glances around the small crowd hanging out at the trailer – the crewmen, drinking black coffee now, an extra who has somehow wangled their way here, and a cameraman who waits impatiently for his bacon. There is an air of something stilted and tense, as though everyone seems to realise that the blind items have gone too far now. 'Doesn't it, though? It almost sounds as if someone is being accused of *murder*.'

'OK, Tipsy, that's enough,' I break in, unable to stand the gossip any longer, especially knowing what I do now about Julian March. 'Just because Oskar isn't back yet doesn't mean that the chatter about the blind items is allowed.'

Tipsy rolls her eyes. 'Oh, Mae. Thank goodness you're here. At least you're not a party pooper.'

'What's going on?' Mae plucks a banana from the fruit bowl on the counter but doesn't start to peel it.

'Another piece in the Last Word,' Vic calls out. 'Want me to read it to you? It's about some new chick in town who may or may not have done away with someone in her hometown.'

'Vic, please,' I say, despair edging in. 'Enough. Enough from everybody. The next person who starts on about the gossip, I'm tattling to Leonard.'

'Jeez, Lily.' Vic pushes himself away from the counter, swishing his hand through his hair in a move that I think is supposed to be sexy. 'I thought you were cool.'

'I'm not,' I say firmly. 'I am very much uncool. So get to make-up before I follow through on my threat to tell Leonard.'

Vic winks and swaggers away. I snatch up the newspaper from where he's ditched it and head around the side of the trailer to dump it in the rubbish bin. As I round the corner, I falter as I realise I am not alone.

'This has to stop,' Bunny is saying as she leans against the cool silver side of the trailer. Cliff stands over her, his hands on the metal siding on either side of her head as if keeping her in place. 'I mean it, Cliff. What if Veronica found out?'

Before Cliff can answer I clear my throat and hold the newspaper aloft. 'Just throwing out the trash.'

Cliff leaps away from Bunny, smoothing his hair down before shoving his hands into his pockets.

'Lily!' Bunny yelps, her cheeks burning a bright scarlet. 'That wasn't…'

I raise an eyebrow at Cliff who has the good grace to avoid my eyes, scuffing his toe through the dirt before he gives Bunny a brief nod and scurries out of sight. Disappointment floods my veins at both of them. Sure, they're adults and can do whatever they want, but Cliff is supposed to be dating Veronica, and I thought Bunny had more self-worth than this. 'Bunny, I—'

'I have to go.' Bunny snatches up her purse where it sits by her feet and slings it over her shoulder. 'I'll talk to you later, Lily. But this isn't what it looks like.'

I think it's pretty clear what it looks like and I feel sorry for poor Veronica, who probably thinks – just like I did – that Cliff is a stand-up guy who'll make an honest woman of her one day, but today I have more pressing things to think about, like who the blind item could possibly be about. If I can just figure out who it's about then maybe we have a chance of stepping in and potentially saving their life. At the very least it might mean unmasking the blackmailer and putting a stop to all this once and for all.

It's not until much later on in the day, when almost everyone else has left, that I manage to get to my desk to type up the continuity notes and deal with Leonard's messages. The day's shoot was fractured and slow going, Mae fluffing her lines more than once, earning such a dressing down from Leonard that she's scurried off to her trailer to practise her lines when she should be going home. There is a weird atmosphere on set that I want to put down to the latest Last Word piece. It's one thing to gossip about secret liaisons in dressing rooms, or scandalous dinners with people who aren't significant others, but Tipsy was right. This blind piece almost felt like an accusation of murder. The inverted commas around 'accident'… and then there was the reference to a fixer, which might point to Freddy Eyelash. I remember the way Tipsy seemed to warn me off digging any further into what happened to Max that night in the Polo Lounge, and a shiver runs down my spine. *Does she know more than she's letting on?* She spends a huge part of her morning every day gossiping and tattling with Veronica in the make-up chair. And she must know Freddy Eyelash because I found his business card in her coat pocket. Before I can really ponder it, an envelope on my desk catches my eye. It wasn't there when I left last night, I am sure of it, and the sight of the blocky, black handwriting and the lack of a postmark makes me drop suddenly into my chair. My hands tremble as I slide one finger under the flap of the envelope and pull out a sheet of unlined white paper. The letter is typed, the M that same familiar wonky style I've seen before.

You think you don't have secrets, Miss Jones? I'm sure I'll find a skeleton or two in your own closet, and if I don't I'll be more than happy to proceed anyway. STOP DIGGING or you'll be next.

A Friend

Chapter Thirty-Two

STOP DIGGING. The exact phrase Tipsy used when she warned me off in the Polo Lounge. Shock makes my teeth feel numb as I sit at my desk, stunned. Part of me thinks I should be afraid, worried that the blackmailer knows who I am and that I am on their trail, but there is another part of me that is filled with pure rage. The only secret I have is that I am not from this time, and there is no possible way of anyone ever knowing that. *Can I die before I've even been born?* There have been a couple of times since I arrived in the past where I thought it might happen, but what would it really mean? Would my mum still have a baby? But it just wouldn't be me? Shaking my head, I re-read the letter, sour saliva coating my tongue. *I'll be more than happy to proceed anyway.* Proceed with what? It doesn't bear thinking about. Taking a deep breath, I try to think rationally. Someone left this note for me in the space between me leaving last night and arriving back here this afternoon. At night, the lot is almost completely locked down unless we're night shooting and there is additional security on the gates, so it would be pretty difficult for someone to get into my office without being apprehended. During the day though…

Shoving back my chair, I snatch up the letter and head into the corridor where Bunny still sits working, surrounded by memos and scripts, her desk an organised chaos.

'Bunny,' I call her name over the tap of her typewriter. 'Bun.'

'Lily.' She pauses, pulling off the black-framed glasses she uses for close-up work, her blonde hair pulled neatly back from her face into a high ponytail. 'Listen, about earlier, I wanted to talk to you about Cliff.'

'Bunny, I need to ask you about—'

Bunny holds up a hand. 'No, Lil, I need to explain things to you. Me and Cliff, it isn't what it seems...' She blows out a long breath, as if steeling herself to continue, but I cut her off.

'Look, whatever the situation is between you and Cliff is between you and Cliff. I don't even know Veronica that well, so it's not as if I'm going to go tattling to her about you two. There's enough gossip on set at the moment as there is.' I thrust the letter into her hand. 'I found this on my desk just now.'

Bunny is silent as she scans the page, the blood draining from her face. 'Where did you get this?'

'I told you,' I huff impatiently, 'it was left on my desk. Someone put it there – there's no postmark, so it's someone who has access to the lot. Bunny, I need you to tell me if anyone has been through here today. Anyone who might have been in my office while I was on set.'

Bunny is shaking her head. 'I don't know, Lily. I wasn't at my desk all day long.' She swallows, her throat making an audible click. 'This is... *threatening*.'

'Yeah, no shit,' I snap. 'Think, Bunny. You really didn't see anyone all day?'

Bunny lets the letter float down onto her desk as she knots her hands together. 'Let me... let me think. Tipsy came by to speak to Leonard but he was in a meeting with Henry Ginsberg. I don't think she came inside the office, but I don't know. I was swamped with typing up the messages and Oskar keeps on calling…' She draws in a raggedy breath. 'Cliff came by to leave the reels from yesterday for Leonard, but I didn't want to speak to him. Oh, and Mae. She was with a tall guy with a moustache. They were just leaving as I arrived, not long before Tipsy came over. Mae said she had something for Leonard, but like I said, Leonard was in a meeting with Henry so she didn't get to see him.'

Bunny is speaking but I can barely hear her. Instead, my gaze is fixed on the pages on her desk, including the one she's freshly ripped from the typewriter.

'Bunny, what is this?'

Bunny frowns. 'Memos, Lily. You know what memos are.'

Yes, I know what memos are, I've typed enough of them myself. Only mine don't carry the wonky M these do. 'You typed these? On your typewriter?'

'Yes.' A note of exasperation leaches into Bunny's tone. 'Lily, what is all this about? Why did someone leave you a note like this? Are you in trouble?'

Looking at her sweet, innocent face, I am almost fooled, and betrayal is like a shard of glass piercing my heart. Because the wonky M on these memos is exactly the same as the one that features in every single of the blackmail letters we've uncovered. 'Bunny, I know what you did.' My heart is crashing in my ribcage and I've never wished harder for Tilda and Louis to be beside me.

'What I did?' Bunny's eyes go to the typewriter, to the letter and then to me, her hand fluttering to her mouth. 'Lily, please let me explain. I need to tell you everything.'

'Yeah, you do.' I feel sick, my stomach swooping and diving, my legs wobbly at the knees. Of all the people I thought could be behind the blackmail letters, Bunny never crossed my mind. She's my friend. A sweet, kind soul who can sometimes drive me crazy. At least, I thought she was a sweet, kind soul.

'It was just a one-off,' Bunny says. 'At first. I never meant for it to happen. He just sort of… swept me off my feet. Anyway, after that first time I realised he was going steady with Veronica and I told him I didn't want anything to do with him anymore, but he was so persistent.'

'Who? Cliff?' I shake my head. 'Bunny, I told you I don't care what happened between you and Cliff. I already told you that.'

'But you said to tell you everything. I'm just saying that I've been trying to shake him off for weeks. I don't know why he thinks I'm so influential. I just type—'

'Exactly, Bunny, you just *type*.' The words are almost a roar as I throw my blackmail letter in her direction. 'I know that none of this was an accident. I know that Ann didn't jump from the Hollywood sign, and that Max would never intentionally have broken his sober streak. You've been sending blackmail letters and when the stars don't comply you've been sending out blind items to that Last Word column anonymously.' My throat closes over and the bridge of my nose starts to tingle. 'How could you, Bunny? I never thought—'

Bunny's eyes are so wide I think they might fall out of her head, and she reaches out and grabs my hands, her palms icy cold. 'What? No, Lily, that's not what happened.' She shakes her head, tears leaking onto her cheeks as her ponytail flies. 'I've never blackmailed anyone in my life. I would never. But…'

'But?' I want to believe her so badly. The thought that someone I love and trust – that everyone at the studio loves and trusts – could be behind the deaths of several Hollywood stars makes my blood run cold.

'The… bl… blind items,' Bunny manages to stammer, her teeth chattering a little as she wraps her arms around her body, hugging herself. 'I did type those. I'll hold my hands up to that, but I had no idea who they were about or the damage they would cause. And I had no idea about any kind of *blackmail.*'

So *Bunny* is behind the Last Word gossip… but there's something that doesn't quite sit right. 'Wait, you typed up the blind items and sent them in to the newspaper?' Bunny nods, pressing her lips together as her cheeks flood pink with shame. 'But you said you didn't know who they were about? How could you type up the blind items and send them in when you didn't know who they were talking about? You must have known.'

Bunny scuffs her foot over the lino, her eyes downcast. 'I swear I didn't know, Lil. I came in one morning to find an envelope on my desk. It had the first blind item in it and a note that said if I typed it up and sent it in to the newspaper I could keep the money in the envelope. There was a hundred-dollar bill inside, Lil!'

My mouth falls open. 'Bunny, your family is wealthy and successful. Your dad hangs out with Spencer Tracy. You don't need to sell someone out for a hundred-dollar bill.'

Bunny almost visibly sags. 'Lily, it's not like that. My father… He's cut me off. That dress I lent you for Tipsy's party? I didn't buy it on my father's account. I used the money from the blind items. And it wasn't really Dior; I just told you it was because I knew you wouldn't know any different. My father doesn't want to pay for my "extra-vagant" lifestyle, and he says if I'm not willing to settle down and be married then he shouldn't have to pay for my choices. It's not that I don't *want* to get married, I just don't want to marry the man he wants me to.' She lets out a sob. 'I was behind on my rent, Lily. The studio doesn't pay big bucks, you know that, and I don't have a room-mate to split the bills the way you do. The morning the landlord told me he was going to evict me if I didn't pay my arrears was the same morning the envelope showed up on my desk. It felt like a sign, Lil. Like the answer to all my problems.'

'And you didn't stop to think about the people this gossip might hurt?'

'No, I didn't,' Bunny whispers, shame behind her eyes. 'If I'd known then of course I would never have done it, but I didn't know and I did do it. I thought it would just be a one-off, and the gossip was so vague that I was sure no one would ever figure it out, so no harm done. But then the next month's rent was due, and there was another envelope, so I just… kept on doing it.' She visibly sags, slumping into the chair behind her desk as tears slide down her cheeks, hitting her skirt and leaving little dark damp spots.

'And whoever it was left you a hundred-dollar bill each time?'

Bunny nods, swiping her hands over her skirt as if to remove a stain. 'Yeah,' she whispers.

Crouching beside her, I take her hands in mine, stop-ping her incessant skirt brushing. 'Bunny, you fucked up.' She gasps at my language, but I carry on. 'If you really didn't type the blackmail letters then we need to figure out who did, because whoever did it wrote them on your typewriter. The last thing you want when all this comes out – and it will – is for the real culprit to say all of it was you.'

'I could *never* blackmail anyone,' Bunny says earnestly. 'It must be someone who has access to the lot because I lock the outside door when I leave. Although...' She frowns, biting on her lower lip as she thinks. 'There was one morning when I arrived and the door was unlocked. I thought you must have got in early, but you weren't there yet. I guess I just assumed if it wasn't you it was Leonard...' She gets to her feet abruptly. 'It's only you, Leonard and I who have keys to this building, Lily.'

Bunny moves to the entry door, stooping to peer at the lock. 'Look. There are scratches all around the side of the lock. Someone could have quite easily picked it, don't you think?'

Having picked locks (quite badly) before, I agree with Bunny's analysis. It does look as though someone has picked the lock, but that doesn't narrow things down at all.

'Do you remember what day it was that the door was unlocked?'

Bunny stands up and moves the desk, pulling out an A4 diary bulging with pages. She flicks it open, flipping through pages and loose leaves of paper until she taps a finger on a page filled with writing. 'This day,' she says. 'I remember because Leonard stayed extra late to view the rushes, and I hung around until he was done so I could make sure everything was ready for the morning. I think that might have been the day Mae fainted. Remember? The day we filmed Tipsy in the pool?'

I remember. I was in the parking lot when Tipsy and Mae left together. Right after I saw Freddy Eyelash headed to the nurses' station. If Mae had left, where was he? Freddy Eyelash, who Bunny also saw leaving the office this morning, just hours before the blackmail note was found on my desk. The blackmail note telling me to back off or else, left for me less than twenty-four hours after I hid from Freddy Eyelash inside Julian March's closet. And who better to pick a lock and get inside anywhere he fancies than a Hollywood fixer?

'Bunny, I could kiss you.' While I'm still furious with her for sending the blind items in to the Last Word in the first place, I can almost forgive her. Bunny might have just blown this whole case wide open.

Chapter Thirty-Three

I somehow manage to get through the morning's shooting, my mind returning over and over to the letter left on my desk. *Does this mean I'm next?*

In the mid-afternoon break, Veronica gossips with Tipsy as she dabs away the sweat at her hairline, before dusting her with a fresh coat of powder.

'I don't know anything about that one, Tipsy, I swear,' Veronica says with a twist of her lips. 'I haven't heard anything about an actress from the East Coast.'

'Oh, phooey.' Tipsy flaps a hand. 'Come on, V, you're not usually this discreet with me. You've been right about all the others.'

My ears prick up at this as I pretend to run a pen over some script pages. *Veronica has correctly guessed who the other blind items have all been about?* My stomach gives a slow roll as I think about the implications. Veronica is just as invisible as I am on set… She could easily have left that letter on my desk without suspicion. And she spends all her time chatting with the stars as she primps and powders them. She must pick up all manner of gossip. My eyes go to her and Tipsy, as Veronica leans in to say something to the actress under her breath. Are they in league together? Are Tipsy's trailer notes built from gossip Veronica has shared?

'Lil? You ready to get back to it?' Cliff frowns at me with concern as he approaches, a clipboard clutched to his chest.

'Uh, yeah.' I pause. 'Cliff? Do you and Veronica ever talk about the stuff she hears when she's working on people in the chair?'

'What… like, gossip? I thought you were going to tattle on anyone who talked about those things,' Cliff teases, before he sobers. 'No, Lil. I try not to pay any attention to it all. Why do you ask?'

I shrug. 'Just wondering if anyone figured out who the East Coast actress is yet.' I had almost forgotten about that blind item until Tipsy brought it up. Whoever the actress is, she is next in line, not me, and I don't have much time to figure out who she might be. 'No one else seems to be able to put the pieces together, but I'm going to do my best to find out.'

—

The set feels eerily quiet once everyone has left for the day, leaving me to finish straightening up before I meet Louis and Tilda. The faint scent of sawdust and cigarette smoke tickles the back of my throat as I lean in to empty ashtrays (ugh, my worst job – I'd rather give Leonard a pedicure) and straighten the cushions on Tipsy's sofa. Working quickly, I feel the prickle of imaginary eyes watching me, the way I always do when I'm left here alone. Ridiculous tales of haunted sound stages have rippled through the studio for years, and I never pay any mind to them unless I'm here late and alone. Winding up some loose cables, I place them into a box and shift it into my arms, huffing under the weight. Taking care to make sure I don't trip over any sandbags, I move towards the centre of the set, casting a quick glance around to make sure I haven't missed anything that Leonard might pull me up on in the morning.

Something that sounds like a floorboard creaking stops me in my tracks, my heart leaping into my throat.

'Hello?' My voice rings out, echoing slightly in the dusty, dim air. 'Is someone there?' My words are met with silence, broken by a thin metallic click. Before I can register it, there is a harsh scraping noise and a clattering of glass and metal, air rushing past my face as overhead – literally, right over my head – the lighting rig comes free and hurtles towards me. There is a sharp shove between my shoulder blades and the box of cables flies out of my arms as I hit the deck, the lighting rig crashing to the floor in the spot where I was stood just seconds earlier.

I lay face down, my forehead pressing against the cool, dusty floorboards as my pulse crashes in my ears and a sob threatens to choke me. *Did the fabled studio ghost just save my life?*

'Jeez, Lily! Are you OK?' Not a ghost. Cliff's voice rings in my ears and then a sturdy hand appears in front of my face. 'Here, come on. Let me help you up.'

Wincing at the pain in my scraped knees, I let Cliff pull me up to standing, and he runs his eyes over me, checking me over for injury. 'I'm OK, I think.' Glancing behind me, I see the lighting rig laying shattered on the floor, glass glinting and the chain overhead creaking.

'Here. Sit down.' Cliff guides me to the sofa, and I sink into its freshly plumped cushions gratefully, my legs suddenly wobbly. 'That was a close call.'

I nod, my mouth dry. 'What were you even doing here? Not that I'm not grateful. If you weren't I'd be brown bread.'

'Brown…?' Cliff shakes his head. 'I was coming back in to check if you needed help with anything. I know you don't like being here on your own after shooting has finished for the day.'

'What the fuck just happened?' I shake my head, my palms stinging from where I hit the floor.

Cliff glances over at the rig. 'It just… crashed down. I don't know what happened. Maybe the chain was broken? All I know is I walked in and saw you underneath it, and then I heard it creak… I just acted. I don't even know how I got you out of the way in time.'

'Well, thank God you did.' I try to smile. 'I could do with a drink.'

Cliff pats at his pockets as if searching for a hip flask. 'Sorry, I'm all out.' He grins sheepishly. 'I don't actually drink. My mom, you know.'

I can't imagine how it must feel to have such a prickly relationship with your own mother. I adored mine, and I miss her every day. Grateful for the change of subject, I ask, 'Do you ever see much of her? Your mum, I mean.'

'Not if I can help it. I have to go back for Thanksgiving and Christmas, but usually she's drinking or drunk and spends most of her time talking down to me, telling the rest of the family how useless I am.' Cliff rubs at one eye, then runs a hand through his hair. 'I have a brother in finance, and she can't help but compare us. If she's not drunk, then I'm pretty much invisible to her. Much like I am to people around here.' He gives a soft huff of laughter. 'What about you? You close to your mom?'

'I was.' I feel that familiar sharp pang I always get in my chest when I think about my mother. 'She passed away a few years ago, and I never met my dad. Are you close to your brother?' Being an only child I've always been fascinated by sibling relationships.

Cliff shakes his head. 'I'm pretty much invisible to him too. And my dad is so busy working that I think all of us are invisible to him. But hey, maybe one day I'll set the world on fire and they'll all sit up and take notice.' He pauses, his cheeks flushing. 'Sorry, Lil. That was a bit much. You don't want to hear about my problems.'

'Hey.' I nudge him gently. 'We're friends, aren't we? Of course you can talk to me about anything… It's what friends are for. And you did just save my life, so the least I can do is listen.'

'There is that,' he agrees, his lips twisting into a smirk. 'I don't know what it is about you, Lily Jones, but I feel like I can be myself with you more than anyone else around here. Where did you come from really?'

I flounder, my mouth opening and closing as I try and figure out how to respond.

'It's like you were sent from heaven. Although if that were the case God would never have sent you down here in those dreadful shoes,' Cliff says with a laugh, gesturing to my Converse. He gets to his feet and holds out a hand to pull me up to standing. 'You should probably get home. I'll clean this mess up and leave a note for Leonard to explain what happened. Is Louis waiting for you? He'll get a shot of booze in you, I'm sure.'

Cliff walks me out to the parking lot, and I turn to him with a shaky smile. 'I can't thank you enough for tonight. You saved my life – you are quite literally a hero. No one can think you're invisible once they hear about this.' Without thinking about it, I reach up and give him a hug, before waving to Louis and running to the car. When I look back Cliff is grinning, and I feel as if maybe, just maybe, he feels seen. For tonight, anyway.

Chapter Thirty-Four

'Lily, are you absolutely sure about this?' Louis's hissed whisper is laced with something that might be annoyance or concern. I'm not entirely sure. Annoyance perhaps because he's given up an important audition for a new band, or concern because we are currently parked outside Freddy Eyelash's office, in the darkest corner of the parking lot, waiting for the yellow glow of light from his office to extinguish for the evening. 'You did just nearly die. Thank God Cliff was there.'

'She didn't die though,' Tilda says with a tut and a roll of her eyes.

'Yes, I'm a hundred per cent sure,' I hiss. The light in the office goes off, and we all slump low in our seats as Freddy Eyelash appears, fumbling with the lock on the door before hopping into an Oldsmobile 88 and zooming out of the parking lot with a throaty roar. We wait until we can no longer hear the engine, and then Louis and I step out of the car, and Tilda slides into the driver's seat.

'You know what to do if someone comes?' I double check. I'm still not sure Tilda is the best person to leave as lookout, but Louis is refusing to let us girls break into the office alone. Part of me wants to swoon at the chivalry, but a larger part of me – the twenty-first-century part – finds it a little sexist. It's not as though Tilda and I haven't broken into places on our own before.

Tilda rolls her eyes. 'Give the headlights a flash three times.' She demonstrates, the full white beams hitting the window to Freddy's office head on. 'And if you guys aren't out, or if it looks like you're going to be caught, I need to pop the hood and hike my skirt up a little – play the damsel in distress as a distraction.'

'Tilda, for Pete's—'

'Relax, Lou. It's a joke.' She gives me a side eye, her lips curving up into a smile. 'I'll unbutton my blouse.'

I shove her lightly on the shoulder and then drag Louis to the door of the main building, as he throws daggers at Tilda over his shoulder.

'I thought her dating that cop guy would tone her down a little bit,' he grumbles under his breath, fumbling in his pocket for one of Tilda's trusty bobby pins. 'Are you sure you feel OK?'

'I'm fine, the rig didn't even touch me. And Ty's a police dispatcher – you know it'll take more than that to calm your sister down.' I peer over my shoulder, checking the car park is still empty. A couple of cars pass by on the main road, but other than that the streets are quiet.

'Aha. Success.' Louis swipes his hair away from his forehead and then gently rests a hand on the doorknob. 'You're sure you didn't see him set an alarm?'

'Well…' I pause. 'I couldn't really see from the angle I was sat at.' In the passenger seat, under a tree, hoping that Freddy Eyelash wouldn't notice us loitering. 'The worst that can happen is it goes off, and then we just peg it.'

'We what?'

'Run off. Get in the car and split.' Nudging him out of the way, I turn the doorknob and creak open the door, pausing to see if a siren is about to rent the air. My pulse thumps hard in my ears and for a minute I half think that

I wouldn't hear the sound of an alarm over it anyway. After a few seconds I let out a long breath. There is no wailing alarm, no screeching siren. There is just silence, and the faint scent of old onions on the air. 'No alarm. We're good.'

Louis raises a thumbs-up to Tilda, who gives a brief flash of the headlights in return and then we slip into the narrow corridor that leads to Freddy's office. It is like a scene from an old detective show – ahead of us a flimsy door with a large window announces *Freddy Carver, Investigator* in neat black letters.

'Investigator?' Louis raises an eyebrow.

'Well, he's not going to say *fixer*, is he?' I tut, testing the door handle. To my surprise, the door springs open under my hand and we step into Freddy's office. Sweeping my flashlight around the room, it's neat and tidy, a legal pad and pencil lined up on the otherwise immaculate desk. A spider plant droops over a filing cabinet in the corner, and the carpet tiles have seen better days. The smell of onions is stronger in here, and when I glance down at the wastepaper basket, a greasy wrapper advertises the fact that Freddy had a hotdog for lunch.

'You really think Freddy was the one who left you the note?' Louis surveys the office, pulling open the top drawer of the desk to find a bottle of single malt. *Oh, Freddy, you cliché.* 'And he's been getting Bunny to type up the blind items?' Lou wrinkles his nose slightly. I know he's struggling to reconcile the Bunny he knows with the Bunny who has got herself tangled up in this mess.

'Yeah, I think he's a definite possibility. So now we're looking for anything that might give us a shred of proof that he's the one sending the blackmail letters. I mean, if he's a fixer then he knows all the gossip, right? And if he's the one leaving the notes for Bunny to type up, what's to stop him from using her typewriter to type his little blackmail letters? If he's an "investigator",' I make quote marks in the air with my fingers, 'then he'll have files. And I reckon they'll all be right there.' I point at the filing cabinet in the corner with the wilted leaves trailing all over the top of it.

'See if there's a ledger or something in those drawers,' I instruct Louis, as I move to the cabinet and yank at the first drawer. It's locked. I should have known it was too easy to get inside the office – if Freddy really is 'fixing' things and indulging in blackmail then of course he'll lock his files away. 'Shit, Lou, do you have that bobby pin?'

Louis tosses it to me and then headlights beam in through the front window and I freeze, my breath sticking in my throat as I cast a panicked glance at Louis.

'Get down!' he hisses and we drop to the floor, out of sight of the windows as the headlights sweep past. Sweat prickles under my arms and I swipe a shaking hand over my face.

'I thought that was Tilda,' I wheeze, a laugh bubbling up in my throat as the office returns to darkness.

'If it was, we'd be cooked,' Louis snorts, and then the two of us are giggling uncontrollably, the panic receding to leave a hysterical kind of relief. 'Why did we hide? Any more headlights and we need to scarper.'

Pulling ourselves together, we switch the flashlights back on and resume our search. I manage to get the filing cabinet unlocked in pretty good time, and as I yank the drawer open the scratches I've made gleam in the torchlight. It doesn't take long for me to figure out I've struck Hollywood gold. Freddy clearly believes that a wimpy cabinet lock is enough to keep the secrets he holds safe, as the drawers are filled with file after file, all neatly labelled. *Barbara Redfield. Hedwig Kiesler. Gretchen Young.* At first glance none of the names mean anything to me, and I pull out the file on Gretchen Young, running my eyes over the scant pages inside. It's only as I reach the part where Freddy references Gretchen adopting her *own daughter* that I realise this is a file on *Loretta* Young. Loretta gave birth to Clark Gable's daughter in 1935 and then 'adopted' her in the hopes of avoiding any scandal. Of course, there was still a scandal, but not until many, many years later when Loretta revealed her daughter was a product of date rape. So, it turns out the baby's 'adoption' was dear old Freddy's idea. And he is keeping his files in some sort of code – the person's real name, not their Hollywood name.

Rifling through the files, I search for Max with no luck. Ann Silver and Oskar also don't turn up any joy. Although I don't know if Ann and Max performed under their own names, I'm pretty sure Oskar doesn't use a pseudonym. I am on the verge of giving up, when a name catches my eye, and I reach in and yank out the file.

'Lou…' I whisper. 'I think I found something.' The label on the file says *Mabel McAllister*, and my pulse spikes under my skin. 'Mae is in here. Remember I found that driver's licence in her real name, hidden away? Freddy Eyelash has a file in that name.'

Louis is beside me in a flash, his torch shining over the paperwork. I don't know what this means now. Is Mae about to be a victim? Or is she in league with Freddy? Either way, we are about to find out.

The file is thicker than Loretta Young's, a bundle of newspaper clippings held together with a paperclip making up most of it. Moving to the desk, we begin to read, my hand creeping up to cover my mouth as we learn Mae's secret.

'Holy crap, Lou. Are you seeing the similarities here?' My hands are trembling as I smooth the article out, ink staining my hands.

MURDER OR TRAGIC ACCIDENT?
Wayne, PA

Residents were left shaken after the body of twenty-two-year-old Eddie Palmer was found lifeless in the pool at his parents' home in the quiet Pennsylvania town. Palmer's body was found by the housemaid early on Sunday morning, following a party Eddie threw while his parents were out of town. Police have not confirmed whether this was a tragic accident or something more sinister, but they are asking to speak with all attendees of the party urgently. Neighbours have expressed shock at the idea of any wrongdoing occurring in their peaceful neighbourhood.

'Like Max,' Louis breathes, his eyes wide. 'This guy drowned in a pool, just like Max.'

'Wait.' I flip to the next article. 'There's more.' The next article is even more damning. It tells how Eddie Palmer threw a party for his friends, but that he was alive when they left. One friend recalled seeing a girl they didn't know there, and that she seemed to be 'obsessed with Eddie'. A photo shows Eddie Palmer front and centre, his arms thrown around two men on either side of him as he stands in a group of people, presumably at another party. The photo has been cropped, and there's something familiar about the man at the edge of it, although I can't put my finger on it. Heavily overweight, with thick dark-framed glasses perched on the end of his nose, the man grins out at me, his eyes almost disappearing behind the thick lenses of his glasses. I run my eyes over the picture again, but I can't place what feels familiar and move on. My heart lurches as I continue reading, the articles growing more and more speculative and overblown as the story grows. Eddie's parents refuse to believe it was an accident, and they speak out on phone calls Eddie was receiving at the house, dropped calls where no one would speak, and then, perhaps most damning of all, they mention letters.

'Blackmail letters.' I point at the page, this time an interview between Eddie's parents and the police. 'Eddie's mum says Eddie received letters from an anonymous person, telling him they would get their revenge on him if he "didn't stop", although stop what, nobody knows.'

A sheet of paper slips out and drifts to the floor. I stoop to pick it up and my heart stutters in my chest. 'Lou, this is one of the letters. And look…' I jab a finger at the signature. 'It's signed "A Friend", just like the others.'

'And then there's this.' Louis holds up the final newspaper article that states Pennsylvania police are looking for Mabel McAllister in connection with the possible murder of Eddie Palmer. 'Jeez, Lil, Mae isn't just a blackmailer. She's a *murderer.*'

Our discovery is the least of our worries, as headlights flash wildly against the wall behind us. Turning, I look out of the window to see Louis's car headlights flicking on and off as another car pulls into the parking lot.

'Lou, we have to get out of here.' The headlights go off, and I scrabble with the newspaper pages, trying to clip them together and slide them back into the paper wallet, but my hands are shaking, my palms are sweaty and my heart is crashing so hard against my ribs I can see black spots in the corner of my vision.

'We don't have time for this.' Lou snatches the sheets out of my hands and stuffs them into the file, throwing it down on the desk before he grabs my hand and pulls me towards the door. There is the clunk of a car door closing outside, and Louis yanks open the office door. As we step out into the corridor, the handle to the outside door begins to turn and I look up at Louis in horror. There is no way we can get out without being seen. We're trapped.

Chapter Thirty-Five

'Get back,' Louis hisses, shoving me in the small of the back. 'Get back inside the office.'

Without stopping to think, I hurry back inside as Louis steps in and pushes the door closed and then guides me towards the desk. 'Under there, quick.' He gives me a gentle shove and I stumble my way beneath the solid oak desk, squeezing myself into the corner so there is room for Louis. He throws himself under the desk just as the office door swings open.

The desk is under the window, so unless Freddy comes around to sit down we are hidden from sight. The only problem is we can't see where he is unless we peep around the leg of the desk, risking discovery. Pressing my back against the desk, I clap my hand over my mouth, trying to regulate my breathing, that familiar wave of panic itching at the back of my throat. Louis reaches out and clasps my other hand, his fingers wrapping tightly around mine, and the two of us crouch there, thighs aching and hearts racing as Freddy moves around the office.

There is the thunk of the filing cabinet drawer sliding open, and then the jangle of the files being moved as if he is searching for something. A small circle of white light beams around the room and I shrink back, as far under the desk as I can fit, terrified the moon of light will land on my shoe or the edge of my skirt, revealing our presence.

Footsteps thud on the dirty carpet tiles as Freddy moves around, and with every step he takes my anxiety increases. Whatever he wants, can't he just find it and leave? I close my eyes, trying to breathe steadily through my nose as there is a shuffling of papers, the click of a lighter and then the smell of a cigar. Bunched under the desk, my thighs twinge and then to my horror the violent grip of a cramp seizes the back of my calf. Letting go of Louis's hand I grab the muscle, trying to massage the cramp away, pain twisting my features as Louis stares at me, panic-stricken. I grit my teeth, knowing that if I let this cramp get the better of me, we are done for. Freddy will know we're here and then he'll fix us. Probably.

The footsteps are coming towards us, and I'm not sure how much longer I can hold my position, the cramp still biting the back of my calf, before Freddy stops on the other side of the desk. Louis pinches the back of my hand hard enough to bring tears to my eyes, and like a miracle the cramp disappears. Seconds later, so does Freddy. There is a rustle of pages and then the footsteps head away from the desk. Moments later there is the click of the door closing, followed by the slam of the outer door to the building.

'Oh my God.' All the air rushes out of my body and the muscles in my legs finally relax, the scent of cigar smoke still heavy on the air. 'That was close.' My thighs cave in and I sink onto the carpet tiles, not caring about the dirt that's probably staining my skirt.

Louis is already at the window, peering between the slats of the blinds. 'He's gone,' he says. 'We need to get out of here before he realises he's forgotten something else.'

Crawling out from our hiding place, I shake out my legs, my eyes falling to the now empty desk. 'The file,' I say, pointing. 'The one with Mae's information in it. It's gone.'

'Why would Freddy come back for that?' Louis frowns, but even as he speaks a thought hits me.

'Why wouldn't he turn the lights on?' I raise my eyes to Louis's face and the sombre expression he wears. 'It's Freddy's office. Why was he carrying a torch as if he didn't want to be seen? Why not simply put the lights on?' A cold hand trails a finger down my spine. 'Louis, we need to leave, *now*. I don't think that was Freddy Eyelash who was just in here at all.'

We run across the parking lot to where Tilda waits in the car, the streetlamp on the kerb casting a sickly amber glow over her face.

'You guys.' She hops out of the car and wraps her arms around us. 'I tried to warn you in time but he just snuck up on me! One minute the coast was clear, the next minute he was at the door, stepping inside.'

Louis slides into the driver's seat and guns the engine. 'Girls, get in. We need to get out of here.' He glances at me. 'Where to?'

'Mae's house.'

Tilda gets in the backseat and I slide in next to Louis, shivering as I finally let the nerves and fear get the better of me. 'That was close. Too close. Til, did you see who it was?' I twist round in my seat to face her.

Tilda shakes her head. 'It was Freddy, wasn't it? At least… that's who I thought it was. It looked like he had a key.'

'The door was already unlocked,' Louis says, glancing at her from the rearview mirror. 'We'd already picked the lock, so the door was open but it wasn't Freddy. Whoever it was stole the file we found on Mabel McAllister and didn't switch the lights on.'

'I didn't see his face,' Tilda says with a groan. 'He was wearing a long coat and a hat pulled over his face, but it's chilly out this evening and I just assumed… Ugh, what an ass. I was so consumed with worry about you two getting caught that I never even suspected it might not be Freddy.' She pauses, leaning forward to grip the head rest. 'Wait a minute… A file on Mabel McAllister? AKA Mae Sinclair?'

As Louis turns onto the main road and begins to head in the direction of Mae's house, I fill Tilda in on what we found in the file, watching as her expression changes from curious to stunned.

'The pool? Eddie Palmer was found in the pool, just like Max?' She shakes her head as if trying to rearrange the information in her brain to make sense. 'And there was a letter? Holy moly, Lil. It's been Mae all along.'

'But why?' That's the only thing that I can't figure out. Why is Mae blackmailing people in Hollywood? She's on the silver screen now, and this movie with Leonard is supposed to be the one that makes her career. Even Tipsy has commented on how talented she is. She has no need to blackmail anybody.

Tilda shrugs. 'Who knows. Maybe she enjoyed the fact she seems to have got away with it in Pennsylvania. Maybe it's a compulsion.'

'Maybe she and Freddy Eyelash are working together,' Louis pipes up, his eyes never leaving the road. 'Maybe he has the information and she has the courage to follow through on the threat. The file on her could be his insurance, to make sure she never sells him out.' He frowns, shifting gears as he takes a corner, turning onto Mae's street. 'Maybe she never got run off the road at all that night. Maybe it was staged.'

I don't know. While on the surface it seems pretty cut and dried – Mae (or Mabel if you prefer) has got away with blackmail, and possibly murder before – I can't see petite, polite Mae offing someone. And I'm pretty sure that Freddy Eyelash is more than capable of doing his own dirty work.

'This is her house here.' I tap Louis on the shoulder, and he brings the car to a halt at the kerbside. Suddenly, looking up at Mae's house, a place that Bunny helped her find, that Leonard wrote her a reference for, a blaze of fury sweeps through me. Mae has taken advantage of people I love, and I am not going to stand for it. Shoving the car door open, I get out before leaning back in to Louis. 'If I'm not back outside in ten minutes call the cops.'

Tilda laughs from the backseat, shrill and inappropriate. 'Oh, bless your heart, Lil. You didn't actually think you were going in there alone?'

–

My nerves are jangling as the three of us head up the path to Mae's front door, the surge of rage coupled with the adrenaline in Freddy's office leaving me feeling drained. The sooner we confront Mae and wrap this up, the better. Leonard will probably want to kill me for ruining two pictures in a row for him, but I'd rather that than someone else end up dead.

Louis presses the small bell beside Mae's name, the chime ringing out in the night air. We wait a moment, but there is no movement from inside.

'I'm going in.' I've already spotted an open window on the side of the building. I won't even need to push Tilda through it. I can fit.

'Wait just a second.' Louis shuffles, glancing over his shoulder. 'What if someone sees us breaking in? Tilda, is Ty on duty tonight? I'm worried we're going to be arrested before we stop any of this.'

'Come on, yellow belly.' Tilda nudges him a little more sharply than Louis was expecting, and he huffs. 'Breaking and entering is nothing compared to what Mae has done.'

Leaving the two of them to duke it out, I make my way to the open window, relieved to see it leads to a laundry room. Standing on the trash can underneath, I manage to get enough leverage to boost myself inside. There is one hairy moment when I get slightly wedged, my legs waving in the air as I squeeze my way inside. After crashing onto the worktop, sending laundry detergent flying, I sit up, rubbing my elbow, and then hop down to open the front door to the building.

'You guys ready?' I open the front door and peer outside to check no one is watching before I usher them inside.

'She's definitely not home?' Louis peers up the stairs as if Mae will miraculously appear at the top of them.

'I don't think so.' Hurrying up to the third floor, we reach Mae's door and I knock. 'Mae? It's me, Lily. Are you here?' Pressing my ear to the door, I try and listen for any sounds of movement or the wireless. 'She's not in.'

'Lily, I can't face picking another lock.' Louis looks sick at the thought.

'There's no need to.' I noticed a small concrete frog beside Mae's door on my last visit to the apartment. I didn't think much of it at the time, but now my gaze drifts downwards and there it is, gurning up at me. 'My mum had one of these. She was forever losing her keys, so she used to keep one in the frog, just in case.' Picking it up, I tilt the frog to reveal a small hole in its butt and a small silver key falls out. 'Here we go. Open sesame.'

'What are we looking for? Besides Mae, I mean,' Tilda says a minute later, as she steps into the sitting room. There is a neat stack of magazines on the coffee table and a scarf draped over the sofa, but apart from that there is no sign that Mae has been home at all this evening. No dishes in the sink, no perfume on the air.

'I don't know.' I pick up a cushion from the sofa and shake it out. 'I don't think Mae's even been back here tonight.'

Tilda drifts out of the sitting room towards the bedroom and Louis moves to the kitchen, leaving me in the sitting room alone. Nothing seems out of place. The church candles still line the mantelpiece. The cosy throw still covers the sofa. But something feels off, although I'm not sure if it's just that I was expecting Mae to be here.

'Lil?' Tilda's voice wafts out of the bedroom, tinged with urgency. 'Lil, I think you should get back here.'

Almost colliding with Louis as we both step into the hallway, I enter the bedroom first. Tilda stands over Mae's chest of drawers. Suddenly nauseous, I swallow hard, not wanting to hear what Tilda has found, but I push myself to ask the question.

'What is it?'

Tilda gestures to the drawer, and the jewellery box that sits empty apart from one thing. A letter, torn into pieces, half of it missing. There is enough left to make out that it has been written on a typewriter with a wonky M, as

Tilda places several fragments together to form two words: *A Friend.*

Horror raises goosebumps on my arms, the soft breath of a chill lifting the hairs on the back of my neck. 'We got it all wrong. Everything. It's all wrong.'

Chapter Thirty-Six

Mae's jewellery box is empty, and when I lift the big, ceramic pig she keeps on the dresser and give it a shake that's empty too.

'Mae was never the blackmailer.' Squeezing my eyes shut, I try to put the pieces together, my brain like liquid sloshing around inside my head. 'God, I feel so stupid. I think Mae might have been thinking along the same lines we were.'

'What do you mean?' Louis looks up from where he is trying to reassemble the remaining scraps of the blackmail letter.

'I found a list in her things, a checklist almost, of the blind items and names scrawled beside them. That put Mae firmly on my list of people who could be responsible… but what if it was the complete opposite? What if Mae made that list because she was also trying to figure out who was spreading the gossip and who might be next?'

Tilda's face drains of colour, and she puts out a hand to stop Louis in his quest to match up the page fragments. 'We already know who's next, Lil. The last blind item… *a little bird from back East says she vanished right around the time a local "accident" made headlines.* Mae is from Pennsylvania, that's East. And now we've seen the articles about Mabel McAllister and Eddie Palmer, it all makes sense. Mae is the next person on the blackmailer's list.'

My mouth goes dry, the full horror of it all hitting me square in the gut. We could save her. We have time – for once we know for sure who the next victim will be. My pulse ratchets, an insistent thud starting in my ears. I grab the pieces of the shredded letter and shove them into my skirt pocket.

'Mae hasn't been home, by the looks of things. She was going to stay late in her trailer and practise her lines… It was a rough shooting day.' Shooing Tilda and Louis towards the apartment door, I slam it closed behind us and we hurry down the stairs and out to the car. 'She might still be there. And if the blackmailer is watching her, they might know that Mae is on the lot alone. We have to hurry.'

Louis turns the key, and the car makes an odd spluttering noise before coughing and dying. He tries again and the same dying sound comes out, a mix between a cough and a groan.

'Louis? Why isn't she starting?' Panic plucks at my nerve endings, and I swallow back the urge to yell. 'We have to get to Mae before it's too late.'

'It's just…' Louis blows his hair out of his eyes and gives it a minute before he slots the key back in. 'It's cold and a little damp out here, and she's an old car. She's usually reliable but sometimes…' He turns the key and pumps the gas hard and finally the car comes alive with a muted growl. Louis guns the engine and we take off through the streets of Hollywood, towards the studio.

We hit every red light on the way, and then there is construction along the boulevard that means we have to crawl through a narrow lane before Louis can properly put his foot down. We screech into the parking lot in a longer time than I would have liked, aware that every minute it takes us to get to Mae is another minute she could be in danger.

'What do you kids want?' The security guard on the gate isn't Bobby, and it isn't anyone else I recognise either.

'Kids?' Tilda draws herself up to her full, still ridiculously tiny height. 'First, we are not kids. Second, we need to get inside, please.'

The security guard shakes his head, his hand going to the baton on his waistband. 'You think you can just rock up here and I'll let you inside? This is a secure lot, ma'am. No one is going inside.'

I step forward, fumbling under my shirt for the security pass that I keep on a chain around my neck. Usually, it's the first thing I remove once I leave the lot, but thankfully tonight taking off my security pass was the last thing on my mind. I tug it over my head and shove it under the guard's nose. 'Lily Jones,' I say. 'I work with Leonard Langford and Oskar Goldstein. These two are with me and we need to get inside, please.'

The guard holds my pass close to his face, running his eyes over the tiny black-and-white photo of my face, my expression sombre, my neat ponytail making me look far more put together than I do right now. He looks me over and I fight the urge to squirm under his gaze.

'Y'all working on the Tipsy Jenner movie?' He hands me the security pass back.

'Yes. So, if you could just…'

The guard taps a pen on the signing-in book. 'Y'all still need to sign.' I take the pen and scrawl my name. 'So, Ms Jenner… What's she like?'

Tilda gapes at him as she signs her own name and hands the pen to Lou. 'Sir, can you not see that we are in a *hurry*?' She pushes me through the gate, and we leave the guard shaking his head after us as we run across the lot to the trailers.

'The lights are off,' Louis whispers as we approach Mae's trailer.

I'm hoping I haven't got all of this wrong too, and that Mae really didn't leave the lot after everyone else went home.

'Lil, I don't think she's here.'

I don't listen, instead approaching the trailer door with Mae's name stencilled on it in thick, black lettering. Moonlight catches the metal siding of the trailer, making it gleam a bright silver, and I press my hand on the door handle, expecting it to be locked. I raise my eyebrows at Louis as the handle moves easily, the door springing open. We step inside.

Louis was right, the trailer is empty, which makes it even more unusual that it would be left unlocked. The only sign that Mae has been here at all this evening is the pair of bright red heeled pumps that she wore in her last scene this afternoon, lying on their side by the daybed as if she threw them off in a hurry, and the clipboard that holds her script.

Disappointment floods my veins, followed by alarm. If Mae isn't here, then where is she? While a part of me knew I could have been walking into Mae being attacked by the blackmailer, at least then I would have reached her in time. Now, I have no idea where she is and no idea how to find her.

'What on *earth* are you doing here?' A familiar voice comes from behind me and I turn to see Tipsy, her hair in a neat chignon and her make-up perfect. Despite the late hour she looks as if she has just walked off set, but I know that can't be right as shooting finished hours ago. There was no sign of her when the lighting rig almost crashed down onto my head. My stomach rolls as I remember the ominous creak it made right before it fell.

'I could ask you the same question,' I say, suspicion sitting squarely on my shoulders. 'Why are you here this late, Tipsy? Shouldn't you have gone home hours ago?'

'I was busy.' Tipsy arches an eyebrow in my direction, before glancing over to Louis and Tilda. 'All three of you are here? Well, well, I can't imagine that all three of you are here by accident. Something must be going on.'

'Why don't you tell us if something is going on, Tipsy?' Tilda puts her hands on her hips. 'You're the one who seems to know all the gossip around here.'

Tipsy lets out a cackle, splitting the air with her shrill laughter. 'Oh, darling, are you worried I'm coming for your job? Silly thing. I only repeat what I read in the newspapers.' She turns to me. 'So, Lily. What *are* you doing here at this time of night, and with your friends too…' She trails off, her eyes narrowing. 'Wait. Was Mae right about you?'

'Me?'

Tipsy steps forward, so close we are almost touching, but there is nothing of the warm and welcoming and slightly bonkers Tipsy that I am used to. Her expression is hard and her eyes are cold. 'Why are you snooping around in Mae's trailer? I thought you were better than that, Lily, with all your talk about not spreading gossip and supporting Leonard in his quest to squash it, but you were in on it after all.'

'What?' Louis laughs the word as he shakes his head. 'Tipsy, you can't be serious.'

Tipsy rounds on him with fury in her eyes. 'I certainly can, young man. I'm not quite sure who you are but I am sure that you probably shouldn't be here. And Lily, once I tell everybody that you're the one behind the blind items, you won't be allowed back here again either. Which is a real shame, because you are a very good assistant,' she finishes begrudgingly.

'Wait a second.' I breathe in, trying to gauge whether Tipsy has been drinking, but all I can smell is perfume and cigarettes. 'You think *I'm* the one behind the blind items? And Mae does too?'

Tipsy's cheeks colour and she shifts her gaze away from my face. 'Well, you never seemed to want to discuss them. It's almost as if you're afraid you'll let something slip. And let's be honest, Lily, you have access to almost *everything* at the studio. If anyone was going to catch wind of rumours it would be you.'

'I—' Speechless, I look to Tilda and Louis for assistance, but they both stay mute. 'Tipsy, it's not me. If anything I thought it was you, or Mae. You had all that... vicious gossip written down in your trailer, and you showed up here with your head cut open the day after Mae was run off the road. The car responsible for Mae's accident had headlights set into the fenders, just like the studio pool car. A car that *you* would have had access to.'

Tipsy gapes at me, before she chuckles hoarsely. 'Lily, you must be joking. First of all, the notes in my trailer – which were private by the way – were a technique recommended to me by my therapist. You know Hollywood can be cutthroat, Lily, and I found I was holding onto a lot of resentment after people treated me badly. My therapist told me to write it all down so I could move on and not become *creatively blocked*.'

'You had blood on your sleeve the night Oskar was attacked, and you were at the hospital before anyone else knew about it. Almost as if you knew ahead of time something was going to happen to him.'

Tipsy shakes her head at me, disbelieving. 'You think *I* was the one to hurt Oskar? Oh, dear girl, I'm not sure what you've been drinking, but that is utterly absurd. I was at the hospital already, visiting a friend. As I was leaving, I saw Oskar being brought in on a stretcher, and of course I was shocked to my core. I grabbed his hand, racing alongside the stretcher as they wheeled him in, trying to see if he was OK. That was how the blood got on my sleeve.' She shifts now, avoiding my eyes. 'As for the cut on my head, that was an accident.'

'Tipsy, you need to tell me what happened. The night Mae was run off the road, the car responsible also crashed. Whoever was driving might have sustained an injury very similar to yours.'

'It wasn't me!' Tipsy half yells, half whispers. 'I was drunk, OK?' She lowers her voice, her cheeks flushing pink. 'I was drunk, and I fell. Mae came by my trailer and found me after everyone went home. I'd had a bad day, that's all. But I realised then that most days were bad… At least that was my excuse. Mae has been helping me stay on the wagon.'

Wow. I was not expecting that. Hearing Mae's name brings me back to the real reason why we are here. 'Speaking of Mae, where is she? We need to find her. It's urgent.'

Tipsy still doesn't seem convinced as she puts a fresh cigarette to her lips and inhales. 'Lily, how do I know—'

'Because everybody who's had a blind item written about them has received a blackmail letter, and almost all of them have ended up dead,' I snap. 'I've never broken the law in my life.' I'm not going to count the lockpicking and breaking and entering I've done since I've been here. It's all been for the greater good. 'So with all due respect, Tipsy, I don't care if you suspect me or not – I'm not the gossip or the blackmailer and I don't know who is, but one thing I do know is that Mae is next on the list.'

'Blackmail? I had no idea!' Tipsy's mouth drops open, the cigarette sticking briefly to her bottom lip before it falls to the ground and Louis hurriedly stamps it out. 'Why didn't you say something before?'

'Because you were too busy accusing us of being the culprit,' Tilda hisses. 'Where is Mae? Her life is in danger, so maybe you could stop puffing on cigarettes for five minutes and tell us where she is. She was supposed to be here.'

Tipsy frowns, and I see the internal battle wage behind her eyes as she fights to tell Tilda to watch her mouth, but her worry for Mae wins. 'She was here,' she says. 'Until about twenty minutes ago. I was helping her run her lines. And then she took a call on the phone bank,' Tipsy gestures to the phones on the wall opposite, 'which I did think was strange, as I didn't think anyone knew Mae was staying late. But here you are as well.'

'Who called her?' Not for the first time I wish I was in my own time when a digital caller ID would show up, or I could at least do *69 to call the person back.

'Well, I don't know *that*.' Tipsy huffs dramatically. 'All I know is that she took the call, and she was as white as a sheet when she came back in. She slipped her rings off and put them into her purse and then rushed out, saying she had to leave.'

Mae left twenty minutes ago, which means she'd already seen the blind item by the time she got to work this morning, and she knew it was about her. She must have brought her jewellery and money to the set today and planned to meet the blackmailer in the hopes that she could resolve things by paying up after all.

'You think it was the blackmailer on the phone?' Louis asks as I pull the door to the trailer closed.

'I don't know. Maybe. Probably. But it doesn't help even if it was them on the phone. We still don't know where Mae is.'

'Yes we do.' Tipsy's voice is sharp and clear, and I thank my lucky stars that today we have clear-headed, sober Tipsy who doesn't miss a trick. 'I overheard her on the phone. She said she'd meet whoever it was in half an hour at Griffith Park Observatory.'

Chapter Thirty-Seven

I could kiss Tipsy but we don't have time. I turn to Louis, adrenaline almost vibrating through my body.

'Lou, you and I will head to the observatory. Tilda, can you make sure Tipsy gets home OK?'

'But—'

'Please? I don't want her roaming about alone, not when… you know.' What if the blackmailer is finished with Mae and comes for Tipsy? Everyone knows that the two of them on set are as thick as thieves. A hot wave of shame runs over me as I think about how I thought they might be in league together.

Tilda nods and holds out an arm for Tipsy to lean on. 'Come on,' she says, 'let me get you home safely. Maybe you can give me some stories for my column. I have to knock Hedda off her perch somehow.' Tilda raises her eyes to mine. 'Be careful, Lily.'

The drive up to the observatory is tense, my knee jiggling as I internally urge Louis to put his foot down. I open my mouth to speak, but he cuts me off.

'Lily, if a traffic cop pulls me over we'll lose even more time.' Louis gives me a sidewards glance, a smile tugging at his lips.

'Sorry. I'm just… *anxious*.' I don't think I'll ever meet another man who knows me as well as Louis – apart from my best friend Eric, back in the twenty-first century. 'If it's not Tipsy and Mae behind the blind items then who could it be?'

Louis taps his fingers lightly on the steering wheel, thinking. 'Anybody. It could honestly be anybody, Lil. I don't think people are as discreet as they think they are… You know Hollywood, rumours are swirling about people all the time.'

Freddy Eyelash pops into my mind, his tall, imposing frame striding through the studio lot as if he owns the place. 'Freddy knows everything, we've seen the files. And he's a big guy, so he could easily overpower any one of the people who've died. Oskar would know of him, if he doesn't know him well already. If Freddy turned up on his doorstep the night of the poker party, Oskar would have let him in.' I feel sick at the thought that if I had just acted instead of wanting to be sure, maybe I could have stopped him.

Louis turns off onto West Observatory Road, the narrow, winding road carved into the hillside up to the observatory. The view as we drive is incredible, the switchbacks that make me feel nauseous revealing a sprawling view of the city, one that I would never get in my own time thanks to the growth of the trees and bushes on the hillside. There is no guardrail as the road winds back on itself, and the steep gradient means the car sputters more than once.

'Come on, come on,' Louis mutters under his breath as the observatory comes into view over the crest of the ridge. Its white silhouette seems to appear out of nowhere, and then the ground levels out and we are racing across the wide-open space in front of the building that serves as a parking lot.

Before Louis even has the car at a complete stop I am fumbling for the door handle and Louis pulls up the handbrake, almost tossing me against the windscreen.

'Wait a second,' he says sharply, nodding towards the building. Or more specifically, to the car parked at an angle across the entrance. 'Is that Mae's car?'

'Yes, it looks like it,' I say, ignoring Louis's instruction to wait. 'Look. There's a service door over there. I'll head inside through there, and you try the main entrance. Mae could be anywhere inside there, so let's split up. We can cover ground more quickly.'

'Lily—'

I knew he'd protest. 'Louis, please. Take the main entrance. If I need you, I'll holler – and you do the same. There's only one car outside so hopefully we've beaten the blackmailer here.' Without waiting for him to try and persuade me otherwise, I skip around Mae's car and follow the path round to the side entrance. It's poorly lit, and my feet skitter over the loose stones on the path as I reach the door and push it open. I head into a narrow corridor, feeling my way along in the dim light until I find myself at another door. I step through into the observatory itself, pausing for just a second as I take in the impressive architecture. The columns, white and Roman-style, reaching up towards the painted ceiling make me want to stand and gawp for the rest of the evening, but I have to save Mae.

'Mae?' I hear Louis's voice from behind me, coming from the gallery. I press on, opening doors into a library filled with old books, a faint musty smell on the air tickling my nose, an office, and then back out into the south gallery. There is no sign of Mae.

'Mae?' I whisper-shout. 'Are you in here? It's me, Lily.' There is no answer, no shuffling of feet, no reason at all to think that Mae is here, apart from her car outside. Shoving open another door, I'm expecting to find myself in yet another little gallery, but I stumble out into the rear courtyard, next to the stairs that lead up to the front terrace. Pausing for a second I try and get my breath back, bending double at the waist as I fight the sharp pull of a stitch in my side. It's as I draw in a deep breath that I hear it. A muffled 'oh' that carries on the wind from somewhere above me. My eyes go to the curving, wide staircase ahead of me.

The front terrace. It lies at the top of these stairs, a vast open space with a wide, waist-height wall where people can look out over the city and marvel at the views. I begin to climb the staircase, a sharp wind cutting through the thin, flimsy fabric of my blouse. The concrete is cold and smooth beneath my hand, and my hair flies around my head as I climb higher and higher, pausing as I reach the top step. The terrace sprawls out before me, and at first I think it's a waste of time and that I am alone up here, but then a shadow moves around the curve of the building. Pressing myself against the wall, I feel a brief respite from the wind as I creep around the curved wall, a gasp escaping my lips at the scene ahead of me.

'You,' I breathe, unable to take in what I am seeing. The last person I was expecting to find here stands in front of me, their back to me, as Mae stands precariously on the wall that surrounds the terrace, her eyes wild, tears streaming down her face. She moves her head the tiniest fraction in my direction and it's enough for the black-mailer to realise someone is behind them, just as Mae's foot slips off the wall.

Chapter Thirty-Eight

'No!' Cliff's head whips around at my cry, just as Mae manages to save herself by throwing her arms out and pitching forward, tumbling onto the concrete in front of the wall. My mouth goes dry at the sight of the revolver in his hand.

'Well, well, if it isn't Little Miss Nosey herself.' Cliff blinks, his eyes watering, somehow managing to make the gesture look sinister. Although that might be more down to the gun he's pointing at me.

I raise my hands in a gesture of surrender. How did we not spot Mae on the wall as we pulled in? Cliff must have only just got her up here, and the thought that perhaps he heard us arrive and forced her up here makes my heart sink. 'Cliff, what are you doing? This is crazy.'

'Is it?' He laughs, a harsh bark that splits the air, and I wonder if Louis is close enough to hear it. 'Let me tell you what's crazy, Lily Jones. You women, that's what. Hollywood, that's what. I'm the only one who *isn't* crazy around here.'

'Please will you put the gun down? We can talk about things properly if you put the gun down. We can fix all of this.'

Cliff waves the gun and my heart stops in my chest, my legs wobbling so hard I'm not sure how much longer they'll hold me up. 'Fix? Oh, dear old Mae already tried to fix things, didn't you, sweetheart? But Freddy wasn't as great as you thought he was. Past it, that's what he is. An old has-been who needs to retire.' Cliff laughs again and there is no sign of the meek, mild-mannered, almost invisible man I've got used to interacting with on set. The man who I thought was my friend.

'You were the one blackmailing people,' I say, quietly. 'And then when they didn't – or couldn't – pay up, you got rid of them.'

'Bravo, Lily.' Cliff claps awkwardly, the gun still tightly gripped in one hand. I swallow, fear sticking my tongue to the roof of my mouth. 'Bet you couldn't guess who started it all though?'

My eyes go to a panicked Mae, who stands shivering in front of the wall, her escape still blocked by Cliff. 'Mae Sinclair.' I hazard a guess. 'Or should I call her Mabel McAllister?' Mae lets out a squeak. 'I found her driver's licence in her real name, but I couldn't figure out why she'd hidden it. I mean, practically everyone in Holly-wood changes their name, don't they? And then I found the file Freddy Eyelash had on Mae, and it had all the details in it about what happened to Eddie Palmer.'

Mae lets out a groan, her legs shaking as she covers her face with her hands. I look to Cliff in fear, poised to charge him if he turns the gun on her, but instead he blinks at me, his mouth opening and closing.

'You know about Eddie?' he says.

I nod. As I spoke about the file Freddy had on Mae just now, I had been thinking about the contents of it – specifically the photograph of Eddie at a previous party. I couldn't think what it was in that photo that felt weirdly familiar to me, but it's just struck me like a bolt of light-ning. 'You knew Eddie,' I say to Cliff. 'You were in a photograph with him and some others at a party. Not the one where he died, one before. I almost didn't recognise you.' The Cliff standing in front of me must be several stones lighter. As he blinks again, I realise why he's been doing it the entire time I've known him. He doesn't have allergies. He's ditched his thick, heavy-framed glasses for contact lenses.

'Almost…' I say, '…but I knew there was something about the photograph that I *did* recognise. I saw what you were holding in your hand.' Cliff looks at me, puzzled. 'The lighter. The one the studio gave out in 1949. They would have sent one to your grandfather, and he passed it on to you.'

Cliff gives a strangled half laugh, half sob. 'What are you talking about, Lily?'

'Did you swipe Tipsy's after you lost yours at the top of the Hollywood sign? After you pushed Ann Silver off? After all, you wouldn't want Grandpa to know you'd lost it.'

'You shut your mouth.' Cliff takes a step towards me, raising the gun again, and I hold my hands up, refusing to look away from him. 'Mabel – that's how I've always known her – is going to get what's coming to her, and it's about time. She needs to pay for what she did to Eddie.'

'Cliff, it was never like—' Mae tries to speak but Cliff cuts her off.

'I recognised her the moment she walked into her audition,' he says through gritted teeth. 'But you didn't recognise me, did you, Mabel? Even when I stopped and gave you a ride to the Beverly Hills Hotel. You never saw me in Pennsylvania, and you never saw me here. Can you imagine how that felt? I've spent my entire life trying to be seen. By my mother, my brother, here in Hollywood.

When I came home from college in Pennsylvania and started work here, I thought I would hit the big time. I've got the surname, right? The contacts? I lost weight – ran miles and miles and lived off portions that wouldn't feed a mouse to do it – and got rid of my glasses. But I'm no higher up the ladder than you, Lily.'

I try not to let the words smart – I think I've done pretty well to get as far as I have. 'So, you knew Mae back in Pennsylvania?' My eyes flick towards her, still standing in front of the wall. Her knees are trembling, her skirt flying up in the breeze to show bruises forming on her shins where Cliff has pushed her against the bricks.

Cliff nods. 'She was always hanging around Eddie, trying to catch his attention.' Mae opens her mouth to protest and I give her the tiniest shake of my head. *God, Louis, where are you?* Cliff goes on, 'And then he started getting the letters.'

'Blackmail letters?'

Cliff nods and behind him Mae hangs her head as if defeated. 'Saying if Eddie didn't "stop" then he'd be sorry. Eddie had no idea what he was meant to be stopping though.' Cliff's hand begins to shake, and he wraps his fingers around his own wrist to keep the gun steady. 'Eddie was my best friend. The only person to ever really see *me*. I finally felt as though I had found someone who appreciated me, who didn't think I was utterly useless. Then Eddie was found dead in the pool, the night of the party, and Mabel had skipped town. Imagine my surprise when she showed up here. I had to teach her a lesson.'

'Wait a minute...' I lower my hands slightly, my shoulders aching. *For the love of God, Louis, think about the terrace and get your ass up here.* 'Max Hayden... He was blackmailed and then found drowned in the pool. You did that to *teach Mabel a lesson?*' Horror is an icy wave that drenches me from head to foot. Who thinks like that?

'At first I wanted to show her that I knew she wasn't Mae Sinclair. I knew exactly who she was and I thought someone might connect the dots… realise that the deaths were so similar that the same person must have carried them out.' He blinks, and I realise this isn't just a funny little tic of his because of the contact lenses. This is his way of getting himself back under control. 'I wrote a letter to your friend, that nosy little redhead, thinking that she would start digging into things, investigating, and it would only be a matter of time before the truth was revealed. But it didn't happen. She ignored me.'

'But Mae knew about the similarities. Which is when she got Freddy Eyelash involved.' Everything is starting to slot into place, and now it feels so obvious. Mae and Freddy weren't in league together. Freddy was trying to 'fix' Mae's problem.

'Max paid up at first,' Cliff says, 'and the extra money was good. And then once Mae didn't get arrested for his death, I felt like I had no option but to carry on. I even tried to run Mae off the road, hoping it would scare her back to Pennsylvania and to tell the truth, but she stayed. Everyone was talking about what happened to Max, and it gave me a buzz. Everyone was talking about something I had done, and while no one knew who was responsible, *I* knew it was me who had caused all this commotion.'

'You liked it? The attention? Or was it all about the money?' Saliva spurts into my mouth, my stomach flipping.

'The money was partly the reason why I carried on,' Cliff says, a smile playing about his lips, 'but you should have seen their faces, Lily. Once they'd received the blackmail letters, I got such a kick out of watching the way their whole demeanour changed, knowing that I was the one having such an effect on them. Little Cliff Marshall, invisible to everybody… I was the one with the power. So the blackmail had to go on. Veronica always had the latest rumours and gossip on the end of her tongue when we went on dates, and I figured if I kept going and made it look like Mae could be involved then eventually someone would figure it out.' He looks me over. 'I never thought it would be you though.'

I raise an eyebrow, trying not to look at Mae, who shifts to step back up onto the wall. I had thought it was Mae. Cliff nearly had me fooled. 'Why get Bunny involved?'

Cliff smirks. 'She was so easy to manipulate. I took her out once and she couldn't get enough… She mentioned that she was struggling with her rent, so I left her a little incentive to type up and mail the blind items for me.'

'So it would never be traced to you; it would come back to Bunny.' Bunny and her typewriter with the wonky M. 'Both she and I thought you were chatting her up, but really you were keeping an eye on her. Making sure she didn't suspect that it was you leaving her the blind items.' A thought strikes me and I go cold. Cliff would have got away with everything if I hadn't shown up and now… now he's confessed it all, which can only mean one thing. Before I can process the thought there is a blood-curdling yell and Mae leaps from the wall, launching herself onto Cliff's back.

She wraps her arms around his throat, clinging on for dear life, squeezing so hard she's choking him, but Cliff is a man possessed as he turns around to try and shake her off.

'No!' I shout, as Cliff whirls towards the wall again, slamming Mae hard against it. Her grip loosens and he takes the chance to whip around and slam the revolver against the side of her head. She goes down like a ton of bricks, slumping into a puddle on the ground.

'Cliff, stop!' I yell, hoping that Louis is close enough now to hear me, as I crouch beside Mae's lifeless body. Her face is a bleached bone white and blood trickles from her temple, a stark contrast to the paleness of her cheeks. 'Mae? Mae, please wake up.'

There is a burning pain in my scalp as Cliff crouches beside me, yanking me to my feet by my hair. 'Cliff, please…'

He drags me to the wall, pressing me so hard against it that the concrete digs into the base of my spine, my hair still wrapped in his fist. The scent of cigar smoke on his clothes catches at the back of my throat, the smell ingrained into the fabric from all the hours sitting beside Oskar as he puffs away. 'You gotta go, Lily. Both of you. I mean, it's a shame because you were the only person who ever saw me. Except Oskar, that time at his house. When I realised he was still alive, I had to play it off as though I'd just walked in and found him there.'

I recall the way Cliff stood in front of me with tears in his eyes at the hospital as he told me he was the one to find Oskar sprawled across the tiles with a head injury. Of course he was. He was the one who put him there. 'Cliff, please. I'm sure we can find a way… This isn't you. This isn't the Cliff I know. The Cliff who was my friend, who saved my life… Remember that? Please…'

'It's too late, Lily. Mae did this to you – look, she even left a note. I'll have to tweak it a little now you're on the scene, but it'll be pretty clear to everyone what happened.'

He kicks at the back of my legs, making my knees give way, then scoops me up and forces me to stand on the wall. The note Mae has written in a shaky hand is pinned to the top of the wall with a small rock, fluttering in the breeze. It reads:

> *I am not who you think I am. This all started back in Pennsylvania with Eddie Palmer. After he spurned me, I couldn't stand to see him with another girl so I made sure he couldn't make eyes at anyone else ever again. I thought Hollywood would be a fresh start, but it was me blackmailing others, me sending in the blind items, and it was me who was responsible for the deaths of Max Hayden, Ann Silver, Julian Marsh and the lady in his car. I can't live with this pain any longer.*

A cloud crosses the moon, blocking out the small amount of silver light that puddles on the floor, and I shiver.

'Cliff, no one will believe Mae is behind it all.' The note sounds nothing like Mae. It might be in her handwriting, but anyone who knows her will know she didn't write it.

'Sure they will. After all, all the evidence is in the file Freddy Eyelash created on her. Only, Freddy doesn't have it anymore. I do.'

I close my eyes briefly, vertigo causing black spots to dance at the corners of my vision. Wind rushes against my shoulders, my hair flying out behind me, and when I open my eyes all I can see below me is a gaping darkness. Of course Cliff was the one who broke into Freddy's office and stole the file. It was the last thing he needed to make his story believable.

'Now,' Cliff goes on, 'the note will read that you figured it out – credit where credit is due, Lily – and Mae had no option but to tussle it out with you up here.' *Is it me, or are there headlights winding their way up the road towards us?* I force myself to keep my eyes on the road below, at the pricks of light that break through the darkness, desperately trying to ignore the pitching of my stomach, the wobbliness of my knees and the gun that I am presuming is aimed at my head. 'You fell, and then Mae threw herself off after you. A tragic end to what has been an incredibly tragic few months.'

'P-p-please,' I stutter, 'what about Eddie? What would he think? He was a good guy, wasn't he?' Desperately trying to keep Cliff talking for as long as it takes for the car to get close enough to see me up here, I fumble on. 'Tell me about him.'

'He was a fucking monster.' Mae's voice comes from somewhere behind me and then I'm falling.

Chapter Thirty-Nine

I don't know how it happens, but one minute I'm standing on the wall, praying for the headlights to reach me before Cliff throws me over, and the next my footing slips. My knees buckle and I pitch forward, slamming hard against the top of the wall, every breath squeezed from my body as my top half hangs out over the vast drop below, the wind slapping my face hard enough to make my eyes water. Gravity tugs me forward, and I fumble for the edge of the wall behind me, desperately hoping to grasp something – anything – I can use to pull myself back to safety, before hands roughly jolt me backwards and I land on the front terrace with a thud that crushes my ribs. Cliff is on top of me, his hands around my throat, and weirdly the last thing I think before I slip towards unconsciousness is, *How is he going to explain handprints around my throat that are far too big for Mae's hands, when I'm supposed to have fallen from the wall?*

Just as darkness descends and I realise that yes, it is possible to die before you've even been born, there is a booming echo and something warm and sticky hits my face, and then the pressure of Cliff's hands disappears.

'Oh my God, Lily, are you all right?' Mae's face appears in my eyeline, hovering over me. She is shaking, her hand coming to cover her mouth before she realises she is still

holding the gun, and she throws it down in horror. 'I...
I...'

There is the thud of footsteps from somewhere behind me, but I am too exhausted to lift my head from the concrete to see who it is, and then from below I hear the faint whoop of a police siren.

'Lily?' The only voice I want to hear comes from behind me. I force myself into a sitting position, my throat and ribs hurting like a bitch. 'Oh, thank God, you're alive.' Louis is there, wrapping his arms around me and holding me tightly as tears begin to course down my cheeks. Over his shoulder I see Freddy Eyelash holding Mae in much the same way, brushing a tissue over her face to wipe away the blood splattered across her cheeks.

'Yeah, I'm alive,' I croak, looking over to where Cliff lays motionless. 'Is he...?'

Louis turns me away so I can't see the body. 'I think so. Mae shot him at point blank range. Jeez, Lil. Why did you come up here alone? Why didn't you wait for me?'

I shrug, pressing my face against his chest and inhaling the familiar scent of him. 'I knew you'd get here in time. You always do.'

'What happened up here? Cliff was the one behind it all, right?'

I nod, the shaking in my limbs finally beginning to subside. I begin to tell Lou how Cliff wanted to teach Mae – Mabel – a lesson after Eddie Palmer died, and that it escalated from there. 'He said something about how he had the Hollywood surname but still no one ever saw him... Not his mother, his family, none of us at the studio. Then Mae came in, someone who he thought was beneath him, and *everyone* saw her, but he knew who she really was.'

'No, he didn't.' Mae's voice is stronger now, but I notice that she's turned her back on Cliff's body so she doesn't have to look at him either. 'He never knew me at all, just as I never knew him. I did know Eddie Palmer though.'

The whoop of sirens is getting closer, so I urge Mae on. 'Mae, tell us the truth, please. Before the police arrive.'

Mae frowns and gives a shake of her head. 'All I have is the truth, Lily. Eddie Palmer was a rotten, nasty man who got what he deserved. I did send him the blackmail letter, but I didn't kill him.' She draws in a shaky breath. 'He… assaulted me, and two other girls in our town. All three of us were stupid enough to go on a date with him because he was handsome, charming and from a good family. But he didn't know the meaning of the word "no", so when I found out about the two other girls I wrote him and said if he didn't stop I would expose him. He laughed in my face, Lily. I called his house to tell his mother what he was doing, but I just couldn't get the words out.' She rubs her hands over her throat as if it hurts to speak.

'It's OK, Mae. You don't have to—'

'I do,' she says abruptly. 'This whole thing has nearly killed me, quite literally.' She takes a second to compose herself. 'I heard about the party, and I thought maybe I could confront him there, in front of everyone, but once again I was too afraid. A chicken.' She gives a snort of disgust.

'Mae, you were assaulted, that's a big deal. It's hard to talk about.'

Mae raises her chin, meeting my gaze head on. 'I didn't kill him, but I was there when he died.'

With that, the sirens screech up to the observatory and footsteps thud up the concrete stairs. Freddy lets go of Mae, and she turns to face the police officers that swarm the front terrace with her hands raised in the air. Louis and I follow suit, as does Freddy, while Cliff remains lifeless on the ground. I wish I could feel some sympathy for him, but he did try to kill me. God only knows how I'm going to explain all of this to Leonard, and who knows how Oskar will react when he finds out that Cliff was the one who tried to kill him. Mae throws a small smile over her shoulder in my direction as a police officer takes her arm and marches her towards the steps. If nothing else, while gossip will never die in Hollywood, at least, today, no one else will.

Epilogue

A few months later

Flashbulbs pop as Leonard and Jean step out onto the red carpet, Leonard leaning back inside the car to bring out baby Redfern. Jean looks beautiful, slim and elegant as she takes the baby and waves to the photographers. She was adamant that she would be attending the premiere of the movie, but she was also adamant that baby Redfern was not going to be left at home with his nanny.

The movie was finished, although not on schedule (which came as no surprise to anyone). Oskar was soon back in the studio, and it was as if he'd never been attacked in the first place as he resumed his shouting and yelling, huffing and puffing. Everything was business as usual.

I stand beside Tilda, her notepad clutched in one hand, pencil in the other, as she prepares to interview the stars as they step inside Grauman's Chinese Theatre. I think she's finally forgiven me for sending her home with Tipsy that night, although I don't think she'll ever get tired of telling me that things would have been resolved a lot quicker and without me almost falling over the wall of the front terrace if she'd been there. She's probably right. On the other side of me, Louis squeezes my hand tightly. Despite the two of us being just friends, it feels as if the invisible connection between us has been stronger than ever since that night.

I could have died. Died, years before I was born. The thought of it turns my brain to mush.

'You OK?' Louis looks down at me, and I realise I'm squeezing his hand far too tightly. He looks like a total snack in his tuxedo, although at any moment he'll complain that it's too tight, too itchy and just plain annoying.

'Yeah. Actually I am.' I grin at him, before turning to see Mae and Tipsy step out of the car at the other end of the red carpet. Bunny fusses with Tipsy's hat, making sure it's on straight, and smooths the back of Mae's tight-fitting silver dress before she gives them the nod and sends them on their way. Tipsy and Mae have been even more inseparable since that night – it turns out Mae had already confided in Tipsy about Eddie, hence Tipsy warning me off investigating Max any further. She was worried that someone would connect the dots and Mae's past would be revealed. It also explained why Freddy's card was in Tipsy's pocket – she'd used him before for her own scandals. Bunny was shaken by the events of that night, obviously, but I didn't see any point in telling anyone she was the one to type up the blind items. As far as everyone else is concerned, it was all Cliff.

Oh, Cliff. He died from the gunshot wound – it was pretty inevitable given Mae fired straight into him – and there was a brief moment when it looked as though Mae might be charged with murder. Once the truth was revealed, backed up by the two other girls who were assaulted by Eddie, and by Veronica who was horrified that her beloved Cliff had taken her idle chit-chat and turned it into something monstrous, the charges were soon dropped and the story will be absorbed into Hollywood legend. The public have already forgiven her, judging by the way her name is called over and over as she makes her way along the red carpet.

'Hey!' Mae reaches us and kisses Louis then me on the cheek. 'Tips, will you let Louis walk you in? I'd like a word with Lily.'

Tipsy giggles, her cheeks flushing. 'Well, of course. I'd never turn down a handsome young man.'

Louis rolls his eyes at me and then takes Tipsy on his arm with a grin. I turn to Mae. 'Is everything all right?'

'Couldn't be better.' She smiles at me, a wide, relaxed smile, and I realise I've never seen her smile properly before. 'I just wanted to thank you. For everything. It's been a rollercoaster. And I'm sorry that I thought you were involved at one point.'

'I'm sorry too. Cliff really played us, huh?' There is one thing I want to ask Mae about before she disappears into the black hole that is the media frenzy over this movie. 'Mae, I wanted to ask you… You said you never killed Eddie, but that you were there when he died.'

Mae's eyes widen for a moment as if she'd forgotten she'd told me that. 'He was drunk and stoned,' she says. 'I watched him smoke marijuana and then drain the rest of a bottle of whisky. I was still plucking up the courage to confront him, see, even after everyone else had left. He stumbled as he walked past the pool and hit the water with the most almighty splash.' She bites her lower lip. 'I could have tried to pull him out. I could have called the emergency services. But I just… didn't.' Mae looks up at me, an odd expression behind her eyes. 'So, you see, I didn't kill him after all. I should head inside, Lily.' She pats me on the arm and walks briskly away, leaving me unsure as to whether Mae just gave me the true version of events. I guess I'll never know.

Lana Turner heads up the red carpet, smiling and waving and looking more beautiful than ever, closely followed by Marilyn Monroe. Two successful Hollywood stars who are about to suffer tragedy in different ways. I wonder, not for the first time, if my time here is up. If I'll wake up in the morning to Eric leaving me a Starbucks pumpkin spice latte on the bedside table before nicking my phone charger. Part of me hopes not. Part of me hopes, despite the bruising around my neck that took weeks to die down, that I get to stay here forever, even though I have no idea how that would work.

'Aww, look at her. Isn't she the cutest?' Tilda nudges me as a little child around six years old, dressed in a pink-and-white frilly dress with her hair in perfect blonde ringlets, dances her way down the red carpet, smiling and waving at everyone.

'Oh, she is cute. Who is she?'

Tilda gapes at me. 'That's Baby June Denver. Only the cutest kid in showbiz.' She grins as Baby June approaches her, a lollipop in one hand. 'Hey, Baby June.'

'Hey, Miss Tilda!' Baby June dimples at me, and even though I've never really thought about kids or particularly liked them in any way, my heart melts. 'You're real pretty, miss.'

As Baby June skips into the theatre, the announcer calls for people to take their seats and Tilda grabs my hand, excitement pouring out of her like water. I can't worry about whether I'll wake up here in the morning. In the words of Scarlett O'Hara, I'll think about that tomorrow.

Author's Note

I've loved being back in Hollywood for a fourth time and I'm so grateful for readers who love Lily and the gang as much as I do! I have taken a few liberties with this story, and any mistakes are my own. Hollywood fixers do exist, and Freddy Eyelash is loosely based on a guy called Fred Otash, who 'fixed' problems for the stars in the 1950s (shout out to my editor for my Freddy's awesome nickname!). If you want to read more about Fred (the real one!) I can recommend *The Fixer: moguls, mobsters, movie stars and Marilyn* by Josh Young and Manfred Westphal.

Gossip has always been rife in Hollywood, and while *The National Enquirer* did exist in 1952, it was originally a mainstream newspaper before being bought by Generoso Pope Jr who turned it into the sensationalist magazine we know today. Henry Ginsberg really was a film studio executive, but seeing as how Oskar Goldstein is a fictional character I'm not sure he was ever called upon to step in at short notice the way I have him do in this book.

I would also never recommend climbing the Hollywood sign. Not only is it not allowed, but it is far more rickety and dangerous than this book would have you believe!

Acknowledgements

I am so lucky to have such an incredible team behind me. Thank you to my editor, Jennie Ayres, for her incredible insight and guidance – you have made every one of these books so much better, and there is nothing I love more than brainstorming with you!

To my agent Lisa Moylett, and Zoe, Izzy and Elena at CMM. Ten years of the dream team. Thank you for believing in me, even when I don't believe in myself.

To my Tedds, who keep me sane, keep me grounded and keep me laughing. One day I will write a book that incorporates all the worst (best) parts of our inappropriate group chat and it'll be a surefire bestseller.

To Nick, Geo, Missy and Mo. For everything, like always.

And lastly, to the readers and bloggers. Lily's adventures have been met with such enthusiasm and I am so grateful for all the love she has received. I read every message I get, and it still feels insane that people I don't know are reading my words! Thank you for letting me drag you back in time…